Assault on the Anchored City

Katherine A Smith

Book Four of the Northnest Saga

Available from author Katherine A Smith

<u>The Northnest Saga</u>

Hawkwind's Tale
The Fledging of Hawkwings
Hearthsraven

Hawktales: Stories from Northnest and Beyond

<u>The Dragonic Voyages</u>

Dragons to Loose
Dragonic Freedom
Dragonic Pride
Dragons to Keep

<u>Children's Books</u>

Otter Twin Magic
Otter Sea Magic

Assault on the Anchored City

Katherine A Smith

Book Four of the Northnest Saga

<u>Kasmith Art and Books</u>
Fort Bragg, CA

To Ginny, the THs, Eva, Kim,
Bob and Christi, Brittany, and Gina,
for encouraging my writing,
but even more for encouraging me.

Chapter 1
Departure

The thaw had come.

The sun shone, dislodging snow that slipped like drips of crystal from the burdened boughs of the conifers. It was a rain of springtime, a storm of sun, and the first day since the cold descended that seemed to proclaim that winter had lost its grip for good—or at least for several months. It wasn't warm yet, though. Vor Hearthsraven stood on the front step of her borrowed cottage wrapped in furs with the air biting at her nose.

A nearby spruce limb dropped a clump of slush and sprang up higher, relieved of the weight that had bowed it down all winter. Vor felt her spirits lightening in much the same way. She had spent several months alone in the mountains, except for her two goats, a smattering of chickens, and whatever beasts of the forest she encountered. The summer and fall had been a busy time: learning from the books Craduticus had left behind how to hunt and gather food to prepare for winter. She'd had to provide for her animals as well.

As if her thoughts had summoned them, her two nanny goats came picking their way through the wet snow, no doubt headed for their lean-to shelter to warm up.

"Had enough, have you?" she greeted them, breath puffing out in frosty plumes.

The white one came to her for petting, which she provided, while automatically checking her ears, eyes, and mouth for any signs of injury or illness.

"You're looking good, Black," she told her. "Come here, White."

The other goat, a black one, obeyed with a goatish grumble, and Vor checked her over, too. Both goats had simple rope halters, decorated with beads that carried mild compulsion spells to keep them from wandering too far and eating the garden—or each other's halters. They'd helped Vor carry her baggage up to the cottage, and provided milk that she had learned to make into butter and cheese. They also grazed down the undergrowth near the cottage, which discouraged predators from sneaking up close and picking off the chickens. Perhaps most importantly, they were someone for Vor to talk to, even if they didn't talk back.

"Alright, you both look good. Go get warm."

Black and White were not loath to obey. The melting snow was surely exposing some of last year's dead greenery—and goats would eat almost anything—but their winter coats were soaked to their bellies and began to steam as soon as they crowded around the stone Vor kept magically hot for them.

Shelters had already existed for both the chickens and goats, and as a mage Vor had no trouble keeping the hot stones renewed, but acquiring enough feed to last through the months of snow had taken as much time as preparing stores for herself. It had turned out that strategic reduction in her population of chickens had been necessary for some to survive, when their food ran low. Unfortunate for the weakest of the chickens perhaps, but beneficial to Vor when she got a few chicken dinners to break up the monotony of what seemed like endless root vegetable-based meals.

At night, and once the snows had set in, she'd read other books left behind by that senior mage of questionable morals. Not that Vor had any right to judge; she had done things she regretted, too: things that made others question her morals as much as she questioned Craduticus's. The cottage shelves had held quite a collection of journals: some about magic, and some about his life, observations of humanity, and own regrets. Those more personal journals Vor hadn't immediately read—not wanting to invade his privacy—but the dark hours with only nightmares for company had eventually led her to crack them, and the contents had given her much to think on.

As for the journals about magic, experimenting with magic from a book, without the presence of a master to pull an apprentice-level mage out of trouble, could be dangerous. Vor had known that, and hesitated long over trying anything other than practicing her own skills. However, the same intrusive thoughts that led her to distract herself with Craduticus's reminisces about his past, combined with her hunger for new magic, had led Vor to cautiously experiment on some of the coldest, darkest days.

Luckily, none of the magic had gotten out of hand—most of the time, if she messed up the spells simply failed—and she'd survived her experimentations with all limbs and sanity intact. The only exception had been a miscalculation that resulted in a minor explosion, but she tried to look on the bright side; now she knew how to make minor explosions. She'd noted down the process in her own journal.

She had no master now to teach her in person, so books were her only option. She might have to get used to experimenting, except—she almost had a way to ask the advice of another mage. Not for anything so complex as discussing the craft, for the communications she sent to and received from a mage called Giri Holster were limited to the codes he'd invented and given to her in a little handbook, but he was one facet of potential for more.

On her finger, the mage-stone ring that accompanied that book was warm. If she focused on it, she could feel a soft, steady pulsing that she had decided must be an echo of his heartbeat. Giri had made the rings so they could talk in code over the great distance between them. By now, Vor had all the codes memorized, but there was one she had never sent. Between the warming sun and the trees dropping their garlands of snow, she knew the time had come to make a decision.

Giri had a master. He was learning. As one of the Wizards of Weldom, his career as a mage was assured. Nearly endless resources were available to him. Weldom provided room and board, education and employment. All he had to do was learn and use his magic for the good of his country.

Vor had none of that. With the death of her master—at her own hands, no less—and new leadership in Northborn—where she'd been living before—she'd been left at loose ends. The sudden upending of her entire life had resulted in the irresistible urge to escape. She would have run off blindly had not Craduticus, her former master's former master, seen the signs and nudged her to take his old hermitage as her own for a while.

It had been the right choice, but she didn't want to stay there forever. She'd had an entire winter to think it over and calm down from the lingering effects of the obliteration of her old life. Also to ponder was Giri himself, who had arrived in the midst of that obliteration and only added more upheaval. Their mutual attraction had led to a rushed and passionate romance mixed with magic and uncertainty, and capped by a mutual confession of love.

Reading Craduticus's journals had given her some other perspectives on that to consider, but the decision at hand was still what direction to take her life. It wasn't the first time her life had been upended, but it was perhaps the first time that the choice of a new direction was completely hers.

Vor sent a firm contact pulse into her mage-stone ring. After a moment, a similar pulse came back to her, indicating that Giri was listening. She took a breath of chill air and sent the pattern of pulses she'd never sent before.

"Spring."

There was no way to include inflection or emotion with the messages. Trepidation and excitement began to stir in her, but he wouldn't be able to tell.

"Yes," Giri replied through the ring. "Spring."

He didn't know where she was; only Craduticus knew. She'd told Giri she was taking some time to sort herself out, and he'd said he would wait for her return in spring. She'd promised she would, but the winter had been difficult. Like a bear that goes into hibernation fat, she was emerging from her winter den lean and hungry, and with purpose. Her clothing was loose on her and whatever softness she'd had was burned away. She had to journey now, on her own two feet, overland, to—

"Weldom," Giri sent to her.

"Yes," she answered. "Weldom."

In late autumn he'd reported that he was back in Weldom, leaving Northborn where they'd met. So now it wasn't just a matter of Vor going back to the capital of Northborn—a place she knew how to get to. She had to make her way across hundreds of miles, into a country she hadn't set foot in since she was nine years old, to find a capital city she'd never been to. It had to be done for the chance to be trained as a Wizard with a talented and trustworthy master of her own, and the chance to find out if the flurry of feelings she and Giri had shared would flourish or flounder.

Vor touched her left shoulder. There were two little scars there, each a thumbprint, one from Craduticus and one from Giri, burned into her skin as the first two of what would be a mark of five if she chose to become a Weldom Wizard. She didn't have to, of course. She had the freedom to remain masterless if she wanted, or search for a master who wasn't a Weldom Wizard. She didn't even have to reunite with Giri—except that she'd promised.

She lamented not for the first time that she had not exchanged some hair with him. They could have attempted to synchronously scry each other if they had such a concrete physical link. It would have been a much larger investment of energy than the rings, and the distance might have been too much for them, but if it had worked they could have seen and heard each other, and had an actual conversation. They could have shared more about their hopes for the future, with the help of his master he could have advised her on the magic she experimented with, and he could have told her exactly how to find him.

"No matter. I will find my way," she whispered to the stirring forest.

Vor went back inside, and began to pack.

It was midday when the most distant of Vor's wards was tripped. It had been a tricky thing, setting up magical wards that would not react to deer, ice-lions, and other large animals crossing over them. Craduticus had designed them to only alert when intelligent creatures—which did not mean only humans—crossed them, but she'd never put such wards in place before. It had been one case where she'd had no choice but to follow a book with no in-person assistance. She also hadn't been out to renew the wards since one bright, sharp day midwinter when she'd wrapped herself up and trudged out to each post, worked the renewal magic for each of them, and staggered back to the cottage just before dark, so chilled she could hardly move to build up her fire.

Luckily, she'd made the effort, so she had advance warning now that someone was nearby. The signal was weak, but undeniable, and she felt it as a prickle on her skin at the same time that she sensed its call like the tolling of a distant bell. When the next closest ward went off quite soon after, Vor found herself alarmed. Someone was indeed approaching, and coming fast—and through deep, wet snow among the trees, too. There was no hiding the cottage and hoping to be overlooked, not now that the snow was in retreat and no longer disguised its presence as an oddly shaped snowbank.

Vor shut the door and barred it, and activated her strongest protective ward out of its passive state. Anchored in the fence poles just outside the front of the cottage, that ward would react with physical blasts of power to anything that tried to cross it. That would protect the front door and windows. The back of the cottage was built into the hillside and there was no back door. If something was strong enough to be tunneling in from that side at the speed her perimeter wards were going up, she was in more trouble than a single defensive ward could fix.

Then she waited, feeling the next closest perimeter ward send its pulse of power at her. There was only one more between it and the house, so soon she would see her visitor. And there went the closest ward, and then there was the intruder—bold as a hungry hummingbird.

Vor blinked a few times, and took a relieved breath. So glossy its fur and feathers shone silver and ebony, a griffin had fluttered down into the snow slush outside her house. No wonder it had approached so fast. It hadn't been fighting through the still-deep drifts of snow in the shadow of the trees; it had been flying. It immediately picked its feet up, almost before it had finished folding its wings, and shook them one at a time like a cat that had gotten its paws wet, not that it did any good since it had to put them back down in the slush again.

Four legged, with enormous hawk-like wings and a hawk-like head and tail to match, coated with feathers above transitioning to fur below, griffins were gorgeous and could be fierce, but were as intelligent as humans and just as reasonable or emotional depending on personality and situation. Vor had met several griffins but didn't recognize this one—and then she did. Not from the events of the previous summer when she'd had speech with several different griffins, but from a year and a half ago. The griffin's coloration tugged at a memory. Her vile now-dead master had invited her down into the Skire's laboratory to look at a captured griffin. It had been grey with dark markings.

Of course, it could be a different griffin. There must be more than one grey and black griffin in the world, and Skire Germaine had repeatedly dissected and stitched up the one in the lab, examining its—her—pregnancy. Princess Jessika with the former Feathyr Hawkwind and some companions had stolen the captive back, but Vor had wondered if she would survive the wounds. Even if she had, why was she landing in front of Craduticus's cottage?

Then a human figure slid down off the griffin's back, from where it had been riding low between its wings. Vor's heart thrilled for a moment, wondering if it might be Giri—but no. This person did look male, but he was too tall to be him. Besides that, Giri had just told her he was currently in Weldom: many days away by any mode of transportation. This man was well wrapped in thick clothing, but as he approached the house he unwound a scarf from his face.

Vor grimaced and involuntarily took a step back from the door; she'd recognized him. The young man reached the edge of her protective ward and, sensing it, stopped. He peered at the cottage, but it was much brighter out there than inside, and Vor knew he couldn't see in. She tried to calm herself, but he was one of the last persons she'd ever expected to see—especially here.

"No matter," she mumbled. "I can handle this."

"Vor?" the young man called.

There was nothing for it; she couldn't stay in the cottage forever, and these people were unlikely to be enemies. They might not exactly be friends either, though. She left the ward up, but unbarred the door and opened it. She stepped into the doorway, where he could see her. He didn't smile, but some faint relief entered his face.

"Karolan," she greeted evenly.

Now he grinned a little, but nervously, ducking his head. "Hi."

Vor contemplated and discarded several different greetings and comments. Finally she copied him. "Hi."

"You're wondering why I'm here," he said.

"Yes, but I'm glad you're looking well," she told him, and meant it.

Last she'd seen, he'd been depressed, despondent, and ignoring her. They'd been lovers, although extremely briefly. It hadn't gone very well, and then she'd fought her master and Karolan's friend-beloved-adoptive-sister had been killed. He had withdrawn from Vor completely, and she had been only a little sad to see him go. She'd had her own trauma to deal with, and hadn't sought to help him with his.

"It's been rough," Karolan admitted with a shrug. "I was hoping I could stay up here for a while. Cray suggested it."

"Up here?" Vor echoed sharply.

"Not together, I mean, um," he stuttered.

Karolan waved behind him at the griffin, who lifted a snow-soggy hand and waved back at the two humans.

"Who is this?" Vor prompted.

"Hawkjoy," Karolan supplied, "my big sister."

The griffin opened its bill in what might have been meant as a smile.

"She's here to take you," Karolan swallowed, "to Giri." Perhaps at her scowl, he revised. "Or wherever you want to go, but everyone assumed you'd be going to Weldom, where he is, so, um."

An awkward silence bloomed. He looked down at Vor as though he thought she might slap him—she had before, once. She'd also broken his nose about a year before that, but that had been when they were outright enemies. Vor gazed back with a tightly controlled expression while another multitude of possible replies rolled through her head.

"I know you never loved me," Karolan whispered, not an accusation but an apology.

"I never said that," she corrected. "I liked you very much for a time, but it was complicated."

He ducked his head again, and said, "um, yeah."

"Do you really want to discuss this?" she asked him.

Karolan rolled a hand helplessly.

"Do you have regrets? Guilt?" she pressed, and he fidgeted. "Do you still want something from me? If there is something that needs to be settled, speak, and let us settle it."

He looked up. "You really love him?"

Vor frowned and forced herself to answer honestly. "I am still inexperienced in the ways of love, and I cannot foresee if what I feel will last forever, or if he and I can become a good partnership, but I want to find out."

"Then why did you leave him to come up here?"

"Why did you run away after Kassandra died?" Vor countered, making him wince a little, and hiding an internal wince of her own. "I needed time to sort out my thoughts, to face my demons in private, and prevent myself from making an impulsive decision when I wasn't in a good place to do it."

Karolan kicked at a lump of snow. "You're in a good place now?"

"I can make the decision now to go to Weldom," Vor allowed, "ready to investigate my options with a clearer head."

"Cray thinks I need a clearer head," he mumbled.

"Maybe you do. He's right about things sometimes," she acknowledged.

Karolan finally lifted his eyes to hers. "I'm sorry," he said. "I was pushy. You're just so confident, and amazing, and—"

"And you were in heat, as your griffin friends call it."

His eyebrows popped up and his cheeks reddened from more than just the cold.

"It's alright," Vor shrugged. "I was a little in heat, too, and I permitted the behavior. I even took advantage of it when it was convenient to me, just like you did anything you could to make me an ally, to destroy Altare. If we both used each other, let's call it even."

Karolan took a deep breath and let it go. "I'm sorry. I didn't think I was using you, but I can see how that's what happened. It was more than that, though. I liked you, too."

"And you wanted company," Vor nodded. "Don't worry. I'm not upset with you. I couldn't have done what I did—I might never have faced Altare—if you hadn't been there. He probably would have killed me, or unmade me, if it hadn't been for you."

"Maybe not," Karolan said weakly. "The wizards might have kept you safe. You might still have gotten together with Giri."

But Vor was shaking her head. "It's impossible to know. We live with what happened." She turned her ward back to passive mode. "Thank you, Rain. I don't regret, and neither should you."

Karolan was chewing his lower lip in apparent confusion. "Really?"

"It's thanks to both of us and all that happened between us that Altare is dead, the mine slaves are free, the Northnest king is free, and I'm free," she expanded.

"Oh, I guess so," he mumbled, face still flushed, and stood for a few moments, shuffling his feet in the slush. "Well, anyway, Craduticus said we should come get you," he explained. "He said Giri sent him a message yesterday, that you said it was spring."

"Ah," Vor uttered, nonplussed at the sudden intervention in her plans.

"Are you packed? You and Hawkjoy should get going, and get to a lower elevation before nightfall."

"Now?" Vor asked.

"Yes."

She blinked at him for a moment. "This is rather sudden. I was going to leave in a day or two when more snow melted, but I suppose I could be ready."

The griffin, Hawkjoy, was walking closer.

"I cannot get through that door," she announced, although her speech was a little strange. Her words were very clear, but they didn't flow as smoothly. Other griffins Vor had heard speak had much the same rhythm and inflections as humans. She wondered if Hawkjoy had a different native language, and this was her second one.

"Vor, this is Hawkjoy," Karolan introduced. "Hawkjoy, Vor Hearthsraven."

"I am pleased to meet you," the griffin said with a polite bob of her head.

"We've met," Vor revealed now that she knew the griffin's name. Jessika had screamed it enough times that Vor wouldn't forget it. "You were unconscious, so you won't remember. My former master took me down into the Skire's laboratory when you were a captive there. I'm very sorry about what happened to you."

Hawkjoy's crest flattened for a moment, but then lifted again a little. "I know your history, Vor. I volunteered to be the one to carry you to Weldom. I wanted to meet you."

"I'm honored, but afraid I know very little about you," Vor apologized. "I hope you will tell me some on the journey."

Her crest fluffed back up to its full height. "I will be happy to."

"One thing I wish to know first," she asked, "did your baby survive?"

The griffin gurgled, and Vor thought it was a sound of pleasure. "Yes. It was a female. I named her Hawkstar. A few months ago I had another, a male. I named him Hawkshine. Hawkwind's sister—you met her, I think—Hawkcall, is the Hawkmother now. The Line raises the chicks, and so I am free to go adventuring again. I am excited to see Weldom."

"I should not delay us then, and I am relieved to know that the Skire did not hurt your baby," Vor said. "Karolan, I'll need to tell you a few things before we go."

And so she invited him in and showed him the use of the stove, sink, and storage locations. She pointed out Craduticus's shelves and piles of journals, and the magical work room in a cave at the back of the cottage. She introduced him to Black and White, and told him about the binding spells in their beads.

"So," Karolan ventured, "you named the black one White, and the white one Black?"

"Don't try to change it," she ordered. "They know their names and will come when you call. Milk them every day."

Karolan wisely said no more about it. The chickens, too, she told him about feeding and caring for, and then walked him to the stream she got all her water from.

"Craduticus left some journals about his time living here," Vor said. "I found them useful. I tried to gather seeds from the autumn harvest, just in case someone would be here in spring to plant. I hope they will be enough to start the garden. I've eaten the larder bare, but since I'll be flying now, not walking, I'll leave behind some of the food I was going to take."

"I can call for help if I need it," Karolan assured her.

He stared at her while she watched the stream gurgling under the patches of ice that still clung to the banks and around the rocks, and she wished he wouldn't.

"You're thin," he said. "Joy will hunt, and you can eat your fill, when you stop for the night. I brought enough food with me for a few days."

It was difficult to keep her voice from becoming defensive. "I'll be fine, and you can get milk from Black and White each day. There are instructions on how to make cheese and butter. The chickens might give you an egg or two, but it's not likely until it gets warmer."

"Vor, I want you to be happy."

She eyed him. "I have a chance for it now and I'll work towards it in my own way. Don't worry about me."

"Alright," he nodded. "Can I hug you?"

Vor frowned for a moment, analyzing how she felt about it, and decided that yes, hugging Karolan would be fine. She put her arms around him, and he did the same to her. It was the first human touch she'd had since leaving Giri on the road, several months ago. They both had lots of layers on against the cold, but it was still good to be held. She hadn't had much of that in her life, not since the war took her parents from her. Both Karolan and Giri—mostly Giri—had provided the opportunity to discover that it was something she liked, from time to time.

Karolan let go first, maybe afraid he would offend her if he hugged her longer than she liked, and Vor stepped back.

"I'd best be on my way," she said.

They walked back to the cottage, where Hawkjoy was waiting. The griffin had scraped four holes in the snow for her feet, exposing rich, damp earth below—which had made her feet dirty and wet instead of just wet, but maybe less cold. Vor fetched her packs and the griffin directed her in tying them onto her harness. Under Karolan's guiding eye, Vor mounted up and strapped herself down. It would be her first time flying griffin-back, though she had ridden on a running griffin before.

"Jessika and Rikah, and some other griffins are in Weldom," he said, looking up at her now mounted, "or still on their way there."

Hawkjoy twitched her feathers. "We shall let them know where you are, Rain."

"Thank you," he said.

"I hope you have a nice time here," Vor wished him. "And thank you for thinking of me."

"Vor, hold on tight," Hawkjoy advised.

Karolan stepped back. "Safe journey."

The griffin spread her massive wings; Vor hunched down small on her back. Then with jerking, thrusting beats, Hawkjoy fought for altitude, clawing her way up to above the treetops. Vor looked down at Karolan, now a small figure standing in front of the cottage. In an instant, he was out of sight behind the trees, as Hawkjoy wheeled and began soaring down the mountain. Vor clung tight to her back, looking ahead for whatever came next.

Hawkjoy landed into the setting sun in a little clearing low on the mountain. The snow was gone from it already but the air was still cool with the dregs of winter. Vor had enjoyed the flight—especially the view—but was glad to be done for the day. Constantly holding on had become surprisingly tiring, and the wind had been bitingly cold. She slid to the ground and unloaded the packs from her companion.

"I will catch us something to eat," the griffin announced. "Perhaps you can start a fire?"

"Do you need one for warmth?" Vor asked. "If not, there are easier ways to cook meat, for a mage."

Hawkjoy tilted her head. "Rain always cooks over a fire."

Vor bit her tongue on what she might have said—that Karolan didn't know any better—and shrugged instead. "I can make one if you want one."

"I do not need one. I am not cold," Hawkjoy said. "I will return shortly."

Vor spelled a stone for light and set it in the center of the clearing. Next, she walked around the perimeter, setting simple wards that would alert her if anything large came near. She cleared away sticks and rocks from the ground and picked a level spot for her bedroll. Then she sat upon it with a sigh, and took a long drink from her water skin. The water chilled her chest and belly. Vor's mage powers had kept her warm through the icy flight, and did not fail her now, but she needed food if she was to recover all the energy she'd spent and have enough for warming herself again on the next day's flight. She'd brought some cheese, but if she was going to be eating only wild game she'd need to portion it out. The fat in the cheese would help her digest the lean meat.

A ward tingled and Vor looked over just as she heard the sound of something large pushing through the undergrowth.

"Vor?" came Hawkjoy's call from the darkness under the trees. "I have a buck deer. I do not want to bring it any closer to camp. Will you come cut yourself a piece or two? You might want to take enough for breakfast and lunch tomorrow, as well as tonight's dinner."

Vor took the light stone and went to do as suggested. The animal was freshly killed, and Vor absorbed the last of its life energy, waste not want not, as she sawed off a large and bloody chunk of haunch. She'd never learned how to prepare food—the servants at Northborn castle had always done that for her—but during her months at the cottage, she'd been forced to acquire many skills she hadn't had before.

She didn't carry the meat back to the clearing, but stayed out with Hawkjoy to keep the scent of the kill away from where they would be sleeping. She was willing to bet that the presence of a large predator like a griffin would keep just about every other animal away, but there was no reason not to take precautions. After all, she didn't want Hawkjoy to have to wake up in the middle of the night and fight something off. Her studies had told her there were other things just as big and deadly—or bigger and deadlier—as a griffin in the world, and she would not tempt fate.

"I don't mind if you eat," Vor murmured, seeing Hawkjoy hesitating over the kill. "It won't bother me."

Indeed, the simple necessity of a predator eating its prey had little chance of turning Vor's stomach, after the other things she'd seen in her life. Her former master had mutilated, tortured, and even eaten alive both animals and humans in Vor's presence—and tried to make Vor do such things, too, a little of which she had done under his pressure. The memories of those instances were some of the ones Vor had spent so much time putting to rest over the winter. By comparison, the buck deer was fully dead and would no longer feel pain, and Hawkjoy had no malicious glee in killing it. Guts and blood Vor had seen many times before; it was no challenge for her to ignore it.

She stepped a little ways away regardless and set her light stone on a fallen log. Hands firmly holding the deer flesh, she began to focus heat into its mass. Fire required gathering wood and preparing a fire pit, and created smoke and wasted heat. It took longer than this direct hands-on method of cooking, and there was always the risk of the fire escaping and burning things Vor didn't want burned. Plus, when she cooked it herself, she could control exactly how hot the meat got, preventing it from getting burned or remaining raw inside. However, it did make the meat rather hot to handle.

Within a couple minutes, she had a fully cooked and steaming lump of meat big enough for three meals, and was juggling it back and forth from hand to hand and cursing under her breath at her frying fingers until she got it securely impaled on her knife. Vor took a bite out of it, burning her lips and tongue a little. The proper way would have been to sit with a plate, knife, and fork—but she didn't have anything but a knife handy at the moment, and there was no one around to care about her table manners.

When she'd eaten a third of it between nibbles of cheese, she searched through the undergrowth until she found a few handfuls of new dock leaves. The moist heat of the meat made the leaves malleable and she wrapped the meat with layers of them, and then ate several more of the leaves herself. Vor licked her hands as clean as she could get them, and carried the meat back to camp. She had no salt to preserve it, but she thought it would keep well enough until the next day, especially in the cold temperatures. Hopefully, wrapping it up inside her pack would be sufficient to keep small animals from getting into it during the night.

"There is water, a stream, not far away," Hawkjoy informed.

"I have water, thank you," Vor called back, "but I'll make use of the stream in the morning."

Stumbling around a rocky riverbed in the darkness trying to get water without falling in was not pleasant; she knew from experience. She wasn't as clean as she'd like, but unless they were stopping at inns, which she doubted, she expected the trip would leave her craving a bath by the end of it, and was prepared to endure.

The griffin called out once more. "I will go wash, and come back."

Vor lay on her bedroll, light stone still glowing brightly and making the stars difficult to see. Hawkjoy returned, sat down on the other side of the light stone, and began to preen her feathers. Vor watched her, wondering if the griffin was inclined to conversation, or preferred silence. Vor normally saw little need for conversation for conversation's sake, but she'd been several months alone in the mountains, with no one to talk to save the goats and chickens, who of course never did her the courtesy of talking back. Besides that, she was curious about the griffin, and thought some conversation would be a good way to build companionship, thus alleviating the uncomfortable feeling of travelling with a stranger.

After a few minutes when it seemed Hawkjoy had tended to her most critical feathers, the griffin paused and looked over at Vor.

"Rain tells me you are going to Weldom to reunite with your mate," she said.

"Ah," Vor uttered. That wasn't the topic she had intended to broach first, but clearly it had been topmost on Rain's mind. "It is perhaps a little early to call him my mate."

The griffin flattened some feathers. "Oh, I see. Forgive me. The mating habits of humans are still somewhat unknown to me."

Vor smiled. "Sometimes I think they are unknown to me, too." She rolled to her side, propping her head up on her hand so she could more easily watch the griffin. "I'm still figuring out what I want, and what I should do about it."

Hawkjoy rustled her bill under her rump feathers to gather oil from her uropygial gland. "Knowing what you want is important," she said when she'd finished, "but not always easy."

"I have to get to know him better," Vor reflected. "We had fun together and I don't regret it, but if we intend to be paired permanently, I have to make sure we have compatible life goals and personalities."

"This is not something I have ever considered," Hawkjoy reflected. "Griffins do not pair permanently, or even temp," she paused as if struggling with the word. "Temporarily. Perhaps I cannot give good advice."

"It still helps to have another person to talk about it with," Vor suggested. "Craduticus left behind a lot of books at the cottage. I read through them, and some of them talk about the nature of human relationships. They can be messy, complicated, difficult to maintain, and difficult to be happy in. Sometimes it makes me wonder why humans do it, and if I want to."

"That is strange to me, too," Hawkjoy observed between strops of her bill. "With griffins it is very clear. When a female awakens, she is the matriarch. She will mate with what males she wants, and have chicks if the Line needs them. When her body goes back to sleep, she stops, and returns to how she was before."

"That is much simpler," Vor agreed. "And how about for the males?"

Hawkjoy flicked her crest. "It is difficult for me to say, as I am not male. They seem happy to mate when they get the chance, if a matriarch they like chooses them. But you humans, you pick one mate and stay with him for many years?"

"Sometimes forever," Vor nodded, "although not all humans do that. Some mate with anyone who will have them, whenever they want, or have one mate for a few years, and then a different one. It seems like a lot of them stay paired to make a family."

Vor found herself frowning at that. The last thing she wanted was to make a family now. She wasn't finished with her mage studies. A family would have to wait. She could only hope Giri agreed, or that could be a problem.

Hawkjoy spoke into the conversation pause. "And Wings said you cannot control when you have chicks—babies?"

"Mages can," Vor said. "Other people can't, at least not easily. There are techniques and medicines that sometimes prevent it. Are you saying griffins can choose when to conceive and when not to?"

"Yes," Hawkjoy confirmed. "All griffins learn this."

"That's lucky."

The griffin nodded seriously. "It is necessary, or we would become too many, and eat all the prey, and then we would starve. We must count the prey, and plan how many chicks we can have."

Vor snorted and flicked at a pebble in the dirt. "If only humans thought ahead like that. After all, babies can always be prevented by not mating. There's really no excuse for families so large that children starve."

"So," the griffin went on, returning to the original topic and settling her wings with a rustle. "You are going to Weldom to see this male, who might or might not become your mate. These bonds between mates that humans have, we do not have them, we griffins. Of course I like the males I have mated with—otherwise I would not have chosen them—but you have something more than just liking."

"Love," said Vor softly.

"We have love," Hawkjoy replied, not sounding offended. "Mothers love their chicks. We all love our fellow Linemembers—those are griffins we are related to through a common line of mothers—but I think the kind of love you speak of is different from that."

"Human parents love their children, too," Vor nodded. "Family members love each other, like your Linemembers. The love between mates is something different, though, as you say. Perhaps it needs a different word."

Craduticus in his writing had suggested it was simply lust mislabeled as love because it could feel so strong and people wanted it to mean more than the urge to mate. Real love, he wrote, involved alliance, friendship, partnership, and companionship that was separate from the physical lust—but could exist together. If that was the case, Vor wasn't sure if her and Giri's confession of mutual love hadn't been a misjudgment. They'd definitely lusted after each other, and enjoyed it, but as far as a friendship or partnership, that was in its infancy between them.

"Whatever you feel," Hawkjoy said into the silence, "it is strong enough to make you leave your home and travel so far to be with this male in a strange place where you know no one, perhaps for forever," Hawkjoy observed, now standing up to shake before resuming preening. A few bits of feather and fluff went flying.

"That," the griffin continued, "is such a strange idea to me."

"Before last summer, it was such a strange idea to me, too," Vor told her. "There is more than that, though. Have you heard the story of what happened at Northborn castle?"

"I have. I have visited there with Wings—that is, Princess Jessika—and seen the wizards and the king, and heard much of it."

Vor took a steadying breath and braced herself, but it was a fact she could not deny and would not exclude. Her eyes were steady on Hawkjoy's slow and rhythmic preening. She kept her voice even. "You know I killed my master?"

Hawkjoy paused and her skin shivered, making a shining ripple move across her fur in the glow of the light stone. "I remember him. He was the one that came and put magic on me so I could not move and could not feel when that woman cut me open." Her voice turned from soft to hard. "I am glad he is dead. I am glad you killed him."

Vor gave a short nod. "I don't want to live there anymore. I am going to Weldom because other mages are there, not just Giri. If it's a good arrangement, I'll learn more magic there and become a wizard like the ones you met at Northborn castle. Maybe that will also allow me to stay with Giri."

The griffin preened a few more feathers up under her wing. "I think this is a good choice you are making."

Vor smiled a little, not sure how to respond, but finally settled on, "thank you. And why do you go to Weldom? Why did you volunteer to be the one to carry me there?"

Hawkjoy's feathers lifted, and Vor thought she interpreted it as a sign of pleasure.

"Adventure," the griffin said. "I have had my chicks and now I wish to see more of the world. Hawkwind is in Weldom, with Hawkwings and Hawkdare, and Thornwing, and Eaglegrace and Snowdark. Now that I am not the matriarch anymore, and there are four new adult Hawks with the Line in Southscree, to help with the chicks, I can be spared."

"When did everyone else go there?" Vor asked. "I mean to Weldom: the other griffins and the princess."

Hawkjoy nibbled at an extended talon while she thought for a moment. "Three wizards went back in the autumn, when new people came from Weldom. Wind and Wings, with the others, flew there only a week ago. I expect they are there by now."

"I wonder what sort of reception they got," she wondered aloud.

"I do not know," Hawkjoy agreed. "Weldom conquered Northnest. I know that. Wings was the Northnest princess."

"Somehow I doubt they will treat her like a princess," Vor said. "I'm from Weldom, originally. I hope they will allow me to stay."

"I have never been there either." Hawkjoy's feathers fluffed up with another sign of excitement.

"You know how to get there? We're going to the capital, right? Anchoria?" Vor checked. "I've never been there, but I assumed that's where everyone we're going to see is at."

All she knew about the capital was that its name was Anchoria. She didn't know what it looked like or how big it was, and had only the vaguest idea of where in the country of Weldom it was located: near the midpoint of the northern border.

"Yes," Hawkjoy confirmed. "That is where the wizards said to go, and they told us landmarks to look for. That is where the wizards train, and where your possible mate is."

"Good," Vor breathed.

Anchoria: where the wizards trained. The two scars on her left shoulder tingled a little. Wizards had five such marks, from five different senior wizards, arranged in a circle like the petals of a flower. Giri had explained that they created accountability. If a wizard misused her powers, those five who had approved her would hear about it. He hadn't explained what misuse looked like to Weldom wizards, but apparently it didn't include killing one's master in a mage duel, or Craduticus and Giri would never have given her their marks.

Vor would have to get three more marks before she could be employed as a wizard, as Giri was. She didn't know if they'd let her stay at wherever wizards lived in the capital, if she wasn't. She also didn't know what employment as a wizard would entail. She'd have many questions for Giri when she arrived—to be asked in between all the other things she planned to do with him. Actually, it might be better to save her questions for those with more authority. She didn't want to depend on Giri as she would depend on a master. He couldn't be her master, since he was still an apprentice himself, and even if he could have been, she could not allow such a power dynamic between them if they were also to be lovers and beloved.

"Did Craduticus go to Weldom, too?" Vor wondered aloud.

Hawkjoy answered promptly. "I think you mean the man we call Cray? Yes, he went, too, but he says he is too old to fly all that way, so he is going to go there by magic."

That was some comfort. The two wizards who had given their approval to Vor so far, would be there, at hand in case they had to justify it, and there to answer all her questions. After all, if she could get them in trouble by misusing her powers, it was reasonable they'd want to make sure she knew what misuse looked like, so she wouldn't do so. Hawkjoy finished preening, stood once more to stretch and shake, and then folded her wings and lay down.

"If you get cold," the griffin offered shyly, "you can sleep under my wing. It is very warm that way."

Vor found herself giving her companion a genuine smile. "Thank you,

Hawkjoy. I will remember, and I'll turn out the light stone now, unless you need it?"

"No, thank you. Goodnight Vor."

"Goodnight."

The griffin curled up, and Vor touched the stone, sucking the remaining magic back out of it. After a few moments, her eyes began to adjust to the night. Vor looked up at the stars that sparkled like dashed sugar across the dark sky. She hadn't slept outside in a long time, and never outside in a forest. A few early insects chirped or whirred, and once in a while Vor heard the soft tread of something small moving among the leaf litter or along the branches of the trees.

With her own power at her call, her wards in place, and a large friendly predator sleeping within reach, the nighttime sounds did not frighten her. It was still too early for mosquitoes, it seemed, and the cool air felt good on her exposed face and arms. For some time Vor lay, just staring at the stars and wondering what they were, how far away they were, and if anyone anywhere knew.

The morning saw Vor get a quick bath in a chilly stream, another belly of venison with dock leaves and a bite of cheese, and then they were airborne for the second day of flying. Hawkjoy did land a few times during the day for brief rests. During one of those rests, Vor ate the last of her meat, and again they landed near sunset. Again, Hawkjoy hunted, although this time she brought back what was unmistakably a pig.

"It was wild," she assured Vor. "It is not from a farmer."

The pig certainly looked rugged enough, not like a cared for meat animal. Vor took her share and cooked it as she had the venison the night before. And so it went. The weather stayed clear and got a little warmer, although some days were windy, which made for exciting flying as far as Vor was concerned, and challenging flying according to Hawkjoy. They made less progress those days, as the griffin explained that it was not a tailwind, which would have helped her, but winds mostly from the south, which only caused her endless annoyance.

They were over land that was partly settled now, beyond the mountain forest, heading west and a little south, but there were still patches of wild land. Some of it was forested, near the rivers, and other areas were more like grassland or marshes. Where the land peaked up in small hills, scrub brush and tenacious trees grew among the rocks. The mostly flat land boasted well-maintained roads and tidy towns and cities. Water seemed plentiful—though partly because of the spring melt, no doubt. Rivers cut across the land, with occasional lakes and ponds speckled with water birds. The dense forests were bright green with their new spring growth. These were the kinds of trees that lost their leaves every year—deciduous trees. Conifers like pines and firs and spruces seemed rare. The hunting was good, although the deer were smaller and redder than the big brown ones Vor was used to seeing.

It was their sixth night, after they'd eaten, that Hawkjoy pulled a stone from one of her pouches. She took it in her hand, and Vor sensed as it activated from her body heat and sent a magical signal. It was not unlike the ring she wore. With it, the griffin was sending a message to someone.

"I am not a mage," Hawkjoy said, glancing up at Vor, who was watching her. "I can only send a simple signal. Cray has the other one."

"And why are you sending the signal now?" Vor asked, though she had a suspicion.

"Tomorrow we will reach the capital," she answered, confirming Vor's guess.

She nodded, not disputing it, but curious. "How do you know?"

"I was told to watch for a lake with an island in the middle, which we flew over today, was the second to last landmark. We griffins have estimated that once it is passed, the capital is within one day's flight." The griffin opened her hand and looked at the stone. "I feel the heat signal. Cray has heard me."

Vor's mouth quirked. "May I hold the stone?"

Hawkjoy willingly passed it over to her, and Vor grinned wider. She took it firmly in hand and sent a series of rapid little pulses, something only a mage would be able to do. After a moment of silence, the same signal came back at her, and she delighted in thinking of Craduticus realizing Hawkjoy must have passed her the stone, for no one but a mage could do more than hold the stone tight to activate it. Craduticus would know now that she and the griffin were together.

Then after a few moments Vor felt both the stone and her ring light up with identical contact pulses at exactly the same moment.

"Hello. I miss you. Weldom tomorrow," came further coded pulses.

Vor smiled widely enough to make her cheeks tight, and felt her skin blush with heat. The coded messages were ones Giri had made, that only she and he knew. Craduticus and Giri were together. The former had announced to the latter that Hawkjoy had contacted him, and Vor had sent the quick set of pulses, which Craduticus had returned, realizing Hawkjoy had given the stone to Vor. So then Craduticus had handed the stone to Giri, who had sent codes back to Vor using both magical contact items at the same time.

Vor replied with both items, too. "Food, yes, warm, yes, safe, yes. Weldom tomorrow, yes. I miss you."

"Goodbye," Giri said through Hawkjoy's contact stone—but through the ring he sent a different message. "I love you."

Vor reached out blindly, felt the griffin's extended hand, and released the stone into it. She clutched the ring to her chest with her other hand, silly grin gone. They didn't use that phrase all the time, and Vor had never heard it from his mouth with her ears. She had it written in the back of the codebook, by his own hand, and she looked at it sometimes. She hoped that even if it wasn't completely true yet, it would be.

"I love you," she replied.

"Tomorrow," he sent again.

"Tomorrow," she agreed.

They didn't say goodbye. The messages just subsided into the subtle, almost undetectable heartbeat pulsing again. Vor relaxed, feeling tremulous anxiety in her chest and belly.

"What was that?" Hawkjoy asked gently, and Vor explained.

"So you can talk with this man, Giri, through the ring?"

"Yes, but we can't say many things. It must be done in code."

"And tomorrow you will be able to speak with him again as you usually do," the griffin said thoughtfully. "It wasn't until my seventeenth year that I became able to speak with my voice. That was a year and a half ago, after I was rescued from the castle."

Vor hadn't heard this before, and regarded the griffin with interest. "Why is that?"

Hawkjoy spoke slowly and quietly. From her posture, Vor thought maybe it was a sensitive subject for her. "I was born a prisoner in a faraway city called Snow-in-lee. My captors were talis, finned serpents able to hypnotize griffins with their coloration and movements. We are weak against them. They cut up my throat, so I could not speak aloud. I spoke with my hands, as all the Snow-in-lee griffins did. Two summers ago, after I was rescued from the Northnest castle, I was dying from my wounds. A unicorn healed me, and that healing extended to the injury from my chickhood, to my throat. So now, I can talk."

"Is it better to be able to speak aloud?" Vor asked.

"Now I can talk to anyone. Before, I could only talk to those who also knew the Snow-in-lee sign language, although there is nothing wrong with my hearing, so I can understand when anyone else talks—once I learned the meanings of spoken words—but they could not understand me. In that way, it is better now."

Vor nodded in acknowledgment. "Are there ways it isn't?"

"It is noisy," Hawkjoy said. "It is less elegant. When speaking with your hands, you must look at whom you are talking to. You must give them your attention. If you both are not looking, you cannot talk. I agree that speaking aloud can be very convenient. You can shout around corners, at people in other rooms, in passing, quickly. That makes it easy, but it also makes it too easy."

Vor was trying to understand, but it felt slightly out of reach.

"Perhaps it is like dancing, when you talk with your hands," Hawkjoy went on. "You and your partner turn towards each other and watch each other. You cannot be distracted. I see people speaking, but they do not give the attention to each other that we who speak only with our hands do."

"I think I can imagine what you mean," Vor said. "It is easy to do something else while speaking aloud. People might be eating or working on something, instead of devoting one hundred percent of their attention to what they say and what the other person says."

"So when you meet this male who might be your mate," the griffin commented, "although you will then have all your language to use, you must be certain to speak with intent and focus, and look at him fully, as though speaking with your hands. I hope he will do the same."

Vor was quiet for a small while, absorbing that. The griffin's words had somehow made a little of the anxiety she felt fade, but not all of it.

"I think that is good advice, Hawkjoy," Vor said.

"You still look nervous," the griffin observed. "What are you worried about?"

"Many things, really," Vor shrugged.

"You are worried this male will not want you."

"No," Vor denied. "I know he does. He's told me he does."

Hawkjoy appeared undaunted. "Then you are afraid he will change his mind."

She clasped her hands around the ring, where the echo of Giri's heartbeat went on unabated. "We don't really know each other that well," Vor admitted.

Hawkjoy flattened her crest. "It is not so important with griffins. We do not have to know our mates well. It is a brief thing, with us. I do understand the worry of being afraid a male I would like to have will not come to me. For us, though, there are always others." A few of Hawkjoy's crest feathers twitched up hopefully. "There is always Rain, if this male in Weldom does not come to you."

"No," Vor said immediately, but gently. "I don't want Rain anymore. I'm just afraid that when Giri gets to know me better, perhaps he will not care for what he learns, or I that I won't care for what I learn about him. We might not have the same goals, or morals. Or we might not be able to live happily together. I think I am nervous that we will fail as a pair."

"I have little mating advice for humans," Hawkjoy murmured. "I am sorry."

"It's alright. I shouldn't be bothering you with it."

She made a trilling sound. "Friends tell each other their troubles."

Vor eyed her cautiously. "Are we friends?"

Hawkjoy eyed her back. "Perhaps we are more than acquaintances?"

"Yes," she agreed, "I would say we are that. I like talking with you."

Her crest fluffed back up again, taking her neck feathers with it. "And I, with you."

"It's getting late, though. We should probably sleep."

Hawkjoy agreed, and so the two closed their eyes, as Vor put out the light stone.

Vor bathed herself as well as she could the next morning, in the nearby river, but there was no way to get perfectly clean, and her clothes were still quite dirty. She only had one wearable set left after the trials of autumn and winter. When she'd been expecting to walk to Weldom, she'd planned to find a shop in a town somewhere to buy or barter for something new, but she and Hawkjoy had stayed in the wild lands so there had been no opportunity.

Considering her appearance, she feared she would not make a good first impression in Anchoria. She tried to spot clean some of the worst stains off her clothes, but it really was hopeless. Resigned, she twisted up her wet hair into a bundle at the back of her head, secured it with a snug knit cap, and went back to the camp where Hawkjoy was getting ready to fly.

"I am very excited," the griffin said. "I have never seen such a city as Anchoria is said to be."

"I'm from Weldom originally, but I've never seen it either, nor heard much about it, other than that it's the capital city," Vor replied.

She strapped the packs onto Hawkjoy's harness and pulled herself up onto her back in movements that had now become familiar. The griffin took to the sky, fighting for height in the still morning air. They flew a couple hours before Vor noticed much change in the land below. The level areas became fewer, the hills steeper, although they did not approach the size of mountains. Great rocks could be seen thrusting up through the soil, sometimes topped with soil of their own and supporting grass and brush, or even stands of trees.

Gradually there came to be more rocky areas than open land. Rivers ran swift and white between the ridges and plateaus, forming deep gorges cutting through the stone. Roads were making their way towards the capital, too, passing through towns full of buildings crowded shoulder to shoulder in the sparse flat land, and climbing sometimes up onto the rocky heights with switchbacking paths, even crossing over the gorges on narrow suspension bridges.

It was dynamic, beautiful land, enough to distract Vor from her anxiety over the destination, but she wondered why anyone would put a capital city up among it. Of course, lots of people would want to visit and probably live in such beauty, but to make a large city in it must have been a challenge. There was little nearby farmland for one thing, so most of the food would have to be imported: no shortage of water, though.

The air warmed as the day went on and became heavy with humidity. The waters below showed no sign of petering out, and looking into the far distance Vor thought she saw a vast range of peaks, snow-capped and vanishing into the sky under wreaths of cloud. Those mountains must have been the source of the rivers, carrying melt water, but the griffin and her rider were not going that far.

The sun was high above when Anchoria came into view.

Vor stared in amazement. The castle in Northborn, fine though it was, nestled among the piney peaks of the mountain foothills, could not compare to the crowning sculptural majesty of Aiguille. The upthrust rocky terrain rose even higher here, forming a sort of peninsula of stone, a slight precursor to the distant mountains, and beyond this semi-circular outcrop the land continued rising, although slowly. The city was perched on this protrusion, and from below the edges of the city waterfalls emerged through gorges deep or shallow on the eastern, western, and southern sides. The rivers that fed them ran through the peninsula like spider-webbing veins.

From above, Vor could see where the water entered the city, from the northern side where the rolling rocky land continued ascending, becoming more and more jagged and forbidding. As the churning rivers passed into the gorges and through the city towards their plunge off the edge, the waters split, parted, and rejoined, leaving pillars and islands of stone between them. Buildings were founded on most of these, with a wide variety of bridges joining them: some arched and carved of stone, some wooden ones utilitarian and flat, some boasting small buildings of their own along their spans, and a few of the suspension type combining strong poles, wooden slats, and cables holding it all together. There were even some rope bridges clearly intended for pedestrians only.

The buildings were largest near the center and the southern edge of the city. A few reached up what must have been a dozen stories or more. The tallest were of stone, but there were fine wooden ones, too. Interlacing supports, arches, and joints linked the buildings together, lending stability. There didn't seem to be any part of the city that was run down or full of hovels. Vor wondered where the poorer people lived, or if they were actually barred from dwelling in the city somehow.

The other inescapable aspect of the city was what flew in the air above it. Drakes were airborne: not a lot, but a few handfuls, in every color of the rainbow, patrolling leisurely. None of them came to confront Hawkjoy, and the griffin sailed over without trouble—but nor did she get too close to them. After her first pass east to west, Hawkjoy made a wide circle and came around to the southern edge. Vor was scanning the buildings, and picked out a high platform on one of the tallest, on which she came to see four griffins and a few humans standing. More than one of the griffins was raising its wings as if waving.

Vor held tight as she recognized the posture Hawkjoy took when she was beginning to angle in for a landing. As they approached, she could see there were three humans; she'd expected Giri would meet her, maybe with Colby and Milsa, too, but none of these people seemed to be any of them. Her stomach, already a little uneasy from the flying, tightened with nerves. Hawkjoy dipped down, below the level of the platform, and then angled up, using a stall as she spread her tail and fluttered her wings to drop lightly onto the stone platform.

The griffin folded one wing, extending the other forward to let Vor get off without disturbing her feathers too much. Vor unstrapped herself, and slid to the ground on legs that shook a little, and then Hawkjoy folded her open wing, and Vor could see plainly the people who awaited her. None of them were Giri, as she'd detected. In fact, she didn't recognize any of them, but they were staring at her with welcoming, even excited expressions.

One of the griffins Vor knew immediately.

"Hawkwind," she greeted as the big brown female stepped forward.

"Joy, Vor," she replied, "I am glad to see you both arrive safely."

Then Hawkjoy and Hawkwind exchanged preening to each other's neck feathers and the other three griffins stepped forward, too. The five griffins dropped quickly into conversation with each other—although one, a rusty red one who seemed familiar, looked briefly at Vor and gave her a jaunty nod. It seemed Vor would have no choice but to face the trio of her own kind that was waiting for her. She unfastened the packs she'd clipped to Hawkjoy's harness and slung them over her shoulders.

Trying to stand tall despite the weight of the packs, her rough clothes, and questionable cleanliness, she turned to the humans and approached. They all looked impeccably dressed, like they were soon to head to a special event. There were two men and one woman, all in about their third decade of life. One man was strikingly tall, with pale skin and bright blonde hair. He was grinning widely and wore mage robes in muted blues. The other man was a bit darker and shorter, with rich brown hair cut at his shoulders, and he also had a pleasant—if less exuberant—expression. He wore a fine jacket over a vest, shirt, and trousers, not robes.

The woman was smaller than them both, closer to Vor's height, but with some added curves. She obviously hadn't been half starving all winter. She was about as dark as Vor, too, with long black hair in braids, wearing a split gown of gold and dark blue. She was smiling excitedly. Her brown eyes shone. In fact, there was something familiar about her face. She looked a little like—

"Vor, you must be Vor. I'm so happy to meet you. I'm Giri's little sister, Andra," the woman glowed, extending both arms out towards her.

Ah, yes. So that was who she looked like, and Vor's heart gave a nervous pulse. Vor didn't shy away, but her hesitation in reaching out to meet Andra's offered double handclasp could only be obvious. Andra pulled her arms back in, but not offended, only smiling sheepishly.

"I'm sorry. I'm just so excited to meet you," she blushed. "Giri sent me, since he couldn't come himself."

"Why not?" Vor asked, even as she knew she should be introducing herself and giving first time greetings.

"You must be so disappointed," Andra apologized. "You'll see him soon, today." She brightened again. "It's actually really lucky. You're just in time to see Colby and Milsa get married. You're invited, of course. Giri is with them, getting ready for it. He's going to be in the ceremony, so he couldn't come to meet you."

Vor struggled against a frown and tried to analyze the sudden upwelling of emotion inside her. Should she feel disconcerted that Giri had chosen his master over her? His duties came first of course—she'd never interfere with that just as she'd never appreciate him interfering with her duties—and yet this would be their reunion after half a year apart. Well, how could he have known when she would arrive exactly? She hadn't contacted him even to tell him; she'd just assumed he'd be here. The greeting party must have been waiting for a while on this platform. Giri couldn't be expected to give up his whole day when there was an important event going on, could he?

Rather, she decided, him complying with his master's needs, yet making sure that there was someone present to meet Vor when she arrived demonstrated both his loyalty to his master and consideration of her. It was a solution like she would make if she had been in his place. She decided she should be grateful, not upset. She'd waited months to see him. She could wait a few more hours.

"Pardon me," Hawkwind interrupted. "We will be going now. Vor, it's nice to see you again. I'm sure we will see more of each other while we are here."

"Oh, are you coming to the wedding?" Andra asked with a little bounce.

"Thornwing and I, at least, intend to be there," Hawkwind confirmed.

"Great, see you then." Andra waved.

Vor nodded to the griffins. "Hawkjoy, thank you for carrying me all this way, and for your company on the journey. I hope we can spend some time together again."

"Yes, surely we will," Hawkjoy replied. She leaned in and butted Vor with her head, gently. "Good luck with your mate," she whispered.

"Happy flying," Andra waved some more as the five griffins dove one by one off the platform, Hawkjoy going last and following close behind Hawkwind. "Aren't they gorgeous? How exciting, you got to ride on one," Andra gushed. "Was it scary? Exhilarating?"

"All of those. It was definitely an experience," Vor allowed.

"Really, you must come along now," Andra urged, still with a smile. "We have to get you ready for going to the wedding, too."

Vor followed slowly as Andra retreated towards the two men, who both straightened from where they're clearly been muttering together.

"This is my husband, Terias," she said, hooking her arm through the arm of the shorter man. "And this is—"

"Darling, let's take Vor's bags for her," Terias said softly, and Andra gave another hop.

"Of course," she gasped.

"We'll go ahead," Terias went on, voice mild, as Andra took one and he took the other bag, unburdening Vor.

She noticed the two men exchange subtle nods, and Vor had a moment to wonder what this tall, skinny, blonde mage—which she was assuming from the cut of his robes—had in store for her. He took a step out to meet Vor as she approached. Andra meanwhile was steering her husband towards the door on the side of the tower from which the platform was built. The tall man gave her a short bow, with a rather flirty grin.

"Dellostrikata Traskitandi," he said. "You can call me Dello, if you like. Really, only my master bothers with the whole thing, and then only when

I'm in trouble, which is always. I'm Giri's best friend here at the Citadel." He straightened up, half a grin still on his face. "And you're Vor Hearthsraven, the woman he won't shut up about."

That took her aback a little, but with an embarrassed delight, and brought a bit of heat to her cheeks.

"I wanted to thank you for bringing that sparkle back to him," Dello said. "He had a couple painful relationships, some years back. I never thought I'd see him interested in a woman again."

Unspoken, but present nonetheless was a warning Vor didn't miss. "Dello," she ventured, "I'm flattered, and glad to help, but you know I can't promise a ballad-signer's happy ending?"

"Oh, I know, I know," he replied with satisfying emphasis. "Believe me, I know about troubled relationships. I know you two might not be a perfect fit; after all, you hardly know each other."

That was such an echo of Vor's own thoughts on the matter that she felt a load of tension slide off.

"But honestly, I wanted to meet you and take your measure, and find out if you were just out to take advantage of him," he shrugged. "Then if you were I could," he shrugged again and frowned, "well, I don't know what I could do. Ask you to leave him alone before he gets more attached? Pay you off?"

"Pitch me off the platform?" she suggested with a hint of her own grin.

"I wouldn't do that," he chuckled, and flicked his hands as he went on, perhaps betraying some nerves. "I don't know. I just don't want to see him get manipulated again. Giri is like my little brother. I watch out for him. He's brilliant, you know, with the magic and the scholarship, but he's not so good with people. He's learning, but he's sensitive. I know you're learning, too, but I just wanted to talk to you about it. Maybe I shouldn't get involved, but."

Dello seemed to be waiting for a response from her, some reassurance that she wasn't about to do the same thing as whatever those women had done to create a couple "painful relationships."

"I don't want to see him hurt, either," Vor said. "And of course I don't want to get hurt, but I am going to be honest with him, tell him what I do and don't want, or if I'm not sure, and I hope he's honest with me, and we can work this out, or not."

Dello was frowning a little, but nodded. "That's fair."

"Where are they?" Vor asked next.

Dello squinted at her. "Where are they?"

"The girls who manipulated and took advantage of him," Vor clarified. "I'd like to," she paused, picking a word, "teach them not to do that."

For a moment Dello stared, and then a fresh grin started in one cheek and spread across his face until he was beaming. He started to reach out his long arms, but then yanked them back and drove his fingers into his hair instead. He tipped his head back, grinning at the sky, while Vor's sudden adrenaline spike that she was about to get hugged subsided.

"I'm so happy to meet you," he insisted and—was he crying?—as he did a sort of spin, pivoting around on one foot. Vor could only assume this was his alternative method of expressing his relief and joy, rather than hugging her, which perhaps he had sensed she did not want him to do.

"Let's get you some clothes," Dello suggested when he faced her again. "Giri brought back your sizes and had a couple things made, but you look really thin. They might be big on you."

"Dello, what are you doing?" Andra goaded cheerfully from the open door into the tower. "Let's go."

"Come on," Dello urged. He turned for the door, and Vor followed him down into the Wizards' Citadel.

"This is Giri's room," Andra announced as she swung open a door along a corridor lined with many similar doors. "He said we could use it, but I don't think we'll all fit."

Vor took a look in, leaning past the passive wards that hummed against her skin. They were Giri's wards, and she recognized the flavor of his magic brushing against her aura. It almost felt like he was near, and made her suddenly long to see him. The room wasn't especially small, but with bookshelves on every wall, a bed, dresser, desk and chair, nightstand, and wardrobe there wasn't much floor space. Andra and Terias were currently filling it, fussing with clothing.

"You'll get your own room when you're a wizard," Dello provided quietly, and Vor raised an eyebrow his way.

He returned her look. "You are going to be a wizard?"

Vor nodded after a moment. "I suppose so."

"I'll give you your third mark," Dello offered, voice low so only she heard. "I'm sure Colby and Milsa will, too, and then you're done."

"You haven't even seen me work magic," Vor objected softly.

"I don't need to. I can sense all I need to know. Giri might be more powerful, but I'm very good at reading auras."

Vor blinked at him. "You've been reading mine?"

He gave an apologetic wince. "I read everyone's. It's hard not to. It would be like turning off my hearing."

"How about this one?" Andra called, swinging around a set of mage robes on a hanger. "Giri said you like grey."

They were closer to silver, with muted lavender accents—and they were true mage robes, not a girly dress, quite similar to what Dello was already wearing.

"We'll need to feed her for two weeks before she'll fit properly in those," Dello objected.

"Well she certainly won't fit my clothes, or Milsa's, or yours, or even Giri's," Andra chortled. "These will have to do. Are they alright, Vor?"

She managed a nod. "They will have to do, as you say. I certainly can't wear what I'm wearing now to a wedding."

"To the baths then," Andra declared, snatching up a satchel to go with the robes. "You men will have to wait for us. Maybe go get some of that food you were talking about."

Andra caught Vor by the elbow and propelled her down the hallway. Vor managed one startled look over her shoulder, back at the men. Dello gave her a wave, and then was out of sight.

Vor at least managed to convince Andra that she could bathe on her own. The woman's enthusiasm seemed to know no bounds, and Vor feared it would carry her on and on unless someone stopped her. The bathing chambers were separated into male and female, but shared by all the wizards at the Citadel and any guests that might come through. The water was plentiful and hot, and there was a wide selection of soaps and cupboards full of fresh towels. It was far more luxury than Vor had enjoyed in several months.

"I didn't know what would fit best, so I brought a few different kinds," Andra explained, shoving the satchel through the curtain blocking off one of the cubbies for those who wished to bathe and dress in private.

Vor took the satchel and found several different options in undergarments. It was just as well. Her own were much darned now and really needed replacing—a thorough wash at least. She found a simple set that fit her and then faced the task of figuring out how to put on mage robes. Her former master had owned a set, but rarely wore them, and he'd never prepared a set for Vor. They were at least easier than a dress, requiring no one to lace anything up behind her.

Once she had the plain inner robe on, which wrapped her torso tightly and fell loosely to her knees, she stepped out of the curtain. Andra clasped her hands together.

"Oh, excellent. I'll help you. It is a little big, isn't it? But wrapping it like that helps."

The outer layer was of heavier material that clasped at her belly, secured with an attached belt that wrapped another layer around her, and then swept down to the floor, and included wide sleeves that reached her elbows. The floor-length hemline could be folded up and back from where the edges met in front, and hooked to the back of the belt, should the wizard need to get it out of the way of her feet. It also had several cunningly concealed pockets for carrying focus objects or more mundane items like snacks. Vor tucked her knife into an inner pocket that seemed to have been placed exactly for such a purpose.

"Now what do you want done with your hair?"

"Braid it, please," Vor said at once, "in the western style."

"Perfect, but I'll have Terias help me. Let's go back up."

They found the two men sitting in Giri's room and with ongoing commentary from Dello, the husband and wife couple combed and braided up the top half of Vor's hair, leaving the rest of it hanging long as was common for young and unmarried people. Dello had also brought up some food, which Vor attempted to eat while keeping her head still. It was good, some kind of stew with vegetables and fish; she'd had nothing but wild meat, her chunk of cheese, and a few wild plants for roughly a week.

"Save some space," Andra chided with a laugh. "There will be food after the wedding."

"She has nothing but space," Dello retorted.

"We should hurry," Terias said softly. "It will be starting shortly, and we have to get halfway across the city."

They were going out in the city?

"You like that, Vor?" Dello prodded from where he was sitting in Giri's chair backwards, watching. "I can see your eyes light up—not to mention your aura. Do you even know where you are?"

"Anchoria," she answered.

"In the Wizard's Citadel," he added. "This is where the rich folk of Weldom send their magic-blessed babies to be trained up. Any recognized wizard can live here, although he has to do work in exchange for the room and board. Wizards employed by Weldom get their spot as part of their salary. The wedding is happening in a private hall in the city. Both Colby and Milsa are nobility, and their families are well off, so they're renting a nice place. Just about every wizard is going, though, since Colby is a State Wizard."

"Are we walking there?" Vor asked.

Dello shook his head. "We're going by carriage. I'm sure you and Giri will go out to see the city. If you end up living here, you'll get to know it well in time."

"There," Andra declared. "You look beautiful."

Vor tightened her jaw but managed not to wince. "We should go then?" she nudged.

"Might as well," Dello drawled. "We might get seats close enough to see the dais if we get there early."

Chapter 2
The Wedding

Vor spent the carriage ride looking out of the window. Her curiosity to see the city warred with her anxiety over meeting Giri again. They crossed over several bridges, and Vor stuck her head out of the window trying to look down into the gorges. Dello copied her, so she wouldn't be doing it alone, while Andra mentioned gently that it was not mature behavior, but took no other action to discourage it. Terias just smiled, as if quietly amused.

Birds flew down there, shining in the sun, and butterflies clung to the rock walls and hanging vines in the hundreds, creativing living draperies in a multitude of glimmering colors. The buildings were less interesting to Vor for the moment, though she supposed if she ever tired of the sheer rock walls draped with greenery and the mists rising up from the frothing rivers down below, dancing over rocks, that she might have some mild interest in looking at the architecture and sculpted decorations that festooned them.

The ride was over too soon, and at the same time not soon enough for Vor's apprehensive heart. They joined a queue of carriages that inched forward, disgorging their occupants one at a time to the broad steps of a majestic stone building carved with pillars and arched windows and hung with bright banners. When at last it was their turn, they descended into a crowd of people, most of them in mage robes, and waded their way through to the flung open doors. The four of them stayed together only by linking arms, and managed to find four seats in a row halfway back in the grand open hall.

"I don't suppose you've ever seen a Weldom wedding," Andra started chattering. "Way up there will be the dais where Colby and Milsa will come out. Giri is Colby's attendant, and Milsa will have chosen someone, a woman, to be hers. There will also be their parents and maybe other relatives of their houses. There will be a lot of talking that we might not be able to hear, way back here. It would be easier if it were a smaller wedding, like ours was, but I don't suppose you can expect that when a State Wizard is getting married."

The press of people—many chattering just as loudly as Andra—was sti-fling, and Vor felt a vague sense of being smothered. She thought she would rather have just waited in Giri's room, alone, for him to get back, no matter how long that took, than to have come to this, where she doubted she'd even get a glance of him, much less be able to talk to him—or anything else.

"The reception will be better," Dello murmured to her.

"The what?" she asked.

"After the wedding, only a fraction of these people will be allowed into the party that follows. We're all invited. It will be mainly Colby and Milsa's friends and family there, although most noble houses that currently have a representative in the city will make an appearance. You'll be able to see Giri then, and talk to him, and dance with him, and maybe even find a few mo-ments of privacy out on a balcony somewhere."

Vor was too stressed by the crowd—which was far greater than she could ever remember seeing, even when the courtyard at Northborn castle was full of people—to blush at the thought of sneaking off into a dark corner with Giri. One thing Dello had said stuck out above the rest.

"Dance?" she uttered.

"Do you know how to dance? There will be dancing."

She shook her head, feeling minute by minute more and more of an un-washed, uncultured, northern barbarian. Dello put his head closer to hers so he could speak more easily into her ear.

"If you dance with Giri, he'll know how, and he'll give you cues," he said. "Listen and I'll explain the steps of a couple common dances."

So Vor listened, moving her feet and arms in tiny movements as Dello did, trying to memorize his instructions. She'd never done anything like per-forming in front of people—except for when her late master had once com-manded her to put on a display of magery at a celebration—and the idea of it made her nervous. Perhaps Giri would not mind if they didn't dance, at least this first time they went to a party—and she found herself hoping they wouldn't go to many. She'd much rather be doing magical works or studying or making medicines.

Then a blare of horns interrupted the quasi-lesson.

"It's starting," Andra gasped.

The crowd quieted. Vor could hardly see over the heads of the ranks of people in front of her, though she could tell there was movement up at the end of the room. She heard voices, too, but had trouble catching more than a few words. As the ceremony droned on, she stopped trying to hear and see, even though she knew Giri had to be up there—she had no hope of seeing him without brazenly standing up to look over everyone's heads. With so many mages in the packed room, she couldn't sort through their glowing auras to try to locate him magically, either.

Only once did she perk up. She couldn't discern the words, but she recognized the voice—Giri had said something. Her heart pounded; she hadn't heard his voice in months, and she sat on the edge of her seat, hungry to hear more. After another several minutes, when he did not speak again, she slumped back a little.

"Don't worry, Vor," she heard Dello whisper then.

She darted a look at him, puzzled and wondering what thing he was telling her not to worry about this time.

"He misses you, too," Dello confided, his usual wide grin substituted this time for a comforting little smile.

Vor's belly flipped and quivered, but she managed to give a weak smile back, and return her attention to the unseeable dais. Eventually a cheer went up, starting at the front of the room and making its rapid way to the back. Music played and people began standing, waving, hollering, and clapping.

"It's over," Dello said in Vor's ear.

She quirked her brows at him, and he nodded.

"My wedding was much smaller," he agreed. "Of course, it couldn't have gotten much smaller. I think there were five people in total. This is ridiculous to the other extreme."

Though that prompted for Vor some curiosity about where his wife was, she wasn't about to pry, and wasn't given a chance to anyway.

"Let's get going," Andra suggested. "Maybe we can get to the reception before it gets crowded."

It took several more minutes before the mass of people started to calm and disperse. They were standing around talking in pairs or clumps, impeding others who were trying to leave. Only a few guests were as yet fighting their way through against the tide of people departing, toward the reception. When at last Vor and the other three made their way to the front of the room, the dais was empty again.

"This way," Andra urged. "The reception is in the smaller hall behind this one."

She led them to a door off to one side of the dais where a man in a suit was standing at attention.

"Names?" he asked as they approached.

"Terias and Andra Holstor, Dellostrikata Traskitandi, and Vorella Hearthsraven," Terias announced.

The suited man must have had the guest list memorized, for he bowed, and reached back to open the door for them. Andra led the way through, exclaiming something Vor couldn't hear as soon as she passed the threshold. Then Terias was going in behind her, but Dello was practically pushing them both out of the way. It was a good thing, too; Vor felt the presence of a magical aura she'd known so well last year, even if for a short time, that her months of solitude had not erased the memory. She strode through the path Dello opened for her—and swept Giri straight up into her arms.

She hardly had a chance to confirm visually that it was he, it happened so fast, but her powers recognized his in a flare of brilliance and surged to meet. She knew the sound of his voice breathing her name into her ear, and she recalled vividly the feel of his arms, his hands, his chest and back and the texture of his hair brushing her knuckles, and his scent of books and cinnamon. Vor clutched him hard, afraid she might hurt him but unable to stop, and he held her just as strongly. A discordant sound came from her; it might have been his name.

Vor had no thought of if others might be watching them, if others considered the embrace odd or improper for the place and time. She had the vague sense that Andra, Terias, and Dello might be standing around them, chatting about inconsequential things, as a shield. She couldn't let go of Giri, even though she wanted to look at him, kiss him. It felt too good to hold him, and the tension in his arms did not relax at all either. As long as he wasn't giving signs of wanting to let go, she wasn't going to, either.

"I can't believe you're here," he said after a time.

"I promised I'd come."

"You did, but it seemed so impossible."

"Impossible things happen sometimes."

She sensed his smile. "Yes, you have a history of making impossible things happen, don't you?"

And they went on holding each other, although the urgency began to subside after some number of heartbeats, until at last a voice intruded.

"Giri," Dello whispered. "It's starting to get crowded. The houses are showing up, people who will recognize you."

His arms relaxed a little, and made herself do the same. She looked at him as they drew back. He was smiling, his eyes full of light. His mage robes were blue and gold and fit him perfectly. His dark umber hair was swept back and braided much like hers. Giri touched her face briefly, but didn't start anything more intimate.

Vor grinned and leaned back in for a moment to whisper. "Do I get to stay in your room at the Citadel with you?"

"Yes, you do," he confirmed immediately, "but there are representatives from Noble Houses here, and I don't want to start any rumors until I've taken you to meet my parents."

Vor felt a surge of alarm, but tried to hide it. She wasn't sure what Giri's words implied. Giri didn't give indication that he'd noticed; he was scanning the room.

His voice turned amused. "Do you mind if we delay putting our hands all over each other until we get back to my room tonight?"

"That would be proper, wouldn't it," she conceded, trying to squash down both the heat and anxiety that had started building in her. "It is Colby's and Milsa's wedding party, after all."

"After all," Giri agreed with a sheepish smile. "Do you want to go say hello to them?"

Their three-person barrier parted as Vor and Giri turned to join them. Dello was grinning ear to ear. Andra beamed with delight, and even the more subdued Terias was smiling.

"You met my sister?" Giri managed weakly, appearing suddenly embarrassed.

"Of course she did," Andra glowed, "and Terias and Dello."

The latter winked.

"Oh my goodness, and did Giri tell you he has a set of twin nieces?" Andra gushed on. "I didn't tell you either, did I? We had a pair of baby girls last year. Of course, they're at home in Croun with their nurses and our parents. We're hoping to have some more. Children are so wonderful. Do you think you and—?"

"Vor's going to go greet Colby and Milsa now," Dello interrupted firmly, taking Vor's elbow and tugging her along. "Come on, Giri. Move your stubby little legs."

Vor glanced back, seeing that Andra had hardly paused and was now talking to her husband about something else. Giri caught up with a quick step.

"Well, that was close," Dello remarked.

"What?" Giri asked.

"Never you mind, my boy," the tall mage said, gathering his shorter friend under his arm on one side, still guiding Vor along by her elbow on the other.

Dello exchanged a covert glance with Vor. She knew perfectly well what Andra had been about to ask, and was not at all prepared to answer such a question. The room was crossed in only a few dozen paces—slightly fewer for Dello's long legs. Colby and Milsa were sitting together between a pair of tables, so each had a spot for a glass of something and a plate of food while still being able to sit or stand and greet well-wishers whenever they approached. Colby saw Vor coming right away, though it might have simply been the sight of the close packed trio with towering Dello in the middle that made them impossible to miss.

"Vor Hearthsraven," Colby smiled, getting to his feet.

He gave her a bow, and she—now freed from Dello's hold—returned it. Milsa stayed seated, but gave her a smirk and raised her glass as if toasting her.

"So you are here at last," the state wizard went on. "Your journey was pleasant?"

"I would say so, sir," Vor replied, "my first time riding a griffin."

"You've lost weight you didn't need to lose," Milsa commented from her seat.

Vor managed not to make any rude reply, but she wished everyone would stop mentioning it. "Congratulations on your wedding," she said instead.

"Our thanks. If he hasn't told you, Giri starts two weeks of leave time tomorrow," Colby announced. "It's only logical, since Milsa and I will be on leave, too."

"As it should be," Dello put in, "and congratulations, by the way, to you both. About time you made it official."

Other people were starting to crowd around the happy couple, eager to deliver their salutations as well.

"Wonderful to see you, Vor," Colby concluded. "We'll see you again in two week's time when you get back."

Dello dragged them away, finding a less crowded spot in a back corner.

"When I get back?" Vor repeated. "Or when we get back? From where?"

"This is where I exit," Dello said, and released both his prisoners, striding away into the milling party guests.

Giri took a step closer to Vor and kept his voice low. "He's assuming I'll use my leave time to visit my family, and that you would go with me," he said without preamble. "The thought has crossed my mind. I usually use my leave to go back home, but if you don't want to, we won't. We wouldn't have as much time together if we went to see them."

Vor's brow knit. The thought was both exciting and anxiety-inducing: meet Giri's parents, just as he'd mentioned a few minutes ago. She wanted to know them, but depending on how he introduced her, it could have a lot of significance for their future.

"You don't have to decide now, either," Giri assured her. "This day must already have been overwhelming for you, especially after months of peace and quiet in the mountains."

She nodded a little and took a calming breath. "You're not wrong. You said it seemed impossible that I would ever be here. To me, too, it's hard to believe I'm here, that you're standing in front of me again."

Vor tried to look at him the way Hawkjoy had told her to, with her complete regard. It helped a little, and she noticed Giri responding in kind. His gaze was steady on hers. He didn't rush to speak. The moment of conscious connection incited a gentle spread of wellbeing in her chest, and some of her anxiety faded. The swirl and noise of the crowd became just so much twittering of colorful birds: unimportant, outside her purview. The past didn't matter, nor the future: just now.

He was here, and Vor felt a lightening of her expression, the cautious curl of a smile. She realized again how attractive she found him, and her smile widened when she saw his cheeks darken a little: a blush. He shifted his weight, ducked his head just the tiniest bit, and gave a lopsided smile. Despite his age—several years more than hers—and his powers and competence as a mage, and his perhaps more worldly life experiences, there were times he exposed an unexpected sort of vulnerability. It was boyish and adorable.

"Let's talk about it tomorrow," Vor suggested gently. "I'd like to spend the rest of tonight just feeling my reality in this new place, as awkward and strange as it might be, and looking at you."

Giri's expression shifted from boyish to manly and he took another step closer, beyond what two chatting acquaintances or even friends would make their distance. That moment of vulnerability was gone as quickly as it had come, and his eyes now conveyed something far different. Vor recognized the look, and it stoked the warmth in her, too. Then he flicked his gaze around the room, found what he apparently sought, and touched the back of her hand.

"Come with me?" he asked.

Vor nodded, and followed as Giri moved past her, heading to the side of the room, where partly open curtains revealed shut balcony doors. There were balconies on both sides of the hall, but no one had opened them yet, and as Giri stepped through the first set of doors Vor saw that the balcony beyond them was empty. He shut the door quietly behind her once she stepped aside, out of view of the partygoers.

"You changed your mind?" Vor teased softly as he stepped up close to her—intimately close.

"Is that alright?" he replied.

"Yes. I'd hoped you would."

Giri's hand swept up the side of her face and they leaned in. He was only a scarce inch taller than her, so it was easy, and wonderful. She'd missed it, and pulled Giri against her, molding her body to his. He was not at all reluctant to comply, slowly pushing her back until she found herself against the wall beside the doors to the balcony, his mouth eager on hers. The pressure of his body made her tremble. In revenge Vor nudged her knee between his and pulled him harder against her, arching into him so he broke the kiss with a groan.

"Can you teleport us back to your room?" she breathed.

"You overestimate my abilities," he chuckled back, now bending his head down to find her neck.

Vor dug her fingers into Giri's back and shut her eyes to better feel the sensations heating up in her body. After having known this, and then being separated from him for several months, she hungered for more. She ran a hand down to his hip, the other encouraging on the back of his head, while his hands slid up her sides—

"So you're a hussy just like your mother."

The harsh voice shocked both Vor and Giri into jerking away. Vor rounded on the owner of that voice, finding an elderly woman standing just outside the now open balcony door. She was about Vor's height and as straight as a spear, with skin far darker than Vor's and well wrinkled with time. Her long braids reached her waist, black at the ends and getting progressively lighter until they were nearly pure white at her scalp, and woven through with red and black ribbons.

She was dressed in the kind of split gown Vor had already noticed was common in Weldom on non-mage females. It was a light gold in color, with darker embroidery, and the blouse and trews she wore under it were cream. The fabrics were pristine and the fit impeccable. The garments brought out her eyes, which were also a light golden color. The woman must have been in her seventh decade, but she seemed bright and spry for all that. She carried a cane, but didn't lean on it.

"I beg your pardon," Vor said coldly. "Could you repeat that?"

The woman's weathered face creased. "Your unwed mother spread her legs for a filthy guardsman." She exaggerated looking Giri up and down. "At least you have better taste. Your name, boy?"

Vor exchanged a quick concerned look with Giri, but he straightened and walked steadily to stand before the intruding woman. He gave a small bow.

"Giri Holstor, madam."

"Holstor, ah yes, and the firstborn then, aren't you?" She sniffed and seemed to think for a moment, not bowing back. Then her gaze transferred back to Vor. "No. Too strong: we'd never keep our name, not now. Come with me, Vorella. I'm taking you home."

"Excuse me," Vor retorted as Giri retreated a few steps, "but I'm not going anywhere."

The woman stabbed the floor with her cane. "You will be grateful," she declared. "Your uncle's daughter has failed to breed. Your aunt's sons both lost their names in their marriages. But you're pretty, young, and healthy enough—too thin, but that can be fixed. You could make a match to save Mrandis House, so we will be generous enough to take you back."

The excitement of Giri's touch was long faded and Vor's heart pounded from a different cause now.

She feared she knew, but asked anyway. "Who are you?"

The woman stuck out her chin. "I'm your grandmother, child, your mother's mother. I don't suppose she told you of me, or my name. I'm Mirassi Mrandis, born a Mrandis, always a Mrandis."

Vor felt a snarl coming on. "I am not a Mrandis," she stated. "You threw out my mother—your own daughter—and me with her. I'm a Hearthsraven, and I will match where I choose or not at all."

The old woman stuck her gnarled fingers at Giri. "You think House Holstor will allow you to pair with their prize boy, the young man half the noble girls in the west have been begging their parents for?"

"They don't get to tell me who I associate with," Giri put in. "I've made that clear with them."

Vor met his gaze for a moment, saw the calm steadiness there, and something trembled in her chest—and then calmed to match him. Giri transferred his gaze back to the matron of House Mrandis.

The woman laughed, although it sounded more like a cough. "Fools and cursed," she croaked. "Keep him as your lover if you will, but make a match for breeding more—"

"I refuse," Vor declared.

The woman lifted her head like an offended goat.

"I would be curious to meet my family," Vor went on before the woman could speak again. "I have wondered if I might travel to Mount Brasson and visit both my mother's and father's side. I expect my father's parents, if they yet live, will be happy to see their grandchild again, who they surely thought dead with their son and his wife somewhere in Northborn. But perhaps there is no point in visiting my mother's family. Is there, Grandmother?"

Now Mirassi Mrandis hunched on her cane with both hands, head shaking. "You know nothing, bastard child lost in war. What have you done with yourself in Northborn all these years? Were you a shopkeeper's girl? A rag picker? A whore—?"

"I was, and am, a mage," Vor avowed. "I was apprenticed to the late mage lord of Northborn."

She seemed mildly startled but rallied. "Were you really? Perhaps you should have died with him," she taunted.

"I killed him," Vor emphasized.

Apparently Mirassi Mrandis hadn't heard that part of the story, or hadn't believed it, for Vor's words drove a nail of shock into the woman's face, but she recovered quickly. "And what are you now? Living on Holstor's charity?"

Giri cut in. "She's State Wizard Colby's apprentice."

The old woman's head jerked up again, making her braids dance, and Vor, too, wanted to startle, but she held her reaction in. For several heavy moments the crone of House Mrandis looked from one to the other of them, and back, and back again. The indignation ran gradually out of her posture.

"House Mrandis is dying," she rasped. "It's your mother's fault; you owe us your help. You won't consider a marriage long enough to have a babe or two for us?"

"It's only a name," Vor said, gentler than she had yet been.

Mirassi made a frustrated gesture. "Who will live in the manor without children to inherit it?"

Giri spoke again. "Explore your family branches. Welcome them back to the manor. After all, situations like yours are what they're for. Show them kindness and generosity, and they might return the same to you. Let yourself love the children they bring, as though they were your own—though it sounds to me like you have not much loved your children."

Her lip curled in Giri's direction as she ignored his suggestion in favor of further defense of her position. "Tell me how House Holstor would treat a daughter that lies unwed with a common soldier, a peasant, and chooses to keep the child he spawns in her—even asks if she might marry him and bring him into the family—when she had already been promised to another."

He shrugged. "I don't know, but I don't think we would disown her."

"Well enough for you then," the woman hissed, stamping her cane on the floor again.

"You didn't get to marry for love, did you?" Vor broke in.

The crone's eyes fixed on her like drawn arrows.

"So you can't stand anyone else getting to do it," Vor concluded.

"Hold your tongue. Your mother said the same, but you are all ignorant, naïve fools," she cursed. She sniffed and lifted her chin again. "With your mother's changeling blood you'd probably cause us more problems than you'd fix anyway, so do as you like then."

She looked Vor up and down once more, and then turned to stomp back through the balcony door and into the hall.

"I shall," Vor murmured after her.

Giri stepped close. "That was a surprise."

"I thought it might happen, since Colby announced it to Strafa and Ylanzo and their apprentices," Vor confessed. "Words, once let out, cannot be put back in their boxes. I just didn't think it would be so soon."

"Vor, I was the one who did the research, who found out who you were. I told my master," Giri confessed. "I'm sorry. I didn't think he would tell everyone. I just wanted more reasons for him to let me help you."

Vor put a forgiving hand on his shoulder. "It's alright. It was bound to happen eventually. I wasn't expecting much from House Mrandis, but I didn't think she'd say things like that."

"Or make that demand?"

Vor shrugged one shoulder and glanced his way with a sly little twinkle. "Colby's apprentice, am I?"

"You're not, but you could be." Giri again winced in apology. "I was going to mention it to you first, but we hadn't really gotten to that sort of thing. He said he'd be happy to take you. Milsa is done. She's been granted master status, so he has time and space for a new apprentice. He's used to handling two."

"And Milsa doesn't want to take me on."

"Do you really think you would get on well with her?"

Vor almost smiled. "Perhaps not, but maybe in time."

"Besides," Giri whispered, "don't spread this around, but," he put his mouth beside her ear, "she's pregnant, and going to be taking some time off magery."

"Oh," Vor blinked. "She could still teach though?"

He shook his head. "She's staying in the Srawn House, here at the capital. She needs to stay away from mage-stone, in case the baby's meant to be a mage, and there's a lot of it in the Citadel. Colby will be staying at the capital, too, of course, for a while, so he could take you through wizard orientation, teach you stuff, and get you ready to start taking assignments, us three, together, maybe with Milsa later. You wouldn't have to agree to be employed by the state, but that would make things easier."

Giri seemed to be watching carefully for her reaction. "But it's only an idea. You don't have to accept him."

Vor, however, was nodding. "It's a good idea. It would allow us to work together, wouldn't it? If I were to become anyone else's apprentice, we might be getting assigned separately all the time, and if I don't pledge to work for Weldom, I don't know how I would be able to go with you at all."

"It would be more complicated, but you don't have to decide tonight, or tomorrow, or even next week," Giri assured her.

She smiled at him and reached out to pet his cheek. "I've been thinking it over all winter. I'm inclined towards this solution," she said. "Of course there are aspects to be clarified before I reach my final decision."

It was amusing; she could both see Giri's hopeful excitement and how he was holding it in, trying not to influence her with it. Regardless of how he felt about it, she knew that becoming a wizard would get her training, occupation, and lodging all in one. That it would keep her near Giri was an extra bonus. Her magic was a part of her so deep, she could no more give it up than she could give up her breath or cognition. Being a wizard would be the best way she knew of to continue using it and learning about it. Of course there were still a lot of unknowns as to everything being a wizard would entail, but the wizards she met seemed well adjusted enough—far better than her late master had been—so she could only hope she could adapt.

Giri swallowed. "Is it what you want? Maybe you should talk with Colby about it first. You should understand everything you're agreeing to."

"I will," Vor confirmed. "After all, I don't know all the obligations and rules I'll be expected to live by." She raised an eyebrow his way. "Killing my own master apparently did not disqualify me?"

"Well," Giri began, "that situation was self-defense, and occurred outside of Weldom, and Altare wasn't a wizard, and he deserved it, but I'd suggest you don't do it again."

Vor laughed, the first laugh she'd had in a long time. That seemed to inspire Giri to gather her into his arms, which she had no objections to in the slightest, and which led to a little more than hugging—until Giri's stomach clenched and grumbled vigorously enough that Vor both heard and felt it.

"Have you eaten today?" she queried, drawing back to look at him.

"You're the one that needs feeding," he countered.

"Let's get food."

Vor and Giri went back into the bustle of the hall. Tables had been filled with food and the smell was tempting, making her belly rumble as much as Giri's had. Dello was standing beyond the end of one of those tables with a plate piled with delicacies.

"There she is," he grinned as Vor and Giri approached.

"Dello," she greeted.

"Nevermind me," Giri remarked, beginning to fill a plate.

Dello gestured towards Vor's shoulders with a stalk of some purple vegetable. "Your hair's a little mussed. Someone been putting his hands in it?"

"It's been distracting him from food," she said. "And he's been occupied with ceremonial duties all day so I need to feed him."

Giri looked up and gave her a teasing smirk. She smirked back.

"Those yellow things are good," Dello pointed.

The pair made their selections with Dello's running commentary and then Vor dragged the pair of them back out to the balcony. Dello immediately took a seat up on the railing, kicking his feet like a boy, as though there wasn't a deep gorge behind him that he could plummet into if he lost his balance.

"Enjoying the party, Vor?" Dello asked, and then snorted. "Silly question, silly me. I can smell the hormones in the air and sense them in your auras. Told you he missed you, too, didn't I?"

Giri had his plate on the railing far enough from Dello to prevent theft, and Vor took a spot just beyond him.

"So you're going to stay?" Dello went on.

"I am thinking so," Vor admitted, "but we'll see."

"Told Colby yet?"

"Not yet."

"You don't want your marks?" Dello asked. "I'll bet Colby would make Milsa give you your fifth, and with me and Colby that's—"

"Let her do things in her own time," Giri interrupted.

Dello lapsed into silence, but only for a few breaths. He took the time to turn around so he was sitting on the railing facing towards the gorge now, instead of with his back to it.

"You two are adorable. Do you have any idea how envious I am?" he commented, his usually vibrant voice oddly flat. "The person you love being a mage and wizard, pretty much your equal with just different strengths, who you'll get to work with all the time, and able to marry if you both want to, just like Colby and Milsa did. You're really lucky. I'm really happy for you."

Vor hesitated, not sure how to respond, and decided to let Giri handle it, which he did.

"Give me your last yellow thing," he demanded of his tall friend, reaching for his plate.

"Get your own," Dello retorted, jerking his plate away and sending half its remaining contents flying into the gorge. "There's plenty inside. You've got super crazy magic powers, the strongest master, good looks, top grades, a great girl, and you want my last yellow thing? Take a flying leap, shorty."

He spun about on the railing and dropped to his feet, winked in Vor's direction, and retreated back into the hall. Vor moved over to stand with Giri at the balustrade, put her plate next to his and they shared out their remaining food. Sunset was approaching, and though the building was not at the eastern edge of the city, it was by one of the gorges, and they could look along it towards the east and glimpse the reddening sky. Giri held her hand.

"Is Dello alright?" Vor asked.

"He's fine," Giri replied. "His marriage was arranged by his house and he doesn't have a love bond with his wife. Still has four kids with her, but I think he's feeling left out."

"Dello has kids," Vor echoed, surprised.

"The house is raising them, as is usual with noble houses," Giri said, somewhat glumly. "I don't really approve, but it's none of my business. I'm born to a house, but I have never felt involved with all their customs. Luckily, my parents never forced me, like Dello's did."

"It doesn't seem right," Vor agreed.

"Don't feel too sorry for him," Giri shrugged. "He's still a wizard, which has gotten him free of his house in a lot of ways. Feel sorry for the ones who can't get even that much freedom."

"Like my mother," Vor nodded. "I suppose that's why she left Mrandis House."

"And why you won't go back."

Giri was watching her, and she turned her head to meet his gaze. "I won't go back. That's one thing I know."

Giri nodded in acknowledgment. "The party will go on a while longer," he said. "We don't have to stay until the end."

"How long do you want to stay?"

He shrugged a little. "I have gotten all I wanted. Wouldn't mind a few more of those yellow things, though."

Vor smiled, but then suggested, "For now. You also want to take me home to your parents?"

He stared at the last bit of herb bread in his hand. "Yes," he admitted. "I do."

Vor closed the distance between them and leaned her head against his. "I suppose you should."

"You're alright with it?"

"I'm not sure, but Andra will tell them anyway, won't she? They'll be curious," she said. "I am with you. Let them know."

"Alright." He leaned his head into hers, counterbalancing. Vor thought he might say more about what meeting his parents might imply, or what they might expect of her, but he was silent for a while. "We should go see your family, too, shouldn't we?"

"Yes, I suppose so. I'm not sure which makes me more nervous: meeting my family or yours."

They stood and ate as the sun sank lower. Around the time they finished their plates, a swell of music came from inside the halls.

"The dancing is starting," Giri said.

"I've never learned to dance," Vor confessed, "though Dello tried to teach me some while we were watching the wedding."

"As good a way to spend the time as any. I couldn't see you in the audience, so I bet you were so far back you couldn't see or hear anything either. If you show me what he taught you, maybe we can add to it."

Giri took a step away, making some space as he spread his arms in an encompassing gesture.

"Would you like to?" he asked. "I'd love to teach you."

She let him. Hand in hand, or hand on shoulder, waist, wherever the dance called for, Giri guided her through the movements and it did not take long for her to catch on. Even had she not been so quick to pick up any learning presented, with their energies mingling, she could sense his intentions, the next coming step, and anticipate it even as he muttered directions. Within a few minutes they were dancing smoothly in synchrony.

"This is nice," she told him. "It's almost like working magic together."

His mouth quirked. "Or doing other things together."

"Or that," she agreed.

"Vor," called a delighted voice from above, bringing the exercise to a halt.

"Let them be," reprimanded another voice. "I think they're courting."

"Oh, I beg your pardon."

Vor and Giri glanced around, locating three griffins on the wing riding the misty breeze that came up from the gorge.

"It's alright," Vor called up. "You can come down."

One griffin dove, dipping down and pulling up to snag the balustrade, and Vor recognized Hawkjoy. The second and third landed on the next balcony over, still within speaking distance—especially for griffin lungs. Hawkjoy clambered up and balanced on the railing, wings partly spread and feathers tugged by the misty breeze every which way.

"Is this your mate?" she asked eagerly.

"Ah, Hawkjoy, this is Giri. Giri, the griffin who carried me here, Hawkjoy," Vor introduced.

As Giri greeted the griffin, one of the others leapt over from the neighboring balcony and balanced beside Hawkjoy. It was the rusty red one who had given her a nod up on the landing platform.

"Thornwing," Giri greeted this one, too.

"Good evening," he replied. "I see you reunited at last."

Vor looked over at the third, again recognizing the big brown griffin as Hawkwind.

"We're late to the party," she called over.

"Go on in," Giri invited. "You will cause quite a stir for those who have not met you yet."

The griffin was unruffled at that. "As it has been. No one has speared us yet."

Then Hawkwind stepped down from the balustrade, and Vor was surprised to see she had a rider. The Northnest princess Jessika had been hidden in the shadow of her wings, and now slid down the griffin's back to find her feet. Vor had forgotten that Hawkjoy had told her the young woman was coming to Weldom. She wore a muted green split gown and a somber expression.

Then a fourth griffin wheeled over and landed on the same balcony as Hawkwind. This one was bigger even than Hawkwind, and it too had a rider. Vor recognized the young man as Rikah, son of Rikan the blacksmith who worked for the Northborn castle. He dropped to his feet and moved quickly to Jessika's side.

"Don't go off without me," he requested, just loudly enough that Vor could hear.

The princess did not respond, did not even look at him.

"Let's go in then, children," Hawkwind chivvied, finding the latch of the balcony doors and pulling them open. "Pet us, will you, so they can see we're not attackers."

The two griffins and two humans walked into the hall to sounds of exclamations and dismay. The music squawked to a halt. Vor smiled a little, and Hawkjoy and Thornwing stepped down from the railing onto the balcony beside her and Giri.

"We interrupted," Thornwing apologized.

"It's fine," Giri said, extending a hand to Vor. "Perhaps we should go in and join the dancers?"

"Ah, dancing," Thornwing nodded. "We griffins dance in the sky, up and down in addition to side to side. How unfortunate you humans must do your dancing only on the ground. If you would be so kind as to walk in with us in a way that might show we are not fearsome beasts, at least not at the moment."

Giri drew the doors wide as Vor went to Hawkjoy, reaching up to put a hand on her shoulder, and the four of them walked in. There was less dismay at the appearance of two additional griffins, since the first two had not ripped any of the partygoers into shreds yet. Inside, it was clear that the humans had already sorted themselves by disposition towards the large feathered guests. Some amount had warily moved to the tables at the far side of the room. Some others continued dancing or talking as though nothing had changed. Another group had approached the griffins with curiosity. Those at the back of that group, who could not get close to Hawkwind and the other, drifted over towards Thornwing and Hawkjoy.

"Enjoy your attention," Giri grinned, and then Vor took his hand and they stepped out to join the dancers.

Dancing really was not particularly difficult, especially since she could—as Dello had said—follow Giri's cues. Once she got completely comfortable with the movement patterns, it was even rather fun. They paused when they got tired and sought food and drink. They danced some more, and in the next pause found themselves chatting with the griffins, who had clustered in one corner. Jessika—and Rikah as her apparently unwanted bodyguard—were out in the crowd, mingling.

"So the dancing is not courtship?" Hawkjoy wanted clarified.

"It is," Giri answered, "or it can be. Many people may dance together, and it is one way to meet people."

"You two dance only with each other," the fourth griffin observed.

Giri bowed. "My lady Eaglegrace, that is when dancing is courtship between an interested pair, and no longer used to meet others."

"So you are mates then?" Hawkjoy confirmed with a lift of her crest.

"Very well, Hawkjoy, yes," Vor told her in surrender. "You may say that we are."

The griffin chortled. "That is good."

Thornwing butted Giri with his head, making the man stagger, but Giri smiled and Vor figured it was some kind of gesture of camaraderie between the two males.

"I'll be staying here in Weldom now," Vor announced, "with Giri and to train as a wizard under Colby if he really will take me, but first I think Giri and I will be going to visit our families."

Giri smiled, and Thornwing and Hawkjoy both perked up.

"Most excellent," the male said. "And where are your families?"

"Western Weldom, in the mountains," Giri provided. "At least, I know my family is there. We will see about Vor's."

"Can I come?" Hawkjoy blurted, and immediately turned to Hawkwind. "Wind, can I go with them?"

"I think I will join you," Thornwing said, "if it would not trouble you."

"You don't need me here," Hawkjoy went on imploringly to the bigger female beside her. "You and Eaglegrace and Snowdark are handling everything. I could go see the western part of Weldom."

Hawkwind's feathers were flat. "You don't need my permission, Joy." She looked across the room to where Jessika and Rikah were making polite conversation with a pair of nobles. "Wings might miss you."

Hawkjoy looked over, too, and even though her raptorial features did not well convey emotion, Vor thought she looked sad—and frustrated.

"She doesn't notice whether I am here or not," Hawkjoy said bitterly.

Then the slender female sat back full on her haunches and lifted her hands. She made some complex, rapid gestures, which Hawkwind and Thornwing watched attentively. It must have been the hand language Vor had heard about. Hawkwind replied swiftly the same way, and Thornwing added a few gestures, too.

Then the male turned his attention back to Vor and Giri. "If it would not trouble you," he repeated, "we would be willing to fly you to wherever you're going. I am not as large as Hawkjoy, but I could still keep up, even with a rider."

"I normally go by horse, but yes, I suppose." Giri glanced at Vor for confirmation.

"Certainly," she concurred. "Going griffin-back is both an exciting and efficient way to travel. Plus, griffins are much better conversationalists than horses are."

Hawkjoy's feathers perked up a little, but she still looked sad.

"In that case, not tomorrow, but the next day?" Giri asked. "Would that be a good day for you to depart?"

"Let it be so," Thornwing confirmed. "We can meet you in the morning up on the platform where Hawkjoy arrived with Vor today. Eighth hour?"

They agreed. By then, full darkness had fallen, but the party went on, with fresh food and drink being continually provided, and the musicians steady on their instruments. The lamps were all glowing, holding back the night. Giri and Vor danced some more, fetched a little more refreshment, spoke again with Dello and Andra and Terias, and returned to sit with the griffins. Vor contemplated going to Colby, and confirming that he would take her as an apprentice, but he and Milsa were constantly surrounded by other guests, so she decided to wait. The room heated and people went about opening the balcony doors to let cool spring air waft through.

Then it happened.

There was no warning, when someone cried out, and then someone else, and then came the thuds and crashes as rocks, stones, and pieces of paving began pelting into the hall through the open balcony doors. People shouted and screamed. The missiles hit the food tables, scattering desserts and delectables, and shattering dishes and pitchers of drink so partygoers were food-pelted and splashed as well as struck. A few dozen magical shields went up at once, Vor's and Giri's not excluded. They spread them to cover the griffins, none of whom were mages. Blocking physical attacks with magical shields was no easy thing, but Vor and Giri merged their energies, reinforcing each other, and the barrage did not last long anyway, no more than half a minute.

"Stay away from the balconies," Colby ordered over the tumult.

"Watch for broken glass," someone else added.

The griffins didn't listen: at least Hawkwind did not. Vor's shield wouldn't stop something getting out, only things getting in, so the brown griffin dashed right out, through the nearest balcony, and out into the air. Thornwing swiftly followed her, but Eaglegrace sought out Jessika where Rikah was trying with some difficulty to hide her in a corner. The big female stood before them both with wings mantled and crest feathers splayed in an unmistakable threat display, and all the surrounding humans cleared away.

The missiles had stopped however, and wizards started lowering their shields. A couple dozen people had been hit, no one fatally, but there were a few bleeding head wounds and lots of bruises. A few hundred rocks and stones lay scattered across the floor. The doors back into the ceremonial hall burst open and a score of armed guards came rushing inside. Then all was "what happened?" and "who did this?" and "who is hurt?"

"That was unusual," Giri said. "Are you alright?"

"I'm fine," Vor answered. "Hawkjoy?"

"Fine," the griffin nodded.

"I assure you, this is not a normal part of a wedding celebration." Giri kicked at the closest rock.

Then Vor noticed an oddity about a nearby stone and fetched it. "There's a note on this one."

Indeed, many people were finding missiles with paper bound onto them with string. Vor untied the one she held and opened the dirty scrap of parchment. Giri and Hawkjoy both crowded close to read what was written on it.

Vor's brows lowered. "Magic," she read aloud, "is for everyone."

Vor, Giri, Dello, Andra, and Terias left together. With rocks, smashed food, and spilled drink all over the hall, there seemed no point in staying later, especially as the maintainers of the hall had moved in to begin cleaning up. The carriage went first to drop off the married Holstors at a friendly house where they were staying, and then headed back to the Citadel. Giri and Vor sat together across from Dello, leaning on each other's shoulders. Dello was watching vigilantly out the windows of the carriage.

"Nothing more will happen tonight," Giri mumbled. "They never prank us twice in a row."

"That was a prank?" Vor asked.

"A bit more violent than usual," Dello said seriously. "This sort of thing has been on the rise over the past decade, but it only happens a few times a year. There's a group of people unhappy with the wizards, so they've been harassing us from time to time. They call themselves the Magic Liberation Front. Some people think they're a joke, but others are getting concerned." He sighed with a philosophic air. "You can't please everyone."

"I should have thought about it," Giri remarked. "I was too distracted. This was a perfect opportunity for them. The wedding of a state wizard, where bunches of other wizards would be attending?"

"Then when it got dark, the lamps were lit, and the balcony doors opened," Dello went on.

"A tempting target they couldn't resist," Giri concluded.

"That paper," Dello grunted to Vor. "That's their slogan: magic is for everyone."

"But it's not," she contributed. "You have to be a mage. You have to have the inborn ability."

"And mages are born only to the nobility," Dello reminded her.

She frowned. "That's right, because of the mage-stone."

He nodded. "Because of the mage-stone that's in all the metal the common people use. It stops their babies from being born with magical potential."

"It's why Weldom invaded Northnest," Giri pointed out.

"Because," Vor agreed, "Weldom was running out of the stone, and Northnest had a bunch."

"Our mines were empty," Dello confirmed. "Are still empty, and so we delve for more. Adding mage-stone to metal makes it brittle and difficult to melt down for reuse, so we always need more. I say 'we' but I don't mean us sitting here. I mean," he made a vague gesture, "the government, I suppose."

Heavy in the air was the thought among all three of them that perhaps—one way or another—the mage-stone would run out completely, would stop being added to cheap metal, and that would change things. For better? Or for worse? Maybe that would depend on the perspective of the person or organization in question.

The carriage came to a halt. Giri took a deep breath and sat up from his slump. They had arrived at the front gate of the Citadel.

"So you two are heading off into the west for a while?" Dello asked as he opened the carriage door and stepped out. He glanced around, as if looking for threats.

"In a couple days, yes," Vor confirmed. "The griffins are going to take us."

Dello made an impressed sound. "Well, I'll be here, doing whatever nonsense my master has me at next."

"We'll be around tomorrow," Giri offered.

Dello elbowed him as the trio walked up the steps to the front entrance of the Citadel. "Yeah, right. You two will be in bed all day tomorrow."

Giri elbowed him back.

"Not all day," Vor said mildly.

Dello snorted as though he did not believe her, and they passed through the entry arch and into the carpeted foyer with the wide desk of dark wood tenanted by a night receptionist, who looked them up and down, and made no comment. From each side led off a corridor. Dello didn't even pause as he gave a magical answer to the ward guarding the one to the left—a ward no non-mage could have passed without assistance—and the trio went on. They climbed some stairs, heading to higher floors.

"Well," Dello shrugged, "come find me then, if you want, if I'm not stuck in a library researching something or other."

"Oh good," Giri teased, "you're getting some more time in the libraries."

The tall man gave the shorter one a shove. "Off with you. Goodnight, Vor."

"Goodnight, Dello," she called back.

He waved blindly over his shoulder and turned off down a branching hall. Vor and Giri headed up to the latter's room, taking each other's hand as they went. Even though night was well underway, there were still a few people in the halls, most in some version of mage robes, a few in bath robes, and the halls were gently lit with glowing stones set into the walls.

They reached Giri's room.

"You put my wards up when you left," he smiled.

"It seemed the polite thing to do," Vor said idly before bringing out a thought that had been dogging her. "What my grandmother said, that you're the prize boy of House Holstor?"

He winced a little and led Vor inside, touching a cluster of quartz crystals on his desk and setting it aglow.

"My parents have been trying to use me for an alliance marriage for years," Giri sighed. "I've been resisting. They've been kind enough to humor me. Andra married well and has now produced babies, which took off some pressure, but their patience is running out. Sometimes mages don't wed, and they know that, but they still want it."

Vor shed her outer robes and leaned back against a bookcase. "Dello said you got your heart broken."

His eyes snapped over to her and for a long moment he stared. Vor was about to tell him he didn't have to tell her when he blurted it out.

"I did," he admitted, "twice, when I was seventeen, again when I was nineteen. It wasn't related to my parents trying to match me up. It was here, with two other mages. I was enamored and wanted it to be love. As far as I can figure, the young women found me convenient, skilled, and devoted, and no risk to getting them with an unwanted child. They let me believe, until I became too clingy, and started asking for more than just their bed time."

Vor crossed her arms. "Dello told me he was afraid I was doing that to you, too."

Giri went on staring at her. "It's possible we might hurt each other," he acknowledged, "but I know it won't be that way."

"It won't be," Vor confirmed.

After another tense moment of staring, Giri let out his breath. "I need a bath."

"Me, too."

"Use anything you want from the wardrobe," Giri invited. "I have a spare bathrobe somewhere."

So they both went off to the separate bathing chambers and Vor stood in the hot water of the shower, awash with contemplations of the future. It was inescapable. Unless one of them did something drastic, she could see now that she would probably end up marrying Giri. The question was if it would be because his house wanted it, or he wanted it—unless neither wanted it. Would it be possible they didn't have to marry?

What Vor's head and heart said about it was that she didn't care—married or not, all she wanted was to be with him—but to keep him for herself, to let the world know that he was hers, and because he was from a house, she figured she would have to marry him. That would mean convincing his parents, or defying them, but she would be with him, and she wouldn't tolerate sharing him.

Was that how Giri would feel about it, too? He was taking her to meet them. If he had meant to keep her as his wizard mistress—as her own grandmother had suggested she do with him—she would never be brought to his ancestral house, right? No, surely he was going to tell his parents that she was his choice; she could see no other way it could be interpreted. The only question was if he would let his parents' arguments sway him. Since he'd resisted their attempts to marry him off for years now—long past when most young nobles were married—she couldn't imagine that he would give in to them, not when he had more to lose than before.

Still lingered some worry: what if her feelings changed in time? She knew it was possible: that such things did happen. She was very inexperienced in the ways of love and pairing. Could she be making a mistake? Well, she figured, of course she could. Her feelings for Giri were strong, and she liked him as a person, and respected him as a fellow mage, and really enjoyed what they did together in bed. She would soon be Colby's apprentice beside him, and that meant they'd be together.

She'd spent all winter considering it, and had decided she'd be with him. Now that she'd seen him again, that decision hadn't changed. She couldn't know the future, but her mind was set. For now, she would be bound to him. In a few minutes, she'd go back to his room and renew those bonds. She'd let there be more bonds if that was what had to happen: being a fellow apprentice, and even being his wife. She had never thought she'd marry someone and if she was honest with herself, the idea still felt foreign, like tying a griffin into a carriage harness meant for a horse, but if she had to, she could do it, just like that griffin could pull a carriage if it had to.

But was that the right thing to do?

It was all so uncertain and had the potential to make Vor's mind confused and heart conflicted—but it could wait until tomorrow. Vor dried off and wrapped up in Giri's bathrobe. She combed out her hair using a little magical heat to dry it, cleaned her teeth, and made her way back to his room on silent bare feet, cool against the wooden floors: cool as other parts of her were not. He was waiting for her in the now dimmer light of the crystal. She slid out of the robe as she slid into his arms and they tumbled down to the bed, where they loved through the night until they didn't miss each other anymore.

Chapter 3
The Citadel

They slept late and Vor awoke in warmth and contentment like she hadn't felt in—like she'd never felt. Since she'd left the cottage, and since she'd arrived in Anchoria, and on a larger scale since she'd left Northborn, since she'd killed Altare, she felt better. Everything felt better, but she knew she couldn't become complacent. She had an upward trend, but it would need tending to maintain. The most immediate aspect of that was currently in bed with her, and she sensed he was awake.

"Giri?" she murmured, voice resonating through his chest where her head lay.

"Mm?" he hummed back.

"There's something I want to tell you."

"Alright," he assured her, with an accompanying enlivening of his aura. "You have my full attention."

She still hesitated for a few breaths before she finally took the plunge. "You know I came to Weldom partly because you're here. I promised you I'd come, and I'm glad I did."

"I love it that you're here," Giri said simply in reply.

"But you aren't the only reason I'm here. I spent the whole winter thinking about it. What's most important to me is continuing my magical studies and attaining self-sufficiency. Altare controlled my life, and controlled me. I'm never allowing that again."

Vor could sense him taking in her words, and growing uncertain about where she was heading with them. She got to the point before his unease could grow further.

"We made it clear with each other, before, what our arrangement was to be," she said. "Obviously, things changed, but we were honest. I want to be honest again."

"Yes, let's," Giri replied with satisfying promptness.

"I'm here for magic. You're here, too, which is perfect, but if you weren't here, I would still be here."

Unspoken, but implied: if it were a choice between being there with magic, or elsewhere with Giri, she'd choose the magic. If he made that connection, it didn't seem to upset him unduly, though his hand moved against her back with a hint of possessiveness.

"Vor, I really enjoy your company, but if it came down to it, I'd probably make the same choice. If you decided you were going to go off by yourself, I'd let you go, like I did before, and if you said you'd come back, I'd wait, but my life is here."

She sensed that in his honesty he'd voluntarily made himself vulnerable, just as it hadn't been easy for her to say either, but it was genuine honesty; she could sense that, too. It relieved her.

Vor went on. "I haven't fully resolved to become a wizard yet, but if I do, that will be my life. If you fit into it, and it seems likely that you would, then all the better. How I feel right now, is that I want us to stay together. Time will tell if that's the best thing for both of us."

Giri nodded against the crown of her head. "If it does come to pass that you become a wizard," Giri postulated, "as Colby's apprentice or someone else's, and you find the studies and work fulfilling, what do you want a relationship to look like? In general, I mean: not necessarily with me, but with anyone you might end up picking."

"You're talking about marriage and family," Vor guessed.

"I am," he confirmed. "Shall I tell you my views first? Or would you rather go first?"

"I'll go first," she said. Now that they had broached the conversation, she wasn't about to let her courage falter, or let herself be influenced in her answer by hearing Giri's expectations first.

"As for marriage, I don't see a particular need. I wouldn't sleep around. If I'm with someone, then I'm with him. Being married or not wouldn't change that. Marriage is something I could consider, but I'm concerned it would add family expectations and obligations I don't want. Colby and Milsa only did it when they were both old and established enough that their families probably aren't trying to put pressures on them, but I don't want any strings of control on me."

"Good to know," Giri acknowledged.

"As for producing a family," Vor charged onward, "It's not in my plan. I certainly wouldn't do it if it interfered with my studies or duties as a wizard. The process sounds extremely unpleasant. I should not be put in charge of properly raising a child. I don't know if my mind would ever change on the topic, but right now, I doubt it. No partner of mine should ever expect it." She took a breath. "Alright, your turn."

"I am in full agreement with you on the topic of offspring," he declared without hesitation. "Though my parents raised me with their expectation that I would, and when I was younger, I thought I would have to, I've never wanted to make children. As time has passed and I've expressed that to my parents, they have backed off. Now it has no place in my life plan, either. I'd never want a partner of mine to expect that I'd provide her with babies. I don't want that kind of responsibility or drain on my time."

Vor sighed with relief, and tried to resist cuddling him tighter.

"Not that my nieces aren't adorable," Giri muttered, "in small doses, but I'm glad they are not my obligation."

"And your expectations regarding marriage," Vor prodded.

"I'm like you that when I commit, I commit, and no signature on paper is needed to attain my constancy," he provided. "Because I'm from a noble house, if I married, there would be many expectations attached, and I don't want those. I also don't want any partner of mine to ever feel that she's obligated to stay with me or provide heirs due to some formal promises before witnesses and signatures in a book. Also, though nobility often marry someone they hardly know, I wouldn't. After years together with unflagging adoration, I might be willing to marry, provided my family doesn't think it means my partner and I are going to live at Holstor House and produce heirs. On the other hand, if a committed partner of mine never wanted to marry, I would be fine never marrying."

Vor absorbed that with further relief. It didn't mean she and Giri would make a perfect pair, but at least their expectations for a pairing were very similar, so they still had the potential to be a good pair. "Thank you," she whispered. "I like that we're largely in accord."

"I think I do love you," he blurted next, some of his composure deserting him, "but we're both still new to this, to each other, and neither of us should feel like we can't walk away if it's not good for us."

That must have been hard for him to say, Vor thought, considering—

Giri plowed determinedly on, as if, having gotten started, he felt he had to get everything out. "Just because those other two women broke my heart, that doesn't mean you should feel sorry for me, or like, if you needed to leave that you couldn't because it would hurt me. Do you sense my meaning?"

"I think so," she said—and another weight of tension left her. This weight she hadn't even realized she was carrying, but ever since Dello had told her about Giri's past broken hearts, it had been there: pressure from him not to do anything to break Giri's heart again. She frowned to herself, a little annoyed at Dello, but Giri didn't seem to notice.

"What I thought was heartbreak then," he went on, "was not that serious of a hurt. I was young. I was new to pairing, and though I thought I loved them, it's hard to say how deep my feelings really went, or didn't go."

He shifted a little, and Vor lifted her head to meet his gaze.

"I just think, I would rather have you get what you need in life, whatever that is," he affirmed, expression intent, "and if I'm getting in the way of that, it would make me sadder to be causing you such trouble, than to be without you but see you live your fullest life."

Vor nodded. "I agree. I would rather have you leave me before I held you back from your greatness. I'm grateful for everything you've said. I was starting to think about bonds and obligations, and preparing to take them on, even as they felt like burdens."

"No burdens," he breathed, "not for us," and their hands found each other between the sheets and clasped tightly. "Andra and Terias, and even Dello, probably expect us to get married," he continued, less emphatically now, "but there's no reason we have to do it."

Vor felt herself relax even more.

Giri reached out his other hand and stroked her hair. "That relieves you; I can feel it in your energies."

"It's not that I'm not very fond of you," she pointed out quickly.

"I know," he replied with a little smile, "I can feel that, too."

"I just worried I would have to marry you to keep you."

She felt the anxiety drain from his body and energy both. He sighed into her hair and wrapped her up with his arms.

"You don't have to," he promised. "I'm not going anywhere, and you don't have to do anything for me but be yourself. Be the most magnificent and powerful and devious wizard the Citadel has ever produced, and I will be proud to cheer you on."

"What will you tell your house?" she asked some time later.

"I will tell them what I always tell them: that I am not interested in making a noble marriage," he replied with a chuckle.

"Marrying would make the eligible noble maidens stop chasing you."

"There is that, but I think if you just grab me and glare at them, that'll get them to stop just as well. Your glare is impressive when you put your heart in it. My parents will have to learn to accept that they aren't going to overrule my own wishes."

"You still want to take me to meet your House?"

"I do." He stroked his fingers through her hair. "But if you don't want to, we won't go. I do have this feeling like I want to show you off to my parents, to show them how amazing you are, and yet you choose to be with me."

"I have that feeling, too," she mumbled against his neck, "except my grandmother apparently disapproves of you as a match for me."

Giri chuckled.

"But I think my other grandparents might have a different opinion."

"I'd like to meet them."

They snuggled for a while, both feeling relieved that they'd discussed the subject and had compatible perspectives. The agreement of course required celebration, so it was another hour before they levered themselves out of bed.

Giri found Dello somewhere and dragged him over to eat lunch with them. He looked as wilted as a light-starved plant.

"You two are sure perky," the tall mage grumbled. "You haven't been in the library for hours reviewing old trade treaties between Weldom and Lackland."

"We're not going to get married," Giri told him flatly.

Dello looked blearily up from his soup. "What? You're not?"

"Or we might, if we decide to, sometime later."

Dello's brows pinched together. "You're confusing me. My brain is already weakened by the treaties, and now this."

Vor smiled behind her forkful of roasted vegetables.

"Your house will take that well, won't they," Dello grunted next. "You paired up with a, uh, with Vor, but no big party or binding vows?"

"It would be easier for them if they did," Giri agreed.

Dello raised an eyebrow and made a dubious face that seemed to say "alright, whatever you want, but you're clearly in love and I can't imagine why you wouldn't make it official, so you must be a little insane. I can only hope you'll eventually snap out of it." The trio ate in silence for a while until Dello finished his soup and bread and pushed away his tray.

"They caught a half a dozen people last night under suspicion of having thrown the stones into the reception hall," he announced. "No evidence of course, just seen running from likely positions where stones could have been thrown. They'll have to let them all go."

Vor shrugged. "No one was seriously hurt or killed."

"I think this was probably their most violent act so far," Giri supplied. "It's a little worrisome."

"There's rumors of mages being born among the common folk," Dello muttered, clearly trying to keep his voice down.

Giri shrugged. "Every now and again that happens. Without a teacher, the talent fades."

"But it's more than every now and again, lately," Dello corrected. "My master's not a state wizard, only works for them, like me, but your master would know more. He hasn't said anything?"

"Nothing in my hearing," Giri said.

"Something might be done about it, so I hear, just rumors, people talking." Dello sat up straighter and stretched. "I just thought, if you're going out to the countryside, you should know. Maybe don't wear mage robes. I have to get back to my treaties, so I'll see you when you get back, if we don't run into each other at dinner."

Vor and Giri finished their food and set to packing for their departure the next day. They took Dello's advice, even though Giri claimed there was no danger, but after all, Giri was off duty and so could wear whatever he wanted. Vor had little of her own to wear, but fit some of Giri's clothes tolerably well, since they were of a height and both relatively slender.

That task done, Giri showed her around the Citadel. On the lower floors he pointed out the dormitories for the younger mages, and the wide variety of classrooms, workrooms, and libraries. The dining hall and bathing chambers Vor knew, but there were also a few different gymnasiums and exercise rooms, stillrooms, and an infirmary. Above those floors came the ones devoted to living quarters for wizards: apprentices and above. Then came a floor of workrooms that could be reserved for work-related magical tasks and projects, not teaching.

They walked up to the grand glassed over greenhouse on one of the higher floors that circled the building like a ring, and then up higher still, passing the floor full of suites for the state wizards, to the open-air teleportation platforms—which were now apparently doubling as griffin landing platforms.

"It's its own city," Vor commented. "You could live in it and never need to leave."

"And there are some who don't," Giri nodded. "Some of the older wizards, the highest master mages: they study and research and never go out on assignments. That reminds me, Craduticus is here. Do you want to go see him?"

"That's right," Vor winced. The excitement of being with Giri again and her internal debate over what to do with him had driven most other thoughts right out of her head. "I should have remembered."

"He's busy sometimes," Giri explained as they turned to descend. "He's advocating for Princess Jessika in front of the ministers, and teaching a little, so he's not always around."

They went back to the floor where state wizards had their suites and Giri took her along to a particular door and rapped upon it. The lock clicked of apparently its own will and the door inched open with a slight groan.

"Master Craduticus?" Vor called, pushing the door open several more inches. She could sense clusters of powerful wards around the door, but they were all passive.

"Vor Hearthsraven," came the call from within. "Enter and be welcome."

They walked in and found the old mage reclining in a padded chair with a teapot and a plate of honeyed seed cakes close at hand. The curtains were all thrown wide, and several glowing statuettes around the room supplemented the light. The room was modestly furnished—for a State Wizard—with a couch in addition to the chair, a desk with a stiffer wooden chair, and a low table in the center of the room. Bookshelves lined most of the walls, except for the windows, the fireplace, and a door that no doubt led to Craduticus's bedroom.

In addition, a large woven basket hung from a hook by the window, currently bathed in sunlight. It rocked alarmingly before two sets of gray fingers and thumbs latched onto the edge. A head the size of a small melon, also gray and finely furred, with large bat-like ears, an upturned nose, and human-like mouth and eyes—though the eyes were a bit large for the head—peered over between the fingers. The creature's gaze raked over Vor and Giri.

"Bad girl," the bat-cat declared in a screechy voice. "Dumb boy. Go away."

"Enough, Breeka," Craduticus scolded lazily. "They are our guests." He marked his page with a large feather and set his book aside.

"Pardon me for not rising to greet you."

"Stay as you are, sir," Vor assured him.

He smiled ruefully. "These old bones are finding it harder and harder to gallivant about."

Giri peered into his teapot. "You're empty."

"Leave it," Craduticus waved. "If you refill it, it will just mean my bladder making me have to get up sooner."

Vor sat down on the edge of the couch facing him. From behind him Breeka continued watching the gathering with what would have been sinister intensity, except that for Breeka that expression was its usual one. Craduticus called Breeka a bat-cat, but Vor had never heard of the species from any other source. With stubby hind legs, one of them twisted like it had been broken and healed poorly, a compact body, and long bat-like arms with a few free fingers and thumbs, all covered in a fine grey fur, it was a curious creature.

Despite the wings, Vor had never seen it fly. Mostly, it rode around on Craduticus's shoulders, or shuffled along in a limping run. She'd also been given to understand that the bat-cat preferred to be called "it" rather than "he" or "she," and if it had any sex organs, Vor had never seen signs of them—not that it was any of Vor's business. Breeka was devoted to Craduticus, called him master, and displayed fierce loyalty. It was also perennially grouchy, and Vor never took any of its insults seriously.

"So you have come to Anchoria at last," the old mage smiled. "And how do you find it?"

"It is a trifle impressive," Vor replied.

Craduticus grinned more widely. "Ostentatious, isn't it? Overblown, pretentious, arrogant—don't look like that Giri, you know it's true. Ah, what can be done when one has magic! Although the city itself was built mainly by honest muscle, it was the magic that made the city possible: the power, the wealth, and the control. Still, that was many hundreds of years ago, thousands even, though these days it takes magic to hold it together, what with the deepening gorges, but largely we enjoy the hard work of our ancestors."

"There will be more humble views soon for us," Giri offered. "We're leaving tomorrow to go to the west."

"Good," Breeka spouted. "Go."

"Visiting your family, or families?" Craduticus presumed, ignoring Breeka.

"Yes. Mine at least, but," he glanced at Vor and she took the cue.

"I was greeted at the party last night by my maternal grandmother."

"Were you?" Craduticus marveled, looking more alert. "And how did that go?"

Vor felt her mouth twist up into a wry expression. "Poorly, I'm afraid. She called me a slut and ordered me home to make an alliance marriage for House Mrandis and provide babies, because the house is dying out. I refused."

"Naturally." The old wizard frowned a little. "There goes a woman with her thoughts and feelings tripping over each other." Craduticus shook his head. "Have you considered that part of her, somewhere deep down, might actually be curious to know you?"

"Not really," Vor stated. "It seemed to me like she just wanted to use me."

"Only rumors of you could have reached House Mrandis, yet they sent someone all this way to find you, and the mistress of the house, no less. It could be she's been living in the city, on the charity of another house, investigating where you might be and waiting for you to appear."

"She sounded rather desperate," Giri mentioned.

"Desperate enough to beg?"

"Not much," Vor said after a moment of consideration.

Craduticus lifted his hands, palm up in surrender. "You'll not know unless you go find out more. Or perhaps you'd rather walk away from that history."

"They threw me out with my mother," Vor said. "I think I might find more of a welcome among my father's family."

The old mage stroked his beard. "That will be an interesting meeting. I wish you luck."

"Bad luck," Breeka commented. "Bad girl has family? No one likes bad girl."

"Enough of that, Breeka." Now Craduticus eyed Giri. "I am more curious, however, what kind of meeting you expect at House Holstor." His eyes flicked between them. "Am I correct in assuming you'll be presenting your chosen bride?"

Vor choked—not at the idea, but at the word: bride. She'd never in her life expected that word might apply to her, and wasn't at all sure she wanted it to.

Beside her, Giri twitched a little. "Not exactly. We're not intending to marry just now. Perhaps someday. We're just going to be," he paused to pick a word, "together, as mages and friends and beloved, too."

Craduticus's gaze did not waver. "How will that go, I wonder?"

"I don't need their approval and I won't follow their commands," Giri declared. "We can find somewhere else to stay. We can—"

"I make a suggestion, and I further suggest you listen closely," Craduticus interrupted firmly, silencing the younger man. "You have this glorious fantasy of striding in, full of your power and frustration with the world, to declare your love for a socially unsuitable woman who you intend to make your life companion in place of the noble marriage they want for you."

He shook his finger as Giri opened his mouth to interject and Giri shut it again. "You think this is some romantic play. You think you must defy and sacrifice for love to win out, but think on this instead. If you march in there and confront your parents, with the expectation that they will disapprove and reject you, well, they might do just that. As is the attitude, so is the response."

"If they do—" Giri began.

"Hush, boy. I'm not done. You think all about giving up everything to be with the one you love, as though that is some ideal to achieve. Bah. Have you ever thought instead about how you might keep everything, including the woman you love?"

Giri shut his mouth with a snap, a crease between his brows.

"Dumb boy," Breeka rasped softly.

"You really want to alienate your family? Ask Vor, who has none, except for one that wants to dictate her future, how that feels."

He seemed to be thinking. It had made Vor think, too. She'd been defensive to her grandmother. Of course she wouldn't agree to go off and marry some stranger and make babies, not when she cared so much about Giri— and had her budding career as a wizard to consider—but she could have been kinder. Craduticus extended a bony finger at Vor.

"You have your five marks?" he asked.

She tried not to fidget. "No, just the two of them, from you two, but I expect I'll be getting the others soon."

A smile tugged at his face. "She's not only a mage, but a wizard. Perhaps she cannot claim to be of House Mrandis legitimately, but there is still status in wizardry. And she is young, not unpleasant to look at, well behaved, strikingly intelligent, and strikingly attached to you. Giri, you need not ask your parents for permission to be with her and abstain from a noble marriage, but most parents have at least some care for their children, and House Holstor is notable, but small, so you probably know them well."

His tone seemed to invite a response, and Giri nodded. "I do, better than most children of the nobility."

Craduticus unfolded a hand. "So nor should you assume you would not get permission, were you to ask. Your parents might be quite happy to see you happy, and happy to see you with Wizard Hearthsraven, even if marrying or not marrying her is something still to be left undecided. And if they must let go of their hopes of using you in an alliance marriage with some other house, well, don't you think they have been bracing themselves for that for years now?"

Giri had his fist pressed to his mouth, thinking hard.

"So I would not recommend you barge and bluster and in general act like a petulant child, but instead put some faith in your family recognizing both the validity of your choice, and how happy you are with Vor. If they are sensible people at all, they will realize on their own that nothing good can come of trying to force you otherwise. If you approach with good will, and they still reject you, well, then you can have no regret that you did not make a genuine effort."

Giri let his breath go. "You make sense, sir."

Craduticus relaxed, looking a bit smug. "I do that from time to time."

"Master, wise," Breeka sniffed. "Boy, dumb."

Vor smiled a little, only to have Craduticus's firm regard fall back into her.

"As for you, Hearthsraven, you are to be a wizard here?"

"It seems likely I am to be Wizard Colby's second apprentice," she announced.

"She's not on the books yet," Giri said. "Once we get back, we'll take care of the paperwork."

"No point in rushing through it now, when you're not even going to be here for a couple weeks, and your new master away besides," Craduticus agreed.

"I'm still not sure how to feel about it," Vor confessed.

"No need for you to decide that yet. You haven't really started working with Colby yet. Just give him a chance. From what I know of him, he is a decent sort."

"Demanding, strict, but decent," Giri put in with a little grin.

"I have faith you will do just fine, Vor," Cray smiled. "Speaking of doing fine, you've reunited with the griffins and the other humans from Northborn?"

"I saw them, at least some of them," Vor confirmed. "Hawkjoy gave me a ride out here, and I got to talk with the other griffins at the party. They are amusing company."

"You saw Jessika and Rikah as well?"

Vor exchanged a glance with Giri.

"Yes," she said, "but I didn't speak with them. They seemed a little troubled."

"Troubled is a good word for it," Cray nodded.

"Giri said you're Jessika's advocate to the ministers," Vor brought up.

He shrugged a shoulder. "The ministers have little time for a girl from Northborn, claiming to be royalty. Even on my word, and the word of others, they dismiss her." He shook his head. "The child is finding herself lost now, with nothing to hold onto, but that is something we all must face in life. We each must find what we wish to hold onto, and keep it if we can, or hold to nothing, and let life take us where it will. Jessika has come to such a crossroad."

"Will she go back to Northborn?" Vor wondered.

"Her father is there, and doing well, much better than any of us had expected. He is a determined fighter, and well enough now that she felt comfortable leaving him with castellan Amlee, to come here. He could not travel like this yet, but perhaps someday. I, after all, made the journey, and there are few more ancient or worn than I. Still, I doubt I shall ever journey in such a way again."

Craduticus laughed at himself, but Breeka abruptly vanished back inside its basket. They spoke of various things, inconsequential and mundane, for some more minutes, and then took their leave.

"You haven't spoken much about your family," Giri mentioned as they checked their packing one last time that evening.

Vor sat with a tunic folded in her lap at the foot of Giri's bed and thought on Giri's observation.

"You mean my father's family?" she confirmed.

"Or your parents themselves, but yes, I am thinking of the family you might have remaining to you, in Trivale."

"After the war," Vor ventured, slowly feeling her way into the words, "after my father and then my mother died, and after Altare took me in, I tried not to think of them. My childhood was pleasant. The family was big. I lived with aunts and uncles and some cousins, and my grandparents. It was a loving family. I was happy."

"And you didn't want to think of them, not even as a way to give yourself some comfort?" Giri echoed, taking the folded tunic from her and adding it to one of the packs. "Wasn't your life as Altare's apprentice rather horrible?"

She shrugged. "Yes, sometimes. That's why I didn't want to think of the time before, or how I'd been so happy, so innocent. If I started to think: if only I'd stayed, if only my mother hadn't insisted we go with my father, that I'd still be living there, blissfully happy in my ignorance and thinking I was just awaiting my father's return, then I could not bear where I really was and what had really happened."

Giri was kneeling now by the filled packs, watching and listening to her with his full attention. She forced herself to meet his gaze and give him the complete truth.

"The weight of my current situation, at the time, became too great. I could not allow myself the weakness of tears, of regret, of wishing life were other than it was," she told him. "If I started to speculate: perhaps my oldest cousin, Glory, is married by now, perhaps she has a baby of her own, and Evalyn, too, perhaps I would be soon to be married if I'd stayed, have Dansen and Juris taken over the cabinetry work yet, are they married with babies—all those wonderings only hurt me. I trained myself to forget, to focus only on the present. Besides, Altare would have taken advantage of any sign of weakness. I couldn't afford that."

Giri nodded a little. "If it doesn't hurt anymore, you can tell me about them now, if you want," he offered awkwardly, "or anytime."

She nodded back. "I might. You'll meet them soon enough, so I suppose you should at least know their names."

Then he smiled, stood up, and went to flop on the bed behind her. "I'm selfishly glad you didn't stay there, or some of your speculation might have come true. You might have gotten married to someone else."

Vor pivoted on the bed and quirked a little smile down at him. "Oh, I'm sure if I'd stayed I'd still have met you, one way or another. After all, my magery still would have come on me, and I'll bet my folks would have found some way to send me to the citadel for training. The Mrandis branch family was still kind to my mother and me. They might have helped."

She crawled over to him, hands braced on the pillow on either side of his head, and her long, unbound hair cascaded down to cover them.

"I'd have found you," she promised.

He reached up and ran his fingers through her hair. "You wouldn't have been the same person."

Vor shrugged a little. "Maybe not, but then, we would have met much sooner, before you were the man I met in Northborn."

"True," he allowed. "Perhaps, if I had met you soon enough, I'd have never had my heart broken."

That got a rueful chuckle from her. "I was about twelve or so when that happened the first time, I think. I doubt a scrawny adolescent fresh from a dirty little village would have turned your head."

"Well, maybe not," he conceded. His fingers slid up under her hair, up the back of her neck. "But you never know. Maybe your presence would have changed things. Or perhaps this is the way it was meant to be."

At his gentle urging, Vor folded her elbows and lay down on his chest.

"Perhaps," she agreed. "At any rate, this is what is, and I am happy with it. I only wish my parents were alive."

"You're sure they're dead?"

"I saw their bodies."

Giri's arms held her close. "I'm sorry. I'm sure, if they could see you now, they would be proud of you."

"Thank you," she whispered, "though sometimes I doubt it. I've done things I regret."

"Me, too," he murmured back seriously. "Master Colby says regret is the sign of a thinking mind and feeling heart. Though we mustn't wallow in it, when we stop being able to regret, it is a sign that we've stopped being able to think and feel."

Vor nodded a little against his shoulder. "Perhaps there is some truth to that."

"We all make mistakes."

"But that's no excuse," she countered.

"No," he agreed, "but it might be a reason."

"And when your mistakes mean people die?"

Giri soothed the muscles of her back, which had started tensing. "So many events conspire, so many people are a part of them, that unless you held the knife, unless you intentionally plotted to bring about someone's death, there is little point and less practicality in tracing the blame."

She gave in to his rational and comforting hands, letting go her breath. "But I did hold the knife, I did plot my master's death."

"He would have killed you," Giri said simply, calmly.

Vor had spent many weeks asking herself if she should have done differently. With Karolan, she'd been so convinced that Altare had to die—and to be sure, he was a cruel man who had done many evil things, killed and hurt many other people. Still she had asked herself: should his sentence have been by her hand? If she'd known the wizards better she would have realized that they would take action against him, but she hadn't. She'd already been committed to her path, and even when Giri had realized she meant to face Altare and kill him, he hadn't tried to talk her out of it or explain her other options.

The wizards had abetted her. Karolan had pressed her towards it, too, but she'd been the one to do it. Vor couldn't blame anyone else. She'd held the knife—spear in this case—and she'd plotted his death. She had to live with that, and it made her question if her parents really would have been proud of her or not.

"Most of my nightmares have stopped," she murmured, "and I didn't have any last night, sleeping with you. I've pondered my actions in the long hours alone in the forest, in Craduticus's cottage, and put many of my fears and regrets to rest, but sometimes they still stir."

"And they might always, from time to time," Giri said. "No one goes through what you did and comes out unscathed on the other side, Vor. It's all right to have those feelings. When you do, you can share them with me, no matter how many times it is. I can't take them from you—and I wouldn't even if I could, because they make you who you are—but I can listen."

She rested against him, listening to the thump of his heart and feeling his every breath. "I've always been alone," she whispered, and suddenly fought a lump in her throat and the prickle of tears.

"You're not alone anymore," he asserted. "And you'll see your family soon; you have them, too. Let's go there first. I'm sure they will be surprised and overjoyed to see you again."

Vor curled up around him. "These are a lot of changes for me."

"Yes," Giri murmured, "but you're handling them beautifully."

The stiff wind ruffled through Thornwing's rusty-red crest feathers as he stretched his head skyward. Hawkjoy was tense and clearly eager to be gone as well, though she didn't seem as happy about it as the male griffin. Vor suspected it might have something to do with the princess Jessika's apathy.

"A good wind," Thornwing coaxed. "Let's get in the air."

Vor tightened down the straps on Hawkjoy's harness holding her bundle of clothes and supplies. They'd gotten travel food from the kitchens, though Giri's stipend meant they could stay in inns along the way. The packs were as light as they could make them, but Vor still worried about burdening her new feathered friends.

"You had better tell Vor's mate how to hang on," Hawkjoy told her fellow griffin. "He has never ridden a griffin before."

Thornwing bent to do just that, and Vor patted Hawkjoy's shoulder in thanks.

"Are you ready?" she asked the griffin. "You seem troubled."

"Hawkwings—Princess Jessika—is going again to the ministers," Hawkjoy reported readily. "From what Hawkwind told me yesterday, the situation is hopeless. Northnest is dead. Wings cannot bring it back."

"You think she should go home?" Vor asked.

"Yes. I think she should be with her father. They could do each other a lot of good."

"I think we should all go home," Thornwing spoke up, apparently overhearing. "The ministers all but drool when they look at us, us griffins. Hawkwind thinks there might be potential for some kind of alliance."

"The rest of us think it is time for griffins to vanish again," Hawkjoy added.

"Well," Giri contributed. "You two will vanish from the capital for a while at least. Are we ready to go?"

Hawkjoy shook her head in that rapid, blurring way that birds do, and rolled her shoulders. "Yes, let us be gone."

Vor mounted up, already feeling nervous not about the flight, but about what waited at the end. They wouldn't reach Mount Brasson today, and she knew perfectly well there was no point in being prematurely nervous, but she couldn't stop it completely. After more than a decade apart, she was on her way to see her family.

"What if they don't like me?" she breathed.

Hawkjoy flicked her head back at her, and she realized the griffin had heard her. "How could they not, brave one? Hold on now."

Thornwing went up first with Giri clinging to his harness and strapped on as well. At first, Vor saw that the young mage had his head tucked down a bit, but after only a few wing strokes he cautiously lifted it and began to look about. Thornwing circled the landing platform before flying away, perhaps in case Giri demanded to get off, but the mage made no such request, so the griffin tipped a wing towards Hawkjoy, who launched off as well.

Vor held tight through the first flurry of sky grabbing flaps. The larger female quickly caught up to the male, and for a few seconds they paced each other in a loop around the tower. Vor looked over at Giri and he looked back, smiling. She couldn't help but return the expression. They were off on an adventure together—or at least a journey. Vor didn't anticipate any danger or—

Both griffins bobbled and suddenly lost altitude before flapping strongly. Vor's heart jerked and she grabbed harder onto Hawkjoy's harness. Then she realized what had happened. The stiff wind was gone. The griffins had been riding it with outstretched wings, hardly needing to flap, but somehow it had been turned off as quickly and completely as someone shutting a book or blowing out a candle.

And there was more—her mage senses screamed warning at her.

"Bank!" she shouted. "Turn, there's something in front of us."

Thornwing and Hawkjoy both pulled to the side, and Vor was horrified but not surprised to see the tips of Hawkjoy's primaries on one wing spark and smoke as they brushed against something invisible in the air. The griffins plummeted back to the platform.

"A shield," Giri declared as soon as they landed.

He unbuckled and threw himself off Thornwing's back and strode to the edge of the landing platform, hands outstretched.

"By all that's green and good," he swore. "Vor, do you feel it?"

She was examining Hawkjoy's burned wingtip, but the damage wasn't spreading now that it was no longer in contact with the shield.

"I feel it," she called. "I felt it."

"And a good thing you did," Giri said. "I was too distracted by the excitement of flying."

"What is it?" she asked as she came up beside him. "There isn't normally a shield here, is there?"

"Definitely not," he glowered. "And it's dangerous to put one there with griffins and drakes flying about. This is either an idiotic mistake, or," he didn't finish his sentence.

Vor extended her own senses. Indeed, there was a curving wall of magical shield extending—extending—

"It's huge," she exclaimed. "It's—"

"It's surrounding the entire Citadel," Giri marveled. "All of it."

Thornwing rumbled from beside him. "I know little of magery, though my brother is a mage, so I have learned some from his endless prattling about it. A shield like this takes power."

"Considerable power," Vor confirmed. "My former master and his mages held shields like these over Northborn castle, but it took six of us, and we were not of inconsequential ability, and it took preparation and regular renewal."

"And why," Thornwing went on, "would there suddenly be such shields over the Citadel?"

"That is the question," Giri nodded. "I don't recognize the maker, or makers. If they were anyone I've worked with before, I could probably tell who was generating these, but I can't."

Hawkjoy made an uneasy trilling sound. She was looking down, far down, at the ground below. "We are not the only ones to have noticed."

Vor squinted downward. The shield was still invisible, but like ants who wouldn't cross a line of salt, little black specks—people—were accumulating on both sides of where the shield apparently touched the ground.

"If this is an attack," Giri nearly growled, "the master wizards will have it down shortly, but why? Why would someone do this?"

"Look at the drakes," Thornwing remarked.

All four heads jerked back skyward. The drakes that circled the capital on patrol were controlled by their collars, which magically linked them back to mages in the citadel who guided their actions. Some of the drakes had ceased their patrols and were circling or flying about wherever they wished over the capital. Others had turned and were flying off entirely, getting smaller in the distance. Habit might keep some obedient, but if they decided to leave or attack the people of Weldom, no one could stop them now unless a wizard outside the shield with knowledge of how the collars worked took action.

"No one would attack Weldom," Giri asserted. "Certainly they wouldn't strike the capital. Sure, this might take us by surprise—"

"Has taken us by surprise," Vor corrected under her breath.

"But the power that will be turned against the attackers, whoever they are—"

"Get back," Vor ordered.

Again her magical senses shrilled with alarm. Giri caught on a fragment of a second later, and both dashed away, around the perimeter of the platform and back towards the doorway to it. Thornwing and Hawkjoy dropped right over the edge, briefly catching the still air, and with a few flaps sent themselves up and over, to land beside the humans just as they reached the door.

"What is it?" Thornwing demanded.

Vor and Giri both pointed. There wasn't much to see just yet, but the air in the center of the platform was shimmering as if with heat waves. Against Vor's senses it was a sudden rumble and a scent of damp earth.

"Something's coming," Giri said.

"But not through that shield, so they're inside it with us, whoever they are," Vor added, starting to feel the pumping of adrenaline. "They're bringing something or someone in. They couldn't send it in through the shield from the outside."

"I doubt it will be friendly. Let's get inside," Giri suggested. "We'll seal the door."

"But if they are already inside?" Hawkjoy stuttered.

Out of the warping air, something landed on the platform, making it shudder.

"You want to stay out here with that?" Thornwing jibed.

Several more somethings landed. They were stocky, human-shaped but taller and much thicker, without faces or hands or clothes—just the tawny color of clay, mixed through with veins of brown and even black, and lighter patches of white.

"What are those?" Giri hissed.

"I've no idea," Vor concurred.

The nearest took a ponderous, steady step closer, and the others began to follow it. There were nearly a dozen of them, all taller than a man and much heavier. Vor heard Giri take a deep breath, and then he flung a hand forward. A torrent of flame burst forth. It splashed against the lead clay-creature—and did nothing. The clay skin of it dried and cracked, but the creature paid it no mind.

"It didn't even flinch," Thornwing observed. "Maybe you should hit it harder?"

Giri didn't pant, but Vor sensed his energies shudder a little before he recovered. He'd thrown a heavy punch, maybe one of his best, and it had gotten him next to no results.

Hawkjoy crouched down. "Let them try me," she growled.

The griffin was airborne faster than Vor had ever seen her move. She whipped around, legs tucked up and vast wings powering her forward. Even her burned wingtip didn't seem to bother her. The clay-creatures paid her no mind, and they were still approaching, as inexorable as sunset. Hawkjoy sacrificed speed for altitude, darting up several lengths, and then immediately stooped on the last creature in line. She struck with her claws in a passing slash. Again, the creature didn't flinch. The griffin circled, but instead of making another pass, she came to land by Vor again.

"I hit it good," she reported, "but the cuts sealed back up. It didn't even bleed."

"Golems," Giri reported then. "I think they must be golems."

The clay-creatures were still approaching. Even moving slowly, large creatures took large steps. Soon, they'd be close enough to touch. Vor didn't get the feeling that they would stop with touching—rather punching, kicking, and smashing.

"How do we kill them, then?" Vor asked.

"They aren't really alive. We can try to rip them apart," Giri answered, starting to draw back into the doorway, the others following. "They are exactly what they appear to be: clay. They have no blood, no bones, no heart. Magic is making them move. They do as their makers bid them."

"So we kill the maker," Vor realized.

"If we can find them. This many golems, there will be many makers," Giri nodded.

"I'd try pushing them off the edge, as I doubt they can fly," Thornwing contributed, "but I'm afraid of getting close enough to try it."

"Do not," Hawkjoy said. "They are heavy. We are strong, but not strong enough."

"I don't know what they'd do if they got a hold of you," Vor muttered, "and I don't want to find out."

The two humans and two griffins went in through the door to the platform and shut it. Giri set his hands against it and Vor sensed him begin constructing a shield of his own. It was tight work, and he was panting this time when he was done.

"Here," she muttered, gathered her own energy, and reached up. She ran a finger along the seam between door and jamb, and sealed the stone and wood together, effectively turning the door into a wall.

"That should hold them," Giri nodded.

Just then came the first thump against the sealed door. The door-wall shook.

"For a while, at least," Thornwing remarked.

Now that they were inside, they could hear a commotion, though it sounded a bit distant. People were shouting, even screaming. The ruckus had reached all the way up the multiple floors and hallways to the top of the citadel.

"More must be inside," Vor observed.

"What in all the world is going on?" Giri cursed.

"Craduticus," Vor said. "His quarters are closest. He may be weak in body, but he's strong in power."

"A good notion," he agreed.

The four of them took off running through the halls.

Chapter 4

Battle for the Citadel

More clay golems had come in through the exits to the other teleportation platforms, and possibly up from below. The two humans and two griffins passed some places where there were streaks of clay on the floors in the pattern of walking steps. They had to backtrack and detour several times to avoid golems blocking hallways and coming inexhaustibly onward. Many of the doors to the suites held by the highest state wizards of the citadel were open. Most had been broken in. The door frames were smeared with clay.

On their way to where Craduticus had his suite, they followed the tracks of the clay golems, passing those smashed doors. They didn't hear or see anyone else, and didn't stop to check in the rooms. They skidded to a halt as they rounded a final corner, to see a solitary golem pounding relentlessly against Craduticus's door. Even as they watched, unsure for a moment what to do, the wood cracked like breaking bones. There was a flash of light and the golem was staggered back a step by an invisible force.

"His wards," Giri observed, "but they won't be much. We don't put wards of killing strength on our doors here, and even if they could kill a human, they wouldn't destroy that clay golem."

The golem recovered and methodically resumed its assault on the door.

"Hey, ugly," Thornwing called out.

"They don't have the freedom to respond to stimuli," Giri said. "They just follow magical orders. They might not even be able to hear."

"We have to stop it," Hawkjoy urged. "Wings was going to come up here this morning to talk with Cray, before the session with the ministers. She could be in there."

The door crunched and collapsed as the golem put a heavy foot on it and pressed. It stepped into the doorway. Then fire—so hot that Vor and the others flinched back—roared forth and wreathed the creature in heat, lighting the shards of the door on fire. Despite the fire, the golem tried to keep advancing. Unlike Giri's flame attack on the golem on the landing platform, however, this fire went on much longer, and rather than just desiccating its skin, the entire creature began to stiffen. Its clay flesh paled, drying out, and began to crack.

The fire died, but the golem was still moving a little. It managed to take another shaky step. Then it was knocked back from inside the room. It fell onto its butt, shaking the floor and breaking into pieces and chunks from the impact. Hawkjoy rushed forward, taking a controlled leap over the remains of the golem and darting awkwardly into the burned out doorway. She misjudged a little and bounced off one side of it; Craduticus's doorway was larger than normal since he had a fine suite, but still tricky for creatures as large as a griffin to get through.

"Wings," she called out. "Cray?"

The air was still hot around the door, but not harmful, and Vor followed in Hawkjoy's wake, with Giri right behind her. Thornwing stood over the still clods of clay, and watched back down the hallway, on guard. Inside, Craduticus was on his knees on his carpet, thin shoulders heaving after his breath. Breeka was snugged against his side, and Hawkwind stood over him with mantled wings. Behind her were Jessika and Rikah, clinging to each other, but calm at least. Hawkjoy exchanged a head-bob with Hawkwind and went immediately to the two young humans at the back. Jessika shrugged off Rikah's arm now that the danger was past.

"Clay bakes," Craduticus wheezed. "Solid objects can't walk about."

"And they're lighter when they're dry," Hawkwind nodded. "You can knock them over. Then they break."

"Sir, do you know what's going on?" Vor asked.

Breeka whimpered and Craduticus shook his head slowly, like an old, tired mule.

"No idea; we've been in here," Hawkwind replied directly.

"I felt the shield go up," Craduticus grunted. "You know who did it?"

"No, sir," Giri answered. "Do you?"

He rubbed his head wearily. "I don't recognize the power, nor that moving the golem."

"There's more of them," Vor said. "We don't know how many in total, but at least a dozen, maybe two dozen, or more."

Giri nodded back towards the door. "There's shouting and screaming out there. Every door on these levels has been smashed in. We haven't checked for survivors. We came straight here."

"Is it an assault?" Rikah piped up. "An invasion?"

"There are dozens of master mages here," Giri asserted, "plus many more apprentices and students. Whoever is attacking can't hope to win."

"They're after me," Jessika quavered out. "They want to destroy Northnest—"

Vor snarled and turned to her. "Everything is not about you," she spat. "You are utterly unimportant, and so is Northnest."

Jessika flinched and her pale face flushed. Then all three mages twitched, though there was no sound or other indication of what they'd felt.

"Someone's hitting the shield," Giri said. "It's holding, so far."

"Good shield," Craduticus shrugged.

"Another one," Thornwing called from outside the room.

Vor and Giri dashed back into the hall. Another clay golem had appeared where the hallway turned. It was walking steadily forward just like the others had. Its shoulders were wide enough to nearly block the hall.

"What do you think it would do if we just tried to slip around it?" Vor wondered.

"The griffins aren't slipping around that," Giri pointed out.

"Shall we bake it?"

He raised an eyebrow at her.

"It's not like we're not fully charged," she whispered back. "Can you sustain a fire blast like Craduticus did?"

"Yeah," he nodded after a breath, "but it'll take a lot."

"I'll feed you."

She slipped her hand into his and stepped partly behind him. With a gentle exhalation, Vor linked her energies into Giri's. That was easy now, approaching second nature, but they hadn't worked much magic together. She'd thought—fantasized—about it, of course, and had known they would eventually, but now, preparing to fight together, her pulse surged and she clenched her jaw against an eager grin.

Giri lifted his free hand, let the golem get a bit closer, and then opened up with another torrent of flame, but this time he didn't stop after a quick blast. He drew on both his own energy and Vor's to sustain it. She felt her energy bleed out of her, but she was offering up all her stored extra energy first, not personal energy, and it was a harmless sensation she was used to whenever she worked magic; the power had to come from somewhere; usually it came from within her.

The golem didn't stop coming, but after several seconds of applied fire, as the heat in the hallway rose enough to make the humans sweat, its steps became awkward and stiff. Then its knee joints began to crack. Vor dug deeper into her reserves, beginning to think she would need to touch her personal power after all, but the golem was drying out, and after a few more seconds it didn't seem able to take another step.

Giri staggered, releasing the fire, and Vor caught him against her.

"Allow me," Thornwing said from behind.

The griffin made a light leap over their heads, his partly open wings brushing the ceiling, and then he danced up to the golem, hopping up to put his feet against its chest—before pushing off. The golem toppled over, breaking into semi-wet pieces when it hit the stone floor. It twitched a little, but could not rise again. Thornwing skidded to a landing and cocked his head at a jaunty angle.

"I think I may like pottery," he grinned.

Then a third golem rounded the corner where the second had appeared. Vor felt Giri sag for a moment.

"I didn't even get to catch my breath," he complained.

"I've got it," Vor told him.

His golden-brown eyes weren't doubtful, just confirming. "Are you sure?"

"I've seen you do it now, so I can, too. Feed me," she said, stepping now to stand just in front of him.

Supplying energy was one thing, relatively easy. Directing, controlling, and applying that energy—no matter where it came from—took skill. It also took effort. Giri squeezed her hand. Vor lifted her other hand. The third golem came walking as unperturbed as any of them had. It stepped right among the remains of its fellow, kicking pieces of hardened clay aside without pause; it probably didn't even know they were there.

Vor gathered her breath. Giri didn't have much more energy left than she did, and they would both have to tap into personal power now, but they could share the load. She pointed her hand, and as she let out her breath, the fire flowed, just as it had for Giri. Vor, however, narrowed her focus, directing it precisely where one leg met the golem's torso, instead of baking the whole hallway. That joint cooked first, broke, and the golem fell partly down, but it caught itself and continued to try to advance, leaning against the wall.

The second hip took another couple seconds. Then the golem fell forward to the floor, but its arms still worked, and it continued trying to drag itself closer. Vor's next targets: one shoulder, then the other. The body and head were still wet, but the creature couldn't do any more than wiggle a little once its arms and legs were broken off. The fire died, and Vor nearly fell to her knees. Giri caught her, but he, too, quavered, and they ended up sliding down to sit against the wall.

"Well," Thornwing sniffed, "I was just starting to like pottery and there you've gone and cut out the fun part."

Vor could feel her head swimming. Her eyes blurred a little. Sustaining a blast of fire that long and that hot, four times, even with another mage to share the energy cost had taken a fair bit out of her. She blinked and steadied her breathing. It had been a while since she'd thrown around so much magic.

"Vor," Giri murmured at her ear.

His arms were still around her, and when she turned her head towards him he fixed his mouth on hers for a kiss, and a little more than a kiss, and—but there really wasn't time for much more.

"Ah," Thornwing grunted, "and then you give yourselves a fun part instead."

But Vor realized at once that it wasn't about fun—or rather, that was just a side benefit, but also essential to get the main objective. As her emotions surged and her body responded as it usually did to Giri, so came an energy bloom: not huge, but enough to make her head stop spinning and vision clear.

"No time for anything else," he breathed to her as they parted, "but it's something."

"Let's hope there's no more golems," Vor replied, grinning a little, "or we'll have to have Craduticus hold them off while we borrow his bedroom."

Giri managed a weak smile. They helped each other up, and luckily a fourth golem had not appeared. Still weaving a little drunkenly they rejoined the others in the old master mage's suite, with Thornwing again standing guard just outside the door—or maybe because Hawkwind and Hawkjoy already made the main room of the suite too crowded to fit another griffin inside.

"What happened?" Rikah demanded.

"Two more golems," Giri reported, not panting too much.

"They're down," Vor added, trying to get her own breathing steady.

The old master mage nodded as if he had expected nothing less of them. "The shield is still up," Craduticus said. "I can tell there are some state wizards hammering at it, but it's enduring."

"Whoever put this up and sent these golems is incredibly strong, or there's a lot of them working together," Giri contributed.

"Or they've been planning it for a long time," Craduticus countered. "You can make and store golems for years." He snapped his fingers weakly. "And then light them all up when you're ready with rather less energy than it took to make them."

"Altare never taught me about golems," Vor disclaimed.

"Eh," Craduticus sneered, "not flashy enough for him, and too much work. Any mage of minor talent can make one, with enough time, but they're not bright, and not useful for much, except things like this—pointing them at an enemy with a single command and releasing them. He liked his magic more personal, more hands on."

"He did indeed," Vor muttered darkly.

"We should join the others," Giri interrupted, "and help bring down the shield."

"There could be more of those things out there," Jessika objected.

"And we're worn out," Vor countered. "This room is not defensible. You'll be safest where the other mages are, unless you want to hide here and wait for another wandering golem to come squish you."

"If we can go by my room," Giri went on, "we could recharge from my horse statue."

"Maybe we can manage that," Vor nodded.

Hawkwind nudged Jessika with her bill. "Get on, Wings. You'll be safer on me."

"I can run," Rikah said.

Hawkjoy knelt by Craduticus and looked up at Vor. "Help get him on me?"

"I'll help," Rikah volunteered at once.

Vor was fine with letting the strapping young man lift up Craduticus; she'd already done some heavy lifting of her own in taking down those golems. Instead, she fetched the old mage's staff that he also used as a walking stick and handed it up to him. Breeka the bat-cat climbed up Hawkjoy's harness on its own. Despite the permanent limp in one hind leg, its clawed wing-arms worked well, and it settled behind Craduticus with a secure grip.

"I'll lead," Giri announced. "I know my way around."

"I'm with you," Vor nodded.

"I'm right behind you," Thornwing added.

"The wizards working on the shield are in one of the big workrooms, on the third level," Craduticus called out.

The train of griffins and humans made their way down the hall, past the remains of the golems, which undulated a little but could do them no harm now. Vor glanced briefly into open suites they passed, travelling more slowly than their first run down the hall. Mostly she just saw smashed, clay-smeared furniture, though in one was a clay-coated body, twisted and motionless on the carpet. The occupants hadn't been home in the others, or they'd managed to escape, or they'd been killed or were hiding in deeper rooms. She winced a little at the necessity, but they just didn't have time to search every suite, and they might walk into wards even if they did try. One did not go searching through a wizard's home without anticipating magical locks and traps.

They encountered no more golems as they made the stairs and started down. They had five levels to go before reaching the third. The stairs were gummed up with clay, so they knew the golems had gone down before them, and they had to watch their steps to avoid slipping on it.

"Here," Giri announced when they reached the fourth level where his room was. "We'll be right back."

Vor and Giri dashed down the hall to his room, which hadn't been broken into. In fact, none of the doors along the hall were touched.

"They're following the master mages," Giri surmised.

"Or first seeking out the strongest mages, and working their way down," Vor suggested. "Which amounts to the same thing."

Giri whipped down his wards and unlocked his door. He'd set the room up to be unoccupied for a couple weeks, so it took him a bit longer to undo all the protections than if he'd just stepped out for lunch, but then he and Vor went for the mage stone statue of a rearing horse he kept beside his bed. It was full, thanks to the past two days of amorous activity that had generated surplus power. They put their hands on the horse's head, and drew out equal portions, depleting the statue and replenishing themselves.

Recharged, they dashed back out, and Giri restored his waiting wards. When they ran back down the deserted hall, they found the three griffins, three humans, and bat-cat right where they'd left them, grouped up and watching nervously all around them. Vor ran to Hawkjoy and put her hand on Craduticus's, where he was holding gamely to the harness.

"Oh no you don't, missy," the old mage scolded, snatching his hand away. "You keep that power."

"You might need it," she whispered. "You wore yourself out with that fire."

"I'll be just fine," he snapped back.

"Bad girl," Breeka hissed half-heartedly.

"Next is the third level," Giri was saying. "That's where most of the big workrooms are, where Master Craduticus says the retaliation against that shield is coming from. There might also be golems. We want to join the retaliation, but we don't want to attract the golems' attention until we're secure."

"Why don't we leave?" Jessika demanded.

"The shield is in the way," Giri informed her, much more patiently than Vor thought she would have replied. "We have to bring it down first."

"Hawkwind, can you fly me out?" the princess asked.

"The shield goes over the citadel like an overturned bowl," Giri explained tightly. "No one is flying anywhere until it's down."

Craduticus reached over and patted Jessika's shoulder. "I'll protect you. Don't worry."

"Me, too," Rikah spoke up, but the princess ignored them both.

They moved down the stairs slowly, Vor and Giri leading and trying not to slip on the clay smears. Soon enough they heard heavy, rhythmic thuds ahead of them, which got louder and wetter as they turned down one of the halls. Vor gestured for the griffins to stay back, and she and Giri went the last dozen yards by themselves.

Up ahead, several clay golems were gathered around a set of double doors. They were pounding their stumpy hands over and over against the doors, leaving smudges and splats of clay, and gradually wearing away their arms—but they had a lot of arm to wear away before it would impede them. The doors were wood, bound with bands of metal, and each thump shook them, but they hadn't buckled yet. Behind the still moving golems were chunks and piles and splatters of clay from what looked like another handful of golems, now defeated.

"That's the biggest workroom," Giri muttered.

Vor trembled as she felt a wave of magical force slam the shields. They flickered for a moment, and then stabilized.

"It's a matter of what breaks first," Giri breathed in her ear. "Those doors or the shields."

"We can't take on seven golems," she breathed back.

"Even trying to distract them could get us killed," he agreed. "They're not fast, but we can't run forever. We can't get out while the shield is up, and there are too many dead ends in this place."

"If we can't get in to help, let's put a shield over the doors, to reinforce them," Vor suggested.

Giri turned a beaming smile onto her. "That's a great idea."

She shrugged, but felt an inward flutter of pleasure at his praise. "The trick is doing it from here, without being able to touch the doors."

"I can probably handle that," he muttered, "unless you'd like to?"

"Have at," she muttered back. "I'll watch and learn."

Giri nodded and lifted a hand, spreading his fingers as though he were pressing his palm to the door. He had been a mage apprentice around seven years longer than Vor had. He'd also had the benefit of learning under both Colby and Milsa, who were highly skilled and had wanted to teach him everything they could—unlike Altare who had taught Vor only certain things, and not always the things she wanted to learn, or the most useful things. Vor acknowledged that Giri's abilities were more finely honed than hers, but she was learning with her every breath, and only had to see things once or twice before adding them to her own repertoire.

"I'll make it as heavy as I can, but it won't last forever," Giri remarked. "Every time they hit it, it will erode a little, until it breaks, but it will buy the wizards inside more time."

Vor nodded. "Just like the shield over the citadel. If the citadel wizards hit it enough times, it will come down eventually."

"The only issue is," Giri added, "when the wizards inside are ready to come out of the workroom, they'll have to break my shield, too, if it's still there. I can make it smooth and tough on the outside, and full of flaws on the inside, so they can crack it and get out."

Vor nodded again beside him, filing that type of shield away in her capacious memory for future use. Then she watched as Giri built the shield, starting at the threshold of the door and weaving it upward. It grew quickly, as fast as the spread of water from a dropped cup. The golems continued pounding, and the sound of their banging didn't change, but they all simultaneously paused, rocking back slightly, as though they could see or feel the shield—and then one turned to face the corner where Vor and Giri knelt all but hidden.

"Time to go," Giri gulped.

Vor heartily agreed, as the single golem that had decided—been elected?—to investigate them began its relentless, ponderous march towards their hiding spot.

"It knew," Vor hissed as they trotted back down the hallway. "It sensed the magic."

"I'll bet that's how they're locating the wizards in here," Giri postulated. "They are tracking magic."

"Perhaps if we get far enough away, it will lose our scent."

"Let's hope."

They came out on the stairway where the rest of their party waited.

"Well?" Craduticus croaked as they ran up.

"The wizards, some at least, are barricaded inside a workroom," Giri reported. "There are six golems trying to get in."

"There were seven," Vor contributed, "until Giri cast a shield on the door, the golems sensed it, and one came after us."

"We could never defeat seven of them," Craduticus stated. "The spare might return to its companions, if it can't catch you. It seems to me like the golems are tracking magic users."

"That was our thought, too," Vor agreed.

Craduticus frowned, deepening his wrinkles. "Not everyone can be in there. I fear the golems may have gone after the apprentices, too. They aren't here, trying to get their masters out, so something must be detaining them."

Hawkwind clacked her bill. "We can't help those wizards, you say, but there are young ones in danger?"

"We can't fight those things," Jessika objected.

Vor decided to just stop listening to anything the so-called princess said.

"There could be," she answered Hawkwind. "We should at least try to locate them."

"We can help protect them until reinforcements arrive," Giri declared. "Maybe we could even get them all up here and together take on those golems. Let's go."

Regardless of what Jessika might have wanted, she was riding Hawkwind, and when the griffin ran, the princess went with her.

"It was still breakfast time," Giri commented as they scrambled down the stairs. "There might have been a lot of wizards in the dining hall."

"Let's check there first," Vor agreed.

There were more clay smears all along the stairs and hallways, suggesting that the golems had indeed penetrated down to the lower floors—or come up from below. They passed a golem blasted into half-baked chunks. A little further on they found a body—a teenage girl twisted and broken with her face coated with clay. Vor gritted her teeth, feeling anger give her energy.

The group turned the corner to the hall for the kitchen and dining areas, and skidded to a halt. Two golems were pounding on the doors of the dining hall. Those doors were a formality, and not meant to stand up to a prolonged assault. They buckled and sagged with every hit, and between hits surged back to their fully closed position.

"They're being held shut by people in the hall," Giri said.

"That'll last only as long as their strength does," Vor remarked.

"Two golems," Craduticus added. "I'm low, but could you two take them?"

"One, yes, but two would be a stretch. I'd rather have more help since it's available," Giri countered. "We're all a little tired and I'd prefer no one collapse. Let's take the back way into the dining hall."

"Why didn't people get out that way?" Hawkjoy asked.

"They picked a spot and made a stand, I expect," Thornwing spoke up. "They had to do it somewhere. At least here, they can all be together." He shrugged a wing, "and there's food. I hear mages need lots of that when firing off their magic. At least, my brother does."

"It helps," Giri acknowledged. "This way."

They had to backtrack and take a different turn. Then they emerged into a wide wood-paneled hallway with trolleys of dishes and barrels, sacks, and boxes of raw food materials lined up along one side of it. Windows along the outer wall let in morning light and gave a view of the city outside. Unglazed windows in the inner wall allowed air circulation through the kitchens themselves.

There were no clay smears on the floor, which Vor took as a good sign. The kitchen doors were standing open, suggesting maybe someone had fled that way, but the kitchens themselves were empty. Partly finished food was left standing on the long wooden tables. Ceramic dishes soaked in soapy water in tubs along one wall or stood drying on racks. Something in one of the brick ovens smelled like it might be burning, but there wasn't any smoke just yet.

The griffins had some difficulty moving through the close quarters. Hawkjoy accidentally knocked over a rack of cooling pies, splattering pastry and various fillings across the floor.

"Oh, I am so sorry," she apologized quietly.

Vor patted her shoulder. "A little spilled pie is the least of the problems here."

"They'll be weeks cleaning up all that clay," Thornwing agreed.

Rikah picked up a fragment of pie that hadn't actually touched the floor and ate it off his palm, getting some of the purple mumfruit filling on his chin. Vor just turned back to the objective of getting into the dining room and declined to comment aloud. There were two service doors just wide enough for the narrower trolleys, and a long serving bar, creating a horizontal window in the wall between the kitchen and dining hall.

"This is why they felt safe," Vor observed, "to hole up in here. The golems can't fit through these doors, or over that bar."

All three griffins had paused to assess the various means of entry, and Vor wondered if maybe they wouldn't fit through either.

Thornwing grunted. "Weldomians don't build with griffins in mind."

"Down, Wings," Hawkwind said, and Jessika slid to the floor.

Craduticus got down, too, and Vor offered him her arm. He merely gave her elbow a pat and hobbled onward on his own, leaning on his staff. Breeka limped after him. Hawkjoy and Hawkwind clambered through the service window while Thornwing eyed the doorway. Giri was already striding into the dining hall to join the cluster of people Vor could hear fulminating inside.

"Griffin males are smaller than females," Thornwing remarked to Vor as he tucked his wings in tight and squeezed through the service door with a wiggle. "There are times I'm glad of it."

Just then Hawkjoy hit her head on a hanging lamp over the service counter, her hand slipped off the edge, and she nearly left a dent in the dining hall floor from her hooked bill as she tumbled out through the window into an inelegant pile of grey and black limbs, wings, and tail feathers.

"Times like this," Thornwing nodded, feathers in carefully calm orientation.

Vor would have smiled, but not all the mages in the room had met the griffins, and some apparently took them to be newly arrived threats. She had to throw up a shield, deflecting someone's bolt of green, crackling power before it hit Hawkwind, who was in the lead.

"I said," Giri declared loudly, apparently reiterating, "they're allies. You all know there are griffins in the city, from Northborn."

"Yes, but—," someone began and Giri promptly argued him down.

Rikah went to Hawkwind and petted her shoulder; perhaps the fact that she did not immediately tear his hand off helped to calm the hotheads in the group. Vor assessed the situation. There were a few dozen people in the room, most of them within a decade of her age. Only a handful were older, and one of those older mages was stretched out on a table, stained with clay, while a couple younger men were trying to splint his leg with found materials. There were a few others who bore signs of having gotten too close to the golems, but the older wizard seemed like the only major casualty.

The rest of the crowd was largely involved in holding the main double doors of the hall shut against the pounding of the golems. Giri was standing near to them discussing the situation with a particularly tall and skinny wizard—Vor recognized Dello. It looked like he'd been half slimed with clay, and his brilliant blonde hair was hidden under a coating of grey. She went over to join them while Craduticus limped over to the leg-broken wizard on the table and Rikah and Jessika gathered with the griffins.

"We're pretty worn out," Dello was saying. "The young ones panicked, started throwing everything they had at the golems—of course it didn't work. So far, we've only found heat to be an effective attack."

"Likewise," Giri nodded.

"I had to throw most of my power at one down by the baths," he lamented. "The steam kept it wet and it nearly got me. Oma, Vor."

"Giri and I might be able to take those two," she nodded, "but it would help if we had a few others to feed us."

"Or we could put shields on the door and wait it out," Giri offered.

"Wait it out until when?" Dello retorted. "Until those wizards up in the workrooms bring down that shield over the citadel? That's strong stuff. I'm not thinking it will come down anytime soon. Even if it does, they'll be tired, and the golems will still be here. Besides, we've been putting shields up when we can, but they keep breaking them, and we're almost worn out. There are only a few of us with some juice left. Now that you're here, maybe we can bake those buggers."

The group holding the doors let out an exclamation as one of the doors cracked. The broken boards twisted and a golem arm poked in.

"Now's as good a time as any," Dello declared stoutly. He rushed back to the defenders. "We're going to cook them," he announced. "Those who can attack, forward. Everyone else, fall back and feed someone what you can."

"Aim for the joints," Vor added. "I think it's the most efficient use of power."

She hustled to the doors with Giri beside her. A few others stepped up, too, and she felt hands grab her arms and shoulders or press against her back. A glance around showed all the wizards in the room linking hands and grabbing their neighbors. As she reached for power she felt a sudden flood of energy. It wasn't limitless, but it came from everyone else contributing a little bit: whatever they could spare. It came in every color, taste, and vibration, and she had to grip it and focus it the same way she would take a moment to strategically gather up an armful of awkwardly shaped branches and chunks of wood, so that she didn't drop any, before pitching it all into a fire.

Then, there was nothing but flame. The doors broke apart under the combined blast of fire from the wizards and the punching of the golems. The heat became abruptly intense, nearly intolerable, and Vor felt her exposed skin dry and tighten painfully. A wizard a few feet away cried out at the heat and retreated a couple steps, eyebrows singed. The golems managed to advance a couple steps before they began staggering. It didn't take long, but Vor could sense it was the last major effort the group could make. The donated energy ran out, and Vor had to finish using her own power.

As the flames died, the two golems were revealed: pale, dry, and immobile, with cracks running through their joints. The defenders let out a relieved sigh.

"My turn," Thornwing announced from behind.

A few people flinched like he meant it was his turn to attack the wizards, but the griffin just leapt lightly over the group, half-landing against one golem, and knocking it over as he pushed off it to land on the other. As he pushed off that one, too, both teetered and fell back, breaking into pieces against the floor. Thornwing touched down back behind the gathered wizards and flicked his wings into place.

"That's the fun part," he informed them merrily.

The group made little response except to begin shuffling over to the tables: apparently relieved that the threat was neutralized. Dello, however, was not so optimistic.

"Do you know what's going on?" he asked Vor and Giri as everyone else slumped, exhausted, onto chairs, stools, and benches. "What idiot would attack the Citadel? Weldom is the dominant country on this continent. There are plenty of wizards outside the Citadel, plus the army, ready to act, and you can bet they're mobilizing already."

"I agree," Giri huffed, still catching his breath. "Whoever is orchestrating this, they'll be put down. I can't imagine what they're trying to accomplish other than inconveniencing us. There won't be more than a few deaths, I don't think."

Dello looked over at the crowd of beached wizard apprentices. "Hey," he called. "Anyone who can walk, go get some food from the kitchen for everyone. You lot will be unconscious in minutes if you don't eat something." He turned back to Vor and Giri with a long-suffering sigh. "Idiot baby apprentices."

"And what are you?" Giri jabbed weakly.

"An idiot older apprentice."

"Inconveniencing us," Vor interrupted, echoing what Giri had said moments ago. She narrowed her eyes. "You mean like a prank? Like those people who threw the rocks at Colby and Milsa's wedding? The Magic Liberation Front? Do you think they're behind this?"

Giri and Dello both stared at her as though she'd suggested unicorns were responsible.

"They aren't this powerful," Dello denied.

"They aren't this organized," Giri added.

"You said there have been more wizards born among the common people lately," Vor pointed out. "Could they have organized? Maybe they're working with the Front. Maybe they are the Front, and all the non-magical pranks were to make you think they were just a nuisance, not a real threat."

"They wouldn't do this," Dello asserted. "What could they hope to accomplish?"

"If they are angry," Vor countered, "they might not be thinking of what they can accomplish, but just what they can do to get even."

Someone brought over a plate full of sausages baked in pastry, and Vor took one, took a bite, and chewed and swallowed. Giri and Dello copied her, both looking contemplative.

Vor pressed her idea. "They don't get training. They don't get employment with the State. They don't get recognized for their abilities. Weldom even tries to stop them from existing by putting mage stone in their metal. You say they keep pulling pranks on you—do you think they think their pranks are supposed to accomplish anything? Have they accomplished anything?"

"No," Giri admitted. "It's only made the government try harder to find more magestone, to stop them from existing, like you say. That probably has made them even more angry."

Dello frowned at the possibility, chewing methodically.

"If this is their doing," Giri said softly. "If they're this powerful now, we have a problem."

The trio looked around at the worn out mages in the room. Someone had distributed food to everyone, and Jessika and Rikah were going around with water pitchers, filling cups and glasses. Thornwing had stationed himself as a lookout by the broken doors to the dining hall. Hawkjoy was by the serving window into the kitchen, watching that way.

Every mage twitched as the shield over the citadel shivered, flickered, and vanished for a moment, only to resurge. Vor took a steadying breath and firmed up her own personal shields as she felt another wave of force strike the barrier. It wavered—and then it fell. They waited, heartbeats passing in silence, and it did not rise again. Vor let out her breath as the room took a collective sigh.

"It's down," Dello said. "Now we'll get some help to finish off the last of the golems." He managed a weak smile. "What a way to start your vacation, eh, Giri?"

Vor felt less mirthful about the situation. "What's going to be done?" she asked. "If this is the work of mages from the common people," she glanced between the two men, "what do you think Weldom's response will be?"

Dello's little grin faded and Giri winced.

"They'll hunt them down and kill them," Vor said, "won't they?"

Dello let his breath out and lifted a hand. "They did try to kill us."

"And managed it," Vor nodded, "in at least two cases that I've seen."

A ruckus approached from the hall outside the dining room. A moment later, Thornwing stepped back, and a few tired looking older wizards poked their heads in.

"Wizard Traskitandi," one, a taller woman with black hair cut at her shoulders, summoned.

"Well done," Giri muttered, "not many can get that name right."

"Yes, Master?" Dello replied at once.

"You alright in here?" she went on, striding into the room.

"A few injuries, one broken leg," he reported, "and a lot of exhausted apprentices."

Dello's master was indeed taller than average, but—like everyone—still shorter than Dello; her eyes came about to his chin. She had the agile build of a dancer, and her simple brown robes flattered her. At closer range now, Vor could see that her thick black hair had a few threads of silver in it, but her strong features showed little sign of age. Her complexion was creamy, and her hazel eyes quick. Her sharp gaze snapped over to Vor and Giri. She jerked her head back at the shattered door and broken golems. "Your work?"

"We helped," Giri said with a brief bow.

The woman's eyes lingered on Vor. "I don't recognize you."

"Vor Hearthsraven," she replied. "Colby Srawn's presumptive new apprentice."

"Ah, I've heard of you." Some of the distrust receded from her expression. "You're with these griffins."

"Well," Vor hesitated. "We came from the same general region of the continent, though I was born in Weldom. I mean, I rode one of them when I traveled here a few days ago."

"You also killed your former master," she said without heat.

"He rather deserved it," Vor mentioned.

"So I've heard, if anyone deserves death. Well, Colby wouldn't have taken you on if he hadn't. Tessalia Himes," she introduced herself and twitched her head in Dello's direction. "I'm this ungrateful lay-about's master."

Her eyes gave a hint of her humor, and Dello smiled like she'd just praised him. What Vor sensed of her aura was carefully composed, and not without strength. Vor decided she might like the woman.

"We brought the shield down," she went on. "Groups are going through the citadel now, searching for any more golems, but we're all low on energy. Whoever was holding that shield against us had a lot of juice."

"Who do you think it was?" Vor asked.

Master Himes opened her mouth to reply, and then every mage groaned, flinched, or cursed. Dello put his hands over his face. Giri leaned back against the nearest wall. Vor hissed through her teeth; she could sense what had just happened.

"That thrice-blasted shield," the master wizard exclaimed in a growl. "They've gone and tossed it back up."

"What in all the," Giri muttered.

"There are wizards hunting for them," Himes went on, "but apparently they haven't found them yet."

"Maybe our reinforcements got inside at least, while it was down," Dello suggested hopefully.

Then Vor rubbed her ear. There was some kind of high-pitched buzzing just at the edge of her hearing.

"Maybe something else got inside," Thornwing called from where he still stood on guard. "Do you hear that?"

"Do you know what it is?" Vor called back to him, now rubbing both ears.

Others in the room were doing the same thing, especially the younger mages.

"It's chirping," Hawkwind said, joining them, "a lot of chirping."

"It sounds like a buzz," Vor commented.

"You might be hearing just the lower end of it," the griffin continued. "It sounds like insects, many insects."

"They let you bring the shield down long enough to toss something new in and then they put the shield back up," Giri surmised.

"Now I hear it," Dello spoke up.

Indeed, the noise was getting louder. Master Himes strode towards the recovering wizards at the tables.

"Everyone up," she ordered, snapping her fingers at them. "Gather together in that corner and get ready to cast shields. Get Master Majisson over there, too."

There were a few groans, but everyone obeyed, a few people helping the broken-legged wizard to hobble painfully into the corner. Vor led Giri and Dello in going to join them. Hawkjoy and Hawkwind went, too, but Thornwing lingered at the door, watching down the hallway.

"Any thoughts on what it might be?" Vor muttered to Master Himes.

The older woman shook her head. "There are many possibilities, and it's always possible our enemy came up with something new."

"How about any idea why this unknown enemy might be doing this?"

Master Himes eyed her from one hazel orb. "Did you have any thoughts, Wizard Hearthsraven?"

The buzzing was getting louder, and Vor could almost discern the chirping Hawkwind had spoken of now. The group was nearly silent, watching the doorways and serving window.

"I'm not actually an official wizard yet, but yes. The Magic Liberation Front," Vor answered her question. "I think it's them. I'm just not sure if they're doing it out of simple emotion, or if they're doing it with some kind of plan."

"Not an impossible theory," Master Himes said archly, "and you point out the relevant issue with it. We know they're angry. We know they're hiding. There have been efforts to root them out, to disrupt their secret organization, with only partial success. Weldom doesn't have any other overt enemies that would be likely to make such a move as this."

"Perhaps the discontented commoner mages have found support from a country that is quietly an enemy," Vor suggested, having to raise her voice now to be heard over the buzzing that was rapidly becoming a whirring, shrill cacophony.

Thornwing retreated from the doorway so quickly his feet slid a little on the tiles and he had to grip with his claws. He dashed over to the corner and tucked himself next to Hawkwind.

"A swarm," he reported, "blue and red and silver and crawling on the floors and walls, moving fast, and flickering as though they're shiny."

"How big are the creatures?" Master Himes demanded.

"Kitten size," the griffin reported, "or squirrel, lots of legs. You'll see in a moment."

Master Himes said a word that made a sweet-faced young apprentice behind her wince. "Blade-tails," she announced.

Her rude word was echoed by several of the older mages, but most of the young ones looked nervously puzzled.

"They seek heat," she explained. "When they find it, they cut into it with their tails to lay their larvae. They like throats and groins. Slipping one into a rival's bedroom at night is usually sufficient to prevent future competition. They can be killed easily if you see them coming and there are only a few. Stomp them, burn them, blast them, but they climb rapidly. They'll climb your clothes—inside and out—cut you if they get trapped or feel threatened, until they find a suitably warm spot to carve out a slit to insert a larva."

Then the swarm burst into the room, and there was no more time for explanations, nor need. The small creatures scuttled on several pairs of legs, much like elongated scorpions, with hooked claws in front, a tiny head, and a flexible tail bearing a natural carapace blade that looked as sharp as any knife. They were striped down their length in a pattern of red and blue. Their hooks, legs, and tail were a shiny grey that looked silver.

Mage shields sprang up along the floor.

"The walls, too," someone cried.

A sweeping blast of fire rushed out over the crawling crowd of creatures, slaying dozens, but dozens more rushed in to take their place, and they were still pouring in through the doorway, spreading across the floor like water and building up against the shields.

Vor took a moment, closed her eyes, and silently sang a cantrip, weaving her mind and magic into the proper patterns as she did. As she opened her eyes, before her materialized a small flicker of flame. About as long as her hand, and eternally burning, the lesser salamander blinked at her with white-hot eyes. She held out her hand, offering a globe of energy.

"Stay with me. Protect me from them," she whispered.

The salamander wriggled, dipping forward to gulp the energy, and flew down to take up position near her ankles. She'd always had a good relationship with fire sprites and salamanders, made better when she saved one from imprisonment in a magical ward. Now, salamanders always came when she called, and served her out of proportion to the payment she offered them. Vor had been taught that elemental beings, summoned from their plane by a mage, were neither good nor evil, but she had to wonder about that. From her observations, they seemed happier doing good works, and angrier—and demanding of more pay—when asked to kill or wantonly destroy.

The blade-tails were crawling atop each other, trying to get over the shields keeping them from the cluster of blood-warm wizards and griffins. Among the mages, outstretched hands were starting to shake with fatigue. Between the efforts to bring down the shields over the citadel and the fights with the golems, most of the wizards were running out of energy. Lashes of force or fire still struck out at the swarm, but despite killing hundreds, the plague kept coming.

"How does someone get so many of these?" Vor wondered aloud.

"You get just a few at first," Master Himes answered from beside her. "Keep them in a pit they can't climb out of, and keep throwing them food. They'll breed as long as they have food and hot flesh to lay their larvae in."

"I'm losing it," one of the other wizards quavered. "Can someone take over?"

Another wizard went to reinforce the shield. Throughout the group, wizards were starting to stagger, and other less exhausted wizards took their places while they rested.

"We can't keep this up," Giri warned. "Shields that stop physical attacks are hard enough, and they usually only get hit by an object every now and then. These blade-tails are pressing against the shields all the time."

"We need to run," Dello said.

"To where, Traskitandi?" Master Himes retorted. "I expect these things are infesting the entire citadel by now."

"And the shield is back up," Giri growled, "so there's no getting out."

"What kind of walls can't they climb?" Vor asked. "Master Himes, you said to keep them in a pit they can't climb out of."

"Smooth inward sloping walls," she replied. "Their own weight makes it so they can't hold on."

"Let's angle the shields like that," Dello pounced. "Here, everyone, do this."

The tall wizard led the group in altering their defensive tactics, but despite angling the shields, the blade-tails still piled up against them, crawling over their companions both alive and dead, to press against the shields. One by one, wizards pleaded their exhaustion. The group crowded back into the corner, trying to squish together so the shields could be smaller. Vor released a lash of fire on the creatures. As they died, she sucked up what little life energy they had; they were only bugs and she had no compunctions about harvesting what would otherwise go to waste.

"When you kill them," she directed, "take their life energy."

Several nearby wizards looked alarmed. Master Himes put a hand on her shoulder.

"That's not really encouraged," she said with a little wince, "with the young ones."

"We're all going to die if we don't get some power," Vor retorted, and with a flick of her shoulder got the older woman to draw back her hand.

Vor lashed the creatures again, and noticed a few others tug in a bit of the freed power. She was still spending more than she was getting back, but she'd rather fight to the end than wait for the masses to overwhelm the shields. Again and again she lashed the blade-tails, and more and more wizards began taking in bits of the energy and even copying her.

Yet, the swarm of blade-tails did not slow.

"It was a good last effort," Master Himes praised, now panting herself.

"We're not going to die here," Hawkwind snarled.

Some of the younger, exhausted apprentices were crying weakly at the back of the group. Jessika and Rikah stood together, not quite hugging. Hawkjoy had her wing around them, holding them to her. Giri stepped close to Vor, his chest half-touching her back.

"We need to make a run for it," Vor said stubbornly.

"Where?" another wizard asked hopelessly. "They're everywhere."

"The direction they're coming from," she insisted. "We might even find the ones doing this at the end."

There didn't seem to be much interest in her suggestion. Wizards that were still holding the shields looked wearily at each other.

"In Northborn, when it snows, the main roads are plowed," Vor said. She put her hands into a V shape, fingertips together. "The plows are shaped like this. We run through the blade-tails with a shield-plow leading. These things are fast, but not as fast as someone running. The shield-plow clears the way, and we run through while the blade-tails figure out what's happening and try to turn around against the flow."

"It's better than staying here," Giri declared. "Let's do it."

The griffins all took passengers: Jessika on Hawkwind, Rikah on Thornwing, and Craduticus and Breeka on Hawkjoy. They gathered behind Vor and Giri.

"Master Majisson can't run," someone objected.

Rikah immediately slid down from Thornwing's back. "I can. Thornwing, will you carry him?"

The griffin cocked his head. "Can you hold on, sir?" he asked.

Master Majisson, dark skin grey with pain, propped himself up against the wall, wincing. "If I fall off, you may leave me."

Thornwing nodded. "On you get, then."

Others helped the old mage on. Rikah used some straps to buckle him down. Meanwhile, others of the group were muttering, glancing around shiftily. Finally, one young man got up his nerve.

"Are you sure this will work?" he asked of the group that roughly contained Vor, Giri, Dello, and Master Himes.

"No," the master wizard retorted. "But I agree with Hearthsraven. It's better than staying here. We'll find somewhere more defensible. Stay if you want, though I don't recommend it. Are we ready?"

"The sooner we go, the more energy we'll have," Dello confirmed.

Vor felt Giri touch her back. A little embarrassed, she pulled him to one side so Hawkjoy was between them and most of the others. He complied, holding her close. For a few moments she was almost able to forget the imminent death frothing against the faltering shields. A little cuddling didn't generate much energy, but it was enough that she thought maybe they could lead the charge, supporting each other with the wedge shield.

"Let's go," Giri announced, striding to the front of the group. "I've got enough power left to run the wedge shield."

"Follow closely," Master Himes instructed the others, "and try to shield whatever side you're on."

Vor went to stand behind Giri, ready to catch him when he faltered, but she didn't know the way through the Citadel like he did. It was only one more floor to the entry level, but if she had to lead—

Master Himes appeared beside her. "I can take over when needed," she said, "and so can Traskitandi."

"Thank you," Vor replied, relieved. "I'll provide as much power as I can to whoever is leading."

Giri had a hand out in front of him as he began to concentrate, and Vor felt the magic move. She sent a silent message to her salamander to ignite any blade-tail that slipped past the materializing plow-shield.

"Get ready," Master Himes announced, no doubt feeling it, too.

In another breath, Vor sensed the shield firm up.

"Come on," Giri called, and then he ran.

There was immediate confusion as those determined to run followed close on Giri's heels, those determined to stay huddled back in the corner, and a dozen indecisive wizards hesitated in the middle. The shields of the staying wizards contracted. The runners pelted away in the blade-tail-free space created by Giri's snow-plow shield. The indecisive wizards were caught in the middle.

A couple jumped back behind the staying wizards' shields just before they hardened. A couple more belatedly sprinted to join the fleeing group, hopping over and stomping on blade-tails trying to close in from behind. The rest were too slow. Vor got one quick look over her shoulder as blade-tails clambered up their legs. They swatted and screamed and ran for the departing group or tried to get through the shields of the remaining wizards—who weren't sure whether to let them in or not. Vor didn't see any further what happened, but there were more screams.

"This is hard," Giri growled from the point position. "I've never pushed a shield ahead of me before while hitting things."

They'd gotten out of the dining hall, where Giri turned to the right, but blade-tails still coated the floor and walls, though not as thickly as before. Vor touched his back, giving him some more power, and he kept up the charge, not quite a sprint, but much faster than a leisurely jog. The group of now about twenty wizards all told, three griffins, two non-mage humans, and a bat-cat trotted behind him.

"I hope we don't run into any more golems," Dello muttered.

"And thank you, Apprentice, for that cheerful thought," Master Himes drawled. "Down the stairs, Wizard Holstor."

Vor could see Giri's hand shaking. Sweat was shining on his neck. Hand still on his back, she gave him yet more energy, again digging into her personal power. The main stairwell was ahead. It was still crawling with blade-tails. Halfway along it was a crumpled, motionless body with several blade-tails clustered around its neck. The stairs below it were coated with blood, visible even though the carpet of blade-tails.

"Nothing we can do for him," Master Himes grunted. "Keep going."

Giri started down the steps, still plowing the murderous little beasts out of the way. Vor's salamander was still at its task, too, flicking here and there around her ankles, but so far it hadn't had to take any action to protect her. Giri slipped on a stair and Vor caught him as he started to fall back. The shield wavered and Vor sent a pulse of energy into him, but during the waver a few blade-tails—pressed up against the shield—had fallen through.

Wizards stomped them, exclaiming, and Vor's salamander flicked at the one nearest to her, instantly charing it into a twisted tangle of legs and tail. It undulated over the corpse, as if celebrating, or perhaps laughing, and then darted back to Vor to zip around her head in rapid circles.

"Very good," she praised it softly, more with magical intent than sounds. "Most excellently done."

Vor offered it a payment of a little more energy, cupped in the palm of her hand, but it just made one more orbit of her head, ignoring the gift, and then flashed back down to her ankle level.

"Loyal little one you've got there," Master Himes muttered to her under a partly raised eyebrow.

Giri had firmed the shield back up, but was visibly panting.

"Let me take it," Dello suggested, and as soon as Dello's shield sprang to life behind Giri's, the latter let his fall.

Dello took the lead now as the group went as quick as it could down the stairs. Vor got an arm around Giri, tucking him against her.

"I'm fine," he insisted between sucking breaths.

At the landing of the stairs the blade-tails were fewer, and Dello went on more confidently. This was the first level, the ground floor, full of the dormitories for the youngest wizard apprentices, those that hadn't been taken by masters yet and were still receiving rudimentary education. During the tour he'd given her, Giri had said some magic-gifted children came to the citadel as young as ten years of age. There weren't any wizards that young among their group.

Master Himes seemed to read her mind. "Hopefully they sealed their doors. The blade-tails won't be able to get in," the lady wizard murmured. "There are no clay tracks from golems, at least. If we can find the casters, we can stop this."

"The shield is still up," Giri pointed out.

"Maybe we can fix that, too."

Vor wasn't confident of any of it, but at least there were fewer and fewer blade-tails now. They were only on the floor, not the walls, and thin enough that she could see the floor tiles between them. The ghastly critters did, however, come straight for the group of trotting humans and griffins, rebounding off Dello's shield. They were headed down the main hallway now, moving at a quicker pace, and Giri managed to get his feet under him and keep up on his own.

"Traskitandi," Master Himes spoke up. "Let me take the lead."

Dello fell back as his master passed him, but kept his shield up in front of her. They approached the entry hall, where the reception desk and the wards over the hallway entrances should have kept anything hostile out. One more turn, and then Master Himes gave a soft gasp. For a moment her steps faltered, but there were still some blade-tails in the hall determinedly closing in on the group, so she kept moving.

Vor saw what she'd seen, and everyone made muffled exclamations of dismay. The entrances to the hallways, and the desk between them, had been broken to rubble and kindling. Perhaps a few golems made of stone could have caused such destruction by punching everything repeatedly, or actual wizards had unleashed their powers directly. There were several bodies trapped and unmoving under some of the wreckage. A few of them were child sized. Directly in the nearest entrance was the remains of what seemed to be an adult in reddish mage robes torn and soiled with blood. The gray-bearded but bald head—still identifiable—suggested an older man. The rest of his limbs were only partly in attendance. The floor around him was scorched black.

"Master Morinder," Dello identified softly.

A lone blade-tail approached the shield. Master Himes stepped over and stomped viciously on the vermin.

"What could take down Stanis?" she sighed, as if to herself. "Come on."

They picked their way through the detritus, having to shove some of it aside, and into the main entryway of the citadel.

"Bust down the doorway on which the wards are placed," one of the other wizards who had come with them remarked, "and you take down the wards. That's one way to do it."

Only a couple blade-tails were in the entry hall, and both seemed to be resting, uninterested in approaching the group. Vor jerked her chin at them.

"What's wrong with them?" she asked aloud.

"They've probably already laid their larvae in corpses," Master Himes answered. "You can drop the shield, Traskitandi."

Dello huffed, and the shield vanished. He staggered for a moment, and his master caught his shoulder, supporting him until he gathered his feet under him. Then Master Himes marched over to the two blade-tails. They skittered a little, but without the energy needed to escape her stomping feet.

"Blessed blue skies," the master wizard sighed, now trying to scrape the squished bugs off her shoes, "how did all this happen?"

"The shield out there is still up," Craduticus called. "Shall we try getting it down again?"

"And the citadel is still full of those blade-tails," Master Majisson added shakily, from his perch atop Thornwing. "They're surely still looking for targets."

"Everyone out," Master Himes ordered. "Head for the shield. Maybe we can talk through it and find out if anyone saw anything, and at least see if there's some help outside. Those blade-tails will come back. They'll keep searching, just as you say, until they've all found a host for their larvae, or they're all dead."

The other fleeing wizards didn't need to be told twice. The shield touched down on the road that encircled the citadel, but there was plenty of room between it and the walls for the wizards to go stand in sunlight at least, and feel psychologically free, even if the shield still contained them. The griffins stood aside in the entry room to allow the humans to stream out. Vor, Giri, and Dello remained, too, watching Master Himes walking slowly through the wreckage.

"I'll just drop you off outside, shall I?" Thornwing said genially to his rider, and followed the other wizards out.

"Can we go out, too?" Jessika begged Hawkwind, and the big female turned to exit behind the smaller male.

Hawkjoy with Craduticus and Breeka remained behind.

"What do you think, Master?" Dello asked once all the others had left.

"I think we lost a lot of wizards today, Traskitandi," she sighed.

"We have only seen a few bodies," Hawkjoy pointed out timidly.

"The ones we left in the dining hall won't have survived," Giri surmised.

Master Himes nodded. So did Craduticus.

"Against all those blade-tails, eventually their shields will have failed, their energy exhausted," she agreed.

"So why didn't they run?" Hawkjoy asked.

"Fear," Vor answered. "And we couldn't make them, and there was no time to argue with them, or we all would have died."

Master Himes gave a little wince. "It was their choice. They were all adults. But I will still regret leaving them for the rest of my life."

"And the other wizards in the citadel," Dello picked up. "Unless they found a room they could seal, will have been overcome, too, especially after they spent so much energy on the golems and the shield."

"Which is exactly what our enemies wanted," Master Himes growled. She flung out a hand at the busted up entry room and hallways. "Magic did this, and not anyone's magic I recognize. I've worked with most of the wizards of the Citadel; I would know if any of them did this."

She pointed a dagger-like finger at the deceased Master Morinder. "The residue of his final magic is almost all defensive, and none of it did this damage. He was fighting someone, other mages. They came in through the front door. They broke the wards over the hallways so they could send in the blade-tails after they'd used the golems and the shields to wear us down."

"So they had to be inside when the shield went up, so they could summon their golems in here," Giri suggested. "Then they opened the shield, stepped out, and sent the blade-tails in?"

"Maybe," Master Himes shrugged.

"But by then people would have gathered, including other wizards who were outside the shield when it went up, and would have come here to try to help," Dello said. "They would have been caught."

"But if they had been caught, by now the shield would be down," Craduticus insisted. "It isn't. They're still in control of it. No one has caught them yet."

Vor tried to listen to the discussion, but her own observation of the destruction in the foyer was troubling her, and no one else seemed to have noticed; perhaps they were so obsessed with magical analysis that they were neglecting visual evidence. She gave Giri's sleeve a tug, and he turned to her.

"You said the other hall leads to the utility rooms," she recalled, "not to dormitories or anywhere lots of wizards would be."

"That's right," he nodded, and immediately began scrutinizing the hall, as Vor had been doing.

"Then why bust it open," Vor went on, "and why is there a cleared path in the rubble?"

"Not much of one," Giri agreed, "but definitely there, compared to the other hall."

"Blade-tails wouldn't make a path," Vor said. "They'd just climb over or around it all."

"So who went that way," he concluded, "and why?"

Indeed, there seemed to be a hint of a trail, winding around the very largest piles of wreckage, with manageable pieces of stone and wood nudged out of the way just as the group of wizards had nudged wreckage out of the way when they came into the foyer from the other hall a minute ago. Vor went over to it. Just like snow, the dust from the destruction had left a thin layer over the floor, and it held footprints, many footprints.

Master Himes suddenly appeared beside her, looking where Vor was looking. "Someone went this way," the woman declared.

"Lots of someones," Vor nodded, declining any comment that might have suggested the older woman had missed the obvious until someone else went to look. "Who would go this way in the middle of a battle, Master Himes? Would they be going to contaminate the water system for the Citadel, perhaps?"

"Possibly," she shrugged, but her expression didn't convey much confidence.

"Could they be apprentices, going to hide?" Giri suggested.

"These are bootprints," Master Himes denied. "Inside the citadel, we just wear house shoes, like mine."

She made a footprint next to the others and Vor could clearly see the differences: her shoe had a flat sole and narrow contours; the other prints had a definite heel and blockier outline, with texture in the sole to provide traction.

"You wouldn't need this many people to poison the water system," Giri stated.

"And what would they want with the furnaces, laundry, or waste chutes?" Dello added. "Going to do our chores for us?"

"And there's nothing particularly valuable in the storage," Master Himes agreed.

Craduticus tottered up beside them, leaning on his staff. "There's no blade-tail tracks, either. They prevented the creatures from going this way." His sigh came out much like a growl. "We've got a problem."

Four faces swung to him.

"What?" Dello shrugged. "They're trapped in there now. It's a dead end that way except for the dumb waiters. I guess you could fit a person on one of them if you tried, but otherwise once the shield is down we just—"

"These people defeated Master Morinder," Master Himes reminded him, "and are probably the ones responsible for the golems and blade-tails and the shield."

"I think there's another group running the shield from somewhere outside," Craduticus corrected, "and another that made the golems, and another that made the blade-tails." He pointed an aged hand down the utility hall. "This is the infiltration group."

"That's a lot of people," Dello muttered.

"But to what point?" Master Himes countered. "As Traskitandi said, they can't get out."

Craduticus cleared his throat with a gravelly sound. "They're going down," he said darkly.

No one spoke for a moment.

"Down?" Vor repeated.

The old mage nodded. "Under the city, under the Citadel."

Master Himes shook her head and seemed to try for a dismissive smirk. "No. They wouldn't. No one would."

Craduticus glanced at Vor. "Young Hearthsraven is right. They're angry."

"You're talking about the Magic Liberation Front? The 'magic is for everyone' people?" Vor confirmed.

The two master mages locked somber stares. "You've seen the signs, Tessa," Craduticus rued, "and everything the ministers have tried has only made it worse, especially the newest mandate. There's finally enough of them, and they've finally had enough. They're done with pranks, and they're acting now." He shrugged a little. "I can't really say that I blame them, but I didn't think they'd take it this far."

"What are they doing?" Vor asked, alarmed by the growing darkness of Craduticus's words.

"I told you that magic holds the city together these days," he said, turning to her. "The gorges are too deep and with the weight of all this city on top of them, would collapse without magical help staying up."

"So killing all the wizards—?" she guessed.

"The spells will hold a while," he explained. "Killing a bunch of us won't cause an instant catastrophe. Someone still alive will just have to renew the spells in a week or two."

Master Himes added a clarification. "We didn't set up these spells; we're just custodians."

"It was long dead wizards who set them, hundreds of years ago," Craduticus resumed, "anchored them deep under the city, far, far down into the bedrock."

"But magic doesn't work well over such distances," Vor said, "or through so much rock. The same as you can't cast spells through a large volume of water, or even a smaller volume of fire."

"Indeed," Craduticus smiled, revealing all his wrinkles. "You have been a good student, Vor. So what is the solution, young wizard?"

"You create a link, using an item," she said. "You magically prepare it to receive the spell, and take it to where you want your spell to go. Then you can touch it from a distance, even through rock or water or fire. That's how Giri and I could communicate all this time over such a great distance, with the rings he made."

"Quite so," he praised. "That is what the ancient wizards did. They sent a team down into the depths of the old city, and deeper, into the caves below, to the deepest point they could find. The team succeeded in anchoring the supportive spells for the wizards who remained behind, up here, to use."

"The legends say," Master Himes interjected with a raised eyebrow, "that the team never returned."

"But they saved the city," Craduticus concluded, "by planting the item, the anchor for all the spells."

"The key to the city," Master Himes nodded.

Craduticus looked down the hallway towards the utility rooms, his neck bones audibly popping. He sighed, exhalation rough.

"And now," he groaned. "I am thinking these disgruntled common-born mages are going to go pull it out."

Chapter 5
The Door

Vor just stared for a few moments, absorbing that.

"And the entrance to the old city is here, in the Citadel," she confirmed.

"One of the last ones, perhaps the very last, that I am aware of." Master Himes nodded, "in the utility wing, down through the water basement."

Vor puzzled at that. "How does the MLF know?"

The master mage shrugged. "Doesn't everyone know?"

"I've heard about it," Giri muttered, "but it's sealed up. Most young apprentices go looking for it in their first year here, but no one has ever found it."

"And we let you," Master Himes revealed. "Young apprentices haven't the skill to find it, much less open it, so we let you think it's a myth, an old story, and give you a vague admonition to stay away from it." She nearly managed a chuckle. "That practically guarantees you'll sneak down there. We allow the tradition to continue of all the young apprentices going to search for—and failing to find—the Door. That way, you don't go looking for it when you're older and more skilled. Can't have anyone opening it by mistake, now can we?"

"So you know how to open it," Vor guessed.

Craduticus and Himes frowned and nodded.

"Do they?" she asked, pointing down the utility hall.

"A strong, experienced mage could probably figure it out with a bit of work," Master Himes admitted.

"Or they have someone helping them," Dello muttered.

The tall lady wizard frowned firmly at her apprentice. "Suggesting one of our own has betrayed us is a serious charge, Traskitandi. People have died."

"Yes, Master," he subsided.

"But not impossible," she allowed.

The group, including Hawkjoy and Breeka, stood for a minute looking down the utility corridor. Breeka hissed softly.

"Well," Vor began, feeling rather hesitant in front of all the older wizards. "We're not going to just let them do it, are we? It would destroy the city, wouldn't it?"

"It would," Craduticus confirmed.

"I doubt they can survive to find the key, and even if they did, they probably wouldn't be able to pull it out," Master Himes said, but she did not sound confident.

"Doubt?" Vor echoed. "Probably?"

Giri sucked a breath through his teeth. "I know Master Colby would never take that risk."

Master Himes huffed out a fragment of a laugh. "Your master would never let such a thing rest. It's a pity he went away on his marital leave when he did."

"No it isn't," Giri retorted, but softly. "If he'd been here, he might have been killed."

Vor took that with a bit of shock at the realization. "We might be some of the only wizards left."

"I'm sure others have survived," Master Himes stated at once.

Craduticus winced. "They did a decent job, thinking up a way to kill or at least inconvenience as many of us as possible."

The griffins, who had gathered again and were standing silently by at a polite distance, suddenly twitched and turned as one, looking back down the main hallway or out the door towards the shield.

"The blade-tails are coming back," Hawkwind announced before anyone could ask.

Then Vor started hearing the buzzing, just as she had before. Master Himes cursed colorfully. One of the other wizards, a young woman, came running inside with alarm painted on her face.

"We know," Master Himes snapped, before the young woman could speak.

"There's nowhere left to go," Dello mumbled.

"There is," Vor disagreed. She pointed. "Down there."

"Here they come," Giri exclaimed.

Perhaps because they hadn't found enough victims, or perhaps just because they had reached dead ends and turned around, a wave of blade-tails was pouring back down the hallway the group of escapees had just come through.

"Get everyone from outside," Master Himes ordered.

But then, like curiously heavy rain, objects started falling from the sky, landing with plops like softly clapped hands. The pouring increased, and the fallen blade-tails were not hurt at all by the drop. Screams erupted from where the escaped wizards had gone to work on the shield.

"Come in," Master Himes shouted.

Dello threw up a low shield as the leaders of the blade-tail wave began to reach them. A few wizards came running inside, dancing about to avoid the blade-tails recovering from their fall outside, or pausing to stomp on them.

"Master Majisson," one of the first arrivals bemoaned. "We had to leave him. A blade-tail dropped right onto him. He didn't even have time to react before it," the young woman swallowed, "before it, um."

There were winces all around.

"Can't be helped now," Craduticus whispered.

Jessika and Rikah had mounted Hawkwind and Thornwing. Hawkjoy, with Craduticus and Breeka, moved closer to the utility hallway. Vor put a hand on Giri's arm. Her salamander was once again on patrol around her ankles.

"We should go," she said. "There's no choice."

The blade-tails kept coming. Everyone inside Dello's shield—some twelve humans, three griffins, and a bat-cat—crept away from the main entrance, finding the meager path through the wreckage, into the utility hallway. Once past the last of the rubble and splinters, they looked back. The blade-tails surged and ebbed against some kind of invisible impediment, and didn't seem able to follow.

"Curious. It's not a shield," Master Himes said. "It's some sort of ward, a subtle one, that makes them reluctant to come any closer. It's good work, but now that there's something on the other side the blade-tails want, it will be truly tested."

"How long will it last?" Thornwing asked.

"It will fall eventually," a tall mature male wizard muttered.

"We should move," Vor agreed.

"Alright then," Master Himes nodded. "Let's go."

Master Himes led them down the hallway at a brisk pace. Dello followed just off her left shoulder. Vor and Giri came behind the pair, with the griffins and their passengers following. The other wizards, five of them, three women and two men, hustled along at the back of the pack.

"Do you know any of them?" Vor asked Giri softly, twitching her head back.

"One of the women was in my year," he said tensely. "Pirossa is her name if I remember. She's the shorter, darker one. She's also from western Weldom, but much farther north."

The woman Pirossa wore mage robes patterned in dark red. Her inky black hair was sharply straight and cut off at earlobe length. Even from a distance, Vor could see her eyes glimmering emerald green from her thin, elegant face that was almost as dark as her hair. She walked with quick steps, probably because she had legs shorter than everyone else, and watched vigilantly around her, an instinct that had probably kept her alive.

"She looks sharp," Vor remarked.

"And bossy," Giri added. "She respects authority though, which is why she hasn't said anything since Master Himes is here and in charge."

"I'm supposing you don't like her?"

"She's a fine mage," he muttered. "I just had too many group assignments with her. She's great at spells of seeing, though, like scrying."

"She might be useful then," Vor supposed.

"The blonde woman I don't recognize," Giri went on.

A young woman perhaps a bit taller than Vor, with medium blonde hair and in pale blue mage robes that looked a little too large on her, she walked slightly apart from the others. Her gray-green eyes flicked nervously all around. She was lean enough, but her hands and face still showed the baby fat of youth. Vor thought she might see tear tracks on the girl's face, and she moved with a tense posture, as though ready to spring away at any moment. She couldn't really blame her after having endured the events of the day.

Vor's gaze went to the third woman, who walked tall in the middle of the party of five wizards. Her robes were a rich, smooth brown and cream, and she wore them as though they were the finest satin and silk gown. Her hair and eyes, too, were rich browns, and her skin a deep umber that glowed with vitality. She had a lovely face: long but nicely symmetrical and balanced in features. Somehow, through all the chaos, she'd kept her fetchingly coiffed hair in place.

"Who is the third one?" Vor asked, oddly feeling an immediate dislike of the woman.

"Lanisala Salasis," Giri said too evenly.

Vor turned her head to examine his profile. "A friend?" She could see the tightness at the outer corners of his eyes which she now knew indicated both stress and distress.

"Not exactly," Giri murmured, and took a steadying breath. "She was the first woman I broke my heart over."

Vor was seized with the sudden and fierce desire to go punch Lanisala Salasis in the face, several times. Whether he sensed that or not, Giri took her hand, and she mastered the desire—for the moment.

"She's skilled with combative magic," Giri continued, voice rough and low. "A lot of the fire getting thrown against the golems and blade-tails was her."

"Is she a threat we need to guard against?" Vor murmured.

"I'm not sure," he said, "but she might say something to us, maybe to you. She's been ignoring me for years now. I just hope she continues doing so."

"So do I," Vor grunted. "We've got a common enemy. I hope we don't end up with an internal enemy."

"I wouldn't want to fight her," Giri said, "though together we could probably withstand her, you and I."

"She's that strong?" Vor marvelled.

"She's very strong," he confirmed. "She's not stupid, either. What she lacks is a heart."

Vor squeezed his hand, wishing she could take the time to hug him instead.

"And the men?" she nudged.

One was definitely older than either of them, but younger than Master Himes. He was tall, quite thin, with grey robes that were torn and clay-stained. He had thick but short brown hair starting to show a hint of grey, and a darker beard and mustache. The expression on his tanned face was focused and worried, but showed no fear, and his long strides were confident and easy.

"The tall one is Ramikar," Giri said. "I don't know him personally, only by reputation. I hear he's a good fellow. He just recently passed his master trial, but I don't think he has an apprentice of his own yet. He's skilled with earth magic and also a scholar of history."

"Then he should be useful down below," Vor hoped.

"I think so," Giri agreed. "As for the last, I don't recognize him."

The fifth and final trailing wizard was shorter than Ramikar and Lanisala but taller than all the others, and surprisingly solid-looking for a wizard. He wasn't obese by any definition, but most wizards were on the lean side if they weren't overlarge, due to a life mostly of scholarship and only light or moderate exercise. This man looked like he could probably swing a battle axe or hefty war hammer around with ease.

His robes were patterned with several colors. He wore his dark reddish hair in a tail against pale skin. His eyes glinted blue-green and unlike everyone else there, he wore a hint of a smile, as though this were any ordinary stroll on a lovely day. He caught Vor looking, and winked at her. She promptly turned her face back to front.

"I wonder what our chances are," she muttered, "down there."

"Me, too," Giri said.

"Here," Master Himes called before they could speculate further. The wizard stood at a pair of open doors. One swayed drunkenly from a single hinge; the top corner was broken away. "We have to go through the water pump room. Beyond that is an access hatch down towards the holding tank. The entrance to the water basement is not far from there, and after that we go down into the old tunnels, and beyond them into the old city, and sometime after that we'll reach the natural caverns. At the bottom we'll find the key."

Craduticus was nodding along. "Somewhere," he added. "No records exist of the path the wizards who planted the key took. We can hope they might have left markers."

"Supposedly, they warded it as they went, too," Master Himes mentioned.

"Let's hope the thieves run into the wards first," Thornwing contributed optimistically.

"More likely the wards have faded with time, but let's hope we catch the thieves before they get that far," Master Himes countered.

"And that they don't prove the stronger," Dello mumbled.

"That's enough from you, Traskitandi."

"Yes, Master." Dello smiled again—as he seemed to do every time his master spoke to him, whether to scold or instruct or praise.

Master Himes turned to look at the five wizards at the back of the group. "You can stay here and hide until the shield comes down if you want," she offered. "No one is forcing you to chase a bunch of invaders."

"If they even exist," the lovely Lanisala said with an elegant roll of a hand.

"I'm sure we'll figure that out soon enough," Pirossa snapped. Her gaze darted from the dubious Lanisala back to Master Himes. "I'm coming and so should we all. It's our duty to Weldom to protect it."

"I'm with you," Ramikar uttered, his voice smooth and deep.

"Might as well," the second man, the one with the red hair grinned, rocking back and forth on his feet. "It could be fun, routing rebels, capturing keys."

Master Himes turned to the young blonde woman in the blue robes. "Iyai?" she asked gently, "would you like to find a safe place to wait?"

While the discussion of who would go and stay went on, Vor called to her own follower, and her little salamander flickered up to her eye level.

"There's water in there," she murmured to it. "Shall I send you back?"

The elemental surged closer to her, and then flew a tight orbit around her neck, its warmth delighting her skin.

"You want to stay?" she asked it.

In apparent answer, it tucked itself behind her right ear and clung to her pinna with all four feet and tail. It was hot, but not painful; lesser salamanders had full control over when they burned things and when they didn't, and this one was clearly choosing to be cautious of Vor's combustible human skin, but it couldn't eliminate all of it's natural heat, and Vor thought if it was planning to ride on her ears, she'd have to make it switch sides from time to time. At least it was the next thing to weightless.

"I guess this means you're staying," Vor muttered.

Then the blonde woman, apparently called Iyai, turned towards the hallway back with a gasp. "The blade-tails," she blurted, "I hear them again."

"Sounds like we're all going then," Master Himes announced. "Come on."

Vor heard the buzzing too, and the griffins nodded in confirmation. Master Himes led the way through the double doors and waited while everyone else went past her.

"They broke this hinge," she remarked. "We won't be able to seal the doors against the blade-tails, but I can put a shield over the doorway. It will last for a while, give us some extra time. Keep moving."

Vor passed through, into a wide and tall room that smelled of wet metal, wet stone, wet wood—wet everything, really, but with surprisingly little scent of mildew or algae. Someone must be cleaning it regularly. The floor was wood, and felt hollow beneath her feet. Two protrusions high on the walls, two of many, were glowing with magical light, giving only dim illumination. Vor could see well enough to detect that the bulk of the floor was occupied by a large square basin that came as high as her knees, around which the floor ran. As she got closer, she saw that the floor was indeed built around it; it did not sit atop the floor, but extended deep down past the floor. From the high ceiling above, many different pipes dropped down, disappearing below the water surface of the still basin.

"The aquins are gone," the blonde young woman called Iyai whispered worriedly as she passed.

Vor recalled from her studies what aquins were: magical creatures of water, not the biggest, nor the smallest, and generally not very intelligent or powerful. They were just smart enough to follow simple orders, and quite placid. They made good servants as long as inventiveness or initiative were not required, but poor allies in combat.

"They were the pumps?" Vor surmised.

"Yes," Giri answered from beside her. "There won't be any water for the citadel until someone comes to summon and feed them again."

Iyai trailed her fingers through the water of the basin. "That's good," she said softly. "The water is poisoned so we can't have it getting into the citadel. The aquins might have left on their own, because of it."

Vor winced, as did others.

"I'll leave a message," Iyai said, and Vor sensed a slight burst of power coating the water. "Anyone who tries to touch the water will feel that they should be cautious."

The blonde girl wiped off her fingers on her robe and hurried on. Vor was a little relieved; she'd worried the girl would be too timid to be useful.

"But we can't drink here," Hawkwind objected.

"There will be plenty of other places with water," Master Himes said from ahead, where she was holding open a trapdoor in the floor. Below the trapdoor stretched a ladder. "As we go deeper, we'll get closer to the rivers. Water we won't lack. In fact there may come times when we wish there were less of it."

Then Hawkwind balked at the trapdoor. "We might reach places we griffins can't fit through," she said, "like this one."

Ramikar was descending down in the gloom, Pirossa following him.

"Are you going to stay behind then?" Master Himes asked. "The blade tails are still following, and the doors back there can't stop them forever."

Jessika and Rikah slid down off their griffin mounts and helped Craduticus down. Hawkwind was examining the floor.

"The gaps between these boards won't stop them either," the griffin said.

"I don't think they will," Master Himes agreed.

"Go through the trapdoor, everyone," Hawkwind commanded. "We'll follow. Hurry. I hear the blade-tails getting closer."

Vor followed Dello down, with Giri coming behind her. The ladder was wood, a little slick and slightly gummy in places from all the moisture, but it didn't feel unsafe. To one side, as she'd thought, the basin from above proved to be an immense water tank that she descended beside, far down to a little landing below. The smooth stone walls of the room above turned to more crudely chiseled rock, glistening in the light of her salamander. The tank met the rocky walls where they curved into a jagged ring-shaped floor, though it was hidden in places by puddles of water.

Just beyond where the ladder touched down on a wooden platform, a dark hole gaped in the wall. It was roughly square, and looked big enough for the griffins to pass through, though it might be tight for Hawkwind. Vor reached the bottom of the ladder. Pirossa, Lanisala, Iyai, Ramikar, and the redheaded wizard whose name she didn't yet know had already moved into the opening, probably because the landing was too small to hold them all. Dello had his hand out to steady Vor as she stepped down. The wood planking was wet here, too, and slipping off the edge would mean a fall onto the raw rock floor.

She was moving into the tunnel opening as Giri came down with Rikah, Jessika, and Craduticus above him on the ladder. Dello conjured a faint greenish light, making everyone flinch, and Vor stepped deeper into the tunnel with Giri's fingertips lightly on her back.

"Ah, you have a salamander," the solid, red-haired wizard commented as Vor moved deeper into the tunnel.

The dim firelight of the elemental was clearly noticeable in the darkness, and with his comment, everyone's eyes turned to look at Vor's right ear.

"Yes," Vor replied neutrally.

"A good idea," the man went on genially, "though I will say this is the first time I've ever seen one riding on its conjurer. Brilliant."

Vor passed the wizard without further comment. The tunnel continued straight for a few paces before starting to curve down. The floor had been smoothed, but not polished, providing some traction. She found a spot next to Pirossa. Across from her stood Lanisala. For a moment their eyes met. Lanisala wore what might have been a bit of a smirk, had the situation not been too distracting.

Then came the sound of wrenching, breaking wood, making everyone look back towards the tunnel entrance. Craduticus had reached the landing, and clung to one side of the ladder. Breeka now was perched on Rikah's shoulder. Master Himes slid down onto the crowded landing.

"The griffins ripped up some floorboards so they could fit," the master wizard explained. "Move in so they have a place to land. Let's keep going. I don't know how far the blade-tails will follow us. Water doesn't bother them, so it's no defense."

She swept between the rows of people aligned on both sides of the tunnel to take the lead again. Others began to follow, sorting themselves out, while behind came the thump of a griffin landing by the ladder. Vor stayed by Giri, and took his hand in the darkness. Ahead of them, Master Himes made light by touching her fingers to the tunnel walls. The faint spots of illumination lasted only a minute, long enough to guide everyone passing, before fading.

The tunnel descended and curved as it went, and most people put their hands out to brace against the wet walls, going single file. It was difficult to see who was where. Vor only knew that Dello was ahead of her, Master Himes in front of him, and Giri behind her. Behind him came everyone else, but she didn't know what order they were in. She found herself hoping that Lanisala was not directly behind Giri. It was irrational, she knew, to be concerned about a woman who was their ally, when there were obvious enemies who had put a shield over the citadel and released golems and blade-tails to kill them all, and were now possibly ahead of them in the dark, heading for the key that would cause the entire city to collapse and probably kill its whole population.

Still, Lanisala's presence in the group was the top worry on Vor's mind, almost strong enough that she wanted to switch places with Giri and make him walk in front of her. She supposed that must mean she was jealous. Vor gritted her teeth and tried to force the image of Giri being intimate with the elegant, confident Lanisala out of her mind. She felt Giri lightly touch her back, and with it felt a hint of concern from him; he must have sensed the turbulence of her emotions. She took a calming breath and tried to still them.

The tunnel steepened, and shallow steps were now cut into the floor, but with the light so low and the rock so damp, many people started stumbling over them. With a whispered request, Vor sent her salamander down to ankle level again to help her see the steps. Then ahead the tunnel widened and within another dozen paces opened into a cavern. The group followed Master Himes onto a smoothed rock path along one wall, and now that Vor didn't need her hands to steady herself against the walls, she wrapped herself with her arms; the air had turned icy.

Beyond the path, the cavern was full of water. It vanished into darkness in the distance. Pillars of rock branched up out of the water, rough and coated with slime. The ceiling came down low; even Vor could have reached up to touch it, making the taller members of the party instinctively duck. When the griffins emerged from the tunnel, their crest feathers brushed the ceiling, and they walked partly hunched down.

Water dripped continually, and in a few places the first proto-stalactites were forming, but the sounds of the drips were lost in the continual susurration of moving water. It wasn't as loud as a waterfall, but Vor sought the source and saw a square opening through which poured a fount of water at least two feet wide. It fell only a handspan to join the lake of water occupying the cavern.

"There's an exit on the other side, too," Giri told her. "It's a spillway, to keep this area from getting flooded."

"This is the source of the water for the Citadel?" Vor confirmed.

"And some of the surrounding buildings, but mostly the Citadel," he nodded.

"The Citadel was built first," Master Himes interjected, "after the city below started to flood and collapse. The rest of the city above gets its water from other rivers and streams running through the area. There's always plenty. Water is one thing we don't lack in Anchoria."

The master mage moved off along the walkway, closer towards where the water was pouring in through the far wall.

"You've been down here before?" Vor asked Giri.

"Just once," he answered. "Like Master Himes said, most new students sneak down here. It's sort of an unofficial rite of passage."

He turned and directed her gaze to the wall they stood along. It wasn't unfinished stone, like the rest of the cavern. False archways had been carved, and in their centers were dozens, hundreds, perhaps thousands, of scratched names, little drawings—some of them crude or rude—phrases, and dates. Some even overlapped each other.

"Mage students have been sneaking down here to make their mark for hundreds of years," Giri went on. "Maybe thousands."

"This way," Master Himes called. "Let's keep moving."

"Can we drink here?" Hawkwind called back.

"I'll check," Iyai said, and knelt by the vast, black lake to dip her fingers in.

Some of the other wizards passed by, following the faint trails of light Master Himes left on the walls.

"Most students are afraid of the water," Pirossa, the dark young woman who had been Giri's classmate, commented as she slowly moved off. "They think there's monsters in it."

"Don't be silly," Iyai whispered. "Water sprites aplenty, but none are monsters."

The pale young woman didn't sound completely confident though, and at any rate, Vor doubted Pirossa heard as she walked away.

"The boys used to dare each other to swim in it," Giri added. "I've heard of some even throwing each other in for a joke or, you know, to bully each other, as some do."

Vor looked out across the gently moving, inky surface, into the distance where all was swallowed up by darkness, and fought a shiver.

"How deep is it?" Vor asked.

"Not even Dello can touch the bottom with his toes."

"He went in it?" Vor said, impressed.

"So did I," Giri nodded, "but only for a moment, and we stayed at the edge. Sometimes boys will challenge each other to swim to the other side, but once you're in the water, you can't see how far away it is, and it gets dark, and you get scared of what might be in there with you. I don't know anyone who has swam all the way across."

"The water's drinkable," Iyai reported, standing up, "but it's fresh snow-melt, so very cold."

The griffins moved to the water's edge and began drinking: dipping and lifting their heads, as birds do. Some of the wizards also knelt, scooping up water in their cupped hands. Vor went to Hawkjoy's packs, which she'd kept on all the way from that morning on the landing platform. She fetched her water skin, took a long drink, and passed it to Giri, who drank, too. He offered it to Iyai and Dello—but everyone else had already moved away to follow Master Himes.

Together they drained the skin, and Vor knelt to refill it. The water was chill on her fingers, and even up close it still looked black. Her salamander tucked itself behind her ear again, then apparently thought that wasn't far enough from the water and hid itself inside her jacket with a little wriggle to get under the collar. It's warmth settled over her sternum.

Vor had the sudden fear that something would grab her hands and pull her below, but except for the gentle motion of the surface as the water moved from the fount to the unseen spillway, the water remained calm. She silently berated herself for getting scared. Hawkjoy and Giri waited for her to finish, but it was just them by the time she stood, capped the skin, and returned it to the pack.

"I guess the door down is this way," Giri mumbled as they went to join the dim gathering of wizards and griffins at the far end of the path.

Ramikar, not Himes, stood in front of the second to last carved archway in the wall. Iyai was just joining him. She held a hand over the graffitied surface of the wall and stared at nothing.

"Someone has touched it recently," she breathed. "No one I know."

"You know very few mages, child," Lanisala muttered from where she was examining her fingernails.

Iyai flinched hardly at all, but Vor immediately felt a resurgence of the need for immediate physical violence.

"The spells are intact," Ramikar announced. "Whoever took them down, put them right back up, skillfully."

"Let's take them down again, then," Master Himes shrugged.

"Hold there," Craduticus ordered. "Ramikar, did they add anything?"

"Add anything?" Pirossa echoed.

"Additional wards or traps," the redheaded wizard nodded. "Smart man and good thinking, I say."

"Give me a moment," Ramikar grunted.

"Let me help," Iyai said softly.

He looked archly down at her for a moment, but didn't comment. Lanisala smirked and shook her head. Vor's knuckles itched to impact that perfect nose. On the opposite side of the cluster, Pirossa was frowning, eyes shut, as if with concentration. Master Himes was focused on the door, too, and Craduticus also was yearning in its direction. At last, after a few minutes had passed, Ramikar let his breath out in a rush and shook his head.

"I don't sense anything other than the sealing spells," he confessed.

"They're considerable enough," Master Himes grouched.

Iyai lowered her hand, silently, and Pirossa opened her eyes, relaxing.

"They don't think anyone is following them," Craduticus surmised. "If we're lucky, when we catch up, we'll be able to take them by surprise and subdue them quickly."

Vor didn't feel the need to mention that their success in that would depend on more than just surprise; the number and ability of their enemy would also be a factor. Master Himes arched an eyebrow at Craduticus in enquiry.

"Go ahead, Tessa," the old mage encouraged. "But everyone else should back up a bit, just in case."

"I'll handle the weight of the door if you handle the seal," Ramikar was muttering as Vor and the others followed orders and retreated down the path halfway to the tunnel out.

Dello stood at the front of the group, watching critically, eyes narrowed. Vor came up beside him and cautiously extended her senses, trying to observe the unsealing of the door without interfering. She could feel the spell that sealed the door; it was like a knot made of ropes larger around than her waist. Untying such a knot required considerable strength. Vor considered it, watching Himes, and wondered if she'd ever have that kind of power. It also made her wonder, if the strongest of them perished below, would anyone in the remaining party be capable of opening the door on their way back out?

"Perhaps we shouldn't shut it behind us," she mused.

Just then the buzzing of blade-tails caught her ear. Iyai gasped and turned towards the tunnel up towards the water tank. All three griffins' heads swung that direction as if pulled by a single string.

"I think we should shut it," Giri said finitely.

Dello strode up to his master, stood behind her and leaned in to whisper something Vor couldn't hear. Master Himes made no visible reaction. Behind the waiting group, by the tunnel, the red-haired wizard had stepped up to the opening and waved a hand. Vor sensed a shield cover the way, buying them some more time. Then Ramikar grunted, and the wall began to move.

It didn't swing out, like a door on hinges would have. It emerged evenly out of the carved archway, like a book being pushed off a shelf from behind. Master Himes stepped away, idly tugging Dello with her, and Ramikar retreated methodically, slowly, hands up wide, though he didn't touch the slab of stone. It floated out, an inch above the floor, and Vor felt her mouth start to drop open.

Moving objects with magic was not an easy trick. Even using a shield to stop a physical object took considerable energy. A mage could more easily move air, and make the air move an object, but there was not a hint of a breeze, and it would be a monstrous wind indeed that could move solid rock. Magic could not ignore the laws of nature; a slab of stone both taller and wider than a man was tall, and as thick as a man's chest had the same weight whether moved by strength of arms or by magic. Ramikar was levitating it over the floor, and Vor had no idea how he was managing it.

The slab cleared the jam, exposing a slit of pure darkness that widened as he kept it floating farther back. The overall entrance was big enough for the griffins, and with perfect right angles at the corners; Ramikar just had to get the door far enough away from it. As the gap widened, the faint light from the water basement seeped in, but Vor saw no danger, only smoothly planed walls, ceiling, and floor. Behind her, the sound of the blade-tails grew louder.

"Might we progress?" the red-haired wizard guarding their backtail asked, a hint of urgency in his voice.

Master Himes stepped up to the gap and looked through. A moment later she pulled her head back and waved the waiting group closer. Everyone obeyed.

"Lanisala," the master mage summoned, "will you go first?"

Vor wondered if she imagined that the woman's skin paled a shade or two, but she nodded, all smirking arrogance gone from her expression. Lanisala stepped up to the gap, and as soon she could fit through by turning her body sideways, she slid in. Master Himes's eyes swept over the group, flicked on Iyai for a moment, then off her, and settled on Vor.

"Hearthsraven," she said. "You're next."

Vor straightened with surprise, but nodded, sensed a moment of distress from Giri, and marched up to the gap.

"Quickly," Master Himes muttered. "Lanisala to counter any dangers; you to guard her back, and guard those who come after you."

Vor gave a sharp nod, and stepped swiftly through the widening opening. It was nearly black inside, and she saw Lanisala a few steps in as a paler shape against the darkness. Vor readied herself to cast a shield—on whoever needed it, even if it was Lanisala. She sensed Iyai come through behind her, and kept herself between Lanisala and the girl. Lanisala, however, seemed to be completely focused on the pit of darkness that was the hallway before her.

Vor sensed Giri step in next. He came up beside her, passing Iyai, who was pressed against one wall, as still as a frightened pheasant. Then came Pirossa, who moved past Vor and Giri to pause just a step behind Lanisala. Dello and then the red-haired wizard came in. Now the opening of the door was wide enough that more light was spilling in. Though it still wasn't bright, everyone's eyes had adapted to the darkness enough that they could see the hallway ahead resolving into walls, floor, and ceiling as it shifted from utter blackness to merely the blackness of night. Vor thought she saw some movement, down low, rats perhaps fleeing the light.

"Move deeper," Master Himes ordered in a nearly breathless whisper. "The griffins come next."

Ahead, Lanisala advanced slowly, like a sleepwalker moving through water. The others followed. A glance around showed Vor expressions that ranged from concerned to frightened. The light was nearly blocked off as a griffin came into the tunnel: then another: then the third. Vor could only assume that now Ramikar would be changing positions, moving into the opening himself, and pulling the door closed behind him.

The light vanished gradually, until Vor could no longer see any of her companions. Giri took her hand, and as she became blind to the world around her, she turned and put her arms around him. He did the same. She heard the soft grinding sound of the door sliding back into place. It settled with the softest of booms.

Then all was quiet, and completely dark.

Chapter 6
Into the Tunnels

Not completely quiet: as sight faded, Vor soon noticed the sounds around her. Closest was Giri's heart and breath, and her own. Someone to her left was breathing tightly, as if close to crying. Someone's foot shifted on the floor. The feathers of the griffins rasped slightly against each other. She could hear Ramikar panting raggedly at the back of the group. There were soft scuttling sounds, maybe the rats she'd thought she'd seen. Someone moved, there were footsteps, and then—

"Why don't you ride, Ramikar?" Rikah whispered, "until you're recovered."

Vor didn't hear an objection, only the sound of someone mounting a griffin.

"Stay calm everyone," Master Himes murmured. "I'll make some light."

Light: Vor summoned her salamander back out with a flick of her will, and the creature wriggled back up out of her jacket and curled itself around her ear again. Everyone recoiled at the sudden light of it, and then leaned instinctively closer.

"Nevermind," Master Himes retracted. "Hearthsraven has handled it."

Vor let go of Giri just as she saw Lanisala turn her head to look over her shoulder at them. The neutral caution of the woman's expression shifted towards something more sly and calculating. Vor let her face be blank and firm in return.

"The old city is deeper," Master Himes announced, keeping her voice low. "We'll have some stairs to go down, or ramps, or something."

"When was the last time anyone was down here?" Hawkwind asked, and Vor saw that she was in the lead of the three griffins. Her shiny bill gleamed bloody in the salamander light.

"When the key was set," Master Himes replied, "as far as I know."

The griffin gave a nod of acknowledgement. "And how do you know what we can expect?"

The wizard shifted. "I don't, I suppose. All I have to go on are stories, legends."

"How will we get out again?" Hawkwind asked mercilessly.

Vor saw Iyai, on Giri's other side, flinch and tremble.

"We come back here, or there are other exits," Master Himes said.

Hawkwind's golden brown eyes gleamed as she tilted her head just slightly. "You know this? Where are the other exits?"

"There must be other exits," Master Himes plowed on. "I don't know where they are—"

Hawkwind cut her off. "No one but a strong mage can open that door. I've considered the weight. Even discounting the spell that seals it, we three griffins together could not move it. It is so thick, it has to slide out evenly, like Ramikar did it. It is not possible to just knock it down."

Master Himes nodded, bravely, Vor thought. "Correct."

Hawkwind regarded the lady mage with an attitude Vor thought the griffin must use on doomed prey animals. "I wonder if I might have preferred our chances against the blade-tails. Perhaps we could have gone into the water for safety, but now we can't go find out, because who else is there who can open the door?"

Master Himes opened her mouth to reply, but Hawkwind silenced her with a slice of her head. "We would have suffered hypothermia staying in the water more than a few minutes, and we are here now. We must move. This place is all but perfectly sealed. The air will not last. We griffins can withstand thinner air for a while, but you humans cannot. Onward."

Master Himes twitched a few times, but didn't argue.

"Frimillin," she called, "will you walk at the front with Lanisala and me?"

The red-haired wizard—hair even redder in the salamander light—passed Vor to go to the front with Himes. At least now she knew his name. Pirossa stiffened as they passed, as though affronted that she hadn't been asked.

"You don't have to be at the front to keep watch," Giri muttered to her as he and Vor reached her.

The dark woman pivoted, falling into line beside Giri. "I can fight, too," she mumbled at him.

"Not as well as they can," Giri said back.

Vor saw Pirossa's jaw and neck muscles tighten. "You know Frimillin?" Pirossa pointed with her chin.

"Never met him," Giri replied. "He seems a cheerful sort."

"Yes, that is how he seems," she acknowledged. "He is a field wizard. I suppose he is talented at handling volatile situations. I still want to help. I'm still useful." She said it like Giri had suggested she wasn't.

"I know you are," he told her mildly.

"I was the best in our class at law and administration."

"I remember," he assured her.

"I don't think those talents will help us much here, though," Vor suggested.

Pirossa seemed to be grinding her teeth. "I suppose not," she gritted out, and glared across in front of Giri's chest at Vor.

"I've never met you, either," she said. "What was your name? Something about a raven?"

"Hearthsraven," Vor said clearly. "Vor Hearthsraven."

"You're from western Weldom?"

"Originally," Vor confirmed briefly.

"Me, too," Pirossa muttered, turning her face back to the front, "but I'm never going back."

Ahead, the leading trio were moving cautiously into the darkness, the only light still coming from Vor's salamander. It made the shadows of the leaders stretch out, merging with the darkness. Vor extended a hand and brushed the wall: dry, smooth, and chill. The floor underfoot was smooth as well and surprisingly clean; if there was grit on it, Vor could neither hear nor feel it underfoot.

The leading trio came to a stop as Master Himes reached out and grabbed the sleeves of her two allies. Everyone else stopped, too, breaths held. Slowly, Master Himes turned her head back towards them, half of it illuminated by the salamander light.

"A stairwell," she said softly.

"Stay close," the wizard called Frimillin added. "Let's not lose anyone at the back of the group."

"We're all here," Rikah assured them from the tail of the group. "I won't let anyone fall behind."

Master Himes nodded once, silent, and led on. The stairs were apparently straight on, not turning off the trajectory of the hallway. The three leaders began to descend. To Vor, it looked like they were stepping down into black water, their feet, legs, and hips sinking into the unilluminated stairwell. Lanisala lifted a hand and made a few sharp gestures. With a flash of flame, another salamander appeared, this one yellower than Vor's. The woman glanced over her shoulder in Vor's direction, wearing a narrow smile.

"Hers is bigger than yours," Pirossa whispered.

Vor kept her face impassive, but Giri gave her hand a little squeeze.

"She's being ridiculous," Giri breathed.

Vor's salamander was indeed smaller than the average. It had always been smaller, though when she thought about it, it was larger lately than it had been the first times she'd called it, as though it had been growing over the past several months. She was pretty sure it was always the same salamander coming to her—unless she summoned multiples—and she was also pretty sure it had been the fire sprite she'd saved from imprisonment in one of her former master's magical door locks. Ever since that day, when she'd called for a salamander, it had come, and it was always the same red with flashes of orange, and the same gradually growing size, and with the same behavior, greeting her like a friend.

She'd never read of such behavior in elemental creatures, and had to question if her salamander could really be some special case. That was research for another time, however. With Lanisala's salamander brightening the way, Vor could see more of the stairwell descending into the darkness. She couldn't see the end, or any variation in its path. In their turn, she and Giri began descending, too. Pirossa dropped back to walk with Iyai behind them, going two by two, and then Hawkwind and the other griffins with their riders, Rikah bringing up the end as he'd promised.

Before the lead griffin—Hawkwind—had done more than set her feet onto the first step, Vor heard a sudden hushed exclamation from the back of the train. Hawkwind paused, tilting her head.

"What is it?" Vor whispered.

Thornfire spoke from further back in the train. "Rikah says he heard something."

"Where?" Hawkwind asked in a low rumble.

"From behind us," Rikah piped up, only to have Ramikar shush him.

"There's nothing back there," Craduticus grunted. "Nothing but a shut door too big to move."

"I'll go check," Pirossa volunteered. "Everyone else, keep moving. I'll stay at the back with that young man."

"Rikah," Hawkwind provided.

The young mage, so dark between her robes, hair, and skin that only the glitter of her emerald eyes and occasional flash of white teeth revealed her in the blackness of the tunnel, squeezed past the griffins, going back to join Rikah.

"Keep moving," Hawkwind encouraged softly. "There can't be anything back there; we just came that way."

Master Himes, Frimillin, and Lanisala had gotten several steps ahead. Dello waited a few stairs down for Giri and Vor to start moving again. They shifted position a little as they caught up. Giri stepped ahead to walk beside Dello, and Vor dropped back to join Iyai, whose pale face and subtle green eyes looked anxious in the inconstant glow of Vor's salamander.

"Your master didn't want you up front with her?" Vor heard Giri mutter to Dello.

"She knows Lady Salasis is going to be better at blasting things than I am," the tall mage replied frankly.

Beside her, Iyai whispered. "I don't want to be here."

"Neither do I," Vor assured her.

"I'm scared," Iyai quavered. "I'm really scared."

Vor was about to try to say something bracing to Iyai, when the leading trio again jerked to a halt. Master Himes was in the center, and shot her arms out, stopping the other two, but Vor saw no other sign of alarm. Master Himes glanced back over her shoulder as Dello and Giri reached her, the others following.

"Doorways in the walls," she announced, "at that little landing ahead. Frimillin to the left, Lanisala to the right. Giri, back up Lani—" she frowned and revised. "Traskitandi, back up Lanisala, Giri back up Frimillin."

The leading trio crept forward, the others following, until Vor could see the ink black square doorways come into view. She stayed close to Iyai, energy gathered around herself, ready to throw up shields or throw forward fireballs. For a long tense moment the leading mages peered cautiously into the doorways.

"Empty room," Lanisala reported, but opposite her Frimillin had recoiled slightly.

"This one's occupied," he announced, sounding almost cheerful, "and has been for a while, by the looks of things."

Everyone crowded forward, including Vor, though she pointedly avoided shoving up against Lanisala and managed to sneak a look in under Dello's arm. Skeletal human remains were stretched out along the base of one wall, encased in crumbling fabric. What might have once been a satchel was beside it. Finger bones rested atop it, where they protruded from the sleeve of whatever garment the unfortunate person had been wearing. There were other little fragments of detritus on the floor, but nothing Vor could identify from her quick look.

Master Himes stepped into the room. "Lanisala, some light."

With a gesture Lanisala sent her salamander after the master mage, who crouched down in the center, hands on her knees, and looked over the ancient corpse.

"Very old, I think," she muttered. "The flesh is completely rotted away."

Vor thought of the rats she thought she'd seen and heard, and wondered if "rotted" was not the whole story. Lanisala's salamander hovered slowly from the head towards the feet.

"It looks like it's wearing mage robes, maybe," Master Himes went on. "No sign of obvious injury to the bones, but if a flesh wound killed him, or her, there'd be no way to know."

Vor gazed around the little room. Except for the corpse and the bits of detritus on the floor, the room was desolate. The walls were lightly textured— no, smooth—no— Vor narrowed her eyes. Two walls were smooth, but the back wall was not. It wasn't textured, either, at least, not by whatever stonemason had originally put it there. She sent her own salamander into the room to hover near it.

"Those are words," Giri declared, clearly having watched Vor's salamander's path.

Master Himes twitched around. "What?"

Then all eyes were on it: scratches in distinct shapes on the back wall, lots of them, covering a large patch of stone. Master Himes stood and glared, hands on hips, examining the scratches.

"They are words," she confirmed, "but it's in ancient Weld script. I can't recognize more than some of the letters. Is Ramikar recovered enough to come here?"

"I'll check," Iyai volunteered in a tiny voice.

"Good with the words, is he, our Ramikar?" Frimillin asked curiously, rocking on his feet a little. "Never had the head for that kind of studying, myself. Hands on, that's my preference."

Master Himes did not reply to him, just continued running her gaze over the scratched up wall. A few moments later, Ramikar came walking through the crowd, his arm over Rikah's broad shoulders. Even in the warm light from the salamanders, his face looked grey.

"Weld script?" he uttered. "I'm fine, young man. Let me go."

Rikah did so, though reluctantly, and stepped back among the other observers. Ramikar straightened and Master Himes moved aside for him. He stood, swaying only slightly, and gazed for several breaths at the wall of writing.

"'Twenty four of us went down,'" he began reading aloud. "'Seven perished on the journey. Seventeen reached the bottom, but eight fell to the death dragon. Marla gave her life to place the key. Ten of us began the journey back, but one by one we fell. When Scathir died, I knew I would never return to the world above. I cannot move the stone alone.'"

Vor listened, amazed and appalled. "No one came to save him?"

"Down here, with all this stone between him—or her—and the surface," Giri muttered, "it would have been next to impossible to send a message if nothing had been prepared beforehand, so no one would have known."

"What a way to die," Lanisala sighed, her smirks and sneers set aside as she looked down on the last wizard of the task force sent to set the key.

"One would think," Vor pressed, "when the group did not return that a rescue party would have been sent."

"Hush," Ramikar interrupted, and resumed reading. "There's more. 'We spent a week descending, but a month returning, due to injuries.'"

"A month," Iyai breathed. "They might have sent someone after a week or two, but if they didn't find anyone easily—"

"They might have given the whole group up as lost, especially if they found a few bodies," Dello suggested. "They probably wouldn't have come back again a few weeks later, when this fellow might have been here, waiting."

"Hush," Ramikar repeated, more strongly, eyes still on the writing. He continued reading. "'Wraiths, screamers in the deep, horned demons, the spine-leeches, the white spiders—they took of us. Other things we could not see: some of my companions simply vanished. Do not seek to recover their bodies. Let these tunnels and catacombs and ruins be their graves. If you go down, they will be your graves, too.'"

Ramikar took a breath that shuddered only a little. Everyone else seemed to be holding their breaths.

"There's a gap," he said, crouching down, "and more writing down low, near the body. I'll read it, but it isn't as clear, and some parts repeat over and over. 'I'm hungry. My water is gone. I lie here, knowing that just a few yards up those stairs, down the hall, beyond the wall, is water and people and sunlight, but I cannot reach it. I tried moving the wall myself. I can't do it.'"

Ramikar cleared his throat. "'I haven't the strength to cast light anymore. I miss the sun. Knowing I saved the city isn't enough. I don't want to die here. It's not enough. I don't want to die here.'"

He turned to glance at Master Himes. "That's all there is, just repeated multiple times."

"Thank you, Ramikar," she whispered.

He stood, nodded, and stepped out of the room.

"Perhaps," Frimillin spoke into the silence, "it would be better not to go down after our hypothetical intruders. If we wait a few hours, surely the blade-tail threat will be neutralized, the enemy shield will fall, and we can just go back up to our lives. From this chap's description I doubt the intruders will make it very far—us either."

Vor exchanged an uncertain glance with Giri. Dello's gaze was on his master, calm and closed. Lanisala lifted an eyebrow in Frimillin's direction, as though she thought his suggestion was a reasonable one. Iyai just stood motionless, clasped hands and pale face looking bloodless with fear.

Rikah had his arms hugging his chest, elbows in his palms. "I don't think I can bring the princess down into this. We didn't sign up for this when we came to Weldom."

"You might gain the favor of the ministers by helping save the city," Master Himes said with a shrug.

"A favor that will do us no good if we're dead," he countered evenly.

"Fair point," Frimillin noted.

Before the discussion could progress further, a sharp hiss came from the top of the stairs, followed by the sound of Craduticus scolding Breeka to be quiet. The griffins nudged into each other as they tried to turn and look back while edging down the stairs, away from the entry hallway.

"What's going on?" Master Himes breathed, leaving the room to investigate.

Pirossa ducked around a griffin wing, her dark skin ashy. "Master Himes," she gulped, panting a little. "There is, there is something, something back there, but I don't know what it is. I can't see it."

"Nothing could have gotten by the griffins," Master Himes assured her. "They fill the hallway."

"I know, but there's something," Pirossa insisted, beginning to show more white around her eyes.

"Calm down," Master Himes ordered softly. "Take slow, measured breaths, like I'm sure you've been taught."

The lead mage stepped around the griffins to get to the end of the train, blocked from view. Vor stepped up to Hawkwind, who had her head turned completely backwards to look behind her. On her back, Jessika was looking back, too, though less easily. Her fingers holding to the harness straps were pasty and trembling.

"Is there something there?" Vor murmured.

Hawkwind's crest gave a little flick. "I can't see well: too many griffins in the way."

Beyond Hawkwind, Craduticus and Breeka were aboard Hawkjoy. The old mage looked to Vor with a pensive frown.

"Nothing there," he grunted, "just feels like there is due to fear of the dark. It's an instinctual feeling: the fear of being watched and hunted."

"Not for griffins," Hawkwind rumbled. "We do the hunting."

Beyond the farthest griffin, Thornwing, the hallway began to glow until it was bright enough to read by. Then it faded again.

Master Himes returned a moment later. "There's nothing there," she reported. "Nothing to be seen, smelled, or heard: just people jumping at shadows, as Master Craduticus says."

But Breeka was still crouched beside its master, wing fingers gripping his robes and eyes fixed back down the hall. Its body was taut as a bent bow.

Master Himes went on. "It's understandable. This place is closed in, dark, and now we know it can be dangerous."

She looked around at the group gathered in a rough circle between the two rooms, with Hawkwind in the hall at one end. No one had filled the opposite hall, instead keeping their backs to the walls, and letting the black opening loom.

"I still think someone came ahead of us," Master Himes said softly. "I still think they're heading for the key, intending to destroy the city—eliminating the Citadel and the ministers, not to mention killing thousands of other people. I still think we should go after them, but the concerns that have been voiced are valid."

She nodded to members as she mentioned their concerns. "I don't have perfect proof of my belief in this enemy group and their intentions, although the broken doors to the water basin room, the unfamiliar footprints in the utility hall, the poisoned water, the secret wall which had obviously been opened and shut again, all tell me that someone is down here besides us. I don't know where the other exits to this labyrinth are. I don't know what dangers are down there. The writing on that wall could be accurate or could be the ravings of a mage gone mad by darkness and fear. Even if they were true when he was here, there's no way to know if they're still true. Maybe the hazards of the trip down towards the key will remove the invaders that I think are already on their way down, so there's no need to chase them, as has been suggested."

Master Himes took a deep breath. "But I don't want to sit in my room, waiting and wondering if my world is going to come crashing down. They killed our fellow wizards: our teachers and students, compatriots and friends. I think there's enough evidence to be pretty sure they're going for the key. I intend to stop them."

"So do I," Ramikar spoke up.

"Well, that's it then," Hawkwind said. "We can't get out without you two, unless?"

The other, younger wizards shook their heads, winced, or just shifted uneasily.

Frimillin tipped his head. "Maybe, but I'd need help with the door. It's possible it could be done as a group, even without two key strong wizards."

"There are other exits," Master Himes insisted.

"Then why didn't that guy use them?" Vor asked, pointing to the room with the corpse.

Master Himes swung her head to Vor. "Because you'd need wings to use them."

A ripple of surprise went through the group.

"There were drakes quartered down here, in the old city," Master Himes explained. "They came in and out through openings in the walls of the gorges. People might have used them, too, but whatever ladders or lifts they used back then are long gone now. I anticipate that once we get deep enough, we could find those exits, and the griffins could fly us up, if they are willing."

"We'd likely be willing," Hawkwind rumbled cautiously.

"If we do go all the way down to protect the key," Master Himes pressed on, "perhaps we could avoid climbing all the way back up, if our winged companions are able to fly us up to the top again. What is a hike of many days through tunnels might be a flight of only a few minutes."

"That makes me feel considerably better," Thornwing contributed, "except that we still don't know what's between us and those exits."

"We won't reach those exits by standing around here," Pirossa stated. "Let's get moving."

The gathered humans and griffins looked around at each other, back the way they came, or down into the lightless corridor ahead.

"We might as well go, then," Lanisala murmured.

"Onward," Craduticus growled. "We're wasting time."

"Capital," Frimillin grinned. "I'll lead, shall I? Lady Salasis?"

The husky wizard pivoted to continue descending the stairs. With an uneasy expression, Lanisala paced him. Master Himes shared an unreadable glance with Dello, and followed them. Pirossa gave a huff of expelled breath and followed her.

"Onward then," Dello muttered, clearly conflicted.

A peek at Giri told Vor that he wasn't very happy about it either, but he followed his towering friend. Vor was about to match pace, when she noticed Iyai, pale as whey, staring into the room with the mage's ancient corpse.

"Iyai?" she summoned.

"It's just," the young woman mumbled, "there's something."

With no other explanation, Iyai knelt by the remains, a hand half extended. Her turned back blocked Vor's view.

"Should I call the masters back?" Vor asked.

Iyai twitched like Vor had startled her, and a moment later stood up, tucking her hands into pockets, head bowed as if guilty or ashamed. She passed Vor hurriedly and went down the steps. Baffled but not inclined to put more stress on the young woman, Vor made no comment. The group continued down the stairs.

"There were a lot of things Ramikar read out that I've never heard of," Vor murmured once she had caught up to Giri. "Spine-leeches, horned demons, the death dragon?"

"I don't know the first two, but you've never heard of the death dragon?" Giri said softly.

Dello turned his head back, salamander glow catching his face in perfect profile, and even Pirossa twitched back for a moment.

"What is it?" Iyai breathed from behind Vor, where she was following almost on her heels. "It doesn't sound very nice."

"I know of it," Craduticus grunted from his perch griffin-back, "but go ahead and tell it, Giri."

"It's proper name is the celestial dragon—" Giri began.

"To know it's proper name you'd have to ask it," Craduticus interrupted.

Giri clenched his jaw for a moment. "People call it the death dragon because they're afraid of it, and it's immortal and invulnerable, but scholarly writings on the subject use the term celestial dragon."

"That has to do with the sky, but it's down here?" Pirossa muttered back.

"Some say it's everywhere, or used to be, or it's a forgotten great power that used to rule our world, above the ground, obviously," Giri explained. "It's a legend of course, that no one has seen for hundreds, maybe thousands of years, if it exists at all. That dead wizard could have been imagining things, or using symbolic language."

"What does the legend say?" Vor prompted.

"It is an immense dragon: four legs, four wings, three tails, and three heads."

"That sounds improbable," Dello commented.

"It does," Giri agreed. "It could be an exaggeration, but the legend says that the celestial dragon—despite having all those limbs and heads—only appears with one head at a time, depending on who it is facing."

"And what determines which head you get?" Vor asked.

Giri nodded as he walked. The stairs were curving now slightly to the left. Lanisala's salamander was throwing huge shadows against the walls. Vor figured her salamander must be doing the same for those behind her.

"It is called the death dragon also because it supposedly judges each person, or being, after death," Giri resumed. "The first head is entirely black, and will emerge out of darkness. If the black head appears to you, you have been judged as one who has done willful evil. It will breathe fire upon you, and you will burn, vanishing entirely from existence. The second head is pink. If the pink head appears to you, you have been judged as one who was thoughtless, and may have done evil unintentionally, but never really meant to do harm, and never really made the effort to be mindful and do good. It will breathe a mist upon you, and put you into a sleep where you will dream of your past from an outside perspective, that you might learn."

"And the third head?" Iyai whispered.

"The third head shimmers silver," Giri said. "If the third head appears to you, you have been judged as one who certainly still made mistakes, since no one is perfect, but who observed your mistakes and learned from them, who thought and pondered, and also learned to set aside thoughts and feel your own self, and the connection to others, to life, to the world. You tried to do good, to have compassion, and you found a way to contribute something meaningful to the world. And you always felt you could learn more, do better. The silver head will speak to you, as the others will not. You can speak to it, and ask questions, and answer questions. If the silver head greets you, then the celestial dragon will take you under its wing when the talking is done, and on to whatever comes next."

"What's next?" Iyai asked.

"Well, that's the big mystery, isn't it?" Giri shrugged. "No one knows."

"No one knows what happens after death," Vor filled in.

Giri nodded. "It's just a story. That dead, ancient wizard was probably just being poetic when he or she wrote that the death dragon did for his friends."

"Unless the death dragon is down at the bottom of this labyrinth or whatever of tunnels and city and what have you," Dello grumbled with a flick of his hand.

"There's always stories," Pirossa sighed from ahead. "People put monsters under beds and in closets and at the bottom of lakes, and the bottoms of chasms and caves, too."

They all fell silent for a while. The stairs went down and down, coated in bits of grit now but quite intact for being so old. Vor began to wonder if they had even been used much, back when people had lived under the rock. The walls were mostly smooth, but there were some chips and scratches caught by the salamander light. She didn't see any sign of life, though. There weren't even dead bugs or spiders. The stairs just went on and on, and after some time of it, she began to hope she'd never have to climb up them.

"Rather a lot of these steps," Dello grumbled.

"Be grateful you have two legs, not four," Hawkwind commented from behind. "You have it considerably easier than we who always feel like we are about to topple forward, moving at this strange angle with our rumps above our shoulders."

The leaders ahead suddenly stopped yet again, but did not exclaim, and the others caught up, coming to a halt. It was immediately clear what had stopped them. The tunnel was broken, caved-in with rock, but some of it seemed to have been cleared.

"Just big enough for humans to crawl through," Hawkwind observed.

"As we can't leave you griffins trapped in here," Himes replied, "it looks like we will be clearing the rest."

"Allow me," Ramikar said, and everyone moved to allow him to approach the fall. He set his hands on the rocks. "I can tell you which rocks are safe to move, that won't cause further cave-in."

With very few complaints, the group got to work. The tunnel wasn't wide enough for all of them at once, so they took turns, replacing each other when people got tired. They had no tools like shovels or pickaxes, so they pulled rocks and boulders with their hands, collecting scrapes and strained muscles. The griffins contributed their strength whenever feasible, but the smaller humans ended up with most of the work. It felt like hours passed before the way was finally wide enough for Hawkwind to squeeze through.

"I suppose this cave-in prevented our friend in the room up there from getting out by some other route," Frimillin suggested.

"And then the MLF cleared it just enough, working together, to get through," Pirossa agreed.

"Possibly," Ramikar shrugged, "but I'm not sure how long ago this cave-in happened—not within the last day, certainly, but it might not be as old as our friend."

"Well, let's get past it and keep moving," Master Himes urged. "We've lost a lot of time shifting all this rock."

As she passed through, Vor saw that the other side of the rock fall let in a trickle of water. It glimmered in the glow of the salamanders, and Vor felt the floor slippery underfoot as she walked across the wet spot; some kind of algae grew down here then, even in the absence of light. The water continued, cascading down the steps broadly, and then against one wall as the steps curved more sharply.

"Stop," Master Himes ordered before Frimillin and Lanisala passed out of a wide wet patch. "Look for tracks."

They all halted, and Lanisala crouched down with her salamander—keeping it close enough to provide light, but not so close its heat would evaporate any wet footprints. Vor tried to crane her head around so she could see, but there were too many people blocking her way.

"There are footprints," Lanisala announced in a whisper.

"Definitely," Frimillin confirmed, also softly.

Master Himes lifted her head, vindicated. "We're following them," she hissed, "and we will stop them."

They pushed on, nearly silent now except for the subtle gurgle of the little water stream. Vor banished her salamander, sending it back to its own plane to rest. Only Lanisala's salamander gave any light, and it was staying in the middle of the group, which ended up being near Iyai and Hawkwind. Vor thought privately that it was a good thing Iyai had some light, however dim. The young woman never ceased her expression of mild terror.

The leaders, meanwhile, had minimal light, but expressed hope that being in near darkness would allow them to see light from the invaders ahead of them, should they catch up. The tail—Ramikar again on Thornwing—also dealt with near absolute darkness. They knew, however, that there was no danger behind them—or at least there shouldn't be, logically—and neither male complained about being at the end. Vor noticed that Jessika walked now between Hawkwind and Hawkjoy, along one wall. Rikah walked opposite her and glanced at her frequently. Breeka looked behind them from time to time, and occasionally bared its sharp little teeth. Craduticus dozed on Hawkwind's back.

Then up ahead, after a couple hours of plodding down winding stairs until feet and legs ached, again the leaders stopped. The rest of the train followed suit. A whisper was passed back.

"The path opens here," Dello said.

Giri repeated it to Iyai, who gave it to Hawkwind, and so on. Then another whisper came.

"Traskitandi, Pirossa, and Iyai to the front," Dello repeated dutifully, even as he began to move forward.

Giri passed on the message. Iyai looked even paler at being summoned, but kept a firm chin and followed Dello. In another moment, Pirossa passed Vor and Giri, following Iyai.

"I suppose those three are the most sensitive," Giri shrugged a little. "If there are multiple paths from here, they might be able to detect which way the invaders went." He glanced at Vor. "Other than a talent for summoning salamanders, Master Himes probably doesn't know what you're good for just yet, but once she figures it out, she'll call on you for help, too, Vor."

His tone was reassuring, as though he was afraid Vor felt she was being left out. She gave him a little smile.

"I'm just glad I can conserve my energy," she confided softly, and arched an eyebrow at him. "And what are you good for?"

Giri actually looked chagrined. "Apparently I'm not very good at taking you on a nice trip to visit your family."

Vor shook her head. "That's not your fault. If we'd just left a few minutes sooner, we'd be well on our way, and probably more people would have died, to the point that there might not be this expedition to catch the invaders before they destroy the city at all."

"Alright, as long as my incompetence is useful," he quipped weakly.

Frimillin cocked his head back, clearly having overheard. "Ah, so it's your fine fault we're down here instead of dead? Although, if it's true we're on our way to the death dragon, well, then we're as good as dead. Ah, and we're going on again."

Up ahead, Master Himes was in the lead with Dello and Pirossa. Iyai followed with Lanisala right behind her. Vor and Giri followed Frimillin, and then the griffins and their entourage and riders came behind. They emerged through a doorway into a wide hall running perpendicular to the tunnel they'd just come down through. The ceiling was a bit higher, and it was wide enough to walk four abreast. The floor looked odd, though, and Vor discovered why when she stepped out onto it.

"Sand," Frimillin commented from ahead of her.

The sand was a few inches deep, dry and silky enough that she didn't leave footprints, only pockmarks behind her—and the entire width of the sandy floor in both directions was covered with pockmarks. Whatever tracks the invaders had left were indistinguishable from all the other pocks. Vor concluded that was why Master Himes had needed Dello, Pirossa, and Iyai to detect the direction. The trickle of water that had accompanied them down the stairs vanished into the sand at one corner of the doorway, wetting the sand dark in that small spot, but it held no prints either.

As she turned to the right, following Giri, and Hawkwind began emerging from the doorway behind her, Vor took a quick look to her left: the direction they weren't going. Then she did a double-take, certain that she'd seen quick movement near the floor. Rats again? Hawkwind halted behind her and looked, too. A little thrill of adrenaline went through her.

"What did you see?" the griffin rumbled softly.

"Nothing," Vor said. "It was just the light of the salamander playing over the puckers in the sand."

All was still now, but the darkness of the hall could have hidden anything.

"What did you think you saw?" Hawkwind persisted.

"Movement near the floor," Vor confessed. "Much smaller than a human, and quick: but it was my imagination."

"It happened as soon as the salamander came into the hall?"

"Yes," Vor said. "It was just the light on the sand."

She turned resolutely to catch up with Giri, who waited for her a few steps away. Hawkwind followed, allowing Hawkjoy to exit behind her.

"It couldn't have been whatever is causing all these divots in the sand, that saw the light and fled, could it?" Hawkwind muttered.

Breeka growled, but no one else replied. Now that she was in the hallway, Vor could see the walls, and almost paused again. The walls were not smooth. Looking both ahead and behind, Vor saw patches of odd pale texture in large clusters. Others were noticing them, too, and several people approached the nearest cluster curiously. So did Vor.

"They're growths of some kind," Pirossa muttered.

"Don't get too close," Iyai worried.

"Water is coming in from above, look," Dello pointed out. "These things are growing where there is water seepage."

Pale, nearly colorless, no longer than Vor's fingers at the most, and curved and twisted more like ears, the growths covered the wall, densely packed. Between the patches a network of tendrils, like interlaced roots, spread out wide and far, connecting the patches together as well as vanishing under the sand. The tendrils lay flat and close to the wall, varying in thickness from that of human hair to nearly the diameter of Vor's pinkie finger.

"It's some kind of fungus," Vor surmised.

"The growths look similar to cave ears," Master Himes confirmed. "I can't tell if they're poisonous though, so no sampling."

"I think they're emitting some light," Frimillin observed, standing in a section away from the salamander and shadowed by a griffin.

"Handy," Dello shrugged.

Giri knelt down. "They're shorter nearer the sand."

"Less water down there," Pirossa said.

"But they look broken off, not stunted."

Vor knelt to look. "You're right," she saw.

"Let's move on," Master Himes summoned. "The fungus gives some faint light but is otherwise useless and harmless."

Everyone obeyed after a final look. Walking on the sand was not as easy as the smooth stone of the tunnel down had been, but at least it was level. Vor's legs were aching a little from the long descent. They continued on for what might have been another hour. They passed branching halls, all a bit narrower than the one they were in, most coated with the wall fungus in patches. In a few places the walls were damaged, creating piles of rubble, and one whole section they passed was caved in.

From brief conferences with Dello, Pirossa, and Iyai, Master Himes kept them in the main hall, but it was impossible not to wonder what might be down those lightless paths. Vor glanced down the side halls as they passed them. Sometimes she thought she saw movement at the very edge of the light. She continued to believe it was a trick of the light, combined with fear and fatigue.

Then behind her, with the griffins, came the sound of a stifled exclamation. Vor looked back, along with a few others. Jessika was getting up from having apparently fallen to one knee.

"Are you weary?" Hawkjoy asked the princess. "You can ride me."

"No," Jessika objected. "The sand moved under my foot and I fell."

Everyone resumed walking, but the nearest companions regarded her curiously.

"You mean—," Rikah began.

"As sand always does?" Vor supplied dryly.

"No," the princess repeated. "There must have been a stone under the sand. When I stepped on it, it shifted, and I lost my balance. That's all."

"Giri, why is there sand here?" Vor asked. "This isn't a shoreline."

"I don't know," he confessed.

"It could have washed in here from somewhere else, like a riverbed," Ramikar commented from the back of the line. "It could also be from the wall fungus wearing away the rock."

"Continue on," Hawkwind encouraged. "The others are drawing ahead."

Dello was peering back at them, brow pinched. Vor and Giri hurried to catch up to him, leaving Frimillin a little behind, where he was puffing a bit in laboring through the sand.

"What is it, Dello?" Giri muttered as soon as they were close.

The tall man made a futile gesture with one hand. "It's nothing, but there's residue of something: hints of other auras here. They're raw and cold."

Vor thought. "Reptiles and amphibians have cold auras."

"And insects and fish, too," Dello agreed.

"So maybe there's some kind of life down here," Giri said, "besides the wall fungus."

Thornwing perked up. "Maybe it's even good to eat."

"I thought I saw rats a few times," Vor volunteered.

"Rats are good to eat," Thornwing approved.

"Maybe whatever-it-is will try to eat us," Dello grunted darkly. "Some of it is big."

"I suspect whatever-it-is eats the wall fungus," Vor contributed, "but it's short, and can only eat what's nearer the floor."

"That makes it smaller than me," Thornwing said in a pleased tone, "and another sign of ediblity."

Dello grunted, but didn't elaborate further. After another spate of walking, the sand began to thin. Master Himes called a halt and everyone was able to gather close in the hallway with Lanisala's salamander in the center.

"We've been walking for several hours," Master Himes began.

"Don't I know it," Frimillin grumbled, rubbing at his thighs.

"I don't want them to draw ahead, but let's take a short break while there's still sand to sit on, instead of hard stone. We just passed a room."

They paced back a few yards to a chamber filled with deeper sand, and most of them sat, though a few people discovered pieces of broken pottery under the sand and had to toss it away before sitting. Ramikar got down off Thornwing, and even Craduticus got off Hawkjoy to take a seat in the sand. Breeka cuddled up with him.

"Griffins are not the most comfortable creatures to ride," the older mage winced to the younger. "Or maybe it's just my old bones hurting in the cold."

Vor and Giri went together to one wall and slid down it to the sandy floor. Hidden between them, he took her hand. Across the room, Rikah was trying to sit by Jessika and she was ignoring him, huddled instead against Hawkwind. Master Himes gestured Dello over to her and spoke quietly with him. Thornwing and Hawkjoy sat shoulder to shoulder in the doorway, watching out into the darkness of the main hall, occasionally preening each other. Frimillin sat with a grunt. Pirossa sat next to him, and then Iyai beside her. All by herself on the remaining wall leaned Lanisala, apparently not fatigued enough to need to sit.

"Hearthsraven," Lanisala purred, as if caressing the word with her mouth.

Minutely, Vor tilted her head to regard the slightly older woman, and said nothing. Lanisala pursed her lips in a smug smile.

"That's not a noble house," she went on.

Vor raised an eyebrow, just a little, and kept her expression unimpressed.

"I heard you were in Northborn," Lanisala continued, apparently unable to take a hint or eager to start a fight. "That was you, wasn't it? You were apprenticed to the mage in charge. That's where my Giri found you."

Vor suddenly found her heart thudding and her body tense and tingling, but she held stone-still. Lanisala wasn't whispering, and nearby some of the others must have been able to hear. Iyai was closest, but had her gaze firmly fixed in her lap. Pirossa, however, had lifted her head and was surveying the situation. Jessika and Rikah, too, made no secret of their awareness of Lanisala's taunts; they were watching with apprehension. Frimillin sat with a little smile on his face, as if mildly entertained.

One of Vor's knuckles popped, and she took a measured breath, consciously relaxing some of her tension. Instead of replying, she glanced at Giri sitting beside her with his arms now folded.

"Lani," he nearly growled. "I stopped being yours a long time ago. If memory serves, you discarded me. You can hardly be upset that I now belong to another."

Lanisala's pursed-lip smile blossomed into a full one. "You are still so adorable."

Vor gritted her teeth as her energies—all on their own—surged within her. Dello strolled over from where he'd been in conference with his master. He took in the situation and stood, hands on hips. Lanisala gave him no notice.

"You've got a bit of power there," the woman went on to Vor, "but you don't want to start a fight in here."

"Vor is hardly the one trying to start a fight," Giri sighed.

"And you're right, Lady Salasis," Dello spoke up. "Vor killed her former master in a mage duel. You definitely don't want to start a fight with her, here or anywhere else. I've a feeling she'd hand you your tail, and there's a couple of us who might help her."

Lanisala's head turned, glaring at him. Her lips even started to peel away from her teeth, but if she had a retort, she held it in. Instead, she swept her gaze back to Vor.

"It seems you've got some friends prepared to fight your battles for you," she said archly.

"Vor hasn't done anything to you," Giri clarified. "I thought we were over and done. If you have some lingering issue, address it to me, not her."

Lanisala gave that pursed-lip smile again and looked down and away, as if demure. After a few moments of it, Giri leaned back.

"Fine, then," he said.

His hand drifted down and found Vor's again. She held on, and even if she looked away from Lanisala, she kept careful watch on the woman with her mage senses. If Lanisala decided to try anything, Vor wouldn't be caught flat-footed.

But the threat did not come from Lanisala.

The deep sand near the snoozing Ramikar and Craduticus shifted and they awoke at once. Thornwing and Hawkjoy exclaimed as well, getting to their feet as the sand below their resting bodies moved. Attenuated shapes the same color as the sand snapped up out of it. They shone with polished sections of carapace and were tipped with hooks longer than Vor's hand. They wrapped around the legs of the two recumbent mages and began pulling them violently towards the doorway, throwing up tails of sand. Breeka was tumbled to one side, screeching.

Everyone shouted in surprise—especially the two sudden captives—and the griffins slashed down through the sand, but their claws couldn't damage the whip-like appendages. The other humans jumped to their feet, grabbing the two snared men, but they couldn't get traction in the sand and were simply towed along or lost their grip. Thornwing and Hawkjoy tried to block the doorway, but more hard-shelled limbs came slashing up out of the sand, digging their terminal hooks into the griffins and pulling them away.

Lanisala scrambled down to her knees, hands searching through the sand until she found a tentacle. It dragged her along, too, as she gripped it, but she snarled fiercely, and a moment later Ramikar was released. The stench of burnt shellfish filled the air and Lanisala flopped over, panting and spitting sand. Another flexible limb whipped up and sunk a hook into her thigh. She cried out and grabbed that one, too, wrestling with it as it started dragging her.

"Get out of the sand," Master Himes shouted.

Frimillin was in the main hall dragging Ramikar towards bare floor, and the griffins had discovered that though their claws couldn't score the carapaces, they could bite through the armored tentacles, so they were freeing themselves one tentacle at a time, but were still too encumbered to help anyone else. Craduticus was still being dragged, and now so was Lanisala—back the way they had come and into utter darkness. Iyai, Rikah, and Jessika floundered through the sand towards Frimillin and Ramikar, but Vor, Giri, and Pirossa went in pursuit of their captured companions. Lanisala's salamander remained behind, probably because it hadn't received any orders to do otherwise.

Hawkwind—the only griffin that hadn't been snared by the tentacles—leapt and landed beside Vor and sprinted ahead. The long, tentacular arms were picking up speed, sending up a spray of sand behind them and their prey, but Hawkwind opened her wings and used them to assist her in long bounding leaps. She landed just beyond the captured Lanisala, bent her head down, and severed the tentacle. Vor and Giri ran right past them, trying to reach Craduticus, as Pirossa stopped to help Lanisala.

Hawkjoy, now freed, came leaping with the same technique Hawkwind had used. She landed past Craduticus, bit—and missed. Craduticus was dragged on, around a corner and out of sight. Thornwing sailed over Hawkjoy, flapping wildly, bounced off the wall, and dove down the narrow hall the old mage had been taken into. Hawkjoy recovered from her miss and followed.

"Light," Vor panted.

Giri grunted, and a moment later his clothes began to glow. They rounded the corner, slipping in the sand, Hawkjoy right ahead of them. Thornwing in the lead screeched with what sounded like unpleasant surprise. Hawkjoy suddenly tried to stop and backpedalled, but couldn't get a grip; the floor angled sharply downward below her feet. Vor and Giri managed to skid to a halt before they went over, but Hawkjoy fell, opening her wings hopefully. Trailing sand followed her and Giri knelt to put a hand into it, setting the grains to glow.

They revealed a gruesome scene. The room below appeared to be the bottom of a long vertical shaft and had a massive hole broken in one wall taller than Dello. Dozens of armored tentacles emerged from it, running up the walls and into doorways that opened into other rooms and halls above. Vor and Giri stood in one such doorway. A few tentacles whipped between their legs and down into the cave, their ends cut off. Other tentacles held Craduticus wrapped tightly at the bottom of the pit. Thornwing was perched on the bundle, biting through tentacles as they tried to drag the wizard—who now looked unconscious—into the gaping hole in the wall. Hawkjoy had fluttered down and joined the male griffin, even as more tentacles snapped up to jab at them with hooks.

"No," Vor growled.

The floor wasn't very far. Before Giri could stop her, she dropped down into the pile of sand below their doorway. A moment later, he dropped down behind her. She'd guessed what Lanisala had done—the same trick Vor had used to cook meat on her journey to Weldom with Hawkjoy. She knelt by a feebling writhing wounded tentacle, grabbed on, but instead of just heating the carapace below her hands, she sent the fire on, up the limb, towards what must be the rest of the body hiding inside the cave beyond the hole.

Vor poured power into it. Flesh was not the most flammable substance, and it took a lot to get the fire to travel. The stink of burned shellfish hit her nose, and then came a raspy squeal. The tentacles lashed. Thornwing bit through another holding Craduticus, and Hawkjoy yet another. Giri was trying to pull the old mage free. As the tentacle Vor held ceased to show signs of life, she grabbed a fresh one, and continued pouring power. A whipping limb came slashing at Vor and she ducked it. Another hit her back and a hook wrapped her side. It started to dig in and drag her, but then Giri was beside her, freeing her.

"Let's go," Thornwing called.

He was back up in the doorway, Craduticus a motionless lump beside him. He must have carried the wizard up there.

"Run up my back," Hawkjoy directed.

The griffin had reared up below the doorway, forelimbs grabbing the bottom of the opening. The still-hidden monster in the cave seemed to have lost any inclination to attack, and Vor dropped the tentacle she held, which weakly dragged itself away. Giri helped Vor to her feet, but Vor swayed as her head went light. She staggered and was only prevented from falling when Giri caught her. She tried to catch her breath and stay conscious, but the room swam before her eyes and she had to shut them.

"And you're out," Giri tsked. "Too much magic today, my love. Come on, you have to climb."

She managed it somehow. Her personal energies were severely drained, but her arms and legs were uninjured. With Giri boosting her from below, she found the strength to haul herself up Hawkjoy's back until she could take Thornwing's extended hand and slump down beside Craduticus.

"Let's get them on, if you can carry them," she heard Giri suggest.

Between Giri, Hawkjoy, and Thornwing, she soon found herself on Hawkjoy's back, in a posture much like Craduticus's ahead of her: lying flat on her belly, head between griffin shoulders, and arms and legs dangling down. They hurried through the sandy hallways and met Hawkwind with Master Himes and Dello, who had been coming to look for them. They passed where they'd made the brief camp, and into the sandless section. In another room some yards ahead, Pirossa was watching for them and waved them in.

Ramikar, Lanisala, Craduticus, and the griffins all had tears and puncture wounds. The others did their best to tend to them. Vor had escaped injury, but seriously depleted her mage energy. Giri half carried her to a corner after he got her off Hawkjoy's back, and lowered her to a seat on the floor. He knelt beside her and took her hands. He didn't say anything—not that she was brave, or foolish, or anything else. In the darkness, she could just see the shine of his eyes, and felt the slight, slow warmth into her palms as he shared with her what energy he had left.

"We need to rest," Giri murmured to no one in particular, but loudly enough that everyone could hear.

Vague mutters of agreement came back. Vor shut her eyes and accepted the trickle of energy until it slowed and stopped, and Giri sat down beside her with an exhausted sigh. They leaned against each other and held hands, but were too exhausted for anything more. In another corner, Lanisala hissed in pain and then gritted out a few flavorful curses.

"Yes, I'll bet that hurts, my dear," Frimillin answered her. "Luckily it didn't hit any major vessels or you'd have bled out by now."

Vor squinted her eyes open and saw Lanisala with her robes hiked up nearly to her waist, perfect long legs bare against the floor and one thigh liberally coated with blood, which Frimillin was wiping away to get a look at the actual wound. Beyond them, Ramikar was conscious and helping Himes bandage his relatively minor wounds. Pirossa, Dello, and Iyai were examining a griffin each, but the griffins looked more concerned with Craduticus, who seemed to be only semi-conscious despite Rikah and Jessika's attempts to revive him. Breeka was nudging and shaking him, whining in distress.

"Craduticus," Vor grunted.

Giri grunted back and pushed himself forward. The two of them crawled on hands and knees through the forest of griffin legs to kneel with Rikah and Jessika. Vor touched the old mage's shoulder and winced. His life energy was dreadfully low. Much lower and he would slip completely into a coma, and shortly death. All the mages were low on energy, but Vor glanced around, wondering who could most easily spare some—

Then her gaze landed on someone whose energy was nearly full. She put her free hand on Rikah's shoulder.

"Rikah," she said. "Craduticus needs some energy."

"I can't," the young man spluttered, "I'm not a—."

"I will take some of yours and give it to him, with your consent," Vor clarified.

A griffin paw landed on her own shoulder.

"Take a little bit from both of us, to share the load," Thornwing suggested.

Another paw landed on her other shoulder. "Me, too," said Hawkwind. "Not you, Joy, you're too hurt."

"Don't mind my injuries," Thornwing chuckled. "They're just scratches."

"I don't get to boss you around," Hawkwind grumbled to him, "as you well know."

"Alright," Rikah agreed. "I get it. I've loaned power to mages before. It's fine."

Vor let her eyes unfocus and reached for the pulsing, swirling energy that was the life force of the three volunteers. Rikah's was strong, solid, and certain, and easy to harvest—it also glowed with strong feelings; Vor guessed they were for Jessika. It came tamely to her and travelled obediently.

The griffins however, Vor hadn't expected. She'd sensed while spending the days riding Hawkjoy that griffin energy was vibrant but she hadn't actually touched it before. Both Hawkwind and Thornwing had energy that surged like mountain streams in the melt, or like wind storms—but orchestrated. It sang through their bodies at a volume and speed beyond that of humans. Touching it sent a shiver through Vor. Capturing some of it took more than the simple sort of magical dipper she'd used for Rikah. She had to spin out a grasping net and carefully drag out tendrils.

Once she did have a globe of energy held within her own meager aura, she redirected it to Craduticus and began to slowly feed it into his depleted powers, much as Giri had just fed her. It went smoothly for some moments, with Giri helping guide the energy to absorb without disrupting the old mage's natural patterns, and then Craduticus groaned, twitched, opened his eyes and focused accusatively on her.

"What did I tell you, presumptive-Wizard Hearthsraven?" he croaked. "Stop that. You, too, Wizard Holstor."

"You need it, Master Craduticus," she murmured back. "You were going to die."

"That happens sometimes," he sighed. "Some time soon it will happen to me, no matter how much energy you try to give me. Now cease at once. I order you."

Reluctantly, Vor removed her hand from his shoulder. "I can give you three back some," she began.

"Keep it," Hawkwind rumbled, removing her hand from Vor's shoulder. "I expect you need it as much as Cray did."

"Yes, keep it," Thornwing agreed, also drawing away.

"Rikah, here," Vor said, and before the young man could also refuse, returned the remaining bit she'd taken from him.

The griffin energy, however, throbbed in her aura, not quite blending yet but slowly shifting to match her own energy patterns. She shut her eyes and found herself longing for wide, open skies—the endless dome of blue. Did griffins feel that urge constantly? How horrible it must have been for them to be trapped there below ground.

Craduticus coughed and sat up with Rikah's assistance, and Vor relaxed back onto her heels.

"Master," Breeka was pleading, and finally calmed only when the old mage let the bat-cat crawl into his lap and cling.

"That was an adventure," Thornwing muttered. "We're lucky no one was killed."

"I expect there will be many more opportunities for that," Craduticus commented dryly.

"Wizard Salasis," Vor heard Master Himes say, "can you walk?"

"She can ride," Hawkjoy offered. "I'm not too hurt to carry a passenger."

"That will have to do, then," Master Himes allowed. "Craduticus, Ramikar, and Salasis on our griffin friends: the rest on their own two feet."

"Now?" Pirossa spoke up. "I thought we were going to have a rest."

Master Himes scowled in the near dark. "A few more minutes then."

✾✾✾

Chapter 7
Descent

A few more minutes turned into several minutes, and then a half an hour, as most of the party drifted into uncomfortable sleep. Hawkwind had stationed herself at the doorway out into the mostly sand-free hallway, but Vor awoke from her own nap—shoulders and hips achy from the stone floor—and saw that the big griffin's eyes had drooped closed. The only light came from a glowing handprint on one wall where one of the mages had spelled the stone to emit light. It was faint and slightly green, spilling over the recumbent bodies in the bare room. Everyone lay as though dead. Even Giri was motionless beside her, breathing softly.

From where Vor lay, she had a good view of the doorway. Beyond the green glow the hall was darker than any night she'd ever known. Not for the first time, Vor found herself wondering how they would get out again. Master Himes seemed confident, but none of them had ever been down here before. The tentacular sand monster was only the first threat they'd faced. How many more would there be? What else waited out in the labyrinthine caves?

Vor's heart gave an extra beat as her eyes told her she'd seen movement in the hall, something low, maybe only a few feet above the floor, just behind the edge of one of Hawkwind's wings. She focused, straining through the darkness. It happened again: something small, bobbing up and then down. More of the tentacles? Vor began to gather her muscles. In total silence she pushed herself up to all fours. Toe tips lifted so they wouldn't drag, knees complaining about the bite of the hard floor, Vor crept towards the sleeping Hawkwind.

The griffin's sides rose and fell with regularity. Whatever was just beyond her body hadn't disturbed her sleep. Vor placed a hand on the wall beside the doorway, a foot carefully flat on the floor. Moving so slowly was a surprising challenge, but she couldn't afford the slightest sound that might send whatever-it-was running off; Vor wanted to catch it.

Something touched her shoulder and Vor nearly shouted in furious fright. Spasms of shock jerked her body, but she didn't make a sound. She whipped her head around—and a puzzled Jessika stood there, hand still extended. Vor's lips peeled back in anger. She'd never wanted to slap the idiot girl as much as she did then, and call her a great many things worse than "idiot" on top of it.

Vor put a finger to her lips, indicating silence, and Jessika nodded. She thought not rolling her eyes at the foolish woman displayed her magnanimous restraint. She pointed towards Hawkwind, but she couldn't communicate more than that and gave up. Returning to her stalking, she inched closer, Jessika right behind her. Hawkwind twitched a little. Now Vor heard a sound, something soft and wet like tiny movements in water. Vor shaped some internal energy into a ball, ready to turn it into a light source or attack as needed.

Cautiously, she rose up on the balls of her feet and leaned a little forward, to look over the waist-high mound that was Hawkwind's body. Jessika's breath was on her neck, the girl's mouth right by her ear, so Vor clearly heard her throttled cry. Vor, too, had to stifle her shock. On the floor beside Hawkwind, where her forearm was exposed before the wrist of her wing was a—a thing. Vor could only compare it to a crayfish, which she knew; the cooks in Northborn had sometimes boiled them up, and they were quite tasty. It was shelled and had legs like a crayfish, and much larger pincers, but there the similarities ended.

It was many times the length of a crayfish—perhaps three feet long. Its abdomen, instead of having a set of fins for swimming, was attenuated into a long tail. It was the bulbous terminal joint that Vor had seen bobbing up and down. It had a barb, or stinger on it, and long fine hairs along its length. At its head end, it had long, long feelers much wider than its own body that were waving gently, and its mandibles were buried in Hawkwind's forearm, where it had chewed a bloody circle half the size of Vor's palm. The wet sound Vor had heard was coming from the bleeding flesh as the creature ate.

The power she'd gathered transformed immediately into a bolt of energy. The crawly creature seemed to sense it or had heard Jessika's cry, and turned rapidly to scamper off, but it was far too late for escape. Vor's blast of power killed and cooked it instantly, lit up the hallway, and sent the beast tumbling with a breathy squeak.

"What was that?" Jessika cried.

Between Vor's display and the princess's exclamation, the whole room roused. Light bloomed from a few different mages, and Hawkwind stirred, groaning. Vor touched the griffin's crown.

"Stay still, Hawkwind," she said. "You were attacked."

"My arm is numb," the griffin grunted curiously.

Vor took a cautious look into the hallway, and then went to where light was now spilling over the steaming leggy creature. Behind her, several voices exclaimed over the bloody sore on Hawkwind's arm. Giri came up beside her and grimaced at the corpse.

"I've never seen anything like that," he breathed. "It was eating her?"

Frimillin joined them, took a look, and hissed. "Parasitic cave scorpion," he identified. "Nice and dead, just the way I like them."

"What did it—?" Vor began.

The colorful wizard pointed. "See the tip of its tail? It has venom in there. It used it to numb her, just a little prick at first, not enough to wake her. Then a little more, and a little more, until it could start chewing. A big set of mandibles it's got. It would have gone right on eating until something woke Hawkwind or it got full. In some cases, the victims can die of blood loss without even waking up."

Thornwing came walking over next. "How long will the numbness last? Hawkwind is going to have a limp until it fades, but it didn't do much actual damage to her, just got through the skin."

"There was a lot of fur for the scorpion to deal with first," Frimillin reasoned. "Good thing Wizard Hearthsraven here woke up and realized something was wrong. Its venom isn't unlimited, but it could have done quite a bit of damage to her muscle tissue before running out."

Thornwing walked up to the body and prodded it.

"Not to worry, it's fully dead," Frimillin said. "Those antennae move constantly, even while sleeping. The only time they don't is when it has not a bit of life left in it. They're nearly blind, only able to see heat, I believe, and those antennae are one of the main ways it understands its world, by touch."

"It stores the venom in its tail tip?" Thornwing confirmed.

"That's right."

With a decisive snip, the slender male griffin severed the last bit of tail and let it drop.

"Thornwing," Giri queried. "Are you going to—?"

He didn't need to finish, Thornwing picked up the body in his bill and carried it over to Hawkwind and Hawkjoy. It wasn't much—no more than a mouthful each—but in mere moments the griffins ripped off legs and claws and tug-o-warred the body in half. It all vanished down their throats.

"Urg," Giri gurgled.

"Waste not," Frimillin shrugged.

Thornwing tossed his head to flip one final leg into his mouth and shrugged. "I didn't think you humans would want it."

"Accurate," Master Himes agreed with a consenting wave of her hand.

"Wind, can you walk?" Hawkjoy queried the older female.

Cautiously, she pushed to her feet. "It holds my weight," she reported. "I just can't feel it."

"The sensation will return," Frimillin assured her, "once your body clears the poison."

"And the wound will heal?" Thornwing asked.

"In time, like any other wound."

Hawkwind settled her wings. "It's not debilitating."

Master Himes gave a grunt. "Good. Why don't we all gather up? I think it's time we discuss our next move."

The group gathered in the room: six human females, six human males, two female griffins, one male griffin, and an indeterminate bat-cat. Master Himes surveyed the circle.

"We've had some injuries and—"

"I want to go back," Jessika blurted.

Rikah put an arm around her shoulder and she shoved it off.

"What are we even doing down here? This is insane," she went on.

"Please keep your voice down," Ramikar cautioned.

"There's been plenty of shouting and screaming," Jessika refuted. "If there's anyone to hear us, which I doubt, they've heard us by now."

"We need to stop the invaders heading down to find the key," Master Himes insisted. "They do exist and our duty is to stop them."

"Fine, then you go," Jessika hissed. "The rest of us will wait here for you."

"And drink what, and eat what?" Dello spoke up. "There are no resources here."

"How do you know there are any anywhere else down here?" she challenged him.

"There's the chance of finding exits and the griffins flying you up to the surface, remember?" Vor put in.

"Exactly," Master Himes nodded her way. "We can't go back because we probably can't get that door open again without finding a way to fully recharge our energies, which we can't do without food and rest. The best option is to continue down. This is not a directional planning session. I just wanted to find out from the injured parties how able they are to walk."

"I'll be fine," Hawkwind said. "The bleeding has already stopped. It is quite a superficial wound for a griffin my size."

"Wizard Salasis," Master Himes requested. "What about you?"

"She should not walk on that leg," Frimillin interjected.

"Are you a healer?" Pirossa eyed him narrowly.

"No," he confessed. "But I am a field wizard and I happen to know what's fatal and what isn't, and those punctures came far too close to her femoral artery. Walking will prevent healing, and if she uses her leg too much, the wound could even tear and rip open the artery. Then she would bleed to death."

"I'm fine," Lanisala glared.

Master Himes glared back. "I'm going to defer to Wizard Frimillin's expertise. Our griffin allies, will one of you consent to carry Wizard Salasis?"

"I will," Hawkjoy spoke up at once. "My wounds don't hurt and I can move just fine."

Both Hawkwind and Thornwing gave her unreadable glances, but did not argue.

"I'm carrying Cray," the male griffin added.

All eyes turned to the recumbent elder mage, who raised a hand and gave a weak chuckle. "The best solution is to leave me here," he croaked.

"Absolutely not," Vor countered, "especially not after I went to all that effort to save you."

"What she said," Giri contributed softly.

"Master Craduticus on Thornwing then," Master Himes declared. "Ramikar, how about you? Will you be walking under your own power?"

"I could carry him," Hawkwind volunteered.

"The rest helped considerably," Ramikar said smoothly. "I am feeling able to go on with my own two feet."

Master Himes nodded. "Our griffin allies are a huge asset, but their energy is not inexhaustible. Except for Craduticus and Salasis, can everyone else walk on their own?"

The others nodded or murmured affirmatives.

"I know we've had some trouble here," Master Himes went on. "Let's see if we can get out of this area and into someplace safer. Maybe we can even find a water source, or an exit into the nearest gorge. Let's go."

The sandy hallways with their associated series of square rooms gave way through a grand archway to a wide set of stairs. The archway had doors also— massive and carved with geometric patterns—but they sat partly open. Their heavy iron hinges were rusted into immobility. The stairs were broad enough that the whole party could have walked abreast, except that the center section was not stairs at all, but a smooth ramp wide enough for a cart.

Handrails were carved out of the stone walls, and when Vor looked closer, she saw that the walls, too, were decoratively carved with geometric patterns. The patterns seemed to flower out from metal lamp brackets secured to the wall at regular intervals. They all stood empty, almost too high up on the wall to reach, but below some of them were the ruins of fallen metal and glass lamps. There were bits of other wreckage on the stairs and around the doors, too. Some were even identifiable as pots, boxes, a wheeled cart, and a chair.

Vor summoned her salamander again and it lit up the stairs. They descended at a fairly steep angle, down into yet more complete darkness. At the farthest edges of the light, Vor thought she saw more scurrying movement, but hoped it was just a trick of the flickering shadows and too much time spent in near blackness. Despite what Ramikar said, Vor felt that the rest hadn't helped much, and she was trying to be cognizant that she was under stress, and couldn't trust her eyes, but she was getting heartily tired of not knowing if she was seeing things that were real or not.

Master Himes squared her shoulders and led the way. "At least there's nowhere for dangers to hide here," she said confidently.

Dello followed loyally just back of her left shoulder. Ramikar, Frimillin, and Pirossa went next, with Iyai hurrying to catch up to them.

"Right," Thornwing remarked, head tipped up towards the ceiling and bill pointing. "No place at all that anything nasty could hide."

Vor followed his glance and with a wave of her hand, sent her pet salamander up to investigate.

"You're right," Giri said. "Something could hide in there."

The ceiling was high, perhaps three times Vor's height, and sloped downward, keeping a constant distance between the stairs and itself, but only a few paces beyond the grand archway was a square hole a couple feet wide on each side. Vor squinted and thought she could see another one in the ceiling near the edge of the salamander's glow, deeper down the stairs.

"Too small for a griffin to climb into," Hawkwind observed, "even Thornwing."

"As we have discovered, things smaller than a griffin can still be dangerous," Vor said.

"Perhaps it's an air shaft," Giri surmised.

"I could send my salamander up inside it, but it can't really speak, so it wouldn't be able to tell us what it finds."

"Maybe Breeka could investigate?" Jessika suggested in a small voice.

"Nasty hole," the bat-cat hissed at once.

"Sounds like a negative," Cray muttered. "Let's get on. The others are getting too far ahead."

Vor followed as the griffins began walking down the stairs, soon discovering that the ramp was easier for them. Giri paced her and reached over to take her hand. She let him, and gave a little squeeze.

"This isn't the lovely vacation we were hoping for," he whispered.

Vor glanced at him and gave a bit of a grin. "Good or bad, we're together, and we'll get through this."

Giri managed a little smile back, too. "Yes, we will."

"Aww," Lanisala drawled from where she was astride Hawkjoy.

The griffin tripped, jarring her rider and making Lanisala grunt in pain.

"Sorry," Hawkjoy apologized. "You startled me."

Lanisala made no reply, but her lip twitched towards a sneer.

"Griffins are flighty," Rikah remarked, "easily surprised. They are predators, after all."

Vor slanted a raised eyebrow at the man, and he gave a wink back.

"You're Rikah, right?" Lanisala taunted, "same name as the bat-cat?"

"Breeka," Breeka declared.

"No," Rikah answered simply.

Lanisala gave an unattractive sniff and looked ahead. Vor also returned her attention to the descending stairs, already noting a bit of an ache resuming in her lower legs. The party went silent as they descended, except for the constant tap-tap of shoes hitting stone with each step. Every now and then, Vor looked up at the square holes in the ceiling, but nothing came dropping down out of them.

Then Master Himes came to a sharp halt, and Vor heard Iyai give a little whimper.

"What is it?" Giri called softly.

"Nothing dangerous," Dello replied, "just a little startling."

The back half of the group caught up to the stationary front half and looked down the steps ahead.

"Shame it's dead," Thornwing remarked. "That could have been a good meal."

"Long dead," Frimillin added.

Pale bones were strung across the stairs in loops: a meters-long spine with hundreds of ribs. Some of it was still relatively intact, but other sections had disarticulated into jumbled piles.

"Right," Vor muttered. "Something like that could come down those square air shafts."

Several people looked up at the ceiling as Frimillin scooted closer and began poking around the bones.

"Certainly possible," Master Himes shrugged. "At least it's dead. I wouldn't have wanted to fight such a creature."

"Somebody did, though," the multi-colored wizard said. "There's a human skeleton here, too, with bits of cloth: could be mage robes again."

The group picked their way along, skirting the mix of bones. The human remains were trapped under the snake, but the skull was facing up, rendered in high contrast by the salamander light. It still looked frightened and desperate not to die. A little further along was the head of the snake, as long as Vor's forearm and as wide as her thigh. Its open jaws were lined with what must have been hundreds of back-curved teeth as long as her hand. Frimillin knelt down by it and began trying to pull some of them out.

"Is that really necessary?" Ramikar whispered as the others began to pass.

"Perhaps leave the dead undisturbed?" Master Himes suggested.

The salamander light playing over all the ribs and vertebrae gave the illusion of movement, and Vor flinched.

"I'd take the whole skull if I could," Frimillin retorted. "It's quite a specimen. I have a collection, you see, and I've never seen a snake skull this big before."

Everyone else passed by without comment, and a few minutes later Frimillin caught up to the group, tucking handfuls of the slender teeth into pockets inside his robes. Vor supposed they might make good needles, but couldn't imagine any other good reason to take them. Master Himes's suggestion of leaving the dead undisturbed seemed particularly poignant in these lightless, unmapped ruins. Vor wished he'd left the snake skull alone.

After going down only perhaps another quarter of an hour, the descent leveled into a landing several paces wide. At the far side was another archway—grandiose doors standing wide—and to the left and right were open doorways. The whole group gathered on the landing.

"I'll take the right," Frimillin volunteered.

Ramikar and Iyai followed him towards the dark doorway. Pirossa turned to the left one, and Master Himes and Dello followed her. Vor and Giri followed Dello.

"Nothing," Pirossa was saying as they entered. "Just some kind of pillar."

There was a circular structure in the dead center of the rather wide room, but it only came up about as far as Vor's waist and was as wide as she could spread her arms. Its top was a circle of metal a couple inches thick, utterly plain and unadorned but tarnished nearly black.

"There are letters here," Master Himes said, crouching down.

Dello crouched beside her. "Looks like more ancient writing, Master. Shall I fetch Ramikar?"

"If you would."

"Nothing but wreckage in the other room, and signs of another member of the original group that set the key," Thornwing reported, squeezing into the pillar room after Dello exited. "Not much except fragments this time, but Frimillin says they're human, and very old."

"Thank you, Thornwing," Master Himes said.

"This isn't sealed down," Pirossa said, walking around the strange pillar and running her fingers at the seam of stone and metal. "We could maybe remove it."

"Why would we want to, though?" Thornwing shrugged.

Dello came back with Ramikar.

"I think the other room might have had bunks, a table, and chairs, once upon a time," Ramikar said. "They're broken to bits, though. It's hard to tell if that's due to natural decomposition or if they were manually destroyed."

"I wonder if it might have been a barracks," Master Himes suggested, "for guards monitoring the grand doors out there."

"Could have been," he agreed. "What have we here?"

"There's writing," Dello pointed.

"So there is."

While they examined the pillar again, Ramikar kneeling down before it, Vor cast her eyes around the rest of the room.

"There's a little wreckage here, too," she said to Giri and whoever else was listening. "Looks like parts of an old crate, maybe sacks, and lots of broken pottery."

"Little holes in the walls, too," Giri contributed. "There might have been brackets for shelves."

"If that was the barracks, it would make sense if this was a storage room," Vor nodded. "Which would make that sort of pillar thing a—"

"Well," Ramikar pronounced. "This is a well for water."

"We could use some of that," Frimillin commented as he and Iyai joined the group. "No telling when we'll get the chance again."

"There's no bucket or rope," Vor pointed out. "How would we get it up, if we could even uncap it?"

"This cap will be heavy, but working together we could move it," Dello said. "We're sort of out of magic energy, but our muscles still work. Someone must have sealed it off when they decided to abandon this outpost, expecting that no one would ever need it again."

"It doesn't appear that the group ahead of us tried to open it," Ramikar mused.

"I expect they are much better provisioned than we are, since they planned to come down here," Master Himes rued. "They also probably can't read the writing, and wouldn't have known what it was. Let's try to shift it. Everyone uninjured, lend a hand."

"Are you sure?" Iyai murmured. "I don't like it."

"What's wrong with it?" Master Himes demanded.

Iyai wilted. "I don't know," she whispered.

"If we can move it quickly, get some water, and go, it will be worth it. If we can't budge it, we'll just go on. We'll find another water source, I'm sure."

The entire group had by then gathered in the abandoned storage room. Himes, Dello, Vor, Giri, Pirossa, Ramikar, Frimillin, and Rikah all gathered around and tried to find a spot to grip, but Jessika hung back by Iyai.

"Push towards me," Master Himes directed, "away from where Pirossa is."

The group strained, and the cap turned out to be much heavier than expected. After a couple minutes of work, they shifted it far enough for a gust of cool, damp air to escape through a little gap on Pirossa's side.

"Smells like water," Dello commented.

Now a few of them were able to hook their fingers in the gap, and they made better progress. In only a couple more minutes, the gap was big enough to lower a bucket through—if they'd had a bucket.

"Let's leave it there," Himes directed. "Pirossa, can you see water?"

"I hope we don't have to put it back," Frimillin grumbled as he rubbed at his sore hands.

Pirossa leaned down to the gap. "It's really dark down there. I can't see a thing."

"Don't," Iyai whispered from where she stood with Jessika.

Vor frowned, wondering if Iyai was just scared, or if she was sensing something dangerous.

"Here." Dello handed Pirossa a pebble he'd spelled to glow.

She took it in hand and stuck her arm into the gap. With a grunt of frustration, she leaned down further and stuck her shoulder and head through. After a moment, she stood back up.

"It's big down there," she reported. "It isn't a straight shaft. Below this neck, it opens up like a big bottle below the floor."

"Could you see water?" Master Himes asked.

"No," Pirossa shook her head. "Let me look again."

"You're sure it's a well for water?" Dello asked Ramikar.

Ramikar nodded. "That's what it says, or something very similar."

"I'll drop the pebble," Pirossa said, "and watch the light. Maybe it will hit water down there somewhere."

Vor was lucky enough to be standing on one side of Pirossa; she leaned in to try to see through the gap, and saw as the young woman released the glowing pebble. She expected a long, dark expanse of nothingness. Instead, the pebble fell down and through a ragged hole in what appeared to be a deteriorating wooden platform or floor several person-lengths down inside the well. Below that, quite difficult to see, was another, and Vor thought she might even glimpse a third below the second one. After that, she no longer had a useful view.

Behind her, Iyai whimpered.

"There are platforms in here," Pirossa exclaimed, "lots of them, and—there. The light is gone. It must have fallen into some water down there, way down there. There's no way to get that water all the way up here, but maybe we could go down through this well and get to the bottom of this place faster? If we had—"

Whatever else she was going to say turned into a scream of fear. Pirossa's body jerked, and Vor instinctively grabbed her. Pirossa's whole upper body was pulled down into the well, and Vor found herself struggling against a mighty strength.

"Pull me out, pull me out!" Pirossa howled, as everyone scrambled to grab onto whatever bit of her they could reach.

Whatever had her was strong. Pirossa's feet were no longer touching the floor and her waist was even with the rim of the metal cap. The group struggling to pull her back exclaimed with dismay and her cries turned inarticulate as her body inched further into the well. She was slim, and her hips weren't big enough to be caught by the opening.

"Let me in there," Hawkwind ordered, her furry arms reaching in among the rescuers.

The griffin pried at one of Vor's hands, and she reluctantly let go of Pirossa's right hip. Hawkwind grabbed on immediately, and managed to grip the woman's left hip, too. Then the griffin anchored her wings and hind feet against the base of the well and began to push, while she leaned back with her body, pulling on Pirossa with all the strength of her massive flight muscles and legs combined.

Pirossa screamed as if in agony. Vor scrambled around onto the cap and reached down blindly into the well, feeling for the woman's shoulders and head. She found her head and neck, apparently uninjured, but one shoulder felt distended: dislocated. Her body was twisted and taut; something was pulling on her left arm. Vor didn't have the reach to get any further than a bit of her upper arm, but her fingertips brushed something slightly slick, cold, and hard.

"Something's got her," she declared.

"Of course something's got her," several someones shouted back over Pirossa's tearing cries.

"Her arm," Vor clarified. "Something, something alive is pulling on her arm, and I can't reach it."

Dello shoved her shoulder. "Let me. These freaky monkey arms have to be good for something."

He had a blade in one hand, and Vor made way for him. Flat on his belly on the cap, Dello reached inside. Hawkwind was keeping Pirossa from being pulled any farther, but didn't seem to be able to pull her back out without actually ripping her arm off.

"There is something there," Dello growled. "Give me light!"

Vor sent her salamander down, though it left everyone above in darkness. Dello exclaimed something inappropriate and Pirossa's screams became more unhinged. Dello grunted and swore, body jerking as he worked out of view in the well—and then suddenly Hawkwind was flung back, Pirossa going with her. Vor's salamander flashed out of the well, obedient to her command.

"Close it," Dello shouted. "Close it now."

The rescuers reshuffled, moving to pull and push on the metal cap. Full of adrenaline this time, they moved the cap more quickly, but before they could close the gap something stuck its hand out of it. Dark grey and slightly shiny, with long webbed fingers and vicious hooked claws, it was bigger than a human hand, but not not as large as a griffin's, and seemed to have too many joints and a few extra digits. The claws glistened with Pirossa's blood. Dello brought his knife down onto it, hard and swift, again and again, but couldn't seem to pierce the skin. The hand flinched away from the strikes, though. A second hand appeared, and then a third.

"Close it," Dello cried again.

Finally, Hawkjoy—having gotten Lanisala carefully off her back—descended on the gruesome hands. She gripped a knotted wrist in her bill, braced herself, and twisted. Bones snapped. A howling shriek came from within the well. Hawkjoy didn't let go. She shook and jerked until another hand slashed at her. She dodged and dropped her prey. The grey hands retracted, and the others pushed the metal cap back into place.

They had carried Pirossa into the opposite room, away from the capped well, even though there were bits of human remains in there; no one seemed to care about that. Frimillin and Himes were trying to tend to her injury. Vor had sent her salamander to hover close and give light. Pirossa had stopped screaming so loudly but couldn't stop her sobs and groans of pain. Frimillin and Ramikar had gotten her shoulder back into the socket, but her hand and arm were not so easily fixed.

"Let me see that," Craduticus grunted as Rikah and Vor helped the old man to sit by Pirossa.

Vor winced a little and looked away. Over in another corner, Giri stood with Dello, listening to his account and helping his pacing friend calm down. Master Himes was digging in one of the pockets of her robe, and drew out a small sack. From it she shook out a few pale pills, took two and put the others back, and delivered those two to Pirossa.

"Can you swallow these?" she asked. "They're for pain."

Vor didn't ask why Master Himes carried a pouch of pain pills with her, but was just glad she had them. It looked like Pirossa could benefit from them. Between sobs, she managed to swallow them down with some water.

"She needs a real healer," Craduticus said.

"Seeing as how we don't have one," Frimillin growled.

Vor stole another look at her arm. How many of those clawed hands had grabbed her, Vor didn't know, but judging by the uncountable tears and punctures in her arm and hand, a lot. Her right hand had some wounds, too, but not nearly so many as her left. Iyai stood, face as white as Vor had ever seen it, trembling, tears running down her face, while she elevated Pirrosa's less injured right hand and applied pressure to the rips in it.

"We have to stop the bleeding," Master Himes whispered.

"If we tourniquet her arm, she could lose it," Frimillin retorted.

"She could bleed out if we don't."

"We're going to have to seal up the worst of the wounds," Craduticus said.

"How?" Frimillin growled back.

"By cauterizing, quickly."

Master Himes winced, but nodded, and then looked up at Vor. "Mage Hearthsraven, would you instruct your salamander to do as Craduticus directs?"

Vor swallowed hard, and nodded. "Are you sure?" she whispered.

"We have to hope she won't get infections," Craduticus muttered back, "and she may lose some use of this arm, but if we don't stop the bleeding, she will die."

"We can't fix the major vessels if they're damaged, and cauterizing could make it worse if they are," Master Himes breathed, just loud enough to hear over Pirossa's groaning. "Those creatures hooked their claws between her radius and ulna. That's why we couldn't pull her back. They ripped everything in there."

Craduticus grimaced. "Vor, bring the salamander close so I can see. Giri, Dello, get over here and be useful. Elevate her feet and give her a piece of wood to bite. Luckily, the two largest arteries in the arm do not run between the radius and ulna, and it doesn't look like they hit the big artery in her upper arm. Frimillin, wipe away the blood here."

Pirossa quivered and groaned, trying to keep still as they worked. Jessika, surprising Vor a little, came over and sat by the injured woman, half embracing her shoulders, and began murmuring encouragement to her. It seemed to take forever as Craduticus carefully examined first one and then the other side of her arm, tracing the route of the two biggest arterial vessels and checking for any place they were damaged. As he went, Vor sent her elemental servant to cauterize the edges of wounds as the old mage held them together.

Pirossa jerked and muffled her screams into the stick of wood someone had found and placed between her jaws. It was obvious that Craduticus's treatment, though potentially lifesaving, was only hurting her more. Giri and Dello had to hold her down, and after the first time she lashed out with her magic, knocking everyone away, Master Himes came and stood over her, magically clamping down on her powers.

"She has been very lucky," Craduticus said, some time later. "This tear here came very close, but neither vessel was damaged. Her arm might still be largely ruined, but I don't think she'll bleed to death."

"But there's so much blood," Iyai whimpered.

"But the bleeding has slowed," Craduticus countered. "We've sealed the worst of the wounds. Everything is of course still a mess and she must be in terrible pain, but I think with pressure and elevation the remaining wounds will clot on their own, which is better than unnecessary cauterizing."

Pirossa's rich dark skin looked washed out and grey, and her face was slick with sweat and tears. Her eyes were shut, but she breathed still. Gently, Dello took the stick of wood out from between her jaws.

"Use the cleanest fabric we have to wrap her arm, and the wounds on her right hand, too," Craduticus instructed.

"I can handle that," Frimillin said.

"I have a spare shirt in the packs on Hawkjoy. It hasn't been worn," Vor volunteered, and went to get it.

The three griffins were standing guard at the door, looking subdued.

"We haven't gotten very far, have we, and already," Hawkwind murmured as Vor approached.

"And it could get worse," she agreed.

"Will Pirossa live?"

"Probably, thanks to you pulling her out. As long as she doesn't get any infections from the wounds, she might be alright, but her arm probably won't be the same again."

Vor dug out her shirt and carried them back to Pirossa. She gave the shirt to Frimillin and picked up the waterskin.

"Pirossa," she urged. "Wake up. Have some water."

The wounded woman twitched and her eyes flashed open. Words spilled from her. "Water. No, there's no water down there. It's death. They pull you down. You fall and fall and fall. Then they hold you under, and you can't get up—"

"You're safe now," Master Himes interrupted. "You're with us."

"They're going to hold me under," Pirossa gasped out.

"No, they won't. But you've lost a lot of blood. You need to drink," Vor repeated.

"I'm going to die. I can't breathe," she rasped, eyes still showing the white all the way around.

Then Frimillin reached out and put a hand on Pirossa's forehead. Immediately, the lady mage relaxed and let out her breath. Her expression calmed and her frantic words stopped.

Master Himes reached out and snatched his hand away. "What do you think you are doing?" she hissed.

Frimillin just shrugged and went back to wrapping Pirossa's arm. "Just doing what was needed, Master Himes."

"What was that?" Jessika asked nervously.

"Mind magic," Himes grunted.

"Just a little," Frimillin muttered. "Not enough to hurt her."

"Are you done there?" the master wizard demanded.

Frimillin tied off the last of the bandage and nodded.

"I will speak with you privately."

The colorful wizard raised his hands in surrender, and went with her to a far corner where they began talking intently in whispers. Pirossa, meanwhile, now complacently accepted the water Vor offered, and drank thirstily.

"She'll be alright?" Iyai asked, shivering.

"I'll carry her," Hawkwind volunteered, coming to join them.

"We'll see," Craduticus answered Iyai, "and thank you, Hawkwind. For now, I think she will rest, but it sounds like she'll be dealing with mental trauma as well as physical."

"I'm not surprised. Do you know what those things were?" Dello asked, still looking paler than normal himself.

"I didn't get a good look. Describe them?"

"Dark grey, slick skin, emaciated, but structurally humanoid: they were clinging to the walls somehow. Their arms were long, with extra fingers, and extra joints. I didn't see any hair or feathers or fur. They had little horns along their heads."

"Tails?" the old mage asked, frowning.

"Yes, I think they did have tails, short and stubby. They were coiled up together, maybe four of them, so I couldn't make sense of all the limbs," Dello answered after a moment. "I was mostly looking at their arms, trying to pry them off of Pirossa. They were terribly strong, and my knife couldn't hurt them, especially not on the dorsal side, but the ventral side seemed tender. That was how I got them to let go, by stabbing at the undersides of their wrists."

Dello swallowed, looking rather shaken. "And their faces—they had huge eyes, round like fish eyes. Tiny nostrils, but wide mouths with lots of teeth—jagged teeth. Their heads were sort of squished, side to side, compared to human heads, sort of narrow. They looked hungry and wild." He shook his head. "They were going to devour her if they could get her. I know it."

"I don't think I have ever heard of such creatures," Craduticus confessed.

"I'm glad," Vor muttered. "I expect that means they aren't common. I hope their claws aren't venomous or filthy."

"I didn't see anything that looked like venom, or signs of it acting on her flesh," the old mage said. "Filth I can't really speak for. They could have introduced a lot of nastiness into her flesh, without obvious signs of dirt or slime."

"And you're sure her main arteries weren't damaged?" Dello asked.

Craduticus craned his neck around to look at Ramikar. "They don't teach basic human anatomy at the Citadel anymore?"

"Dello's talents are not with bookish learning," Giri put in quickly. "They do teach it. Our instructor was quite good."

Craduticus gave Dello a little glare. "Let's hope you never have to bloodlet for emergency power and accidentally exsanguinate yourself, Wizard Traskitandi."

Vor almost chuckled. Master Himes rejoined them then, though Frimillin had gone to stand with Hawkjoy and Thornwing at the door.

"Let's get moving," the lady master said gently. "There is no benefit to staying here: no resources."

No one argued, though a few of them frowned or scowled. Vor, Giri, Dello, and Iyai helped position Pirossa as comfortably as possible on Hawkwind's back. Riding a griffin couldn't compare to resting in a bed, but there was no bed, either, had they stayed. Lanisala and Craduticus, too, continued to ride. Together, the group went back out onto the landing, and then through the ancient and massive double doors, to find only more stairs.

Chapter 8
The Old City

These stairs did not go far. After only a couple minutes of walking they reached another landing, this one with no doors. Beyond it the tunnel forked. One path continued straight, while another, narrower hall, went off perpendicularly to the left. On the corner where the halls met were carved signs in ancient writing.

"Ramikar," Master Himes murmured, and the tall man stepped forward at once to read in the light of Vor's salamander.

"West wing," he read, indicating the narrower passageway. "City center," he pointed down the wider path.

"We need to get below the city," Master Himes mused.

"Not that way," Iyai blurted.

Everyone turned to look at her, and she was staring down the hall to the west wing, perfectly still except for her trembling fingers.

"Not that way," she repeated, voice harsher. "Everyone down there is dead."

No one spoke for a few breaths. Then Thornwing cleared his throat.

"Well," he said, "let's not go that way."

"On another day, exploration might be enjoyable," Hawkwind contributed wryly, "but I vote for heading to the city center. I suspect this west wing will have no exits."

A few others made sounds of agreement, and the group continued straight on, except for Iyai who didn't seem able to move until Ramikar went and gently tugged her into motion. At his touch she hid her face against his shoulder. As they passed the dark narrow hallway, Vor glanced down it—and then did a double take, pausing for a moment before walking on.

"What?" Giri asked.

"I thought I saw someone," Vor confessed softly.

"Should we go check?"

"No," she replied. "It's not the first time. In the dark, with all the stress, fatigue, lack of food, I think everyone is seeing things."

Giri nodded, and they continued on, passing the side hall. "What did it look like?"

"Just a lighter shape in the dark," Vor told him, "passing by, like it walked through a door or into another hallway, almost like it was a reflection of us."

"Maybe it was a shadow in the salamander light," Giri suggested.

"Maybe," she allowed, "but it wouldn't have been to scale. Shadows from here would have stretched out and wouldn't look like a normal person at that distance. Still, my mind could have interpreted a bit of moving shadow like that."

Giri slid his hand into hers and interlaced their fingers. Vor held on, a little uneasy at all the flickers of movement she'd seen, but not truly scared, since he was with her. If she'd been alone in this place, it would have been different. She'd have probably been terrified.

They walked on, and the hallway turned slightly to the right and began to slant downward at a gentle angle. There were still brackets in the walls for lamps and the decorative carving. Up ahead, Master Himes was leading, with Ramikar and Iyai beside her and Dello just behind her. Abruptly, she came to a stop, but gave no signs of alarm. The others caught up to her and saw what had given her pause.

"Water," Dello said.

A portion of the wall was soaked dark with water and deformed where the trickle had worn it away. It started at the ceiling and coated a section about a yard wide. At the bottom of the wall a few small depressions held puddles. The water collected, overflowed, and then ran down the inclined floor where the wall met it, in a tiny little rivulet.

"Wizard Iyai," Master Himes summoned, "can you tell if it's drinkable?"

The pale girl stepped up before the wet wall and sniffed a few times. Then she held a hand out—an inch shy of touching the wall. After a few moments of that, she ran a fingertip over the saturated rock, wetting it, and finally brought it to her tongue.

"I think it's safe," she whispered, "as safe as any raw water, anyway: no poison or anything."

"It will take a long time to collect enough to drink," Giri observed.

"And it won't be easy to collect, either," Master Himes agreed. "Let's go on. If we get desperate, someone can come back up here and sit with a waterskin."

"What?" someone asked.

"I said—"

"Not you," Frimillin grunted.

Everyone clustered near the wall turned towards the rest of the party: the ones who had been at the back of the group. Jessika, Rikah, and Hawkjoy carrying Lanisala had been bringing up the rear, following Frimillin, who had been walking by himself in the middle. All four at the back looked at the least confused, and Jessika had turned to look back the way they'd come, as if searching for something. It was she who had spoken.

"Someone said something," Hawkjoy said, sounding puzzled about it herself. She twisted around her flexible avian neck. "But no one is there."

"I was explaining about collecting the water," Master Himes said.

"No, it was something else," Rikah contributed. "I think it was a man's voice, but I couldn't understand what he said."

"The invaders might be near," Master Himes whispered, suddenly serious. "Everyone gather up. Vor, dim the salamander."

The group tightened together and Vor hid the salamander inside her jacket, where it was warm against her belly. Doing so plunged the hall into darkness—but not complete darkness.

"Light, from the right," Dello breathed.

"But that's not where they heard people," Ramikar rumbled softly. "They were to the left, in the direction of the stairs and the hall to the west wing."

They waited, silent and still, alert for the sound or sight of movement, but after a couple minutes nothing happened.

"Who feels they can send a scout?" Master Himes breathed, barely audible.

"A silent, invisible one?" Ramikar added, just as quietly.

Vor knew what kind of scout that would have to be: a dark elemental. At least, an elemental of the element of darkness would be the best scout, but there were possible other options. An air elemental would produce the sensation of a breeze, and might also emit light. An earth elemental might work, but would be ground bound, so its footsteps might be heard, unless it could pass through stone, but the weaker elementals couldn't do that. Water elementals required being in water, and fire and light elementals would both glow.

She did know a cantrip to summon a minor dark elemental, because her late master, Altare, had taught it to her right along with all the other summoning cantrips. He'd had no compunctions about embracing all the elements, but Vor knew that some schools of thought excluded the dark. No element was inherently evil, however. Nor were any inherently good. Still, she had rarely ever summoned a dark elemental, and didn't have the good relationship with them that she did with her fire elementals. No one else was volunteering though.

Silently, she dismissed her salamander. "I can do it," she whispered.

Several pairs of eyes gleamed at her in the near dark. Master Himes gave her a little nod. Vor closed her eyes and recalled the cantrip; she hadn't used it in a long time. Doing it without speaking would be a challenge, but she didn't want to alert any possible enemies by saying it aloud. The group waited while she worked the summons through in her head: weaving threads of power into the proper calling.

Her call was answered, but she could tell only by a slight pressure floating in the air before her: amorphous, and nearly invisible. Still silent, she offered a morsel of power— payment—and imparted her request along with it: search the nearby area and indicate the presence of other living creatures or elementals, without being detected.

The elemental went about its assignment. It simply floated through the air, without any sign of propulsion: just a fuzzy shadow moving as easily as thought. After only a few breaths, it returned with its report: negative. Vor released a held breath and banished the elemental back to wherever it came from.

"There is nothing living nearby," she reported in a normal but soft voice. "Nor are there any other elementals that mine could detect."

"Then what did we hear?" Jessika argued.

"I don't know," Vor said evenly.

"Mage Hearthsraven, that was a dark elemental," Master Himes pointed out.

"Yes, and it was perfect for the task and completed it as ordered."

"It could have hurt someone," she scolded softly.

"So could my salamander," Vor countered, "but I didn't tell either the salamander or darkling to do so, so they didn't."

The master wizard did not reply, but Vor wondered if she heard the sound of her clenching her jaw for a moment.

"Let's move on then, shall we?" Frimillin suggested, almostly brightly.

Vor let him head toward the faint light. Ramikar followed with Iyai, and then Master Himes and Dello, though the latter did make a slight glance back at Vor.

"They disapprove of the dark," Vor muttered to Giri.

"Nothing wrong with it in the right application," Craduticus put in, a little too loudly, as Thornwing walked past, carrying him.

Vor gave him a nod of thanks, but as she did, noticed Breeka was staring fixedly behind them. Its tail twitched. Hawkwind and Hawkjoy passed, too, each burdened with their wounded. Jessika followed them closely, body tense, and then Rikah. Just as Vor was about to follow, someone said something into her ear. She jerked around, but there was nothing there. Giri, too, looked sharply back into the darkness.

"Did you hear something?" she asked him.

"Maybe," he said.

Jessika had stopped walking, so Rikah almost ran into her. "I told you," she gritted out.

"I couldn't understand the words," Vor nodded, "but I heard a man's voice say something: conversationally, not angry or mean or scared, just like he wanted to tell me something."

The fine hairs on the back of her neck stood up.

"Let's catch up to the others," Giri encouraged.

"I agree," Vor said.

They discovered the source of the light. The hallway turned left and ran straight far into the distance. Along the right wall were regular openings, one about every ten paces, through which daylight streamed. As Vor rounded the corner, she saw that most of the rest of the group was already clustered at the first window.

"Impossible for a griffin to get through," Hawkwind was saying, "but it's nice to see light and get some fresh air."

The openings were square, and only a couple palms long on each side. They were also deep, plunging through several feet of stone.

"Maybe a skinny human could crawl through," Master Himes pronounced, "but there's no telling what's on the other end. If there's a balcony, that would be something, but if not, then there's no point."

"Unless we could collect some water out there," Dello suggested. "I can hear it."

"If the inhabitants of this city had wanted exits here, they would have built something else," Frimillin declared.

Vor noted that he wasn't facing the square opening in the right hand wall. He was looking the opposite direction, and as she followed his gaze, she saw why.

"That 'city center' sign didn't lie," she said.

The left hand wall was not really a wall. Numerous door-sized openings lined the full length, with what looked like some widened portions, double doors, and larger archways. The ceiling was also two stories tall. There were carved balconies and second floor windows looking out over the hallway. Artisans had chiseled out geometric moldings and frames for the doors and windows. Except for the dimness, it looked like a proper city.

"People really did live here," Giri wondered. "How remarkable."

"They must have had a water source," Master Himes asserted, apparently unimpressed by the boulevard of buildings.

"Something other than that chasm full of monsters," Dello muttered.

Iyai abruptly gasped.

"What?" Master Himes demanded.

The young wizard pointed. "Someone is in there."

"Everyone back around the corner."

The group retreated.

"Are you sure you're not seeing things?" Vor asked. "I thought I saw something, too, but there was nothing there. I can summon another—"

"You will not," Master Himes ordered. "No more dark elementals. The invaders could be hiding in the city, though. Maybe they are resting here, or searching for water, too. We also don't know where the exit down to lower levels is located. We have to keep going; this isn't our final destination."

"Maybe there is an actual exit to the outside," Jessika spoke up, "like you said there should be."

Master Himes nodded firmly. "So we'll divide into pairs and search the city."

"We have injured," Ramikar mentioned.

"They can stay here, or maybe back where the water drips in and fill waterskins."

"If this was a human city, we griffins might not fit through the doorways," Hawkwind cautioned.

"Well, who is still able to go exploring?"

Vor and Giri exchanged a glance. "We'll go," Giri said.

"And Traskitandi with me," Himes nodded.

"I can take Wizard Iyai," Ramikar offered, "if she's willing."

Vor thought she'd probably prefer to stay, but Iyai lifted her chin, skin still as pale as milk, and nodded. She went over to stand next to Ramikar, quite close, as if for protection.

Frimillin spread his hands. "I am willing to go alone."

Thornwing flicked his crest. "I'm the smallest of us griffins, with the best chance at fitting through human-sized doorways. I'll come with you, if you'll have me."

The multi-colored wizard smiled and gave a bow. "Gladly, Thornwing."

Master Himes's gaze landed on Rikah and Jessika.

"These invaders are mages," Vor pointed out. "You don't send non-mages to find mages."

Master Himes frowned but didn't press.

"Plus, someone needs to take care of Pirossa, Lanisala, and Craduticus," Giri added.

Lanisala smirked, but Pirossa was still largely despondent, and Craduticus just shrugged.

"Joy and I will guard them, too," Hawkwind said. Then the big female gave Thornwing a glare that seemed to say "get yourself hurt and I'll yank out your tail feathers and shove them up your nose."

Thornwing posed in reply, arching his neck and fluffing his feathers, and winked at her. Hawkwind snorted.

"Let's get on with it," Master Himes urged. "I don't know how big this place is. Traskitandi and I will walk down to the end of the hallway and investigate the farthest reaches. Ramikar and Iyai, take the next nearest quarter, then Frimillin and Thornwing, then Vor and Giri."

Each pair made sounds of assent and began walking off.

"Giri, Vor," Craduticus grunted. "Take care of each other out there."

"You can depend on it," Giri replied.

They turned the corner, following the others, and entered the nearest doorway.

"Iyai said she saw someone down here," Vor murmured.

"Iyai was just seeing things," Giri replied. "I don't sense any other life in this city, other than insects or rodents, maybe."

"Neither do I, but it is possible to hide somewhat from other mages."

"Do you want to summon back that dark elemental?"

Vor gave Giri a glance in the near darkness. "Are you sure? I don't want to make you uncomfortable."

He didn't wince or flinch. "You're not. It's the correct servant for the job. There is a stigma attached to using the dark element, but it has its uses. Considering who your former master was, of course you would have learned to use it. Honestly, I think that gives you an advantage over a lot of other mages."

Vor felt her chest warm, glad to know that Giri was accepting all her skills as valid. She paused to repeat the cantrip and bring the elemental back. She told it to scout ahead and report back every couple minutes—immediately if it found large life forms. They began to walk through the hallway, glancing in doors and windows. Stairs went up to the second level in places, and they carefully climbed them to check up there as well. There were little courtyards, too, and places where the hall turned, widened, or narrowed. Bits of detritus rasped and crackled under their feet. Vor kept her senses extended, and felt nothing alive.

"Colby never taught you to use the dark?" she asked Giri.

"He did, actually," he replied, "but even though he knows the spells, he never uses them, and I got the impression that he didn't want me to, either, so

I mostly have forgotten how."

"Well, well," Vor teased. "I know something you don't know. What a reversal."

Giri gave her a smile. "I'm sure there are other things, too. I can't possibly know everything."

As they walked, they looked into each room they passed, but saw only old wreckage of what might have been furniture and possessions.

"No one has been here for ages," Giri observed. "The dust is undisturbed."

"You're right. The main hall out there didn't seem to have much dust though," Vor mused. "I am supposing that's because wind and weather gets in those air holes and keeps it from settling, maybe blowing it all back here."

They'd reached the end of the first hall, and were about to leave the last room when Vor whirled at a sound of movement, like a footstep or an object moving slightly on a rough surface. They hadn't made any lights because the faint light from the air holes had been enough to search for human-shapes by, and Vor hadn't seen anything move, but it was so dark she could have missed something. She stood perfectly still, Giri equally still beside her.

"Did you hear that? Something moved," she whispered.

"There could be small animals in here," Giri breathed. "I would expect bats to use these caves."

"It wasn't on the ceiling." Vor's dark elemental checked in with another negative for people or magic. The room was still and silent now.

"Rats maybe," Giri suggested.

"Could be," Vor allowed, staring into the dark, "and food for the griffins if it is." Nothing more made sound or movement, so she turned away. "But it's nothing we need to worry about, whatever it is."

Giri nodded. "That's the end of this street. Let's go back to the main hall and search the next one."

The next hall, or street, since they appeared to be linking homes or businesses, was longer, and branching. The buildings they searched on this larger street all shared walls and were two stories in some cases as well. The stairs up were often stone, but if they had been wood, they were largely falling apart. Once Vor and Giri got deep enough again that dust and dirt settled, they were able to check for footprints to know if anyone else had come this way, without having to look into every room. They often checked the rooms anyway, even if there were no footprints, but they didn't climb any rickety old stairs.

"This is a little bit creepy," Vor confessed as they moved deep enough that Giri had to make a couple stones glow so they could see their way. "People lived here thousands of years ago. They had families and plied their crafts in these rooms. They must have had a lot of lamps, or light stones, if they had mages. Back here it's dark all the time. What a way to live."

"And then they all went away," Giri said.

"Someone said these cities flooded?"

"That's one of the legends."

"Was it overnight? Were the people suddenly trapped here? We haven't seen human remains."

"I don't know. I suppose there could have been a cave-in that released a river. On the other hand, maybe they were aware that the waters were shifting and would soon impact them. They might have had time to leave, but chose to abandon a lot of stuff and make new. I wouldn't have wanted to haul all this stuff up those stairs."

Giri's foot touched a pile of spindly wood—maybe once a chair—and it clattered a little as it fell over. Vor felt a sudden chill and took a quick step back.

"I feel like we're disturbing something," she whispered. "There are no invaders here. They went past this city."

Giri stepped back and stood close beside her. "I think you're right."

She felt his arm go around her and she was obscurely grateful.

"I don't feel comfortable here," she told him. "The darkness is getting to me."

"I feel uncomfortable, too," he confessed. "I think, if the dust isn't marked, and your elemental doesn't sense anything, we can just pass the rooms, without going in."

"I agree," Vor said at once.

Said elemental returned to her then from a search of the current house with inconclusive news. It didn't speak in words, but was able to convey impressions to her mentally carried by magic, the same way she gave it orders.

"It says it feels something here, but it's not magic, and not alive. Let's go, Giri."

They backed out of the house and into the narrow street before it. Immediately, Vor felt a little better. They turned without a word to go check the dust around the rest of the houses on the street. Luckily, the street made a loop, and they didn't have to cross back in front of that house again.

"There was something in there," Giri murmured as they came again within range of the light from the air holes. "Something was left behind in that house, and it knew we were there, and didn't like being disturbed. I shouldn't have knocked over that chair."

"I got the same feeling," Vor admitted. "I think this city, these caves in general, all of them, might be inhabited by something, by spirits, maybe, of past residents."

"Haunted, you mean?"

"I've heard of places being haunted," Vor shrugged, as they turned down the next street in their section. "I never experienced such a place myself, except sometimes the Skire's laboratory felt spooky, like the walls kept memories of the pain that happened there."

"The human mind is powerful," Giri said. "It could also be that we're all short on sleep, food, and daylight, and we're seeing and feeling things that aren't there."

"That's more likely, isn't it," Vor nodded. "Our brains are trying to protect us from threats that could be there, because it's better to make us cautious in case there is danger, than to let us get hurt through carelessness."

Vor tried to keep that in mind through the next couple streets. They didn't go into any more houses, and that seemed to help. The dust and debris was all undisturbed, and they saw no signs of any life. Vor was able to start to relax a little when after a good couple hours nothing more exciting happened. Giri, too, seemed to regain his ease.

What Vor judged to be the last street in their quarter of the city turned out to have different sorts of buildings on it. These didn't seem to be houses or businesses. They were individual rooms linked by internal doors, one to the next, like beads on a string.

"These might have been offices, or school rooms," Giri muttered, "even storage rooms, or communal dining. I'm not sure."

"At least looking into them doesn't feel like invading someone's home," Vor commented.

"Yes, whatever they were, I think this was a public area."

They kept going, towards the end of the street, and there they found one of the things they had been seeking. Instead of another doorway into a square room of some kind, the street widened out into a semi-circular basin with a high arched ceiling. The walls and ceiling all were highly carved with floral designs. The basin was several yards across, and there inside it was—

"Water," they said together.

The pool was black and still in the pale glow of their mage-lit stones. Ringing the room were numerous lidded pots, most of them cracked or broken, but still shining with a hint of colorful patterns wherever dust hadn't settled.

"It could be dangerous," Vor whispered. "There could be things living in it."

Giri knelt to find a rock, and tossed it into the pool from where they stood, a ways down the street. There was no response. With a gesture, Vor sent her obedient elemental ahead to check the area.

"Nothing living, no magic," she reported after the elemental did so.

"Alright," Giri said. "Hold my right wrist tightly. We'll approach, and I'll touch the water with my left hand."

They did so: Vor braced to yank him back if anything stirred. The very peacefulness of the space and the water made her hyperalert, wondering if this was a trap, but even as they got closer, nothing moved or made a sound, except that then Vor began to hear the trickle of flowing water that must feed the pool.

Giri reached the edge of the water, knelt on one knee, and touched the surface. Nothing sprang up or out or in any other way menaced him. He dipped his fingers deeper. Still nothing. He splashed the surface, slapping his hand down. Nothing.

"Now as soon as I say it's safe is when something nasty jumps out to grab me, right?" he chuckled uneasily.

But nothing did.

"It might actually be safe," Vor dared to voice.

Still nothing.

"The water is cold," Giri reported, "and I'm no Iyai, but I don't sense anything wrong with it."

"Call a water elemental into it," Vor suggested.

"Good idea."

Giri sat for a couple minutes, and then finally a ripple told of the arrival of an undine.

"Sorry," he muttered. "Summoning is not my strongest suit, and I rarely work with water."

Vor found herself cracking a smile. "Really?" she murmured. "First there's something I know that you don't know. Now there's something you're not incredibly amazing at?"

He glanced back at her, also smiling. "Plenty of things," he assured her. "Dello kicks my ass at staff fighting almost every time, for starters. Plus, I'm tired."

"Forgiven," she teased, "so what does it say?"

"It says the water is fine, though high in mineral content."

"Well, it did filter down through a lot of rock to get here," Vor acknowledged. "We can drink it?"

"Yes," Giri confirmed. "Yes, we can."

He banished the undine and stood up, and moved to wipe off his hand, but Vor caught it first. His face registered confusion, until she lifted it and licked the water off his fingertips. His face no longer registered confusion.

"There are rooms back there beyond the main pool," she breathed. "The darkling reported them to me. They have water, too. Private bathing rooms, I expect."

"Should we check them," Giri said at once, eyes glinting, "make sure they're safe?"

Vor found herself smiling again. "Yes, I think we'd better, and perhaps test the nicest pool. A bath would do us both good."

He smiled back. "You have the best ideas."

"Where are they?" Rikah was saying as Vor and Giri approached the corner before the waiting spot. "We should go look for them."

"Both Holstor and Hearthsraven are quite competent," Craduticus croaked back. "I'm sure they will return shortly."

Then the pair rounded the corner and had every eye on them.

"And here they are," Thornwing nodded, "safe and sound."

"And back up to full power, I sense," Lanisala crooned with a smirk. "Found a cozy corner, did you?"

"We found water," Giri spoke up. "We should relocate there and fill all our waterskins. There's also enough for us all to bathe."

"Explains why you both look so clean," Master Himes said. "Good enough. No one else found anything of note, but several of us had instances of thinking we saw or heard things. Nothing was there of course: just the mind playing tricks. Let's go to your water source and regroup."

Vor and Giri led the way, and found the big basin with several other little pool rooms just as they had left them. The group spread out to drink, and decided they'd use the smaller pools for bathing to avoid contaminating the large pool. The ladies went to one, the gentlemen to another, and the griffins to a third. Vor found herself with Iyai, Master Himes, and Jessika, checking over the wounds on Pirossa and Lanisala.

"It's really nothing," Lanisala was insisting. "If it weren't for the location, it would be no trouble."

"But Frimillin is right," Master Himes declared. "The puncture is too close to your femoral artery. You must rest until it heals some more."

Pirossa was a different matter, and all of them gathered around her to check on the status of her wounds. The young woman herself remained quiet and wary, like any grievously injured creature in a dangerous place.

"The bleeding has stopped," Master Himes said softly. "That's an excellent sign, Wizard Pirossa. Can you move your fingers at all? Here, right hand first."

Pirossa made no verbal reply, but was able to wiggle a few of her right hand fingers.

"That's good. I'm worried about the tendons being damaged," Master Himes said. "Often, they don't recover if severed completely."

Her left hand, however, Pirossa could not move at all.

"It's probably due to the swelling," Master Himes suggested. "We won't be able to tell how well you'll recover until you begin to heal. Give it a few days at least. There was quite a lot of damage."

Gently, to avoid dislodging scabs, they washed all but the worst of Pirossa's injuries, helped her bathe in total, and wrapped her back up. The others took turns bathing as well, though the water was quite cold. The whole underground was cool in general, but once dried off and dressed, they huddled together and shared body heat to warm up. They sipped some water and Master Himes again gave a couple of her white tablets to Pirossa, and this time swallowed one herself.

"What are those for?" Lanisala demanded.

"For pain," Master Himes answered.

"Are you hurt?"

"None of your business."

"Why does she get some and not me?"

Master Himes gave Lanisala a mild look. "I wasn't under the impression that your wound caused you that much pain, compared to what happened to Pirossa, but you can have one if you need it."

"I'm fine," she declared.

"Master Himes," Vor ventured before Lanisala could find another way to be abrasive. "What Frimillin did to Pirossa, the mind magic; you didn't like it."

"He sedated her," the older woman replied after a moment. "It's wearing off already, and he might be right that it was the best thing for her, but I don't like it."

"Mind magic can be destructive," Vor agreed. "I've seen it used in horrific ways."

Master Himes stared at her for a few breaths. "I read the report about what your former master did to the king of Northnest."

Vor nodded. "That wasn't him alone; other Weldom wizards contributed, but yes, he kept it going. He did a number of other things you might not be aware of."

"He made an imposter of their princess. I heard about that one, too."

"Yes," Vor shuddered, remembering the process. "I was there. That was all his doing, but he used my energy for it."

Master Himes stiffened beside her. "You helped?"

Vor shook her head. "It was a punishment for me. I had recently failed him."

"Failed him how?"

Vor looked over to where Jessika sat at the far end of the cluster, beside Pirossa. "I allowed Jessika, the real princess, to escape his clutches."

The princess heard—Vor hadn't been keeping her voice quiet—and glared over at her. "You tried to kill Koki," she accused. "You didn't allow anything. You would have done anything to keep me a prisoner."

"That's not what Rikah told me," Vor replied evenly. "He said you thought I let you get away."

"Koki would have died," Jessika hissed.

Vor had to face the fact of that. "It's true. I didn't know he was a faun and had poor grip on the roof because of his hooves, and I didn't know he'd fall off the edge, or that a griffin would catch him. I just acted, and my action would have killed him if it hadn't worked out the way it did. Luckily, he didn't die."

Jessika seemed to be seething, and didn't reply.

"Of course, your griffin mage Starbright knocked me off the roof, too," Vor mentioned. "Preventing my landing from being fatal was not the easiest thing I've ever done."

"You deserved it," Jessika whispered. "You tried to kill Koki."

The partially true jab pricked Vor, and she tightened her jaw against a wince. Then the princess began quietly weeping.

"Where is the faun these days?" Vor asked, trying for some sympathy. "Is he alright? I thought you two were a pair."

Jessika sobbed aloud, and then appeared to try to get herself back under control. She wiped her face on her sleeve. "He went back to be with his own people. I," her breath caught, "I don't know if I'll ever see him again." The tears returned. "And now I'm stuck down here in these caves full of monsters and ghosts, and I don't even have my clubs. I'm helpless. If even you wizards can get hurt, what could happen to me?"

"Did I just hear right?" Lanisala whispered. "You were bedding a faun?"

"Wizard Salasis," Master Himes scolded.

Lanisala leaned towards Jessika. "Faun's have the lower bodies of what, goats? Deer? So are they like men down there, or do they have—?"

"Enough," Master Himes ordered.

Lanisala scoffed. "Come on. If we ladies can't sit in private and talk about our men and what they're like in bed, when can we talk about it? So which is he, Princess? Like a goat or like a man?"

Jessika scrubbed tears off her face to snarl at the lady wizard. "Fauns are their own species," she hissed. "It's not like taking a human and cutting him in half and cutting a goat in half, and sticking them together."

"That's why I'm asking." Lanisala spread her hands innocently. "Explain the differences to me between a faun and a man."

Jessika ducked her head and echoed Master Himes. "None of your business."

"Oh?" Lanisala gaped after a stunned moment. "Oh? Oh, I see. You don't know, do you? Really? You've got that Rikah following you around like a puppy, and you haven't taken advantage of his devotion to try your own species?"

"Wizard Salasis, shut your mouth," Master Himes commanded.

The two glared at each other, with Vor glaring, too, over Master Himes's shoulder in Lanisala's direction. Then the shadow of a griffin appeared in the half-circle doorway to the bathing room.

"Wings?" Hawkwind called about as softly as a griffin could call.

Jessika twitched, looked up, and got to her feet. She stumbled a little and almost plummeted back into the pool, but Hawkwind stuck a wing out to catch her, and used it to gather the young woman into her furry chest. The she-griffin gave a polite nod to the remaining five women, and took Jessika away, presumably to join the other griffins.

Lanisala did not seem abashed. In fact, her smirk widened a little. "You know, Vor, I taught Giri a few things. Does he still—?"

"Shut up, or I'll make you," Vor stated flatly.

Lanisala changed direction as swiftly as a swallow in flight. "What about you, Master Himes? Vor and Giri managed to find a quiet moment to themselves, but you went off with that handsome apprentice of yours and have come back just as drained as when you left."

Master Himes shoved to her feet. "Traskitandi is married."

Lanisala shrugged. "That hasn't stopped many another master-apprentice pair, now has it? I'm even surprised little Iyai here and Wizard Ramikar didn't make some power. They're both virgins, after all. They could have—"

Master Himes snarled. "If you do not keep a respectful tongue in your head, I can arrange for you to be left behind because it's too difficult to continue carrying the wounded. I am in charge here. You will do as you're told. Cease trying to cause dissent in the group."

Gradually, Lanisala's playfully malicious leer faded, and she gave a barely polite nod. Through the whole exchange, Iyai had sat beside Pirossa, utterly silent, but her blushing cheeks were almost bright enough to emit light.

"Who cares?" Pirossa gritted out, the first thing she'd said in a long while. "Such nonsense. Sex is rotting your brain, Salasis, and men are selfish, greedy, thoughtless asses. I've no use for them."

"Dello did save your life," Vor mentioned softly.

Pirossa's snarl faded. "He did. I mean, no use in bed. I think," she gasped, "I'm going to be sick."

Vor and Iyai helped her bend over as she heaved up the little in her stomach. Lanisala finally fell silent, and Master Himes let go a weary sigh.

"These painkillers aren't easy on an empty stomach. I hope some of it got in her." She put a hand to Pirossa's forehead. "No fever yet. I'm not sure what else we can do for her. But speaking of men, we should see if the menfolk have had their baths," Master Himes said, "and decide on our next moves. Vor and Iyai, will you assist Pirossa? I think I had best help Wizard Salasis."

The group reconvened in the large water basin room around a glowing rock spelled by Giri. Jessika had fallen asleep in the cluster of griffins, cushioned by their bodies, and Pirossa, too, was dozing, but everyone else made a good attempt at appearing alert. Vor, after a quick conversation with Giri, had dug their travel rations out of the packs on Hawkjoy and Thornwing, and was evenly distributing them to all the humans.

"A decision needs to be made," Master Himes was saying, "about whether we should all keep going, or leave the weak and wounded here, at a water source, while the strong carry on. I worry we're not catching up to the invaders."

"There is no food source here," Craduticus pointed out.

"After business is handled with the invaders, those who went ahead would come back, and we'd then all get out together, either back up, or out whatever exits we found lower down."

"So we'd starve until you return?" Lanisala asked. "I'm assuming as one of the wounded, I get left behind here."

"Starve while waiting or starve while walking," Ramikar muttered.

Iyai, sitting beside him, gave a hesitant nod. Vor had to admit, so far it seemed likely. The only food they'd encountered was the cave scorpion that had tried to eat Hawkwind—which the griffins had eaten in return.

"I think we should all keep going," Hawkwind contributed. "In fact, I think we should take a good rest here, and sleep for a while, and then start fresh."

"The invaders will get even farther ahead," Master Himes objected.

"Do they know we're following them?" Hawkwind countered. "They will need to rest, too."

"If they reach the key before we do, they could destroy the capital," she insisted.

"Perhaps a scout should be sent ahead to find them, or even to get to the key first, passing them, if possible," Hawkwind mused, "but we should not abandon anyone behind. Everyone should keep moving forward. We will find water again."

There were several nods around the circle. Master Himes shrugged.

"Very well. We'll all rest a short while, and then the healthiest of us will go on. The injured can rest a while longer, and then follow at a relaxed pace. Is that an agreeable compromise?"

More nods, with murmurs of agreement met her suggestion.

"Everyone get some rest, then."

"Vor?"

Giri was asleep, curled up on the softest bit of cave floor they could find—which wasn't very soft, at all. Vor turned to find Iyai standing a short ways away and looking as uncomfortable as if she were about to force herself to wring the neck of some poor defenseless animal.

"What is it?" Vor went to her, noting that her furious blush was back in place.

"I'm sorry," she stuttered. "I didn't want to ask Master Himes, and Pirossa is hurt, and, and—"

"Certainly not Lanisala, and not a non-mage nor a griffin nor a male, I'm guessing," Vor finished for her. "So, what is it?"

"Um," she prevaricated, "I just thought, since you have packs and were about to travel, you might have supplies for, um?"

Vor frowned and ran through possible scenarios, and then touched Iyai's aura to check her most likely hypothesis, since the girl herself had fallen silent.

"Ah," Vor said, "is that it? That time of the month, as they say: yes, I have something you can use."

Iyai hung her head and put her hands over her face.

"At least that means you can replenish some of your energy," Vor went on, going to the pack she'd taken off Hawkjoy and was going to use as a pillow.

"What do you mean?" Iyai whispered miserably.

"When you shed blood," Vor murmured back. "It releases energy, even if it's involuntary. You collect it and add it back to your own personal power."

But Iyai was silent, face twisted up between tears and a frown.

"You do add it back to your own power, don't you?" Vor checked. "Iyai, you're not letting it go to waste are you?"

She shook her head a little. "What are you talking about?"

Vor straightened. "Your master didn't tell you?"

"I," Iyai hiccoughed. "I don't have one. My parents say I have to go back, and get married for my house. I'm the firstborn. They need me there. I don't get to have a master or be a real wizard."

She brought a shaking hand towards her mouth. Vor grabbed it as the girl began dissolving into tears.

"Come now, you don't know that for sure, and you don't need to worry about it right now. Take a breath. Focus. Here's what you need." Vor put the supplies into her hand.

"No one," Iyai choked, "no one told me I could get energy from this. It doesn't matter. It's just for having babies for my house."

"It does matter. No other teacher told you about the advantage you get by being female?" Vor pressed. "Even my master—former master—horrible as he was, told me that. Look. Look, Iyai. Look at your energies."

Surprising Vor a little, the girl did.

"You see that power dropping? For the sake of all that's good and green, pick it up. It's yours. Keep it. Use it. You know how to gather power right?"

"Um," Iyai uttered. "Yes."

"Well?"

To Vor's relief, she did so.

"I didn't know about that," she whispered. "I feel stupid."

"Don't feel stupid," Vor told her. "I suppose if you'd never looked before, you wouldn't have seen it."

"I just," she breathed, clenching her robes tightly about her. "I don't like it."

"I don't blame you," Vor said. "I don't like it, either. I can't imagine anyone who would. You can't stop it though, so don't torture yourself in your head about it. Take advantage of the extra power, and just deal with the rest."

Iyai nodded. "You're right. Thank you, Vor."

"You're welcome. Anything else I can do for you?"

"Um, just, I have a question."

"Alright."

"Is," she said, voice so soft Vor could barely hear her, "is it true, you and Giri did—something—to restore your power? What Lanisala was talking about?"

"Of course," Vor replied simply. "Sex makes power. You didn't know that, either?"

She trembled. "Should I have done that with Master Ramikar to—"

"Iyai," Vor said sharply, making the girl look up. "Do you want to have sex with Ramikar?"

The young lady shook her head hard enough to make her blonde hair swirl. "But he's kind, and it would be alright if—"

"No," Vor said. "No. You only have sex with someone you want, understand? You don't have sex because you think you have to." She sighed, almost turned away, and stopped herself. "Look, I'm not the best person to talk to you about this, because I've made dumb choices myself, but I can tell you this much. You should want him—or her—whoever it is you want—before you consider it. And of course the other person should want you back. Alright?"

Iyai nodded, eyes on the floor.

"Did Ramikar suggest you two have—?"

"No, no," Iyai refuted at once.

"Did he try to pressure you into it some other way?" Vor persisted.

"No. He was a perfect gentleman," Iyai affirmed. "He didn't act that way at all. I wasn't scared, or pressured."

Vor hesitated a moment. "What Lanisala said, that both you and he are virgins, that's alright. I haven't looked at him to see for myself, because that's rude, but if he hasn't had sex, he probably has a reason, and probably wouldn't try to make you."

"I think you're right," Iyai agreed.

"But you should know that the first time for anyone releases a lot of power," Vor said. "If you ever decide to do it, you'll want to gather it, so just be aware."

Vor trailed off, and stared at the pale, trembling young woman a few moments longer, but she didn't say anything else.

"Alright," Vor subsided. "If you need anything else, let me know."

"Alright," Iyai echoed her.

Iyai left, stepping around a corner for a couple moments of privacy, and then going to lie down beside Hawkjoy. Vor was relieved to see the female griffin rouse a little and open her wing, tucking Iyai next to her like a chick. Vor went to lie down by Giri, trying to plump the pack into a decent pillow. As she set down her head, Giri snuggled up to her.

"Who's a good big sister?" he teased, nuzzling into her.

"You shouldn't eavesdrop on women's business," Vor chided.

"I'll let you eavesdrop on me and Dello sometime in return."

"I do not want to know what men talk about among themselves," Vor retorted.

And then Giri wrapped himself around her, and there was no more talking.

Chapter 9
<u>Splitting Up</u>

The next morning—though no one could tell what time it was—they sorted themselves into two groups. Master Himes stood with Ramikar and Frimillin to one side, looking over those who remained.

"Vor and I should join you," Giri said. "We're both combat trained, and uninjured. We can move swiftly."

"And I am coming, Master," Dello put in.

Master Himes grimaced a little. "You're all logical additions," she admitted, and the three of them crossed over.

"I wish I could come," Lanisala groused.

"As do I," Craduticus grunted, "but I do not have the physical agility or strength needed."

"However, you can both provide magical protection to those not joining the advance party," Dello soothed.

Pirossa sat quietly, eyes glazed with pain, and made no comment. She was more aware today; it seemed that Frimillin's little mind magic had worn off with some sleep. Still, with her left arm swollen and severely injured and her right hurt, too, there was no way she could join the advance party.

"Iyai," Master Himes said, "do you want to come? You have some useful skills."

But Iyai shook her head. "I'm sorry," she stuttered. "I couldn't sleep, and I, I—"

"That's alright," Master Himes soothed, and the girl lapsed into silence.

"Six is a reasonable size," Frimillin said. "Any more might be too many."

"You should have a griffin with you," Thornwing spoke up. "I'm the smallest, and the oldest, the most experienced. I can fit through smaller spaces than the others, and discourage any monsters we encounter that might think humans are tasty."

"Thornwing is competent," Hawkwind vouched.

The male griffin didn't turn to look at the bigger female, but Vor wondered if she was interpreting correctly the slight alterations in the lay of his feathers that indicated both amusement and weary annoyance. Even Thornwing's bluff good nature could wear thin.

"Alright," Master Himes agreed. "As long as you can fit through the passageways, you're welcome to join us, but will just two of you be enough to carry all the wounded?"

"I can walk," Pirossa mumbled. "They didn't hurt my legs."

"Wizard Pirossa and I can alternate riding," Craduticus said. "Now that the pace will be more leisurely, I don't think we'll have any trouble."

They re-sorted the packs, taking only a few essentials to be carried by Thornwing. Thus, they said their goodbyes, and Master Himes, Ramikar, Frimillin, Vor, Giri, Dello, and Thornwing went on ahead, moving briskly, past the entire searched city, to the exit at the other end.

"No surprise," Master Himes said softly, "more stairs."

They'd reached another set of double doors, but only one was open, and this one only partly. The opening of it had also been done recently, as there was a collection of debris behind it, and a clean section of swept floor before it, where it had been pushed open.

"They came this way," Master Himes continued.

Ramikar laid a hand on the door frame. "There was a ward here, but very old and very weak. They probably hardly noticed it."

Beyond the door, the stairs were fairly narrow—only wide enough for two people to walk down side by side. They went single file, however, Master Himes first and Dello behind her with a dim light. Unlike previous stairs these also had recent detirus. Fallen leaves had blown in somehow, even some twigs and other bits of plants. Bats also hung from the high, rough cut ceiling, and their droppings and bits of uneaten prey thickly speckled the steps. The air didn't smell very nice, because of all that, but Vor thought she felt a draft through the stairs, and a hint of outdoor air.

"If that door was just recently opened, then the bats weren't getting in through the city air holes. There must be another opening below," Vor mentioned.

"I expect we'll find it soon enough," Master Himes agreed.

In another few turns of the staircase, Vor began to hear a rushing sound.

"Water," Dello said.

They came across it as they emerged into a tiny cave, like a bubble in the solid rock. The stairs leveled into a bit of hallway, and then crossed over a channel in the stone like a bridge. To their left, water tumbled down a natural tunnel, rushed under the path they stood on, and away again into another tunnel, vanishing into the rock. The path turned back into stairs after the cave, but narrowed alarmingly before widening out again.

"Tight squeeze," Thornwing commented from where he was bringing up the tail of the group. "Hawkjoy can probably fit, but Hawkwind might have some trouble through here."

"It can be enlarged magically," Ramikar said, "if necessary."

After another turn they came into a much larger cave. Here, several rivulets and streams emerged from different places in the cave, mostly on their left side. The path they stood on turned into a natural cave floor, which was cut across by the merged waters, dotted with stalagmites and patches of sand. A few stalactites descended from the ceiling as well, and in one corner were hanging layers of wet stone that resembled rippled curtains—another living cave formation.

"This is beautiful," Giri murmured.

"Footprints in the sand," Master Himes said. "They crossed through here."

"I hope they didn't touch anything," Ramikar breathed. "The oils from our skin will kill these formations so they never grow again."

Dello froze, hand outstretched, about to stroke a stalagmite. He pulled his hand back and put it in a pocket.

"This place is strong with earth and water magic," Ramikar went on reverently. "It's a true treasure."

"I hope the group behind us knows not to touch," Dello offered.

"Craduticus should know," Ramikar nodded, stroking his short beard and gazing around. "Perhaps, after all this is over, I'll come back here, just to enjoy this cave for a few days. There are elementals all around us, just waiting to be called. They would appear easily here, in their place of power. I might be able to reach some of the more elusive varieties, some I've never seen before."

"Hop across everyone," Master Himes encouraged. "They went this way, out that hole over there."

Vor obeyed, following Giri in a graceful leap over a wide, shallow section of pale sand that shimmered in the faint mage-light. The others followed, except for Ramikar, who still stood on a damp rocky shelf, eyes shut. Everyone paused to wait for him. Master Himes cleared her throat.

Then a nearly subsonic rumble buzzed the stone around them.

"Ramikar," Frimillin hissed.

But the tall, lean wizard's eyes flashed open with surprise as great as anyone's. "I don't think that was me," he whispered.

"Come along," Master Himes ordered.

"Master, what was that?" Dello asked.

"I don't know, Traskitandi," she snapped back.

"What were you doing?" Frimillin demanded as Ramikar made a long-legged leap over the water.

"I wasn't doing anything," he replied, a trifle tartly. "I was just reaching out to sense what was around. I didn't touch anything. I just wanted to see. There's a lot of earth and water magic here."

The husky wizard huffed and shuffled onward into the exit hole.

"I know. That's of little interest to you," Ramikar soothed.

"Just don't touch anything," Frimillin retorted. "I want to get out of here alive."

Vor, just ahead of the two men and following Giri, found her footing unsteady. The stairs here were poorly cut and slick, and narrower than before. Some of the water was escaping down them, instead of through the other outlets.

The walls of the tunnel were rough, too, and the ceiling low enough that Dello and Ramikar both ducked in places. Then the stairs turned sharply to the right, and a few steps after, opened up into a cave much larger than the one they'd just left—large enough to be called a cavern. The stairs they were on hugged one wall, with no railing, and descended to a fairly flat floor wide enough for a dozen griffins to stand shoulder to shoulder and twice as deep.

Water ran down the walls in many places, forming a few small waterfalls, and collected in pools before running either into unseen tunnels or to the far right, where green-tinted daylight percolated inside. Fresh damp air flooded in as well. Everyone stopped on the stairs to gaze over at the opening in the cavern wall.

"That's a way out," Master Himes declared, "an opening into the gorge."

"It certainly is," Thornwing agreed.

The hole was as tall as three men and almost as wide, but greenery hung over it in overlapping strands, and there didn't appear to be a balcony extending out. There also seemed to be—

"A lot of water though," the griffin went on. "Not that it's impossible to fly with damp feathers, but it doesn't exactly help."

"Let's take a closer look," Master Himes suggested. "Even if you can't fly us out this way, this is a good spot for the injured to stay and await our return."

The group moved carefully down the slick stairs. Vor's shoes were getting soaked, but there was little help for that. She'd summon her salamander later to dry them out for her. Once on the main floor of the cavern, Thornwing went towards the cave mouth. Master Himes and Dello followed him.

"There will be a path deeper," Frimillin said. "This was the only way down out of the city, so there has to be more tunnels."

"Don't you suppose other paths could have existed in the past, but have been closed off?" Ramikar countered.

"I suppose there could have been other doors that have since been sealed," Frimillin admitted, "the way the door from the water storage was sealed. We didn't check every length of stone for that."

"We didn't explore that west wing area."

"But my darkling said it was a dead end," Vor pointed out.

"Then this was the way all the people of that little city came in?" Giri mused. "They brought all their food and supplies in through this cave? I wonder how they managed it."

Frimillin had started walking deeper into the cavern, away from the mouth.

"I wonder why they lived down here at all," Ramikar murmured. "Even for one like me, who loves the Earth, this would be a difficult home."

Frimillin didn't reply, but Ramikar started to follow him. Vor watched the floor, picking dry places to step in an effort to avoid further saturating her shoes—and came to a halt as she saw something the eager wizards had missed. Her heart gave a nervous thump.

"Giri," she hissed, and he stepped up beside her.

Frimillin and Ramikar were several yards ahead now. To reach them, she would have to raise her voice, and she thought that wouldn't be a good idea.

"That's a footprint," Giri confirmed, "a drake footprint, still wet. Only wild ones would live down here. I'll tell Dello and the others."

He turned to dash as safely as possible across the uneven floor to where the griffin and two humans were examining the exit. That left Ramikar and Frimillin for Vor. She hurried ahead, and reached out to catch their robes, giving a tug and getting them to stop.

"Mage Hearthsraven?" Frimillin asked.

"Keep your voice down, please," she urged. "We found tracks from—"

And then a long, shimmery neck with a skinny, serpent-like head lifted up from behind a little hill of rock. It was iridescent violet shading to deep plum towards the head. Plum-colored bat-like wings extended, and then the creature got to its feet from where it had apparently been napping. Cold eyes looked down upon them.

"Retreat slowly," Ramikar instructed.

"You can't control it without a collar, can you?" Vor whispered.

"Correct."

The three wizards backed away as the rainbow drake paced eagerly forward. It wasn't much bigger than a griffin, and much more slender, but then another—this one burnt orange and umber in color—emerged from what must have been a cave behind the rocky outcrop.

"How do we fight them?" Vor muttered on. "Fire?"

"We haven't fought drakes in ages," Frimillin objected. "We breed them and collar them right after hatching."

The violet one snapped forward, quick as a snake, and Ramikar dodged but slipped on the slick floor and fell half into a pool, landing hard on his hip. A scarlet red drake, a bit smaller than the other two, dropped down from either a ledge or a quick flight above them; Vor hadn't noticed it before. It lunged forward—and a crackling spark of power struck it on the nose. It yelped and jerked back. Vor glanced over and saw Dello helping Ramikar out of the pool; the older wizard limped a little. Master Himes and Giri stepped up behind Frimillin and Vor.

"Three is bad," Master Himes said, "but we should be able to—"

Then four more drakes, the same size as the scarlet one but each in different bright colors, rushed out to join—

"Their parents," Frimillin surmised. "This must be a breeding pair and their latest clutch. Seven, Tessa? You think we can handle seven?"

The drakes were agile, darting up and over the six humans and climbing easily along the walls to encircle them.

"Thornwing?" Vor asked.

"He's already gone out the exit, seeing if he can reach the open air," Giri answered, sending another crackle of energy to discourage a lime green drake. "He'll have no idea we're facing drakes unless he hears the fight or comes back on his own. The gorge is tight here. These drakes can surely slither through, but a griffin is heftier. It could take him some time to return, but I'm sure when he gets back, he'll jump right into the fight."

The drakes were tightening their ring, and the wizards were clumping together in an outward-facing circle.

"Maybe we could make a fuss," Dello suggested, "so he hears?"

"Shouldn't be too hard," Master Himes grunted agreement. She sent a popping spark at the nearest drake. "They don't like lightning. It's how we punish disobedience in the captive ones. If you all can guard me for a few minutes I can build up a big charge and then—"

"Oh, there won't be time for that," a stranger's voice announced.

Vor whipped her head around towards the back of the cave, though from where she was standing, she faced the stairway they'd entered by and a bright yellow and gold drake that had perched on it. A tall, dark-skinned woman with long, silvery hair held back in braids stood calmly behind the pair of adult drakes. Her clothing was utilitarian: tough dun trousers and a tightly laced brown jacket, but Vor imagined she could make any clothing look good. She was lean and long limbed and carried herself with utter confidence.

She smirked a little and lifted a glass globe the size of a mumfruit in one hand. "Goodnight," she sang.

Then she threw it, and it shattered at Frimillin's feet, releasing a pale mist.

"Don't breathe," Master Himes ordered.

Vor immediately held her breath, but then the drakes leapt. They didn't bite, didn't claw, just barreled their bodies into the circled wizards. Vor let loose a bolt of fire instinctively, but barely scorched the yellow-gold drake. It knocked her to the floor, kicking the wind out of her, and though she fought the urge, though she tried to crawl away towards the cave mouth, the drake bit down on her foot and dragged her back. Her lungs screamed for air, and she couldn't help it.

Vor took a breath, and instantly the world around her faded.

Someone was tugging at her shoulder. Vor twitched away and the unknown tugger jerked her back.

"Hey," she mumbled, fighting to get her eyes open.

"Oh, you're a new one: only two," a voice said: a voice she vaguely recognized. "A pity, that."

Vor managed to squint, getting a look, and saw several people standing or sitting around her. She was sitting herself, legs stretched out and back against a cold rough wall. Light shone in from her right. Someone squatting in front of her was tugging at her sleeve—and he had a knife. Her hand flashed out and caught the man's wrist.

"Aw, look at you," that same voice crooned. "The baby wizard can fight a little, too."

The man she'd grabbed didn't struggle with her, just gave her a cold, indifferent stare. He was a little scruffy, brown haired with a good tan and strong blunt fingers. Vor ran her eyes around the cave, locating her companions all spaced equally around the perimeter, several feet apart so they couldn't touch, each with a couple guards watching them. Their captors were a mixed bag of men and women with a variety of physical types, but Vor thought they were all younger than thirty years of age. The one who'd been doing the talking was the same elegantly tall woman who had thrown the sleep potion at them. Despite her silver hair, she was no older than the others.

"Is everyone awake now?" she asked with a mockery of courtesy. "You tripped our ward in the door down from the city. Thought it was an old one, did you? Left over from the legend of when the ancient wizards set the key? How stupid can you be? Well, we had to come meet you to find out for ourselves."

Vor could see that none of her companions appeared seriously injured, though Frimillin had a pretty good scrape on his face, and all of them had their eyes open with varying degrees of alertness. She found Giri's gaze from where he was propped against the wall to her right, on the other side of Ramikar. He seemed calm, but made no reaction. Vor figured that was a good idea, and schooled her expression into one of blankness, but subtly she sent a little pulse through her ring to—and flinched as the tiny pulse of power backlashed and stung her aura. She flinched at the strange sensation and her personal powers quivered, like an energy spasm.

The tall woman immediately pivoted to face her and clasped her hands. "Ah, yes, now is the perfect time to tell you all that you shouldn't try to use any magic, or you'll feel just like this baby wizard here felt. Anything you try to cast bounces right back against you. Did it hurt?"

Vor made no reply, but yes it had.

"I'm not a very good mage," the woman went on with mock humility, turning about a little to look at each of them, "but I am really good at one thing: putting magic into objects. I've given each of you a gift. If you look at your feet you'll see a pretty little anklet. I made them and you should feel honored that I've given them to you. You see, they are so difficult to make and each one took months and months of work. I don't have very many, and yet I've given them to you. They contain your energy so you can't use any of it for magic. If you try, it just bounces it right back, like a mirror. Go ahead. If you don't believe me, give it a try."

"Don't," Vor muttered. "It works."

"One of you can speak," the woman grinned. She walked over to stand just out of Vor's kicking range. "I'm Vittara," she said. "I'm one of the leaders of our little expedition. It's sort of a joint venture; I can't take all the credit. Would you mind letting go of Granken? He's not going to stab you."

Vor still had a grip on the wrist of the man with the knife. Reluctantly, she let him go and he stood up and sheathed his blade.

"I would apologize for having those drakes attack you and knocking you out and imprisoning you here," Vittara went on with acidic sweetness, "but since you are the evil ones I don't think we, as the heroes, are obligated to do so."

"Excuse me?" Master Himes said softly from where she was forcibly seated across the cave from Vor. "You are the ones trying to pull out the key that holds Anchoria together, which would cause the death of thousands. You sent golems and blade-tails to kill everyone from the youngest apprentice to the oldest master in the Citadel. You are calling us the evil ones and yourselves the heroes?"

"Tessa, perhaps let them have their delusions?" Frimillin suggested. "They clearly don't know any better and can't be blamed for their ignorance."

Vittara drew a knife from her own belt and pointed it slowly around the circle of prisoners. Her false cheer dripped away.

"You are all wizards," she accused, as though it were a filthy word. "Every one of you has the flower mark, except the baby here who is still missing a few petals. You are the evil in this world."

Vor noticed then that the left shoulder of everyone's clothes had been cut open, not just hers. Indeed, she could see the mark of five thumbprints arranged like petals of a flower on each of her companions. They certainly all were wizards, but Vor thought it incredibly unfair to decide that made them all evil. The marks were supposed to create accountability, not give them permission for murder and rapine, or some such nonsense.

"How can you say that without knowing us?" Vor challenged evenly. "You would label an entire group of people even though each individual is different?"

The man called Granken snarled a little. "You're all noble pigs. You're all indoctrinated at the Citadel. Maybe it's not your fault, but you're all wizards, all made to do the bidding of the scum in charge of our country, in charge of our fates."

"You're the tools of the evil ones," another woman spoke up. "Maybe you don't know any better, but even now you do their bidding."

"We chose to come down here and stop you all on our own, actually," Master Himes retorted, sitting up straighter and looking like she might be gathering herself to stand. "Or rather, I made the decision. I led the charge. I didn't get any orders from anyone higher up."

"Then you are evil," Vittara grinned in satisfaction.

"Evil for trying to stop you? If I have the power to stop death and destruction, I should exercise it," the master wizard replied.

"And do you?" Vittara goaded. "Do you stop them from oppressing the common people? Do you use your power to help lift us up? Or do you stand by and let them embed shards of magestone in our bellies to keep us from spawning mage-talented babies?"

Vor's face pinched with confusion. She'd never heard of that. Master

Himes, however, did look vaguely ashamed.

"That wasn't a decision I had any power over," she explained quickly. "I do not make policy. None of us do. We do have a voice, but not a choice. I argued against that procedure, but I'm not a state wizard, so my voice meant little. The ministers decided that since the magestone was running out, the most efficient way—"

Vittara ran right over her words. "To keep the power in the hands of the nobility was to put bits of the stone inside us, to make sure the common people kept having common babies."

The tall woman approached Master Himes where she sat on the floor. "And wizards did it," she continued venomously. "They used their magic to place the stones so deep that if we tried to dig them out we'd hurt, and bleed, and get wound fever, or maybe lose the ability to have babies at all, and maybe even die."

Vittara tugged up her shirt, showing a messy pale scar against her bronze skin.

"But we tried," she whispered, "and those few of us who were born mages, against all the odds, we got teaching, and then we learned to remove them, the same way your wizards put them in, with magic. So then we started having mage babies, and now there are a lot of us, and we found each other."

She stood now over Master Himes, staring down at her with raw hate in her eyes and a furious tear on her cheek.

"When we pull out the key there will be very few of you left," she promised. "Hold her."

The invaders moved swiftly, drawing out knives and brandishing them at the wizards. Two of them grabbed for Master Himes before she could rise. Vor started to get up, but then Granken had his blade out again and another man joined him. Vor hesitated—two on one, with her unarmed and unable to use magic was not good odds. Plus, they were standing and she still wasn't on her feet. Granken shook his head, as if in respectful warning, making Vor think he didn't actually want to have to stab her.

Vor flicked her gaze over to Master Himes. Vittara had apparently dodged the wizard's kicks and had her knife at her throat. The two other invaders had the wizard's arms twisted up against the joints, so if Master Himes struggled she'd risk dislocating her own elbows and wrists.

"Let her go," Dello ordered, although two more invaders had him at knife point, too. "I mean it: leave her alone."

"Throw your best shot," Vittara encouraged. "Make it strong enough and the backlash might even kill you. I'm curious to see if that could happen."

Dello had his teeth bared and eyes fixed on his master, but he didn't cast. The elegant lady leaned down closer to Master Himes, almost nose to nose, and carefully removed the knife from her throat.

"No more wizards," Vittara purred, "not even you."

Then she gripped Master Himes' shoulder, where her robes had been split to reveal her wizard's mark, and with one swift cut and a few tugs, sliced it away.

Master Himes winced, tried to jerk away, and groaned in pain.

"No," Dello cried out.

The tall wizard surged to his feet, taking a cut on the arm where one of his captors menaced him with a knife, but then three closed in around him. Dello grabbed for their wrists, trying to take control of the blades, managed to get one, but another shoved her knife at his face, making him flinch away.

"Sit down," one of the men ordered.

Frimillin acted, too, with a sudden roll as slippery as an eel he escaped the grip of his guards. Vor clenched her jaw, about to join the fracas—when sudden electrifying pain shot into her ankle from the anklet there, and she choked down a whimper. Everyone else seemed to feel it, too. Dello and Frimillin both staggered and their guards shoved them down to their knees.

"Tie them up then, if they won't sit quietly," Vittara commanded, panting, and Vor assumed the sudden surge of pain had come from her, linked into each anklet.

She still held Master Himes' severed flesh pinched in her fingers, and Vor saw her put it almost reverently into a sack at her belt. Vittara noticed her watching and smirked.

"I have a collection," she confided. "I'll be adding all of yours' to it."

"Vitta, really?" one of the other women grumbled at her. "Would you stop with that? It's gross."

Dello was still struggling as he was tied up. "Master," he called.

"I'm fine," Master Himes gritted out. "Don't be an idiot."

She wasn't tied yet, and had her right hand pressing the cloth of her robe over the bloody wound on her left shoulder.

"Master," Dello pleaded.

"Traskitandi," she shushed back. "Compose yourself."

"So you're a master wizard?" Vittara said archly. "You teach others to be minions of the government. Like this beanpole over here?" She gave Dello an appraising once over. "Too tall for my taste. I don't like my men taller than me. Still, I suppose I could make an exception. Shall I cut some bits off him?"

"My assignment," Master Himes hissed between clenched teeth, "has long been maintaining the trade agreements with Lackland. I suppose you think that is evil, too? Making sure both sides are happy with the exchange? Bringing in fresh fish and other ocean products to our land? Making sure Lackland gets the lumber and ores they are owed in return?"

Vittara didn't seem to have a good reply to that, but after a few breaths she came up with, "you are part of the problem, keeping the power in the hands of the nobles, away from the common people."

"Look," Frimillin spoke up, as two men finished binding his hands together, "we are all aware of the magestone situation. We know it has long been used to keep the common people magic-free. We know things are changing, too, and that the balance is shifting. You may think we have power, because we were born with the talent for magic, but we are not the ones who set the laws and rules. That is a power we don't have, no more than you do."

Granken poked him with the tip of his knife, not enough to do major damage, just hurt a little. "But you have enough power that you could have stopped it, could have stopped them, and you didn't. You liked the situation the way it was."

Now it was Frimillin who seemed caught without a reply.

"There is truth to that," Ramikar murmured, "but it would have been messy, and as you say, we had little reason to make such a mess, when the current situation was all to our benefit. I think that is the natural instinct of most creatures."

"Now you'll make a mess," Vittara pronounced. "It will be very messy. You'll stay here in this cave, and when we pull the key, you'll all be crushed by the falling rock."

"And so will you," Giri pointed out.

She smirked. "No, we'll teleport out. One of us has specialized in it, and is ready to get us all away before the rocks start falling. You poor little wizards, though," she mock-pouted, "can't use magic anymore."

A few of the invaders began exiting the cave through a tunnel at the back, opposite the hole to Vor's right that let in light.

"Don't bother trying to climb out," Vittara said, twirling her blade. "The cliffs are far too sheer and you wouldn't want to fall, would you? You will have enough water to stay alive until you get crushed though."

The tall woman's eyes began wandering over the remaining five wizards that still had their marks. Her eyes settled on Giri.

"You're a handsome fellow," she said. "I think I want your little flower before I go."

Vor tensed as Vittara approached, hips swaying. She knelt in front of Giri, and then slowly turned her head to eye Vor.

"You've got a thing for him?" she teased.

Vor couldn't decide how to reply to that. Vittara smirked and returned her gaze to Giri, looking over his mark, and then staring into his eyes.

"How about this?" she suggested, tapping her still-bloody knife against her palm. "I'll take your little flower, or a kiss—a good one. You know what I mean?" She leaned in. "Like you mean it, like you give her."

Giri made no reaction, but Vittara slid her gaze back to Vor.

"You want to decide, Miss Baby-wizard?"

One of the women about to exit stopped and returned to stand behind Vittara. "Would you stop playing with them?" she huffed.

Vittara snarled at her. "They play with us. Why shouldn't we get a turn?"

"It's cruel," she declared. "Don't be cruel like them. And it's disgusting."

"We'll never get wizard marks," Vittara emphasized, "so I'll take theirs."

The objecting woman grabbed Vittara's arm, pulling at her, and Vittara complied, standing up and turning about to confront her.

"There's lots of things we could do to them," Vittara frothed. "They can't use magic now; they're practically helpless. What do you want to do to them to get back at them, hm? Want to cause a little pain? Or a lot? Want to humiliate them? Want to scar them like they scarred you? Go ahead. Whatever you want you can do; I don't care. Come on, Tallie. I'll help you."

"You take this too far, Vitta," the other woman, Tallie, shook her head, making her utilitarian brown ponytail wave. "This isn't what balancing the scales means."

"What's going on?" a man Vor hadn't seen before had entered the room, and Tallie immediately backed off.

The newcomer wasn't especially tall, but he was solid and looked a bit older than the others. His dark blonde hair was cut short so it stood up in a short fuzz, and he had a tidy blonde beard, too. His eyes were small and dark and flat like stones. He was pale, and a little dirty, arms bare and well muscled. At his arrival, Vittara's calm confidence returned.

"You want to play with them a little, don't you, Kardy?" Vittara smiled wickedly.

The stocky man, Kardy apparently, looked around at the six wizards. "If we had time, Vitta, but—"

"There's always time for a little revenge," Vittara growled. "They're wizards; they deserve it. There's a couple girls. You like girls. That one's even a master. She deserves it most of all." Vittara leaned up close to Kardy and murmured in his ear. "Make her scream."

Vor hadn't been tied, only Dello and Frimillin, so she got to her feet finally, and put herself in front of Giri where he still sat calmly.

"Oh," Vittara crooned, "the baby wizard with spirit. Are you protecting him from the big bad commoner?"

"I'm common, too," Vor replied. "You have what you want; we'll die a messy death. Go. Try to torture any more of us and you'll have a fight on your hands."

"I can put you to sleep again and take your marks while you're unconscious," Vittara said.

"But you don't want that," Vor refuted. "You want to see us in pain. You want to stare into our eyes as you cut us. You'd like to hear a scream or two; you just said so."

Vittara's face went stony. "How are you common and a wizard?"

"I grew up in Northborn. My father was a soldier. When I finally met proper wizards they were impressed enough with my skills to let me join them. I can see the problems here, and I can see that the situation is changing. It will change. You don't have to destroy Anchoria and all the people in it to make the change happen, and hurting us won't give you any productive result."

Vittara growled—through it was almost a groan. "But it would make me feel so much better. You don't know how Weldom commoners are treated. You don't know what wizards have done to us."

Behind the slender woman, Kardy was looking around at the various wizards. Ramikar had remained almost motionless, just observing. Frimillin was tied now, and looked like he might be in pain. Maybe the scrape on his face indicated a blow to the head. Master Himes remained sitting, blood seeping between her fingers as she tried to stem the flow from her sliced shoulder. Her face was paper white.

"Hurting others won't make your pain go away," Vor told Vittara. "I learned that a long time ago."

Kardy was staring at Master Himes. The lady wizard stared calmly back. Dello had been tied, but he rolled, levered, and pushed himself over to a kneeling position in front of her. Blood of his own had soaked the sleeve of his robes, where he'd been cut during the struggle, and it looked like he'd been hit in the face—a bruise was forming on his left cheekbone.

"Leave her alone," he said evenly. "You want to hurt someone, you hurt me."

Kardy just snorted. He grabbed Vittara's arm and gave her a yank. "Let's go. Let these pathetic little wizards get crushed. We're wasting time."

The other woman, Tallie, and a few others who had remained watching the interactions, fled the room. Kardy shoved Vittara out first and gave them all a long last look.

"If somehow I do ever see you sorry excuses for humanity again," he threatened, "I will take some revenge, so see to it you die here like you're told."

He stepped back out of the tunnel opening, and a moment later came a deep rumble as the rock reshaped, forming a solid wall. Vor let her hands drop, and felt Giri reach up and take one. At the touch, she let her tension go. Ramikar got up and went to untie Dello and Frimillin. As soon as he was free, Dello knelt beside his master, put an arm around her shoulders, and carefully examined her wound. To Vor's surprise, Master Himes let him, and even leaned into him and hid her face against his chest.

"Well," Frimmilin sighed.

"Well," Thornwing echoed but much more brightly, sticking his head in through the cave mouth, "are you all ready to go?"

The opening into the gorge was too small for Thornwing to climb in through, but the others could climb out through it and maneuver onto his back while he clung to the cliffside.

"I hope you'll pardon me for not sticking my beak into that little gathering between you and the invaders," the griffin said as Ramikar picked his way out through the hole. "I can't fit inside to add physical emphasis to any words I might say, and I didn't want to reveal myself since they didn't seem to know I existed."

"Perfectly done, Thornwing," Ramikar replied, mid-clamber.

"It also took me a little while to find where you'd gone. There were drakes in the big cavern when I returned, and I didn't think they could have eaten all of you in such a short time, so I searched our backtrail a ways, and when I didn't find you, assumed you must have gotten past them, but I couldn't do the same by myself. I, of course, didn't think you'd leave me behind without a farewell, so I admit I was a bit perplexed. Luckily, I heard raised voices and came to search along the gorge."

"Thank you, Thornwing," Vor spoke up. "We might have ended up dead without you."

She reached out to point out the best places for Ramikar to hold onto the harness.

"Nah," Thornwing drawled. "I've no doubt you all are resourceful enough that you would have found a way out. Ramikar, I'll drop you back in the big cavern, but I hope the drakes have retreated or left, or can you keep them off alone?"

"Not with this anti-magic anklet on," Ramikar grumped.

"A what?" the griffin asked.

"One of the invaders is apparently a mage-smith," Giri contributed, and lifted his left foot to show off the anklet. "She gave us unwanted gifts that trap our power inside us, so we can't use any magic at the moment."

"I tried breaking mine," Vor confessed, "but it's too strong for me."

The anklets were no delicate jewelry. They were made of forged links of chain as big around as her little pinky, each inscribed with runes, snug to the skin so there was no slack.

"We'll need a tool to remove them, I think," Giri said, "but I'm not sure what we have."

"I'm sure we can solve it somehow," Thornwing said heartily. "Now, there's a little ledge outside the cave up there, not really a balcony, but you should be able to drop down into the cave from it without too much trouble. I can drop you off there. Hawkwind and Hawkjoy should catch up to us soon. With their help, we can handle the drakes, at least to drive them off."

"I'm ready," Ramikar said, and Thornwing gave a nod, beginning the half-flight, half-scramble across the gorge wall up to where the other cave entrance was.

"How hurt is everyone?" Vor asked timidly, when no one else seemed interested in further assessing the situation.

"I'm fine," Giri said.

"Frimillin?" Vor said.

The redheaded wizard was striding around the room, wringing his freed hands. "Those common-born brats," he seethed. "The presumption: to lecture us? To accuse us? We run ourselves ragged keeping the country safe for them, for their muddy, dirt-grubbing lives, stopping the plagues, the wild beasts, the wild fires, catching the criminals, making sure they have the resources they need to do the simple task of making food."

He threw up his hands, looking around at the others in appeal. "Of course they can't have magic. Look at what happens when they have magic. They try to kill us all and destroy Anchoria. How can they be so reckless, so moronic, so ungrateful?"

Thornwing came fluttering back, and Master Himes spoke up. "Why don't you go next, Frimillin?"

"Didn't see the drakes," Thornwing reported, "but Ramikar is hiding on the ledge just in case."

Frimillin went, still grumbling under his breath.

"Master Himes," Vor called softly as Thornwing took off with Frimillin, "do you want to go next?"

Dello had bound the wound on her shoulder, but it was already bleeding through the improvised bandage. Such an injury, with the skin sliced away over an area almost as big as Vor's palm, wouldn't heal easily. Luckily, Vittara hadn't cut deeply into the muscle, but Vor could only imagine it must be terribly painful nonetheless. Master Himes was standing under her own power, but Dello still stood anxiously close, biting his lip and looking more upset about the wound than she did.

"Very well," she said, and went to mount Thornwing when he returned.

Dello helped belt her on this time, since she had a little difficulty hanging on with her left arm. Ramikar and Frimillin could help undo the straps on the other end.

"Please go gently," Dello murmured to Thornwing.

"Shut up, Traskitandi," Master Himes scolded back. "I'm not an invalid. I'm ready, sir griffin."

Thornwing took her at her word, and as soon as they were out of sight, Dello turned away, hands pressed over his face.

"She'll be alright, Dello," Giri assured him, going to pat his back.

"They took her wizard's mark," Dello growled. "The mark her master gave her, the mark from others who helped her learn and grow." He took an uneven breath. "Her master passed away some years ago. Now they've cut away her respect and admiration and faith—all she had left of him. When she touched it, she could still feel him, you know?"

Vor was a little surprised to see the shine of tears on Dello's cheek, and didn't know what to say. Giri seemed struck without words, too. Dello's hands clenched into fists.

"And they hurt her," he breathed. He rubbed his sleeve across his face, and when he lowered his arm, his anguish had transformed into cold anger. "They hurt her. I should have stopped them. I should have fought harder. I won't let them touch her again."

Giri still stood, apparently unable to choose how to respond, but Vor stepped forward.

"I know you won't," she said. "Now to make sure you can, you'll need to be as healthy as possible. Let's bandage the cut on your arm. Giri, do you want to go next?"

That made Giri twitch as if he had forgotten Vor was there, and he looked between Dello and Vor with a puzzled expression.

"Go on, Giri," Dello said.

Thornwing landed again outside the cave mouth. "Next?"

Giri turned and went without a word. Vor rolled Dello's sleeve up to look at the cut. It had mostly stopped bleeding, but it wasn't all that shallow, so she tore some of the sleeve off to wrap it securely. Dello stood like a statue, jaw clenched, not watching her work, and not flinching as she tugged the bandage tight. Vor let her hands do the job, wondering if she should say anything. She wanted to—to confirm her theory—but she didn't want to upset Dello any further. Then Dello relieved her of her internal debate.

"I love her," the tall mage murmured. "Tessa. I love her, more than just the way an apprentice usually loves their master."

Vor nodded, as she'd suspected, and said nothing.

Dello continued staring at the nearest wall. "She knows. How can she not know? We share magic all the time. All the time. Sometimes master and apprentice pairs sleep with each other, but she won't let anything happen because I'm married."

"She loves you, too?" Vor asked gently, and borrowed his words. "More than just how a master usually loves their apprentice?"

"I," Dello stuttered, "I'm not sure. She's really self-controlled. She could be hiding feelings, even from me—from me! No one is better at detecting auras, no one—well, alright maybe someone is, but I'm really good at it, and I can't tell," he hissed.

"She does have a point," Vor offered. "You are married."

Dello scoffed. "With noble marriages—most noble marriages—the children have to be legitimate, so you have to be careful, but when you don't love each other, you can have a discreet lover on the side. My wife even told me she's fine with it, but Tessa won't—not that I've asked her. I haven't said anything to her, but I know she knows how I feel."

Finally he looked down at Vor as she finished tying the bandage, and they heard Thornwing's talons scraping on the rocks outside.

"It hurts, Vor," he whispered. "And I let her get hurt. I let them hurt her."

Vor reached up and wiped away his fresh tears.

"It wasn't your fault. It's just the way the situation worked out. She's a master mage. If she couldn't handle it, you probably couldn't have either," Vor told him softly. "Stand by her. Be strong and let her lean on your strength as she needs."

"I know." He clasped her hands and managed a little smile. "Go ahead. I need a moment."

Vor went to Thornwing and climbed around until she got situated on his back, taking a firm grip on his harness.

"Ready," she told him.

He pushed off, doing a sort of jump-flap-flap-grab, to the next jutting rock in the narrow gorge, trying to avoid bashing his back—and thereby Vor—against the other rock wall.

"Dello is alright?" Thornwing asked casually.

"Hm," Vor muttered. "The matriarch he wants is declining him, even though they are friends and his feelings are true."

"Interesting," the griffin grunted, jumping for the next perch. "Is there a reason?"

"She considers him claimed by a different matriarch, even though the other is willing to share."

"Not a situation griffins would likely have, but I appreciate your efforts at an analogy, Vor," Thornwing praised.

"And now she is injured and he is distressed."

"Naturally he would be." Thornwing went carefully now. The gorge was narrowing further, and they approached the light waterfall that fell over the opening to the drake cavern.

Vor ducked her head to keep water out of her eyes. "And he blames himself for not protecting her."

"As would anyone who sees someone they care about get hurt, even though it's not his fault."

Thornwing reached the crowded ledge where Giri, Ramikar, Frimillin, and Himes were waiting. Vor managed a dismount and Thornwing immediately dashed out of the waterfall to find another spot to cling. He shook himself, shedding as much water as he could before going back for Dello.

Frimillin was peering around the corner of the opening and into the gloom of the cavern. "I don't see the drakes," he whispered.

"Let's go back up the stairs to that cave with the stream running through it," Master Himes suggested.

"I'll go first," Ramikar muttered.

Vor watched him carefully drop down from the ledge to the rim of the opening, cross the floor and sneak up the stairs on silent feet. He was limping a little from where he'd fallen on his hip earlier, but not seriously. Frimillin followed, and then Giri.

"Go ahead," Master Himes told Vor.

Without objection, Vor followed in Giri's footsteps just as Thornwing approached with Dello.

❁ ❁ ❁

Chapter 10
Reunion

They regrouped in the cave with the stream—the one where they'd felt a tremble in the rock and Ramikar had claimed it wasn't his doing.

"We may have to face the drakes," Ramikar was saying, "and the group coming after us was going to use that cavern for shelter, but not if it's full of drakes. I do hate to kill them, but even if we just drive them off, they might come back and attack our injured."

Frimillin had been standing at the back of the group, and now cleared his throat. "Speaking of the following group," he said.

Then Vor, too, heard the sound of careful footsteps coming from the tunnel behind them. Giri skipped over to it.

"Hello?" he called. "Master Craduticus? Iyai? Hawkwind?"

Three voices answered, and Giri stepped up the tunnel to meet them. A moment later, Iyai came down, picking her way along the uneven floor. She had a little air sprite hovering by her shoulder that was giving off a white glow.

"There's a problem," she said timidly. "Hawkwind is too big to get through the tunnel."

"I can help with that," Ramikar began, and then swore softly. "I could have helped with that, but my powers are locked."

Just then, Jessika and Rikah came down the passage and joined the group with expressions of relief and confusion—probably at their presence when they'd said they were going ahead and yet, here they were.

"Your powers are locked?" Iyai echoed curiously.

Vor and the others indicated the anklets they unwillingly wore.

"We found the invaders," Frimillin chirped, "or rather, they found us, knocked us all unconscious, and trapped us in a cave with this pretty little jewelry on us. We can't use our magic while wearing them, and they are too substantial to easily break."

"I might be able to help," Rikah piped up. "My father is a blacksmith, and I've sort of heard a lot about metal."

Jessika stopped beside Iyai as Rikah hopped the stream to look at Ramikar's anklet.

"Can Hawkjoy get through?" Vor asked.

"We think she can," Jessika answered, "but Hawkwind is in front of her. They'd have to back up all the way out and switch places."

"I was worried about that," Thornwing mentioned. "I barely fit so it'll be difficult for them. I'd best go fetch Lanisala. She'll have to dismount for Wind and Joy to fit through, and she shouldn't be walking."

Vor and the others stood aside so the male griffin could pass, but he balked at the tunnel entrance to let Pirossa and Craduticus emerge. Breeka followed in a limping shuffle behind them.

"What's happened to all of you?" Craduticus barked at once.

Frimillin repeated the explanation, and the old mage gave a heavy sigh. "Unfortunate, but all is not lost."

"I know how to remove the anklets," Rikah reported, standing up from his examination, "but I need pliers, preferably two pairs, and I don't suppose we have any."

"There was a blacksmith's shop in the city above," Ramikar said. "I can go see if there were any left behind."

He headed up the tunnel, following Thornwing.

"I hope he can get around the griffins," Vor muttered, a vision of him crawling on his belly between their feet suddenly in her head.

"I," Iyai stuttered, "I should go with him."

She went as well, close on Ramikar's heels. A few moments later, Thornwing came back with Lanisala perched on his back. Vor graciously helped her down near where Pirossa had gone to sit.

"Tell me about these invaders," Craduticus requested as he moved to find a dry rock to sit on. "And what happened to you, Tessa?"

He'd noticed Master Himes, who was leaning back against a wall with Dello close beside her. The improvised bandage was soaked through with her blood.

"After they caught and immobilized us," Dello spoke up quickly, "one of them had a big tirade about how we were all evil. Since my master is a teacher of apprentices, she said she was the most evil, and cut off her wizard's mark. There were too many of them, and they had knives, and I couldn't stop them."

Craduticus's face creased in concern. "That is unfortunate, but I am most worried about the bleeding."

"It's a big, shallow cut," Dello muttered. "It took off a lot of skin."

"Once those chain things are off, and you all have your magic back, we'll address the injury. For now, tell me more about the invaders."

So Frimillin and Dello took turns recounting what they could, with Master Himes staying mostly silent. Vor thought that the two men were doing a fine job and so had little to add. Instead, she went to see how Pirossa was doing, and found the young lady in considerable pain, her left arm badly swollen and hot with what was probably wound fever, but there was nothing she could do other than sit with her and wait for everyone to get through the tunnel so they could move on.

After perhaps an hour, Iyai came back down the tunnel with Ramikar behind her. Each carried a few blacksmithing tools and presented them to Rikah.

"I think some used to have wooden handles," Ramikar said, "but they must have rotted away."

"Hm," Rikah grunted as he sorted through the selections, "maybe these will work."

It took some experimenting, and Rikah needed a second pair of hands to help hold the chain, but then he was able to pry open a link from Ramikar's anklet and then the magic-blocking jewelry was off.

"See," the young man explained, "every link is just a little bar of metal curved into a circle, and there's a seam. If you twist the ends in opposite directions, you can make enough of a gap to get the neighboring link off."

Rikah moved on to Frimillin's anklet while Ramikar went up the tunnel. Shortly after, Vor sensed Earth magic moving, and a moment after that, a shudder went through the rock—identical to what they'd felt before. All the mages felt it and paused in their actions or conversation, even those still wearing the anklets.

"It happened again," Frimillin mumbled.

"What did?" Rikah asked.

"That feeling," Iyai whispered, "like the rock buzzing."

"Sorry about that," Ramikar said as he came back down the tunnel. "It seems that I have that effect on this area. If I use any kind of Earth magic here, something resonates to it."

"You widened the tunnel then?" Craduticus assumed.

"I did, sir. The griffins can get through fine now."

Rikah had freed Frimillin and was working on Master Himes's anklet. Hawkwind, and then Hawkjoy, came down the tunnel, making the cave overly crowded.

"Shall we press on?" Hawkwind suggested.

"In a moment," Ramikar said. "There is a large cavern ahead, and it has an exit to the outside, but there might be some drakes in it."

"How many?" Hawkwind asked evenly.

"Seven," Ramikar said, "two adults and five juveniles, but they are nearly as big as their parents."

Rikah came to Vor to remove her anklet. All the others except Giri were free now.

"With eight or nine mages and three griffins, we might do alright," Frimillin said.

"I've no doubt we could get past them," Ramikar agreed, "but we were hoping the wounded could use the cavern for resting. If six of us mages keep going deeper, those remaining won't be able to hold them off."

"If it has an exit to the outside, then we can just leave," Jessika said.

"Maybe," Hawkwind nodded, "if the drakes aren't airborne outside. Plus, we can't all get out at once. Splitting the group leaves us all vulnerable. Griffins can't fight well with a rider."

"Lanisala can't run," Vor pointed out. "She'll need to be carried."

"I won't be of any use," Pirossa rasped. "I'm in so much pain, I can't focus enough to cast magic."

"Pirossa at least needs to get out," Craduticus emphasized. "She needs medical attention we can't provide."

"I'll go scout the cavern," Giri suggested. "We need to know if the drakes are there or not, and where the exit deeper into the caves is, so we know where to run to."

"No," Iyai said tremulously. "Let me go. I can veil myself almost perfectly. They won't catch me."

Vor was impressed. She'd heard of veiling—the ability to hide one's presence from sight, sound, even smell—but it was a challenging skill. Most mages couldn't do much more than blur their image or hide the sound of their footsteps.

Ramikar frowned slightly at Iyai. "Are you sure?"

"I'm very good at it," the pale young woman nodded.

He seemed concerned, but nodded solemnly. "I'll go with you to the end of this tunnel, so I can help if you get into trouble."

Iyai moved off with Ramikar in close attendance.

"Whether the drakes are there or not," Hawkwind began softly, "one of us griffins must escape with Pirossa. I'm the strongest and fastest, so I suggest it be me. I'll have the best chance of evading any airborne drakes."

"Without you we probably can't fight them off if they're in the cavern," Thornwing mentioned.

"We don't know if we'll have to, yet," Frimillin said. "Let Iyai come back and report before we worry about that."

"Lanisala should probably evacuate, too," Craduticus added.

The lovely dark lady scoffed. "What about you? You have to be carried also."

"If we can manage it, all the wounded and weak will go up," Frimillin affirmed. "Isn't that right, Master Himes?"

He turned to look back to where the master wizard stood against the wall, and everyone else looked, too. She'd been silent the whole time, but Vor thought she might have been whispering with Dello—or at least, Dello might have been whispering to her. She looked at them from eyes tainted with pain and sorrow, but her jaw was firm and her posture stubborn.

"We have to stop these rogue mages," she said. "Everyone willing to fight should stay. If we have to, we run past the drakes. Master Craduticus, Lanisala, if you want to get out and have your injuries tended to, then perhaps a griffin can carry you. If you stay, or can't manage to escape, maybe you can find somewhere to wait, or do everything you can to keep up. We can't really plan until Iyai returns."

They settled in as comfortably as they could to wait.

Iyai returned an hour later with Ramikar at her side, looking tired but accomplished.

"I located the exit down at the back of the cavern," she began, "but it isn't easy to find. There are lots of other little dead end tunnels and caves. I will have to show everyone."

"And the drakes?" Master Himes asked.

"I didn't see the adults, but the five young ones are there, in a hollow near the back."

"It's not going to be safe for the wounded to wait in the cavern, not unless we kill all the drakes, and I'm afraid we'll take more injuries and wear ourselves out if we try it," Master Himes proclaimed. "Iyai, can we get past the hollow with the drakes without them seeing us?"

"I don't think so. A few were sleeping and the others were grooming when I went past. It's also getting near sunset outside. I don't know if that means they will sleep or not, but when the light fades, we'll have to use lights of our own, and they'll probably notice."

"Drakes use sonar for echolocation," Frimillin said. "They have no trouble flying at night or detecting us in darkness."

"We should go now," Master Himes directed. "Pirossa on Hawkwind, and try to escape. Lanisala, will you stay or go?"

"I'm not that badly hurt," she insisted. "My leg is healing. I want to stay."

"Master Craduticus?"

"I'll be staying as well," the old mage said. "I must protect the princess Jessika."

The princess whirled on him. "But I want to escape," she declared. "Joy, will you take me out?"

The griffin twitched, started to respond, and then hesitated, looking around at the group for consensus, and then to Hawkwind.

"At most, only three can go," Hawkwind said. "There are only three of us. Maybe we can come back for more, but with so many drakes, I think it will be unlikely."

"If Jessika goes, so do I," Rikah said firmly.

The princess whirled on him now. "Do as you like," she told him, "but I have to get out of here."

"Keep your voice down, please," Frimillin urged.

"I have to get out," Jessika repeated, only slightly quieter. "I can't stay down here. I don't care about Weldom, or this city. There's no food, no light, and everyone," she made a helpless gesture to Pirossa and Lanisala, and then again to Master Himes and her blood-soaked shoulder. Her voice went tight. "Everyone is going to die."

Vor huffed a breath out her nose. "And I always thought you were braver than I."

Jessika turned on her. "You're a mage," she accused. "You'll be fine."

"Like Pirossa and Lanisala and Master Himes are fine, you mean?" Vor retorted. "Or maybe you mean like Master Craduticus, who almost got dragged into the maw of a tentacular sand beast? Not to mention that all six of us who went ahead—all mages—would have been left to die if it hadn't been for Thornwing rescuing us, so don't go thinking we're invulnerable because we can toss some magic around. But go, why don't you? You've been the least useful member of this group."

Rikah frowned at her, but didn't argue. Jessika, however, opened her mouth as if about to start shouting or crying.

"Vor, really," Craduticus scolded softly, and Jessika pulled back, keeping her words in.

The cave fell quiet. Vor squirmed inside at Craduticus's scolding, but didn't think she'd lied. Maybe, she admitted to herself, she could have said it more tactfully. Jessika sniffed and swallowed, and then nodded.

"You're right," she whispered. "I'm dead weight to all of you. That's another reason for me to leave."

"Get Pirossa strapped onto Hawkwind," Master Himes interrupted softly. "She can't hold on very well by herself."

Ramikar, Iyai, and Frimillin turned to the task, while Rikah convinced Jessika to step away into the opening of the tunnel they'd come down through.

Giri gave Vor a conflicted look.

"That was accurate," he muttered to her, "but—"

"But not very nice," Vor muttered back. "I know. Cosseting her hasn't been productive. I thought maybe a prod would get results, and I let my own frustration color my words. Maybe it wasn't the best thing I could have said."

She looked over her shoulder. Jessika had her arms crossed over her chest, hands on her own shoulders, facing Rikah but not looking at him. Vor strained her ears to eavesdrop on them.

"I should never have come to Weldom," Jessika was whining. "It's useless. No one listens, and now I'm trapped down here. I can't do this, Rikah. There are things down here."

"Princess Jessika has never given up," Rikah replied gently. "You've always faced every challenge."

"But I can't. I'm so afraid."

Rikah gave a little shrug. "You want Joy and Thornwing to fly us up? We can go. We can send help. Maybe the ministers will be grateful and—"

"They don't listen to me," she hissed back. "They ignore me, but I'm the princess of Northnest. They have to listen to me. I'm royalty. But they don't, they won't. They say there is no Northnest, so I'm not a princess."

"Well," Rikah said slowly, "I probably shouldn't be agreeing with them, but maybe they are right. Perhaps Northnest is gone. Perhaps you're not Princess Jessika anymore."

Jessika made a sound as if she'd gasped with horror. "Of course I'm the princess," she spat back. "I should be the queen. Princesses become queens."

"You were the princess," he emphasized carefully. "I'm not denying that, but your father isn't a king anymore. He was, but the kingdom fell. He's no longer in power. That makes you not a princess anymore."

Jessika spluttered. "How can you say that? No, I'm—"

Vor snuck a look back and saw Rikah take her hands. Jessika made only a token twitch of protest.

Rikah spoke softly. "Maybe the princess wants and needs to be the princess, but what about Jessika? What about Hawkwings?"

"What about—?"

He didn't give her a chance to argue. "Maybe that's why it's hard to be brave right now. Maybe you know the princess is just a shadow now: a shadow that is fading, that no one else sees anymore. I see you clinging desperately to being the princess. Have you ever thought about just being you?"

Jessika shook her head. "But that's who I am. I am the princess. What else is there? What else can I do? I'm nothing without—"

Rikah shrugged, his expression softening into a little smile. "I'm not a princess. I manage."

Jessika frowned, brow pinching, and seemed to look closely at him, as though she hadn't seen him before. "You're—"

His smile widened and he shrugged again. "What? What am I? A commoner? Wings, how have our lives really been that different? Sure, you were born in a castle, and I in an ordinary craftsman's house. For a few years we each lived differently, but both with the same child's wonder for the world, with loving families, without caring what we supposedly were. And since the invasion, we have been the same. Hawkwind rescued us both. We both grew up in the Hawk Line, eating the same food, in nearly identical rooms, being treated the same way. The only difference is in your mind."

Jessika stared at him for a long minute. "So what are you suggesting I do? Give up?"

Rikah shook his head. "They won't let you win, the ministers. I can see that. So can you. The princess can do no more than she has done. She's fought hard, but she's fading and everyone knows it."

"Then what would you have me do?"

Rikah leaned a bit closer to her. "Go back to Northborn. Be with your father. Be his daughter. Be yourself. Start with that, and go from there."

Jessika narrowed her eyes. "You called it Northborn."

He nodded with no trace of regret. "That's what it is now. Northnest is passed. We all have to let it go. It's Northborn now. Weldom will probably take that name away, too, and call it something else, since it's going to be just another part of Weldom soon. If you keep holding onto it, you will sink and disappear along with it, but if you let go, you can float and find your way to the shore."

Vor thought that would be a hard pill for the princess to swallow, but after a few moments she seemed to get it down, and some of her scowl faded.

"And what's on the shore?" Jessika asked. "What's waiting there for me?"

Rikah rubbed her hands gently "Well, your friends, for one, your family, for another—both your families actually. You've got a father. Plus, all the Hawks love you, and most of the Thorns and some of the others, too. I know Joy misses you terribly, and Wind is fretting herself to pieces over you, even if she doesn't show it. You know, Rain is in the same place as you, trying to see what his future holds." He paused, took a breath, as if steeling himself. "And there's me."

They stood looking at each other. Rikah shifted his weight, but having taken the leap he couldn't help but complete the fall.

"There's me." His voice cracked and he swallowed to clear his throat, taking several moments to do it, while Jessika stood suspended and waited for him. Finally, he got the words out. "Wings, I've loved you since we were kids."

Jessika's eyes widened, but Vor didn't think she was truly shocked.

"I know you miss Koki and I'm not asking for anything except your friendship," Rikah went on quickly, voice lower, "but know that I'm waiting on the shore for you, too. I'll always be waiting on the shore for you."

"Today's been full of confessions," Vor breathed, quieter than anyone could hear. "Is it something to do with mortal danger in haunted caves that brings them out?"

Giri had gone to help finish strapping Pirossa onto Hawkwind, so he wasn't nearby to hear her anyway, but Vor saw Craduticus watching the pair in the tunnel from the corner of his eye. The old mage seemed pleased. Rikah was still speaking, but he was leaning closer to Jessika now, and Vor couldn't hear him anymore. She saw Jessika give a little nod to something he said.

Then he leaned back. "You don't have to be the princess to be brave. Hawkwings can be brave, too. Or look at it another way. You say princesses become queens? Well maybe it's time you did that. Maybe you're not queen of Northnest, but there are other ways you can embody what it means to grow from a princess into a queen."

Jessika took a deep breath. "Do you think we should stay down here?"

"What do you want to do?" Rikah said. "If you close your eyes and ask yourself what you want—."

"Of course I want to leave," she replied at once. "But maybe we should be helping?"

Craduticus sat up straighter. "Jessika," he summoned. "You're in danger down here, and I have sworn to protect you. The best thing I could do is encourage you to leave. Take the griffins and go up. Don't land until you find someplace safe outside the city."

"But what about you?" Jessika countered, apparently not upset that he was listening in on their conversation.

"I will protect you by making sure these disgruntled common-born mages do not destroy the city."

Rikah and Jessika both seemed to think about that for a minute, biting their lips and eyeing each other uncertainly.

"You should go," Master Himes added, coming over to stand by Craduticus and glare at the pair of non-mages. "Now that we know what we're facing, we can't waste energy trying to protect you from other mages."

"It is possible that there might be ways we can help," Rikah offered, "like how I knew how to remove those ankle chains."

"More detriment than benefit, I'm afraid," Master Himes said. "I'd like you to get on Thornwing and Hawkjoy and go with them, please."

Jessika clenched her jaw, but then nodded, and tension ran out of her shoulders. "Alright. Let's go, Dare."

Rikah nodded, too, and went to Hawkjoy to begin getting on. He was the heavier of the two, and Hawkjoy was larger and stronger, which left Thornwing for Jessika's mount.

"I will miss your companionship," Giri said to the male griffin as he began helping Jessika strap herself on.

"And I yours," the griffin replied, "but we shall meet again."

Vor meanwhile went to Hawkjoy to help Rikah, handing him straps and tightening buckles on the female griffin's harness.

"Vor," Rikah said as they worked, "you should take some of my energy. You might need it, and I won't."

She raised an eyebrow his way. "Are you sure?"

"Not all of it, of course."

"You might consider giving it to someone who can't easily generate more," Vor said quietly to him. "Giri and I can make more together, but no one else is doing that."

"Oh." He blushed.

"I'll take it," Lanisala purred, stepping tenderly up on Hawkjoy's other side. The griffin eyed her with distaste and flattened her crest.

"You?" Rikah uttered. "Uh, alright."

"Give me your hand then."

Vor tried to keep a scowl off her face as Rikah set his hand in Lanisala's. The woman closed her eyes, Vor felt energy move, and Lanisala's lips curved in a pleased smile. After a few moments, just as Vor saw Rikah start to sag, Lanisala stopped pulling and opened her eyes.

"You are a strong one," she murmured, her thumb rubbing the back of Rikah's hand. "Your power fills me—"

"Enough," Vor found herself commanding. "He's with Jessika."

Rikah drew his hand away, and Lanisala looked across Hawkjoy's shoulders to smile at Vor.

"You are such a killjoy," Lanisala grinned.

"Excuse me?" Hawkjoy growled.

"Didn't mean you, darling," Lanisala laughed.

Hawkjoy clacked her bill at the lady wizard, who twitched, her smile fading a trifle. Lanisala took a few prudent steps back.

"We need to get moving before full dark," Master Himes called. "Griffins in front, Thornwing leading since he knows the way. You'll head straight for the outside exit. There's water falling in front of it, not a lot, but you will get wet so don't be surprised by it. Everyone else will follow Iyai to the back exit out of the cavern. No lights. Move as swiftly and silently as you can."

There was a murmured chorus of assent.

"Frimillin," Master Craduticus requested, "might I ask you the favor of letting Breeka ride on your shoulders?"

The hefty man raised his eyebrows, but then nodded. "I am probably the best able to bear the weight. Come up then, little one."

Breeka climbed the arm he extended down to it, and settled itself securely on his shoulders.

"Are we ready then?" Master Himes whispered.

Packs that had previously been on the griffins were shouldered by the fittest humans. Vor carried one, and so did Giri.

"Let's go," Master Himes directed.

Thornwing went ahead, and then Hawkjoy, and then Hawkwind. The humans filed after, with Vor and Giri in about the middle of the line. Iyai led the humans, with Ramikar behind her, and then Master Himes and Dello. Frimillin, Lanisala, and Craduticus brought up the tail. Without light, they wound their way through the tunnel by touch, headed again to the cavern of the drakes.

The cavern was dim—sunset was clearly in progress—but Vor could see the irregularly rough circle of the tunnel exit as a paler gray-green, mostly blocked by the people and griffins in front of her. Thornwing paused at the exit, everyone else pausing behind him. He lifted a hand up by his head and made a gesture. Hawkwind turned her head and whispered as quietly as she could.

"He doesn't see any drakes."

The wizards nodded back.

"May you have a safe flight," Ramikar breathed over Iyai's head.

Thornwing launched. Vor didn't see him hit the cavern floor, but he must have at some point, so he could pull in his wings to get through the opening into the ravine. Hawkjoy rushed after him, and then Hawkwind. Over the sound of the waterfall and other dripping water, Vor could hardly hear their claws on the rock or the rasp of their feathers.

When they were gone, Iyai crept forward with the others following, and began the descent down the rocky ledge. As Vor emerged onto the ledge, she saw a final flick as Hawkwind's tail feathers disappeared out the exit. She stepped carefully down the stair-like rocks and onto the damp floor of the cavern. Iyai was already heading surely towards the back, away from the exit to the gorge, towards more darkness and danger.

Vor began to follow Giri, Frimillin with his burden of bat-cat behind her. His feet scraped and slid on the slick stones, possibly because he was trying to balance the extra weight of Breeka. The group moved across the cavern floor, dodging pools and puddles by the faint shine of their ripples from drips of water.

Then came the shriek of a drake—from outside, where the griffins had gone.

Everyone startled, and hurried their steps. There was nothing they could do for the griffins or their riders, but an answering hiss came from ahead of them. Frimillin swore softly. The juveniles were awake. Iyai kept going, drawing a partial veil around herself, though what use that might have against the echolocation of the drakes was questionable. Vor gathered energy, and sensed the others doing the same, preparing to fight.

The cavern swelled out large like a belly, with hollows and tunnels of many sizes peppering both sides. The floor became more uneven, with broken dips and jagged teeth of stone poking up taller than even Dello, but Iyai led them along the easiest path. The hiss came again, and from the right, from a dark hollow wider and taller than a griffin's wingspan, came a questing drake nose in lime green. Iyai ducked behind a tall tooth of stone, Ramikar, too, but the others were strung out in a line and had nowhere to hide. They hurried to catch up.

The hiss became a raspy, eager growl, and two more heads—one scarlet, one a ruddy orange—poked out with the first. Vor was just reaching the tooth of stone when the lime green drake lunged forward with a snap. She released a blast of fire right in its face, and it shrieked in objection, pulling back. Frimillin sought shelter behind her, and Lanisala, too, wincing with each step. Vor couldn't see if Iyai was leading them on, or still hiding, but five juvenile drakes would be a lot for them to handle. Better to run, she thought.

"Onward," Master Himes commanded, unknowingly echoing Vor's thought.

The remaining two drakes of the clutch of five—one golden yellow and the other emerald green—crowded up behind the others, and though Vor had stung one, the others apparently weren't deterred. The scarlet one began scampering after Iyai and Ramikar, the latter of whom paused and sent a punch of flame much like Vor's into its face. She had to stop watching though, when the orange one made a feint towards her. The lime green one still seemed cautious, but the golden yellow crowded up beside its orange sibling.

"Come on, Vor," Giri urged.

She saw that Craduticus had made it behind the sheltering tooth of rock, so she slipped behind it, too, just as the orange drake darted its fangs at her.

"Remember, use lightning," Master Himes instructed.

The orange drake was following her around the rock and she backed away, obedient to Giri's tug on the back of her tunic, but not taking her eyes off the enemy. She readied a lightning strike—starting to build up the charge. Then the golden yellow drake came over the top of the rock. Giri shouted and Vor twisted, directing her lightning up at the yellow drake instead, just as the orange drake rushed her. Giri shot under her arm, hitting the orange drake with a quick spark that made it flinch enough that its snap missed Vor by a handspan.

The yellow drake squalled its displeasure, halting its advance and claws slipping on the jutting stone, but the less injured orange made a second strike. Only a sudden blast of lightning from behind saved Vor from getting bitten, and prompted a true scream of pain from the orange drake.

"Quit playing with those drakes and get moving," Craduticus ordered— the source of the lightning. "The others are getting ahead."

Frimillin had followed Dello and Master Himes, leaving Lanisala and Craduticus behind with Giri and Vor. With both the yellow and orange drakes now rethinking their decision to attack the mages, the group of four was able to move off together. Vor looked ahead and saw Ramikar holding off the scarlet drake with sparks of lightning, but each flash showed his face taut and weary, with sweat dripping. Vor recalled that his expertise was earth magic, while lightning was a combination of fire and air—which was not his speciality.

Then Dello stepped up beside him, said something, and Ramikar retreat- ed to where Iyai was waving for everyone, leaving Dello to take over the rear- guard. Vor and Giri let Lanisala and Craduticus go first. Both were moving more slowly, and the lime green drake Vor had initially scorched took interest.

"No, you don't," Giri growled, and sent out a strike of lightning, blasting it in the side.

Vor followed up with one of her own when his only made the drake pause. That was apparently enough for it, and it ran off, towards the exit into the ravine, wings smoking a little. Craduticus and Lanisala caught up to Master Himes, who had stopped, watching her apprentice spar with the tena- cious scarlet drake. She waved them on to where Frimillin and Ramikar had reached Iyai.

"Watch out," Giri cried, and Vor felt him send another lightning strike just as she spun around.

The yellow drake had charged them again, but Giri struck it directly on the snout and it hissed in pain and broke off. Vor hurried on, passing Master Himes with Giri right behind her. The master mage had started walking, slowly, keeping an eye on her apprentice, who was snapping off discouraging sparks at the persistent scarlet drake. Ahead, Vor saw that Ramikar must have gone ahead into the tunnel where Iyai had been waiting for them. Frimillin was directing Craduticus and Lanisala down the tunnel, too.

"Smack it a good one and be done, Traskitandi," Master Himes ordered.

The scarlet drake was stubborn and wouldn't back off for more than a couple seconds at a time, despite all the little lightning shocks it had taken. It was also very quick, so some of Dello's strikes had actually missed. Dello threw both hands forward, releasing two sparks at once and making the drake recoil. Then he clasped both hands over his head and Vor sensed him building the charge. The drake gathered itself to pounce, and Dello built more. It took a short step, another, and drew its head back for the strike, and still Dello built his charge. It leapt.

"Traskit—" Master Himes shouted.

Dello cast, blasting the drake with a fierce bolt mid-leap, and then had to scramble to get out of the way of its pouncing path. It nearly snagged him with its claws, but the drake had finally had enough. It landed in a smoking tumble and flailed weakly. After a moment, it gathered itself enough to stumble away. Dello staggered, and Master Himes strode to him and grabbed his shoulders.

"My stupid apprentice," she scolded. "It almost got you."

"But," Dello began.

"Timing," she went on furiously, now shaking a finger in his face, "and it didn't have to be that big. You do not have the energy to spare."

"But you said—"

"Get moving, and take some of this."

"Master," Dello protested weakly.

Vor figured she must have donated him some energy. The master mage passed him, heading for the tunnel Frimillin still guarded. Vor and Giri made it there first, entering the hole just wide enough for them to walk side by side. The walls were rough and pocked as though splashed by acid, but the floor was fairly smooth and coated with fine gravel. All of it was damp.

"The others are ahead, that way," Frimillin called to them.

Giri gave him a nod and they headed down the path—only to hear a frightened shout from behind them, followed by an angry yowl. Vor whirled, gathering power. The fifth drake, the emerald green one that hadn't entered battle yet, had knocked Frimillin to the floor and pinned him there under its claws. Breeka had gone flying and landed in a sprawl several feet down the tunnel. The drake drew back its head, snake-like, to bite. Dello shouted, waved his arms, and ran at the beast. It redirected its attention to him. Easily within its striking range, Vor had the sudden fear that she was about to see him killed.

She released a shock of lightning at the drake, Giri not a second behind her, but someone else got there first. A torrent of mixed fire and lightning, blinding white and furious fiery blue, in a beam as thick as Vor's wrist, hit the drake mid-strike and blew half its head away in splatters of steaming gore. It shrieked, writhing, and in an instant collapsed to the floor, twitching in death.

Dello had already been leaping away when the drake started to strike, which was probably a good thing, or his hair might have been singed by the magic. Master Himes all but ran to him this time, let out a string of colorful expletives referencing Dello's apparently worthless appearance, intelligence, personality, and parentage, and fisted her hands in his robes, shaking him with every word. Dello bowed his head meekly, but didn't look especially chastised. Vor checked on Breeka, but the bat-cat was getting up and putting its limbs in order; it didn't seem hurt. Giri went to help Frimillin get out from under the twitching body of the drake, and Vor joined him.

"You have my thanks, but I'm fine," he was protesting breathlessly.

The drake was only a juvenile, like the others had been, but it still weighed a couple hundred pounds. Once Vor and Giri got it off him, Frimillin lay for several breaths. Vor extended her senses towards the corpse, and since no one else was doing it, drew in the last of its fading life energy. If Giri or Frimillin sensed it, they didn't comment.

"Hit me and knocked the air out of me," Frimillin panted. "Clawed me a bit, too, but just little punctures from when it stood on me. I'm fine, really."

Giri helped Frimillin to his feet, where he stood, still breathing fast and shallow, a hand pressed to his ribs. Vor looked over towards Master Himes and Dello, where the former had apparently stopped haranguing the latter. In fact—Vor looked away. Master Himes had grabbed Dello in what was undeniably a hug, one hand pulling his head down against her uninjured shoulder. For his part, Dello didn't seem to know where to put his hands, but he wasn't resisting.

"Well," Frimillin grunted loudly, and Master Himes was suddenly by the drake corpse, giving it a kick or two.

"Looks like we have food," Master Himes said evenly.

"Food?" Vor echoed.

"The flesh isn't poisonous," Frimillin agreed. "Might as well."

Vor's mouth suddenly watered and her empty stomach clenched voraciously, even though roasted rainbow drake was not something she ever thought she'd find appealing. Craduticus came shuffling back to them, with Ramikar behind him.

"Got one, did you?" the old wizard nodded. "Good. We're all hungry. Nice shot, by the way, Tessa."

"I have a knife in my pack," Giri said, eyeing the body, "but it's not very big."

"Hold," Master Himes said idly. "Let's drag it deeper, to prevent attracting the others, or other scavengers."

Vor, Giri, Dello, and Ramikar each found a grip, and they dragged the slain beast down further into the tunnel, and Iyai and Lanisala came over to join them. Vor spared a few breaths to summon her salamander back, and it lit the way.

"This is far enough," Master Himes said after a minute.

"The way gets narrow," Ramikar mentioned, "so we'd have to stop soon anyway."

"Wizard Holstor, you have a knife? Anyone else?"

Several of them carried a blade—most mages did—but those who had been wearing their blades had lost it when captured by the invaders, who had taken all their weapons. Vor got hers out of her pack, as did Giri, and Iyai and Lanisala both had their knives. Between the four of them they cut into the muscular parts of the drake, not bothering to bleed or gut it. They'd leave all the remains behind and just take what they could eat. Ramikar found a flat shelf of rock and began stacking the drake steaks there. Vor volunteered herself and stepped up with her salamander.

"Cook these?" she asked of it, offering magical energy as payment.

The salamander wiggled in consent and set to work. Vor had a dark thought that she had paid the salamander with the very life energy she'd harvested from the dying drake, for the purpose of cooking its own flesh. As the first steak was cooked through, she handed it off—nearly burning her fingers—to Craduticus.

Breeka was with him, and had its eyes fixed on the meat. "Good food," the bat-cat declared.

The next steak went to Iyai, and then Dello, and eventually everyone had their hands full with a steaming steak. The meat was surprisingly tender, and richly flavored, almost to the verge of being rank, but no one was complaining.

They'd eaten little over the past day or two or three, or however long they'd been under the rock.

"Don't eat too fast," Master Himes admonished between her own eager tears at the meat. "It could make you sick, and make sure to eat the fat, too."

Everyone was so hungry, Vor doubted anyone was concerned about too much fat intake, and probably saw it as a bonus.

"Can we take some with us?" Iyai asked as she licked her fingers clean.

"Cook the skin, too, and wrap the meat in it," Craduticus directed. "Then it can be carried in the packs without being too messy. The scales on the outside should protect the packs. Here, Giri, help me with this."

Craduticus snagged Giri to drag him and his knife back to the remains of the drake. Vor cooked what she was given—or rather, the salamander did—and all the cooked meat that could fit was stashed in the packs. Leaving the offal for whatever scavengers lived in the caves, the group prepared to move forward again.

Iyai led the way. The tunnel did indeed narrow, so most of them had to turn sideways to fit through, or crouch down in places. It was just as well that the griffins had left; they would never have fit through the passage without some major magical rock sculpting. The way was mostly dry, although trickles of water did dribble down the walls in a few places—or onto the heads of the wizards.

As they passed a large version of such a trickle, this one closer to a stream and carving itself a twisting path through the rock, they emerged into a clearly chiseled out circular room several yards in diameter. It was empty except for a few random stones and some wreckage of fabric and wood and other detritus piled in one spot. The junk looked neither like the remains of a body, nor like anything useful. In the center of the room was a perfectly round hole just a little larger than the girth of an average adult human—another place the griffins would not have been able to pass without reconstruction. The whole group filed in, and then stood looking at the hole: the only exit.

"Down there, eh?" Frimillin said after a few seconds of everyone staring at it.

He slumped down to take a seat on the floor. The fine gravel from the tunnel was nearly sand here, but only an inch or two deep. A rim around the hole kept it from falling down into whatever was below. There was no rope, no ladder, no sign of how to get down through that hole, and no telling how deep it was. Iyai slumped down to the floor, too.

"May we have a rest, Master Himes?" the young mage asked. "I feel like I haven't slept in ages."

"And you just had a big meal, so of course you're sleepy," the master mage sighed. "Fine then. We'll rest a while before we go down, but then we must make up time. The invaders have a big lead on us now."

"At least," Ramikar offered, "they won't be expecting us to be following them anymore."

"That is true," Master Himes admitted. "Maybe that will mean they relax, slow down, and make mistakes."

In ones and twos the wizards began finding places to sit or lie down against the circular walls.

"Tessa," Craduticus summoned. "I have something to help your shoulder."

"Do you?" she replied warily.

"Show me the wound, will you?"

Her eyes narrowed. "Tell me what you have first."

"You'll have to trust me," the old wizard said with a little smile, and pulled something out of his pocket. It was rolled up like a little scroll and seemed to be dark green. Vor moved her salamander closer.

"That," Master Himes flinched. "That's fresh drake skin."

"Yes it is," Craduticus confirmed. "I'm going to lay it against your open wound."

"Excuse me?" she retorted.

Vor found herself widening her eyes, too.

"I know it sounds strange, but it will act like your own skin for a little while, while your body starts growing new. It's better than a cloth bandage."

She eyed him seriously. "Are you sure about this?" Master Himes growled.

"Yes, Tessa," the old wizard smiled. "I'm sure about this."

She didn't look convinced. "This will help?"

"It will help you heal. Wizard Traskitandi, will you unwrap her shoulder?"

Dello complied, ignoring the hostile glare his master aimed at him. The wound was still weeping blood, slowly but steadily. Craduticus lifted the drake skin to it, bloody side to her exposed muscle tissue, and pressed it in place. Master Himes gritted her teeth, and Giri handed Dello new strips of cloth to wrap the wound with.

"Ideally, we'd replace the skin daily," Craduticus said, "but you'll have to settle for a single treatment."

"I can't believe I'm letting you do this," Master Himes groused.

"Trust me."

"I do," she grumbled. "That's why I'm letting you."

"Now," he went on as Dello finished bandaging her. "There is the question of if you'd like a new set of marks. You do have another shoulder."

"I don't want to give those kids an excuse to cut up my other shoulder," Master Himes huffed.

"They won't get close enough again," Dello murmured.

Vor glanced at him. His gaze on his master's held the heat of a sworn vow. She was staring back at him, and after a few breaths gave a little nod.

"Master Craduticus," she said, "would you?"

"Gladly," he smiled.

Master Himes shifted her robes to expose her uninjured right shoulder, and Craduticus pressed his thumb there. She didn't even wince as he applied his mark. The other wizards in the room seemed to sense it, and looked over.

"Wizard Ramikar," Master Himes called when Craduticus was done. "Would you be willing to confirm me as a wizard?"

Her tone was slightly joking—as she had already been confirmed, decades ago—but Ramikar nodded amiably and came over to do as Craduticus had done. Frimillin stood up and rubbed his thumb on his robes, as if cleaning it off, but Master Himes shook her head.

"No, thank you, Frimillin, but I do not need your assistance," she said.

For a moment, the hefty wizard looked offended, but then he shrugged and quirked a smile before sitting back down.

Master Himes straightened her robes. "Two is enough for now. I'll get the others once we're back up top."

"Master," Dello mentioned, "I am more than willing to—"

"You're my apprentice, Traskitandi," she cut him off. "It's not appropriate. Wizards who are older, or at least equals, should be the ones to confirm and take responsibility for a fellow wizard."

No one argued with her. Vor certainly couldn't have given her a mark; she didn't know how yet. Well fed—perhaps overfed after days of famine— the group quickly settled down to sleep. Iyai had already stretched out on the sand, and most of the others were lying down to follow her example. Ramikar touched a loose rock on the floor, setting it to a very faint glow, but closed his eyes for sleep. Craduticus had gone and placed a ward over the tunnel entrance and the hole in the floor, enough to give him warning if anything approached. Vor dispelled her salamander from where she lay beside Giri.

From her position near the path in, she could see Master Himes and Dello still standing together in the dimness. Dello was making sure her new bandage was snug, but she brushed him off and turned to step away. Dello stepped around in front of her again, and Vor noted Master Himes's sudden change of posture in response. She was tall, but he was taller. Still, it seemed she was trying to stare him down. He said something that the little waterfall just beyond the doorway drowned out. They spoke for a few minutes, the music of the water covering their words, during which time both of them softened their confrontational body language.

Vor continued to watch their shadowy shapes through her lashes, too curious to see what was going to happen. Shortly, Vor saw Master Himes adjust her robes again, exposing her shoulder with the two new marks. Somehow Dello had talked her into it. Surely, Vor reflected, it must have been a one-of-a-kind event, for every apprentice would be matched to a master who had been confirmed as a wizard long ago, probably before their future apprentice was even born. Most likely, that master would give a mark to his or her apprentice. To have it be the other way around could happen only in a situation like this, where the master somehow lost her original marks and needed replacements.

Dello stood there for several long moments. Another surprise, Master Himes stepped in and rested her head on her apprentice's shoulder, and put her free arm—even though it was injured—around his back. Dello reciprocated, putting his free arm around his master's shoulders. Dello might not be able to tell what Master Himes felt for him by reading her aura, but Vor thought it was pretty clear she had been distraught at seeing him almost killed a short while ago, and trusted him enough to be vulnerable before him now.

Then Master Himes drew back a bit, and lifted her head up to look him in the face. Dello dropped his chin. Vor saw their mouths move, briefly, saying something. Dello took his thumb off her shoulder and tugged her robes back into place—but then he lifted a hand towards her face.

Master Himes took a swift step back, and his fingers touched nothing but air. "Go to sleep, Traskitandi."

The master wizard moved to an empty spot along one wall, leaving Dello standing by himself and vibrating like a plucked harp string. Eventually, he went to lie down, too, across the room from his master, and all was quiet.

Chapter 11
The Pit

When Vor woke, the circular room looked the same as when she'd gone to sleep, except at some point Iyai had huddled up against Ramikar, who was sleeping sitting up; and Lanisala, Craduticus, and Frimillin had also clustered together. The groupings didn't seem intimate, but more like scared animals finding security in company and numbers.

Breeka, however, stood alone in the center of the room. The bat-cat was peering down into the central hole as if mesmerized. Its tail tip twitched every few breaths. As silently as she could, Vor crawled over to Breeka. The bat-cat flicked an ear, obviously noticing her, but didn't object. Vor still wasn't sure just how intelligent the bat-cat was, but Craduticus spoke to it like it was another human, so Vor did, too.

"Do you know what's down there?" she asked.

Breeka bared its cat-like teeth. "Same," it said. "Same all places. It waits ahead. It follows behind."

Vor tried to interpret the simple sentences. "Something followed us here and now it's waiting down there for us?"

Breeka just bared its teeth again, briefly. Vor figured that meant yes.

"What is it?" Vor asked.

Breeka tipped its head and scrunched up its face as if it didn't know. "Big, old," it said.

Vor tried for more detail. "Is it evil or good?"

Breeka nodded firmly. "Yes."

Vor didn't dismiss the answer as nonsensical. After all, most entities were a mix of both—humans especially. She didn't think whatever Breeka was talking about was a human. In Vor's brief experience, Breeka tended to show petty disdain for most humans, but the way the bat-cat was behaving now reflected both awe and fear.

"Do you think it plans to hurt us?" Vor asked.

"Not yet," Breeka said simply.

"What do you see down there?" Frimillin interupted, coming over to kneel by the whole as well. "Horned demons, maybe? Or spine-leeches? What else did that dead mage up at the top write he'd seen?"

Breeka hissed at him. "Stupid man."

The bat-cat limped over to Craduticus and crawled into his lap.

"Don't be bothered by Breeka," Vor said politely, though she disliked Frimillin's flippancy. "It treats everyone like that."

The rest of the mages began waking. Someone dug out a drake steak from a pack and they all tore pieces off for a quick bite of—breakfast? Vor had no idea what time it might be. They had traversed the drake cave around dusk, so they must have slept at least part of the night, but whether they'd awakened after a brief rest in the pre-dawn hours or slept on to noon she couldn't tell. Her head was proclaiming it hadn't slept properly in a week. She ached physically, both from the hard floor and exertion. Plus, she discovered her foot felt bruised from where the drake had bit it yesterday. It hadn't broken the skin, or any bones—probably because she was wearing sturdy shoes for travel—but it hurt to walk on now.

"We're really going down there?" Iyai said tremulously.

"Yes," Master Himes replied in a voice that brooked no argument.

"But how will we get down? There's no rope," Iyai mentioned with great hesitancy.

Frimillin nodded. "It looks like there might have been a ladder here, or something, a long time ago, but it's gone now."

There were indeed a few little punctures in the rim that might have once held bolts, and scratches that could have been caused by a ladder. Craduticus waved a hand over the hole, removing the ward he'd placed there, and everyone peered down into the utter darkness. There was no shortage of shivers from the assembled wizards.

Master Himes frowned down at the hole as if its very existence was an insult to her. "How's everyone's levitation?"

"I've never levitated," Vor confessed at once.

"Wizard Holstor can do you."

Lanisala snickered and Vor resisted the urge to roll her eyes at the woman.

Then Giri gave a little cough. "I can't say I'm very good at it either." When Master Himes turned incredulous eyes on him, he protested. "It's not an easy skill. You're telling me you can move enough air to make yourself float?"

Before Master Himes could unleash whatever response she had to that, Vor spoke up again. "I have, however, prevented a fall from killing me before. I could probably do it again."

Master Himes gave a half-reluctant, half-impressed nod. "I suppose that would do."

Vor took a steadying breath. "Do you want me to go first?"

"First," Iyai interjected, voice breaking, "I mean, before you go, will you tell me how to do that? How to land safely?"

So Vor tried to explain, and it ended up that the other mages chimed in with their techniques and thoughts, turning it into an impromptu levitation and falling clinic. Vor demonstrated the basics by just jumping in place, and others copied her or modified to fit their strengths, so soon enough everyone—even Iyai—expressed at least a timid confidence that they would be able to land without dying.

"Alright then," Lanisala said smoothly, "since you're the expert and you said you would, you're going first, right Miss Hearthsraven?"

Giri gave her a subtle but anxious look, but Vor wasn't about to back down in front of Lanisala—which was probably what Lanisala had wanted.

"Alright," she replied, perfectly calm, at least outwardly.

No one objected, though it might have made more sense for an older and more experienced wizard to go first—not one who hadn't yet even been granted the title. Vor thought maybe Ramikar would be a good choice; after all, he'd levitated the door. She knew perfectly well, however, that he'd had an advantage since the door had been stone, and he was strong in Earth magic. Plus, it had been an object outside of his body. Levitating one's own living body was a bit different.

Vor went back to the hole, which they'd all moved away from in order to practice jumping and landing, and summoned back her salamander. With a gesture she sent it down into the hole, and knelt to see what its light would reveal. The other mages crowded around, too, to get a peek. Vor did what she could to keep her jaw from dropping open.

First was a long tube—the opening in the floor just continued downward, though a bit wider than the initial hole itself. It was perhaps ten of Vor's own body lengths, but it was difficult to judge exactly. After that, the space opened up; she could see the edge where the tube ended. How big the chamber below the tube was, she couldn't tell. All she could see at the bottom was some kind of surface, textured, she thought, and probably pale in color because the red salamander light made it somewhat pink and reflective.

"I can't tell what we'll be landing on, except it's neither water nor a smooth floor," Vor confessed, "and it's a long way down. That's two or three times the distance I survived falling in the past."

She felt Giri grip her shoulder, but he didn't tell her not to go first. It was true that she had survived a fall that would have killed her before, from the top of the multi-story Feathyr barracks back in Northborn. However, she knew there was a terminal velocity any falling body would reach if it fell long enough, and she didn't think she'd reached it that time. This fall was longer than her previous fall. By the time she hit the floor she would be falling faster than she had before, so the impact would be harder. She began to worry if the magic she'd used to save herself before would be enough this time.

How had the Magic Liberation Front invaders made the descent? Possibly they'd had a rope, but there was no rope here now. Maybe one of them had jumped down with it once everyone else had used it, whoever was best at levitation or making magical soft landings.

"I might suggest," Frimillin spoke up, "that you inch your way down the tube with your feet and hands on the walls, and only drop when you reach the bottom of it."

"That's a great idea, thank you," Vor told him fervently.

The tube was small enough for that, though it wouldn't be easy—but at least going down that way would be easier than if she'd had to climb up like that instead. Vor took a deep breath, trying to keep fear from making her tremble, and sat down on the rim of the hole, swinging her feet in. Her foot throbbed and reminded her that it wouldn't like this. It probably wouldn't like the landing, either.

She called her salamander back up to her and instructed it to pace her as she worked her way down. She gripped the rim firmly, and was about to lower herself in when she felt her magestone ring pulse.

Vor stopped, and looked at Giri. He'd sent the pulse pattern she still remembered from their months apart. "I love you." His face was grave where he knelt just behind her. Vor smiled, leaned over, and gave him a quick kiss.

"It'll be fine," she said. "If you can give me an updraft, maybe it will slow my fall."

Then before he could hold her back, she gripped the rim tightly with her hands, slid her hips off the rim and into the hole, and carefully extended her arms, lowering herself inside. Nothing immediately leapt up and grabbed her. Her salamander stayed by her, lighting up the walls. She could tell now that they were made of shaped and mortared stones, the same color as most of the underground rock.

Where some parts of the journey had been through rough or natural caves and tunnels, and other parts looked carved and smoothed, here the inhabitants must have made the tube and finished it with fitted stonework for aesthetic purposes. At least the regular rectangular shapes—many with crumbling mortar between them—provided easy traction, she just hoped they weren't so old they were going to fall off with the pressure of her hands and feet, or she might be dropping down sooner than expected.

Vor got her feet secure against the walls, and one at a time transferred her hands to the walls, too, and then adjusted her feet lower, and then her hands, and again, and again. The tube wasn't wider than her arm span, thankfully, but it wasn't much less than it, either. That did allow her to lock her arms one at a time, which made the going a bit easier. Several feet down she encountered a spot where, as she'd worried, a patch of stones had fallen off the wall, but the rock behind was rough enough that she still had traction.

As she went further, broken patches became more common, and she noticed herself stretching more to reach the walls with her arms. The tube was gradually opening—not a lot, but enough to make it more difficult. The taller members of the group would have no trouble, but Iyai and Giri might struggle a little. It was actually good that Pirossa, the shortest of the bunch, had been sent out with the griffins, not that she could have made the climb with her injured arm anyway.

The missing stones became more and more common, so that soon there was more bare rock than stone-covered rock, and Vor was struggling to keep traction. She wasn't quite at the bottom of the tube, but she didn't think she could make the descent any further without slipping. She'd have to drop regardless, but she'd rather take a moment to get ready for it and prepare her spells, than be surprised when she slipped.

One spell was to put a dense column of air where she landed, to slow her. The other spell was to soften the floor where she landed, so it was like hitting a mattress instead of hitting rock. Doing those two things had prevented her from breaking bones when she fell off the Feathyr barracks. She was older and more experienced now; she hoped she could do it better than she had before.

She peered down again, even though it gave her adrenaline a kick, to try to see again what the floor was like, now that she was closer. She was hoping for no spikes, rocks, or slavering monsters. Vor found herself squinting, wondering if she was seeing what she thought she was seeing. She sent her salamander down—and caught her breath.

The pale, textured floor was no floor at all. It was bones: piles of bones. They were human sized, and she could pick out human skulls. She guessed this was where the people above had dumped their dead. The round room above must have been ceremonial. That was the only explanation she could come up with. Drakes living in the caves above certainly wouldn't have made an effort to drag the remains of their kills here, and as far as she could tell, she saw only human bones, which were uncommon prey for drakes. There was no smell of rot, however, so these were old enough for all the flesh to have dried out at least.

And she'd be landing on them.

"Maybe it'll be gentler than a solid rock floor?" Vor muttered to herself dubiously.

But how to cushion a fall on bones? Could she use the same technique as she would with dirt or rock, or even a wooden floor? Vor extended her senses down towards the pile below her, but it was too far away. She instead decided to address the bones she had nearby—her own. Vor closed her eyes and focused. The biggest difference would be that her bones were full of water. The bones below were dried. Take away the water and what was left was—

"Earth magic," she breathed, "like stone, minerals. Like falling into a pile of lighter weight stones."

In fact, if she could just decrease their weight a little with some air magic—she had to go soon. Her arms and legs couldn't keep her suspended much longer and were starting to tremble. Vor's heart pounded as she took slow breaths, concentrating, drawing on her stores of energy, calling on the air around her to condense. She couldn't levitate—but hopefully she could slow her fall.

Vor took a final breath, and let go.

The tube rushed past her for a bare second, and then she was free falling through the open chamber, her salamander still down below so she could see the piles of bones racing up towards her, and she wrapped her air magic around her feet, keeping her from falling much faster. With another application of will, she sped her power, as fast as thought, to the bones below, trying to make them soft with earth magic, and fluffy with air magic. She crossed her legs tightly, hoping none of the bones would get between them when she hit, which—male or female—could hurt considerably.

Her feet smacked into the first bones with a shock that jarred her whole body and she choked on an exclamation, but instead of breaking her feet, her magic worked. Skulls, ulnas, femurs, parts of spines, and even pelvises, went flying as she plunged into the pile, magically lightened and softened so they were more like autumn leaves than bones. They still lashed at her, bruising her body through her clothes, smacking her jaw and forehead, and they closed above her as she sunk into the haphazard mountain of remains.

At last she slowed and stopped, whole and safe, but all around her were bones, old and yellow and brown, some cracked or broken, a few still articulated with dried out ligaments. Her spell wore off, and they returned to their natural weight and solidity. Vor tried to move and found them settling around her, fitting themselves to her shape as if accepting her into the pile, prepared to sit another thousand years with her inside.

Vor's courage fractured a little. Logically she knew she wouldn't be left in the pile. Giri—if no one else—would come find her. But death stared at her from every side: her future. One day, she too, would be nothing but bones like these. And it was dark down there; her salamander was above the pile still. She called to it and it wove its way between the bones to her, hovering inside the bowl of a pelvis above her right shoulder.

She had to climb out, but the weight of the bones above her crushed her down. She couldn't even move her arms more than a wiggle. Her heart pounded hard. She had to get out, and panic started to rise in her head. Vor struggled, but it only seemed to make the bones settle more tightly around her.

Then came a sharp, bright pulse through her magestone ring: Giri.

That gave her pause, and she forced herself to stop for a moment, to try to get a handle on her racing emotions. She could still breathe. She was alright.

"Safe?" he sent.

"Wait," she replied, actually a pattern they had used before to say they couldn't talk yet, but she hoped he'd understand she meant "do not jump yet."

If someone jumped down on top of her before she could get out, there would likely be injuries. She thought about yelling, to try to communicate what had happened, but didn't think her words would be intelligible up at the top of the tube. Just to be sure, she sent the pulse pattern again to tell him to wait.

"Think," she scolded herself. "You're a mage. Magic yourself out."

There was no possibility of dematerializing—though she supposed if she were good at teleporting she could have done that, if she'd had a chalked out departure and arrival rune circle, except she'd never teleported herself before. She hadn't even started learning to teleport small animals yet. Maybe she could have teleported the bones above her someplace else—but doing so many would exhaust her—and why was she still thinking about teleporting when it wasn't a viable option? She shook her head a little and kept her breathing steady.

There were, however, a few other options. She could have her salamander burn the bones above her to make way, but that would be a lot of bones, all the cinders would fall on her, and she'd only summoned a lesser salamander, not a greater—which she wouldn't do for several reasons. She could try the spell she'd just used, making the bones light and soft like autumn leaves again. She'd have to be very careful where she applied that spell, though, or she might make herself sink deeper into the pile, and it was difficult to make it last more than a couple seconds.

Another option she could think of was to blast the bones away. If she built up a good charge, a blast of wind or even fire or lightning would do it. Fire or lightning would risk hurting herself, though. Wind then, she'd try wind. Just as she started to concentrate, she heard a frantic flapping sound and the impact of something smaller than a human on the bones above and to her left.

"Hello?" she tried. If that was who she thought it was—

"Bad girl is stupid," Breeka hissed.

Then the bat-cat began digging away the bones. Vor immediately sent her salamander up to provide light.

"Breeka," Vor praised. "Thank you. You've saved me."

"Bad girl be quiet."

Vor obeyed. The bat-cat was not big or strong—not much bigger than a large house cat—but the bones weren't heavy one by one. Only en masse did they become a problem. Vor could hear Breeka dragging them away one at a time, and though it took several minutes, Vor then was able to look up through the remaining bones and see Breeka working, using the finger and thumb on its bat-like wings to grab bones one at a time and fling them away, or dragging them off with its jaws. The weight on Vor's head and shoulders lessened. She shifted her arms and was able to open one from where she'd had it crossed over her chest.

Now she could push the last of the bones away, and begin to dig herself out, as Breeka stepped back to watch, panting from its efforts. Within a few more minutes, Vor levered herself up and out of the pit of bones. They shifted under her feet, and she moved on all fours to get out from under the hole in the ceiling.

"That got a little frightening," she told Breeka. "I'm glad you thought to come down here and help me."

Breeka bared its teeth and said nothing. She began filling the pit back in, restoring the surface of the bone pile to something more level.

"The next person to come down, I can help cushion, so hopefully they won't plunge deep like me," she said.

Vor sent her salamander up to signal that the next person could go, and additionally sent a confirmation pulse through her ring to Giri, conveying that she was safe now. She sat down on the bones a few feet away from the place she'd landed to wait. Breeka stayed close and kept looking around, occasionally baring its teeth and switching its tail. Without the salamander, which was guiding the next person down the same way it had done for Vor, the bone pit was dark. Distant salamander light caught only the top edges of the bones.

For Vor, she was just relieved to no longer be trapped under and among the bones. Sitting safely atop them, even in the dark, didn't bother her much. Gradually, the next jumper reached the end of the tube. It looked like Ramikar. Despite her comfort, Vor was still wary about raising her voice to call out, but felt she had little choice.

"I'll help," she called, and left it at that.

She gathered power and began building a column of dense air, to make Ramikar fall slower. After a few moments, he dropped, and Vor poured in power. He too, plunged into the bones, scattering some, but only up to his waist. Vor helped pull him out.

"That was terrifying," he said simply.

Vor sent her salamander up for the next person and signalled Giri. Frimillin came down next, and between Vor and Ramikar, he had a safe landing. Iyai came next, then Dello, and by then the mages dropping had so much help that they practically did float down. That was a good thing, since Craduticus came next, and he might not have survived a harder landing. Giri followed, and Vor took a moment to hug him tightly. Being trapped under a ton of human bones in a dark cave underground, alone, was probably an experience that would come back in her nightmares.

Lanisala dropped next, getting carefully lowered because of her leg injury. Last came Master Himes.

"You're alright then, Wizard Hearthsraven?" the master mage asked bluntly.

Vor blinked for a moment at the title, but managed to answer. "Yes, thank you, Master Himes. Breeka dug me out. I did get trapped under rather a lot of bones."

"That must have been unpleasant. I commend you for your bravery in going first."

Vor bowed her head a little at the praise, but was more interested in looking around now that everyone was safely down. The mages cautiously spread out, walking carefully over the shifting piles. Vor sent her salamander in a circuit around the walls. The room was a couple dozen yards in diameter, circular, like the smaller room above. The walls were lined with rectangular openings just a few feet wide and less tall, each only a handspan away from the next to the sides and above and below. The walls were packed with them to the ceiling. In a few places, they had collapsed on each other.

"This was their mausoleum," Master Himes whispered.

"So those are all—?" Dello began, pointing at the holes in the walls.

"Crypts," she nodded.

Frimillin turned a skull over with his toe. "I'm guessing they filled the crypts, so just began dumping their dead down the hole, instead of coming down for a proper ceremony."

"Any idea how deep these bones go?" Ramikar asked.

"We can find out," Giri said swiftly. "Over here. I think the invaders, or someone, dug down to a door."

Ramikar helped steady Craduticus, and the group picked their way to one side, where indeed the bones had been excavated into a trough shape and piled even higher on either side. Master Himes led the way, slipping down a steep incline of bones that got more dense and crumbly and brown the deeper she went. The remains looked to be piled around twenty feet deep, but at the bottom, between more revealed crypts, was a skinny dark doorway, no wider than the crypts themselves.

"I wonder how they knew to dig here," Dello mused.

Master Himes raised an eyebrow at him. "They didn't have to know. The wizards who came before, who set the key, would have done this excavation."

"Of course," Dello revised. "I'd forgotten. Then, I wonder how those wizards knew."

Vor looked around. It was a good point. Even the squared archways—not much more than narrow, slightly decorative grooves in the walls—over the packed crypts were identical at a quick glance.

"Perhaps there was some indication in the piles of bones that we can't see, now that they have been dug up," Ramikar offered. "Or perhaps they just dug randomly until they found it."

"However they did it, it seems there is no doubt where they went," Frimillin said.

"Another place the griffins couldn't have fit through," Vor muttered.

Master Himes cautiously approached the black doorway. Dello slipped and slid down the bones to join her and she didn't even give him a quelling look. Ramikar began to follow, with Iyai tagging along behind him.

"There's no door," Master Himes murmured, "just the opening. There are some bits of bone that have fallen inside, but not as much as I would have expected."

"Maybe the old wizards, and the invaders, cleared them away," Dello suggested.

"Do you want my salamander?" Vor asked softly.

Master Himes made a negative gesture, so Vor instructed the creature to stay close to her. She began to follow Iyai with Giri at her back. As she approached the doorway, she flared her nostrils, detecting a new scent over the odor of old bones.

"Water, and something else, something foul," Master Himes breathed. "Douse that salamander."

Vor invited the salamander into her jacket, where it made a warm spot by her collarbone. The darkness swallowed the group, and Vor felt her eyes begin to strain to adjust. The only sound was the old bones shifting under feet as the others began following them down into the trough. After a few minutes of waiting, Vor began to be able to detect the pale bones versus the medium gray wall and the black doorway, so there must have been some light source somewhere—maybe just whatever ambient light made it all the way down from above. Master Himes began easing forward into the doorway.

Vor heard her toss something, and a faint light appeared ahead, a bone fragment spelled to glow, revealing narrow intersecting hallways of dark stone that shone faintly as though they were damp. Guided by the light, Master

Himes took a more confident step forward and the others began to follow her in. The ceiling was low, and the walls in there were indeed wet when Vor put out a finger to gently touch, and they felt textured, like they might have once been covered with carved designs now worn away by water. It was a few paces until they reached the first intersection. Master Himes glanced down the cross halls.

"They turn," she murmured, "both of them, after just a few feet."

"Split up?" Dello breathed.

"Stay with me," she told him. "Ramikar, left. Giri, right."

Master Himes passed the first intersection with slow and measured steps. Ramikar turned left, and Iyai followed him. Vor was in front of Giri, so she turned right, with Giri behind her, and let her salamander peek out of her jacket to provide light. The hall did indeep turn promptly, to the left, paralleling the central path down which Master Himes and Dello still presumably moved. Vor found herself holding her breath, tensing in anticipation of menace. Her steps got shorter. She could sense Giri's prickling energies behind her.

"I feel it, too," he whispered. "There's life down here, but it's cold and slow."

Vor could see nothing moving, just the damp, lightly carved, dark grey walls. They inched along perhaps ten feet before she saw another cross path. Vor cautiously led the way into it, looked to her left, and saw Craduticus and Breeka in the central hall. They paused to look over at her. This time the hall continued to the right as well. Beyond Craduticus, Ramikar appeared where the cross hall ran all the way to the hallway he'd been exploring with Iyai.

"This is an expanding grid of halls and cross halls," Vor observed.

"We might assume symmetry, and that this central hall runs through to the exit, but it's impossible to say for sure until we've explored all the way," Craduticus said.

"Nasty place," Breeka remarked, where it was walking gingerly by its master.

"Why don't you turn and explore the perimeter?" the old mage suggested.

Vor nodded and turned right, though it would take them further away from the wizards taking the central hall. She felt Giri take her hand. The hall turned left again, still at a perfect right angle, to make them again parallel the central hall. Another ten feet and there was another cross hall.

"They laid these out very mathematically," Giri said. "I wonder why."

Vor paused, Giri stopping behind her, and she looked more closely at the inner wall, one of the long, rectangular blocks of stone formed by the cutting out of the grid-like halls.

"Maybe these aren't solid," she whispered. "Maybe they're storage, or more tombs."

Over however-many centuries, the water had deposited minerals all over the walls, the same way water formed cave formations like the stalactites and stalagmites and rippling curtains of rock in natural caverns. The mineral deposits had obscured what Vor thought was carving. If there were doors or seams, they'd been sealed over. She kept walking.

They turned again, and stopped. Stones had fallen from the ceiling, partly blocking the hall, and letting in a stream of water. As the salamander light moved over the scene, Vor saw movement, not rapid, but languid and pervasive. The walls seemed to be moving—no, crawling. She heard Giri draw a breath in disgust.

"What are those?" he breathed.

Sluglike, as long as Vor's forearm, the same dark grey as the walls but shiny with slick skin, creatures of some kind slowly rippled their way away from the light. They seemed to be clustered around the running stream, which had made a large puddle on the floor. There must have been a few dozen of them. Vor couldn't tell their tail end from their head end. They were more flattened in shape than tubular, and seemed to have a sort of skirt of flesh around their edges where they met the floor or wall. Some had paler freckles along their sides or backs.

"They don't look good to eat," Vor commented, "but at least they don't appear dangerous."

"They could exude a contact poison. I've read about slugs and salamanders—your garden-variety salamander—that do that to discourage predators," Giri mentioned.

"I don't intend to touch them," Vor assured him. "But let's not go that way."

"I agree."

The puddle of water stretched into the hall, a couple inches deep, and ran off in the direction they were traveling. They tried to skirt it as much as they could, and get to where it ran along more thinly. As they went, they saw a few more of the slug-like creatures along the edge of the floor. These ones shied away from the light, too, so they must have had some way of detecting it even without obvious eyes, but Vor noticed that when they fell into shadow, instead of flinching away, the end that must have been the head actually quested towards her and Giri.

They continued trying to take the farthest perimeter path, but began encountering more and more water seeping through the walls or dribbling from cracks, until rivulets of it coated the floor. The gray slugs were plentiful in such areas, and Vor was able to get consistent behavior from them depending on whether they were in light or shadow. The creatures began to give her a crawly sensation she disliked intensely, and she made sure none of them got near her.

Eventually there were no more right turns away from the central path. The overall grid of intersecting halls appeared to be quite symmetrical, as Craduticus had thought. They began to make left turns inward, and unfortunately all the water was being funneled inward as well, until there was no escaping it and they walked through a few inches of it, soaking their shoes. Gradually, that brought them back to the straight central hall that Master Himes and Dello had been following. They exchanged nods.

"Nothing out of the ordinary?" Master Himes asked.

"Except that we don't know what's ordinary down here," Vor replied.

She looked down and kicked away a questing slug. They were moving easily through the deepening water.

"I don't like these things," Master Himes commented, nudging another away from where it seemed about to start climbing Dello's ankle.

Ramikar and Iyai appeared across from Vor and Giri, looking a little uneasy, but also uninjured. Frimillin, Lanisala, Craduticus, and Breeka were accumulating behind Dello.

"No sign of the invaders, then?" Frimillin summed up.

"They must have gone onward, as expected," Master Himes confirmed.

The water wasn't rushing, but definitely flowing, through the exit doorway. A few mages had made softly glowing lights, and Vor still had her salamander, although it was acting agitated at all the water around it. The other light sources reflected off the water and sent dancing glimmers against the walls. Vor followed Dello as his master moved through the doorway and into a narrow hall. After several yards they reached stairs, where the water cascaded down in tiny waterfalls. The steps were worn almost to a ramp by the passage of the water over however many years it had been passing this way, and everyone had to go carefully or risk slipping.

Then the hall opened into a square room perhaps ten feet wide. The water filled the room wall to wall. Something dark was floating on the surface, and Vor sent her reluctant salamander forward and followed Dello into the room. Behind her Iyai whimpered, and Vor felt a bit like whimpering, too—or possibly vomiting.

"So we found one invader," Master Himes said.

The dark shape was a drowned body, but more than that, the slugs were moving slowly, almost tenderly, over and into it. The bloated flesh rippled where the creatures had burrowed under it, making it look like the corpse was alive and moving.

"That is profoundly nauseating," Frimillin commented tightly, "but no more than the scum deserves."

"Look out," Lanisala said suddenly, slapping at the water.

Vor turned to see that the tall lady mage had just smacked a slug that had been investigating Ramikar's legs. The water was deeper now, halfway to their knees.

"My thanks. There's a lot of them in here," Ramikar remarked, "no doubt because the food is here."

"Where's the exit?" Giri asked. "I don't see any doorways out."

"Down there," Master Himes pointed. "The steps keep going down. The way forward is flooded."

"So the invaders tried swimming, and at least one didn't make it through," Frimillin said.

"And the others," Vor added, "could also be dead, trapped under there somewhere, if there's no exit. If this just keeps going down and down, then this is the end of the journey."

"I'm not sure if I like that thought or not," Dello commented.

Iyai suddenly stepped forward, extending her hand to gesture away a slug, which complied with remarkable docility.

"I'll send a minor undine," she said. "It will tell me if there's an exit."

"That would be useful, Wizard Iyai," Master Himes nodded.

She bent to put her fingers in the water, and a few moments later a ripple and a flash of pale green skin indicated her success. The little creature—an odd blend of human and fish and no longer than Iyai's hand—flickered in the various glow lights. Vor sensed Iyai pay the little elemental with some energy, and then the undine swam swiftly away, disappearing into the gloomy water across the room. Meanwhile, Vor dismissed her salamander with a thought, already suspecting that it could not make the next stage of the journey with her.

"We're going to have to swim," Ramikar murmured, "provided there's an exit beyond that isn't flooded. Can all of us make such a swim?"

His hooded eyes slid subtly towards Craduticus and Breeka.

"If only we had a rope," Dello said. "One of us, the best swimmer, could swim through and anchor it on the other side. Then everyone else could use it to help pull themselves through."

"Yes, but seeing as how we don't, Traskitandi, any other suggestions?" Master Himes retorted.

Vor chilled, and not just because she was nearly up to her knees in cold water.

"What is it?" Giri asked her softly.

"I have never swam," she answered. "I just never had the opportunity to learn."

She felt him put a hand on her back, no doubt meant to be encouraging.

"I can swim well enough," he whispered. "We'll go through together."

Then a flash of pale green announced the return of the water sprite, and Iyai knelt, extending a hand into the water, and the undine made its report to her.

"There is a way through," Iyai relayed. "It sounds like these stairs go down a ways, a long ways, but part way down there's a shaft that goes up. She says it's smooth, made by humans. If we go up that, there's an exit to a place with air."

"But is that the way the invaders went?" Master Himes asked. "What happens if we keep going down instead? Is there another exit down there?"

"She says there are more human places down there, but no air," Iyai reported. "The water drains into cracks and crevices that we can't fit through."

"What if the key is down there?" Master Himes persisted.

Iyai silently queried the undine again.

"It didn't sense powerful magic down there at the bottom," Iyai said. "She also says there is the stink of humans in the water, probably from the invaders passing through, and it goes mostly up the shaft, but she didn't see any humans."

"It sounds like that shaft is our path," Ramikar commented.

"There are other rooms on the way," Iyai went on. "She thinks we might get lost."

"Can she guide us?" Master Himes asked. "And how far is it? Can we even hold our breaths long enough to get there?"

"The invaders must have," Frimillin pointed out, "except one of them."

"Undines swim much faster than humans," Master Himes grumbled, "and some of us are probably not the best swimmers."

"I can summon a selkie," Iyai offered, just a little hesitantly. "It could help tow us through, one at a time."

The older mages all levelled firm glares at Iyai, and Vor could guess why. She'd read about selkies, but never seen one. They were not as powerful as greater elementals, but they were capricious and could be difficult to strike a bargain with. They didn't tend to violence, but to put oneself in a selkie's care underwater could be dangerous. It would take little effort on the selkie's part to drown the mage so foolish as to trust it.

"I have a good relationship with water elementals," Iyai insisted. "I've summoned selkies before. They've always done what I asked."

"And will they be so kind to those of us with more fire in our natures?" Lanisala suddenly spoke up.

"I'm a strong swimmer," Dello proclaimed. "I grew up in the lakes and rivers around the Traskitandi estate. Pay your minor undine to guide me through. Then I'll swim back here and report on how easy or difficult it was, and we'll have a better idea of if we'll need extra help."

Master Himes eyed him. "How do we know if the invaders didn't all require help? It could be too far for you."

"You know I'm not a slouch with water magic, Master," Dello replied evenly. "I can give myself some extra propulsion if I have to."

"That may be easier than levitation but it's still going to exhaust you, especially if you have to do it three times—going, coming back, and then going again."

"Someone has to try it, Master," he insisted. "Give me some energy if you're so concerned."

She scowled up at him, and then darted a hand out to grip his shoulder. After a few breaths, she let go and turned to face the watery stairs. Iyai had apparently given further instruction to her minor undine, because it swam over to float in front of the tall mage's feet.

When Dello hesitated, Himes barked at him. "Well, get going. The invaders are pulling ahead while we stand here debating."

Dello shed his outer and inner robes—down to a lightweight tunic and drawers—and handed them to Giri. "Just for the first trip, I want to be as agile as possible," he said.

He began stepping down the stairs, deeper into the water, and Vor saw his pale skin turn even paler and pimple with cold.

"Don't die," Master Himes said suddenly.

Dello smiled a little, walked on into the water until it was up to his chest, and dove, the minor undine going with him. Then a few dozen of the grey slugs that had been poking around the floating corpse but not actually eating it, darted after him with surprising speed.

"Shit," Master Himes cursed.

She drove her hands into the water, and a second later a bright ball of light streaked after her vanished apprentice. When she stood back up, everyone was looking at her.

"They hate light, right?" she growled, as though they had questioned her actions.

"I hope it doesn't alert the invaders to his presence," Frimillin mentioned.

"I know," she snarled at him, and then repeated her curse under her breath.

Pacing was a waste of energy when the water was so deep, but Master Himes seemed to give the impression of it by rocking back and forth on her feet and periodically hissing through her teeth or cursing again.

"He's been gone too long," she declared after several minutes had passed.

"It seems like it's been longer than it has," Ramikar soothed. "Give him time to recover from the swim on the other side. He'll be back."

Master Himes just made a growling noise in her throat.

"Tessa," Craduticus spoke up, "do you feel that he's died, or is in any danger? You've shared magic; you will sense it. Use your head, girl."

Master Himes took a few deep breaths and appeared to force herself to calm down. "I think he's alright."

"See?" Craduticus smiled gently.

Vor glanced at Giri. "You think he can make however-long this swim is?"

"He is a good swimmer," Giri replied. "He wasn't lying about that."

Then a glow began below, got brighter, and then Dello burst up out of the water, clawing at his back. Almost everyone leapt forward to help, ripping slugs off him and pitching them against the walls with brutal force. Dello collapsed into a seat on the stairs, the water halfway up his torso, panting. His tunic seemed to have helped somewhat, but there were a few holes in it now, and a few places on his back, near his spine, where his skin was bloody.

"They have teeth," he coughed out. "Only the light kept them from completely mobbing me." He gazed up at his master, strands of bright blonde hair plastered to his face. "Thank you."

"Of course," Master Himes gritted out.

"These must be the spine-leeches that the dead wizard wrote about," Lanisala suggested.

"Whatever they are, we'll all need bright light to keep us safe," Dello rasped.

"Can we all make the swim, do you think?" Frimillin prodded.

Dello rubbed water off his face. "Iyai for sure, with her penchant for water magic, should have no trouble. It is a long way, but you can push and pull yourself along using the walls as well as swimming. One good deep breath is enough. Giri, Ramikar, Frimillin, my master, can probably make it. Vor, if it were just swimming you might have trouble, since you haven't swam before, but you can use the walls, so probably you'll be fine, as long as you can stay calm. Wizard Salasis, how's your leg?"

Vor looked over, and saw Lanisala looking a bit nervous.

"I can make it," she said through a clenched jaw.

"But I'm not sure I can," Craduticus confessed. "In my youth, it wouldn't have been a problem."

"Should I summon a selkie for you?" Iyai asked.

"Even if a selkie could pull me through in time, I'm not sure Breeka can hold its breath that long."

The bat-cat was riding Frimillin's shoulders, since its weight was too much for Craduticus now, but it didn't flinch.

"Master mustn't worry," Breeka said softly.

"Let's start making the journey," Master Himes directed. "Everyone, remove your robes, or outer clothing or whatever, to make the swim easier. Wizard Iyai, will you summon a selkie to bring through the bundle of clothes and packs?"

"Yes, Master Himes," she complied, and put her hands in the water again, beginning to chant softly.

"There are rooms along the stairs, as the undine said," Dello informed, "but they are all in the walls. The shaft up you're looking for is in the ceiling. Just roll over in the water, belly to the slanting ceiling, and swim down it until you reach an opening. That's what you want. Turn into it and climb up. You'll emerge in a pool in another chamber. I got out long enough to get the leeches off me, but I didn't look around, and no one else was there."

"I'll make the swim," Ramikar announced, handing his robes to Giri, who apparently was the official robe-gatherer now, because everyone was giving theirs to him.

"Put your light on your back," Dello suggested. "My master's went straight for my chest, so my front was lit up, but they seemed to like my back."

"Perhaps that is just because that area was in shadow and available, because your lit front was towards the ceiling," Ramikar remarked, and when he finished his spell, his under-tunic glowed in its entirety.

Without another word, he descended into the water, took a deep breath, and dove. The slugs, or leeches, made pursuit, but gave up the chase after only a moment, probably because of the glow.

"Wizard Salasis," Master Himes summoned, "you can do this?"

She'd stripped, too, down to her tunic and leggings, which only confirmed Vor's early assessment that she was elegantly proportioned. She handed her robes to Giri with a smirk, but he averted his eyes.

"Not like you've never seen it before," she purred.

"Get in the water," Dello ordered.

"I'll manage," Lanisala replied to Master Himes, ignoring Dello.

She moved with apparent fearlessness into the water up to her neck, performed a light spell identical to Ramikar's, and sank out of sight. By then, everyone else had stripped down to their undergarments and Giri was trying to bundle the outer clothing up with their packs inside. Vor helped, knotting sleeves and trouser legs until the bundle wouldn't come apart. Vor glanced over as Iyai made a sudden gasp, and the water stirred.

"Frimillin, get going," Master Himes directed, and the hefty wizard passed Breeka to her before taking his dive. "Dello, go ahead again whenever you're recovered."

Craduticus, Giri, and Vor approached behind Iyai, who was now sitting on the stairs with water up to her chest. Vor had never seen a selkie before, and illustrations of them in books she'd encountered had been vague. This creature—elemental—was beautiful.

Its hide was amber and brown, freckled with pale green on its belly and deep forest green on its back. In length it was as long as Vor was tall, but its fins made it look bigger. Its tail was wide, flexible, but also apparently strong, and webbed. It had pectoral and dorsal fins, too. Its neck was short and muscular, and its face a sweet combination of puppy and fish, with large eyes and a profusion of whiskers. Its ears were tiny flaps behind the bend of its jaw, which was deep set, so when it opened its mouth, Vor could see a fearsome set of sharp teeth. Iyai was trembling with cold now, but the selkie nuzzled up against her like a loyal dog.

"Will you have it take the bundle of robes and pack first?" Master Himes asked gently.

Iyai nodded wordlessly as Giri set the bundle in the water. Swiftly, the selkie snatched the bundle in its teeth and vanished into the depths.

"I'd rather not swim while that's in the water," Dello whispered. "No offense intended, Iyai, but just in case."

"Of course," Iyai breathed back.

"Master Craduticus, will you trust yourself and Breeka to it?" Master Himes asked.

"We've little choice," the old wizard replied.

He'd shed his robes, too, and Vor was shocked at how thin he looked in his undergarments. She knew he'd had significant injuries in the past few years, including spending some time in a magic-induced coma. Those injuries, plus his age, had clearly taken a toll on his body.

"I hope those who have gone through already will have the robes dried by the time we all get over there," Vor commented.

Craduticus gave her a raspy chuckle. "Not to worry. I am perfectly capable of drying and warming my own robes."

The selkie reappeared, floating languidly to the surface and swallowing one of the grey slugs, or leeches, or whatever they were, with apparent relish. Craduticus came to sit by Iyai, and Breeka dropped into the water to swim awkwardly over to him. Iyai petted and praised the selkie, and then sat for a minute with it, apparently introducing it to the old mage and the bat-cat. At last, it allowed Craduticus to give it a pat, and then he eased down into the water and embraced the selkie around its shoulders, before the pectoral fins. That left its powerful tail free to propel them along. The pair floated to the center of the pool, over where the stairs descended under the water. Craduticus took a deep breath, and the selkie dove, pulling him with it.

"I hope this works," Master Himes muttered.

Breeka had been left behind. It would go on the next trip. Vor just hoped the bat-cat could hold on. The selkie had no hands to grip it.

"After Breeka goes," Master Himes went on, "does anyone else think they'll need the selkie's help?"

She glanced at Vor in particular, and Vor sensed Giri's concern, too.

"I would hope I can make it on my own," Vor said.

"How about if you go with me and the selkie?" Iyai suggested. "The rest of you are confident of your swimming, right?"

"That's an excellent suggestion," Master Himes said.

Vor nodded. "Alright. We'll go after Breeka, correct?"

The selkie returned then, snacking on another grey slug. It tossed it up playfully, caught it, and swallowed. Iyai gave it a minute to relax, letting it come to her when it was ready for its next task. She helped Breeka take hold of the elemental, getting its wings wrapped all the way around its neck and helping it hook its thumbs and fingers together. Breeka was also able to hold on a little with its feet.

"Take a deep breath and hold it," Iyai told Breeka.

For once, the bat-cat did not have a snappy response. Instead, it looked terrified, and did as commanded. Iyai tapped the selkie, which immediately dove.

"I hope Breeka can hold on," Dello muttered.

"Vor?" Iyai asked.

She came to stand next to the pale young lady.

"I think you should go in front of me and the selkie, so we can see if you need help. Just go as fast as you can, but try not to panic. Hurry, but don't rush."

"I understand," Vor replied.

She felt Giri squeeze her shoulder and appreciated the comfort. She focused on staying calm, keeping her heart slow. She trailed her fingers through the water, thinking watery thoughts, and put a glow on her tunic, to hopefully discourage the slugs—though since the appearance of the selkie, they were keeping their distance—and to provide her with some light, since she'd need to be able to see where to put her hands.

While they waited, Vor got further down into the water to practice submerging herself before the actual swim. The water was cold, and pushed on her from all sides. She took a breath and ducked under the surface for a few seconds. Opening her eyes hurt a little as the water hit her eyeballs, but she decided she could tolerate it. What she didn't know was how long she could go without a breath. She practiced moving herself about with hands and feet, pushing herself along the stairs, but that was still in the shallows.

She surfaced and faded the direction they'd be swimming in—down and down and down. That she'd never swam at all before—much less navigated through underwater passages—suddenly seemed like a major hole in her education. She took a deep breath, let it out, and then took another. Getting her body to do the thing it was petrified of—diving down into unknown darkness full of water—now seemed impossible.

"Let me go first," Giri spoke up. "Vor, you can follow me, then Iyai and the selkie."

"Why has no one invented a spell to allow humans to breathe underwater?" Vor groused softly.

Giri took her hand under the water and drew her deeper.

"We're going to swim for that wall—actually the ceiling of the stairwell," he said. "You're going to go head down, not feet down, with your hands on the wall. Try it just a bit. Just go down and touch the wall, and then come back up. I'll go first."

So Giri took a breath, dropped under, and positioned himself head down, towards the stairwell. He stayed there a moment, and then surfaced.

"Your turn," he told Vor, with a little encouraging smile. "You can do this. Just down for a moment, and then come back."

"Just for a moment," she nodded.

So she took a breath and sank under. It took her a little flailing to figure out how to get herself head down, and she came back up.

"Let me try again," she said at once.

The second time was easier. She did it once more, and this time stayed under for a few seconds. She surfaced and rubbed water from her face.

"You're doing well," Giri told her.

Then the selkie returned. It seemed agitated, and went straight to Iyai, who stroked it.

"Something happened, but the selkie can't tell me what exactly," Iyai reported. "It doesn't appear hurt."

"Let's get going. Maybe whatever it is, we can help," Vor said.

"Alright then," Iyai agreed. "After you. Get a big breath before you go under."

Vor nodded. "I'm ready."

The selkie made a loop around her, and she extended a hand, but didn't touch it. Instead, she let the elemental come close on its own. It nosed her fingers, and then swam so it got a pet along its back.

"Alright," she said. "Let's do it for real. Giri, you should probably go as fast as you can, because I'll be scared and probably going as fast as I can, even as I try to stay calm."

He squeezed her hand. "Got it."

"We'll be right behind you," Iyai added.

"I'm going then," Giri said.

He stepped forward, took a deep breath, and sank under. Vor didn't hesitate, following right behind him, took a breath of her own—straining her lungs to full capacity—and went under. She gave a push off the steps with her legs, rolled over, and reached for the slanted ceiling. She could see the glow of Giri ahead of her, already moving steadily down the incline. Vor followed, kicked her feet, and discovered whether trying to pull herself along the ceiling with her hands or use them to swim with was faster for her. She ended up doing a bit of both, since her natural buoyancy kept pushing her into the ceiling.

By the time they reached the turn and she saw Giri make the corner to begin swimming upward in the air shaft, her lungs were tight and burning—but there was no going back, and the rise to the surface would be swifter than the descent. She made the corner, beginning to feel her throat clenching, and was relieved to see that the rougher air shaft had better hand holds than the smooth ceiling.

Fear began rising. She needed to breathe. Vor pulled herself along as fast as she could, and began letting a thin stream of bubbles escape her lips, which provided some relief, but she knew that once her lungs were empty, they'd scream for a breath in. Up ahead, she saw Giri pause for a second, and then keep swimming. She was closer to him now, almost in range of his kicking and pushing feet. Her lack of air burned, but she couldn't go faster because he was there and the air shaft just wasn't big enough for her to pass.

She slapped his foot. Then as she watched him through the murk and haze of panic she thought she saw a dark shape partially obscuring the glow of his tunic and hose. She couldn't imagine what it was. It didn't matter. All that mattered was that she needed air or she was going to pass out. Terror was flooding her mind. How much farther could the surface be? She'd been swimming an eternity. She needed air.

Then a slick swift body slipped into her weakening arms and she grabbed on. With strength born of desperation she hugged the selkie's neck and it shot her up, knocking hard against Giri—who had for some reason stopped swimming.

And then the pressure of the water came off her face and neck. Her skin chilled and her ears cleared, and she gasped in the biggest, sweetest, best breath of air she'd ever had in her life. She immediately coughed, hacking and gasping though there should have been no reason for it. Hands grabbed at her shoulders. She was blinking water from her eyes as she was pulled roughly onto stone, scraping her skin through her underclothes.

She felt Giri pat her back, and she realized why he'd stopped swimming; he'd reached the surface. The air shaft had opened up into the room, at the bottom of a pool of water a couple feet deep. Now, the other mages had pulled her out of the pool, to where the rock slanted up. There was a lot of hushed but urgent talking. Someone was asking her if she was alright, but Vor was still recovering from her coughing fit and could only nod.

Iyai climbed out beside her, trembling and dripping water. The selkie had nearly beached itself behind her. Vor reached out and patted its head, offering some of her energy in payment for its help. It accepted, absorbed the gift, and nudged Iyai's foot. Iyai didn't seem to have the strength to turn around and give it a farewell pat; the elemental just vanished into a slosh of water when she silently dismissed it.

Vor wrestled herself around so she was sitting instead of lying, and took a look around the cave—for a cave indeed it was. Someone had lit a rock to glow and the light shimmered on the water. There was the sound of trickling water, either into or out of the pool Vor couldn't tell. The cave seemed natural except for the air shaft full of water, but it was not a perfect hermetic globe. Tunnels, holes, and crevices peppered the walls, some only big enough to stick a finger in, others large enough for a cat to crawl through, and a few large enough for humans. The floor was slanted down towards the air shaft, and everything was covered with rock formations from all the running water. Vor felt bad for sitting where she was, on a beautifully rippled shelf of stone that circled the pool, but she had little choice.

Besides Iyai, the other mages were all gathered where Giri had hauled out.

Giri seemed fine, on his knees still half in the water, so she focused her hearing to listen and realized what the problem was.

"Flip it over," Frimillin was saying urgently. "Hit its back. Yes, like that."

Then she saw what the dark shape that had blocked some of Giri's glow had been, and why he'd paused for a second in the swim, and how she'd caught up to him. Vor's throat choked for a different reason now. The gathered mages were frantically trying to resuscitate Breeka, who Giri had found floating in the air shaft and pulled out with him.

"I see," Iyai breathed. "The bat-cat must not have been able to hold on or couldn't hold its breath long enough. That's why the selkie was so upset. It couldn't have taken it to the surface without biting it, and apparently it chose not to because I told it not to hurt Breeka. I'm so sorry."

"We knew this could happen," Vor whispered back.

Master Himes broached the surface, gasping for air, and Vor swam out to help guide her to the shelf around the pool. The master mage seemed to have made the swim well enough, and recovered quickly with only a little coughing.

"Can you help?" Vor asked her. "It looks like Breeka drowned."

Master Himes slogged through the water to where the others were trying patting, slapping, little shocks of magical lightning, heat, and whatever other magical aids they could think of, and started trying to assist. Giri moved over to where Vor and Iyai sat, getting out of the way.

"They're doing far more than I could," he mumbled, but he remained watching, probably following what they were doing the same way Vor was.

Dello broke the surface next, with almost casual style and grace. He saw Giri and Vor, swam over, and Giri told him what had happened to Breeka.

"Poor little mite," the tall mage lamented. "I worried it wouldn't make it. Iyai, are you alright? Let's find the clothes and get them dry."

"I'm really tired," Iyai admitted, "and cold."

"We'll dry the clothes and everyone can get warm," Dello insisted.

Vor stood and located the nearest dry flat space. Giri and Dello found the water soaked bundle of robes, and they began untangling them while the others kept working on Breeka.

"It's been too long," Giri muttered. "If Breeka hasn't come back by now—"

Then a raspy coughing, gurgling, hissing hit the air, and all turned to see the bat-cat thrashing weakly and spitting up water. Vor, Giri, and Dello shared relieved smiles and put themselves to separating the soggy clothing.

"I think I might have the most power left, so I'll dry them," Giri said, "but wring them out first, if you can."

Vor and Dello did as he said, and Iyai got up and came over to help also.

Frimillin joined them, now that Breeka was back in the realm of the living, and began sorting out the packs, shaking out water, and seeing what was ruined. Vor glanced over and saw that Ramikar was holding Breeka now, with Craduticus using his magic to warm the bat-cat up and dry its fur. The old wizard, too, looked bedraggled. His sparse hair was pasted to his head, showing age spots through it, and his wet under-robes clung to him, revealing even more than before how skinny he was.

"Do Craduticus's robes first," Vor whispered to Dello, searching through the pile.

He helped her find them and after wringing them, passed them to Giri. They went after Iyai's next, since she was beginning to shudder with cold even as she tried to help. Vor paused to put her hands on the younger mage's shoulders and send heat down through her underclothes, helping to dry and warm them. A few moments later Giri was able to hand over her clothing and she found a dry spot to stand to get dressed.

Dello switched to helping Giri heat the robes since they were wringing them out faster than he could dry them. Lanisala came over to help Vor, and Iyai began carrying dry clothes to the others. Vor eyed the elegant lady mage cautiously, expecting her usual ribald comments. Lanisala smirked at her, confirming Vor's expectation.

"Nice to see Giri unclothed again," the taller woman winked.

"Wizard Salasis," Vor said evenly, "can you please not?"

But Lanisala just chuckled. "You're not bad yourself, a little skinny, but I don't think that's the most important thing to him. Giri likes fiery women."

"I asked you nicely to keep your thoughts to yourself," Vor nearly growled, and twisted the current robe in her hands with all her strength. "Why do you do this?"

She gave a big satisfied smile. "See what I mean? I can see why he chose you."

Vor gritted her teeth. "He didn't choose me. I chose him."

"Come now. You must at least admit to a mutual choosing. I see why you like him, too. He's cute, isn't he? And he's got so much power," she purred.

Vor shook her head. "It's not about either of those things."

"You're telling me you'd like him just as much if he were some homely merchant or farmer, ugly and magicless?" Lanisala scoffed.

Vor eyed her with distaste, but even to someone like Lanisala, she didn't like withholding truth. "I do like doing magic with him. It's something we have in common."

Lanisala winked. "It's arousing, isn't it?"

Vor fought not to roll her eyes and mostly succeeded. "I am not talking with you about this."

But that seemed only to make the other more pleased. "Are you jealous? Jealous that another woman had him before you did? Jealous that I taught him things, that maybe he even had a better time with me than with you?"

"Enough of that," Vor did growl now. "It's irrelevant."

"It wasn't only me, either. Giri went through a period of searching, experimenting: call it what you will. Didn't you? Or are you too young yet? How many men did you have before Giri?"

Vor squared off against her: hating that she had to look up at the taller woman. Why couldn't she have had just a few more inches of height? "Lanisala Salasis, please desist."

Lanisala winked again. "Were you a virgin with him? Is that why he wanted you?"

Vor took even breaths, but her hands had fisted around the current robe she'd been wringing. What energy she had left began to heat. "No, and it doesn't matter."

Nothing she said seemed to get her to stop. Lanisala just shrugged. "You're quite taken with him, but you know this first blush of intoxication runs out eventually. Then you're left with boredom and it's time to move on. You'll get used to the pattern. Giri won't be your last."

Automatically, Vor felt herself jump to refute it. "He will."

Lanisala leaned closer, apparently ignoring the way Vor's energy was gathering. "Don't tell me you're going to marry him?"

Vor lifted her chin, wondering if perhaps she'd found a chink in Lanisala's armor. "Are you jealous now? Seems like there was a time he wanted to marry you and you turned him down."

But Lanisala gave a quick scoff, and turned away, to wring out some more water. "I could never have married into the Holstor House."

Vor sensed the shifting in the conversation, and pressed. "Why not? Is Salasis not a noble house?"

"It is," she snapped.

"You're young and beautiful and a mage. Your family isn't trying to marry you off?"

Lanisala twisted the garment she held, as strongly now as Vor had been twisting hers before. "That is none of your concern."

Vor felt her own tension lessen, her feet back on higher ground—she'd found something Lanisala didn't want to talk about. What a nice change of direction. "Sounds like we're both speaking of things that aren't our concerns.

Let's leave this now, shall we?"

"Hey," Dello interjected. "Any of those ready for drying?"

Lanisala pivoted and shoved her bundle into his arms.

"What have you two been talking about?" he asked, and then sardonically, "Do I need to separate you?"

"Go dry that, Traskitandi," Lanisala ordered. "I think it's your lover's, oh, no, I mean your master's robes."

Dello glared at her. "You're being more of a bitch than normal."

Lanisala bared her teeth. "Go drown yourself."

Dello spared a glance for Vor, but Vor wasn't worried. If Lanisala ever did come after her with magic or a physical attack, she wasn't sure she could defeat her, but she thought she could defend herself until she got backup. She gave Dello a quick grin, and he nodded and walked off. Lanisala watched him go, and then went for the pile of wet robes, but there were no more.

She scowled at Vor. "You'll learn, little House-less Hearthsraven. The shine rubs off. Don't think you're getting a happily-ever-after. No one gets that."

Lanisala walked up the slope, away from the water's edge, towards the dry area in the largest exiting tunnel where everyone had started gathering.

"Where's my robes?" Vor heard her demand.

Vor finished wringing the last garment. It actually looked like it was Giri's shirt, although in the low light it was hard to tell. Then she sensed him, looked over her shoulder, and there he was, still in his underthings.

"I think this is yours," she said.

"I dried yours," he replied. "They're up there. Are you alright? Dello says you and Lanisala were having words."

"The usual," Vor nodded. "She's just needling me about you because of her own frustrations."

Giri set a warm hand on the back of her neck, and it made her shiver.

"If you come out of the water, I'll dry you," he offered.

They walked up the incline, and Vor felt a wave of heat move through her.

"You're using a lot of energy," she commented.

"I'm alright."

"Tell me about Lanisala. She's House Salasis, but said she couldn't have married into your house."

Giri seemed to hesitate, and then stopped her before they got any closer to the others. He put his mouth by her ear.

"It's a secret, although the heads of most noble houses in the west know, but most of the other mages at the Citadel don't. She'd be furious if she knew you know. Lanisala is a bastard. Her father is now the master of House Salasis, but her mother was a maid in the household. Her father insisted on giving her the name, and since she turned out a mage, he sent her here, to be trained like any other noble brat, but he'll never be able to use her for an alliance marriage since she's not legitimate. Plus, he has three other true born heirs now. When I thought I was in love with her, I offered to marry her. I thought my parents would allow it, since they were so eager to see me wed. Lanisala refused."

Vor could sense him tremble within, and put a hand over his heart in encouragement.

"She left me and never came back." Giri took a deep breath.

"Thank you for telling me," Vor whispered.

"Let's get dressed. Not that I don't like what you're wearing."

Vor shot a look at him, feeling a smile tugging at her mouth. He suddenly leaned over and kissed her, and she didn't resist, so his hands went to her cheeks, and soon one kiss turned to more.

"I thought I loved Lanisala," Giri breathed when they parted for a breath. "I was wrong. I need you to know that."

Vor nodded, forehead against his.

"I was so scared when we were swimming," he went on, "that you wouldn't make it through. When we get out of here, I'm teaching you to swim."

She smiled. "Right, because we're likely to be in this kind of situation again where I'll need to know how."

"You never know," he shrugged.

"You can teach me to swim," she promised, "once we get out."

"Lovebirds," drawled a voice.

"Shut up, Dello," Giri called back.

"Keep your voices down," Master Himes ordered in a hiss. "And get over here and get dressed."

Chapter 12
The Caves

They gathered, dry and warm again, though somewhat depleted in both magical and physical energy, in a broad sandy area at the mouth of the largest exiting tunnel from the pool room. Breeka was huddled in Craduticus's arms now, but wheezing with every breath. Vor suspected the bat-cat was sick from water it had inhaled when it drowned. Although the water hadn't looked especially filthy, there were all those leech-slugs living in it, not to mention the recently dead body of the invader. Vor knew well enough that even water that looked clear and tasted fine could cause sickness. That was why it was always boiled or used in a fermented beverage before drinking. She worried about Breeka, but there wasn't anything anyone could do other than try to keep it warm and safe.

"There are footprints," Master Himes was saying as she surveyed the sandy floor. "The fools didn't cover them."

"I think they think they got us, that we're still trapped in that cave," Frimillin suggested. "They don't think they're being followed: over-confident morons."

Master Himes gave a nod. "It looks like the caves become natural from here. That will make the going harder. Try not to slip or bang your head, and please be quiet. No talking now except for absolute essentials."

There were nods all around.

"No lights. Our underclothes are still glowing, and even with our robes on top, that should give us enough light. I'd like Ramikar to lead," Master Himes went on.

The tall, mature mage didn't look surprised. It made sense, Vor thought, since he was so good with earth magics, and there wasn't a place much earthier than this. He began to move towards the tunnel.

"Here," Giri spoke up softly, "let's eat the last of the drake meat we brought. It won't last now that it's been soaked. Maybe then Breeka can ride in one of the packs."

Craduticus looked up. His eyes were mournful in the dim light. He didn't speak. Giri just went ahead handing out pieces of meat. It wasn't very good anymore, but it was all they had. Vor used a touch of magic to heat up her share to the point of scalding her fingers—hoping to negate any sickness in the water that now soaked it—and ate it. Others were doing the same. Giri offered the pack to Craduticus, but the old man turned away, Breeka in his arms, and fell in behind Ramikar as the group began to walk. Vor realized then that he must have lost his staff in the run from the drakes. He limped a little without it.

The way was mostly flat at first, and then began to angle downward, and continued to do so steadily. The path, such as it was, narrowed and widened in turns. The ceiling dipped low in some sections, and soared up in others. Spurs of rock jutted in from the walls in some places, making the wizards turn sideways, twist and contort, or even climb over, and other places the walls swelled outward. It was all rough, except where trickling water had deposited sediment to form rock curtains, spires, and towers of all kinds of rounded shapes.

They passed signs of rock falls and cave-ins. In a few places they had to climb over rocky debris, but handy for them the invaders had already cleared the path. Steadily, they moved down and down. There were other paths running off from the one they followed. Some were so small they would have had to crawl through them if they'd wanted to go those ways. There were points where their path got small, too, so they had to go to all fours or squeeze through narrow gaps. Their robes, or regular clothing in the case of Vor and Giri, which had been somewhat sluiced clean by the questionably fresh water, became smeared with mud and dirt.

Vor tried not to think about all the stone around her. When she pushed through tight squeezes she focused on staying calm, and not imagining that she might get stuck. Nor did she let herself think about what the climb back up would be like. She'd have to do it. She'd have to swim that passage again—but how would they get back up out of the bone pit? No. Not now. She couldn't worry about that now. She had to focus on each step, each place she put her hands, and avoid banging her head on the low ceilings.

It was slow going, even though she knew Master Himes was in a rush. Frimillin had a large frame, and sometimes needed help getting through the tight spots, and Lanisala still needed to be careful she didn't stretch or twist wrong and tear open her leg wound. Plus, Breeka was still being carried, although Craduticus had relented and put it in a pack now, and had to be passed back and forth when it got in the way of navigating through tricky sections.

The tunnel seemed to go on and on. After several slow hours of it, they took a rest in a spot where the rough tunnel widened and was almost level. Everyone slid down to a seat on the floor, which here was coated with gravel and sand and a few larger stones that they avoided. They passed around waterskins, each person only taking a swallow. There were occasional water sources in the form of trickles of water down the walls, and used them to fill the waterskins periodically, but they couldn't depend on them to keep appearing. If the tunnels suddenly went dry, they would want to have a reserve of water.

"How deep is this going to go?" Iyai murmured.

"Cracks and caverns can go down for miles," Ramikar answered her.

"I'm scared," she added breathlessly.

"It's important to remain calm," Master Himes instructed. "Panicking will not improve anything."

"Will the air stay good down here?" Iyai went on.

"I'm monitoring it," Dello said. "Don't worry, we're still safe."

"Let's keep moving," Master Himes ordered, obviously impatient.

"We should try to sleep, Master," Dello said. "We haven't slept since before the bone room."

She eyed her apprentice with disfavor.

"He's right, Tessa," Ramikar whispered. "I know you're in a rush, but we're no good if we hurt ourselves from fatigue, and this is hard going for all of us. We'll also regain a little energy."

She looked about to argue when Craduticus spoke up. "We'll rest, Tessa."

He didn't look at her. He was petting Breeka's head. The bat-cat had its eyes shut, and its breathing was an audible rasp.

"Alright," Master Himes consented. "A short rest."

Vor was already leaning against Giri, but now they adjusted until they found the most comfortable position possible given the rocks. The others were trying to get comfy, too, but she noticed Dello and Master Himes step back up the path, around the corner before the wide spot they were going to sleep in, and out of view.

Vor wondered what that was about, not that it was any of her business. Still, she was the person seated closest to the back path where Dello and Master Himes had just gone, and as she closed her eyes intending to try to sleep, she heard the whisper of voices.

Master Himes was saying, "Traskitandi, what did you want to talk about?"

Dello retorted, though calmly. "About what I told you above the bone room."

Master Himes's reply was a moment in coming. "I cannot reciprocate. I thought that was clear."

"But why not?" His voice had nearly turned whiney.

Her voice, on the other hand, remained plain and simple. "You're married for one thing."

"It's just for my house, for children, and I have four now. I'm not going to be master of the house. I'm a wizard. My place is here with you."

Vor could almost hear the raised eyebrow. "What would your wife have to say about it?"

Dello's tone was exasperated. "We talked about it. I told her I didn't mind if she had a lover and she gave me permission in return." He paused. "And since we're mages there's no risk of babies."

Master Himes let out a puff of air, the sound louder than their quiet talking. "On top of that, I'm barren."

"You're what?"

Her tone became slightly derisive. "You know what that means. Don't act dumb, Apprentice. It doesn't suit you."

Dello sounded more subdued. "Yes, Master. I'm sorry, or, ah, is it, does it bother you? I suppose you never had children—"

She cut across him, voice stronger but still level. "You've never wondered why I'm not married? I was. My parents married me off like any girlchild of a noble house. I was second born and showed mage powers. They were able to get a great spouse-price for me. I was sent away to my husband's house instead of to the Citadel, where I wanted to go." She took a deep breath. "After a few years, with no babies, not even a miscairrage, they sent me back. They asked for the spouse-price back, too."

Dello's response came quickly. "But that's not right. Everyone knows that can happen sometimes, but the Houses honor their agreements. Even if you can't—"

Master Himes spoke over him. "My husband accused me of withholding children from him on purpose, because he knew mages could do that. He thought I wanted out of the marriage so I could go be a wizard. He was half right. I did want out, but I wasn't preventing conception. I thought, if I had a few babies, then I could go to the Citadel, but it just wasn't happening. He didn't believe me. There were other difficulties, too. I wasn't well suited to being married."

Dello didn't speak for a few moments, so Vor wondered if he'd lowered his voice so much that she couldn't hear him. Then he asked. "Did he hurt you?"

Master Himes, too, hesitated in her reply. "I was too spirited. He was too immature. He saw me as someone to conquer and a means for getting heirs. I saw him as a grudging obligation. He slept around the servants to punish me. One even got pregnant—poor girl—and he used it as proof that everything was my fault, which I guess it was."

"It wasn't," Dello retorted at once. "His behavior was not proper, but I'm glad he sent you back."

"It was upsetting at the time, but my parents finally consented to send me here. I took double classes. I fought to make up lost time. My master changed everything for me. He was the father, brother, friend, and teacher I'd never had, and never knew I so desperately needed."

"He was a fine wizard," Dello said. "I could always see how proud he was of you."

"I miss him, but now I have you to be proud of."

Dello muttered, almost too quiet for Vor to hear, "I'm immature, too, like your husband was. Is that why—"

Master Himes's voice turned warm. "No. No, you are incredibly sensitive and aware, kind, generous, and loyal. You have a lot to learn, certainly, but you are well on your way to becoming a wise old wizard one day."

"You praise me too highly," he objected.

"And you wonder, if I admire you so much, am not married myself, and you are free to have a lover on the side, why won't I take you? We all know it is not uncommon among master-apprentice pairs. Milsa even married her former master."

Dello sounded grumpy now. "I do wonder. That's why I asked."

"You like me too much, Traskitandi."

"What do you mean?"

Master Himes' voice was nearly too quiet to hear. "From the beginning I suspected an infatuation. It's pretty normal. I was warned about it, but was told it usually wears off. With you it didn't. It just grew."

"You knew." Vor could almost sense his exasperation and embarrassment. "You knew how I felt? That was before my marriage, before everything. You could have," he trailed off.

"You were too young."

"I'm not now," he nearly growled. "Why is it a problem now?"

Master Himes's tone turned a trifle sharp. "I don't want our bond altered with that kind of intimacy. That's not what you were assigned to me to learn."

"I don't think it would hurt anything," Dello argued. "It would make us stronger."

Master Himes went silent again for several long moments, or had dropped her volume so much Vor couldn't hear—but no. She spoke again.

"I don't get involved," she muttered. "I don't have lovers."

"I noticed," Dello said promptly.

"There's nothing wrong with that," she hissed back. Now she sounded exasperated. "You know I take my pills, but I've never told you why. I have pain in my belly, and sex makes it worse. With my husband, all I could do was bear it and hope I'd kindle from it, so I wouldn't have to bear it again. Once they told me the pain was part of the same thing making me barren, I refused my husband. Of course he sent me back, and I could never handle having another lover, even if I wanted to."

She went quiet.

Vor was surprised again, but it made sense. That was why Master Himes was alone, and stayed alone, restricting her relationships to purely platonic. It wasn't something Vor had heard of before. It felt to her like a great injustice of nature, for something that was supposed to be so enjoyable to hurt.

Dello finally seemed to get up the nerve to speak again. "And you don't want to. You don't want me."

"Dellostrikata, listen to me," Master Himes said softly. "You are the most important person in my life, and I love you deeply, as the son I could not have, as the younger brother of my heart, as my beloved student and fellow wizard. I would gladly die to keep you safe." She paused, and confessed apologetically. "But I will never take you to my bed."

Vor heard his sob and felt a wave of grief wash out from him.

"Dello, you have my love in many ways, just not my lust," Master Himes whispered. "I do not have that to give to anyone."

"Then what am I supposed to do?" Dello mumbled.

"You might not like my suggestion, but if you're really asking: spend time with your wife. Talk to her. Get to know her. Do things together outside the bedroom. She gave you permission to have a lover, but do you think she's taking one?"

"No." His reply was grudging.

"You've made four children together, so I can't imagine you find each other unpleasant, or you'd have stopped at one or two. I can't be the lover and beloved you need, but if you try to build bonds and find common ground, you might discover your wife is a lovely person who can also be your friend and partner in ways I cannot."

Dello didn't reply for a while, but finally muttered, "I dunno."

"Think about it, Apprentice," Master Himes urged. "Now I'm going to sleep. You should, too. Please don't sit up and sulk. Not only do I need you capable, I also care about your health."

Vor pretended to be asleep as she heard Master Himes walk back into the wider tunnel they were all sleeping in. Dello's reluctant feet followed a minute later. Maybe now she could get to sleep, and yet Vor was glad for Dello's sake that they had talked, even if she'd been stuck overhearing. He had confessed—and she had, too, though not passionate love—and communication was happening. Dello was undeniably disappointed, but Vor thought they'd both be more comfortable having the truth open between them. She snuggled closer to Giri, who seemed to already be asleep, and focused on getting there herself.

What seemed like a moment later, Vor snapped awake at the sound of a cry. All around her in the dimness, the other wizards stirred, too. Vor reached out her senses and felt something heavy, thick, and old pervading the center of their resting cavern, as though an ancient spider hung there, ensnaring them all with suffocating webs, but she couldn't see anything there. She realized she was cold, shivering.

Iyai cried out again, practically screaming, and Vor saw Ramikar scurry over to her and gather her into his arms. She huddled against his chest, sobbing. Near the center of the chamber, Dello was on his back on the floor, staring up, eyes wide. His chest was heaving with rapid breaths, but otherwise he didn't seem able to move. Master Himes had awakened at Iyai's cry, too, assessed the situation, and threw herself across him on all fours, snarling upwards.

Vor tried to gather power, but her reactions felt sluggish, like in dreams where she tried to run or fight, and could barely move. The presence in the room seemed to hang there, suspended, but had recoiled slightly when Ramikar and Master Himes acted. Beside her, Vor heard Giri grunt, as if trying to move a heavy load.

Then Craduticus lifted his arms, palms pressed forward, and shouted in righteous fury. There was a flash of light, making all the wizards wince—

And the presence vanished.

Vor didn't sense it flow out one way or another, or dissolve. It was just gone like the pop of a soap bubble. Everyone slumped in relief. Iyai was sobbing into Ramikar's chest, and he was rocking her like a child, murmuring comfort. Vor could sense now that he'd thrown his shields around her. Likewise, Master Himes had a shield so strong it was nearly visible over her and Dello. He was stirring now, his breathing calming, exchanging mumbled explanations with his master.

"What was that?" Giri asked aloud.

"A phantom of energy," Craduticus said, voice rough.

"A spirit?" Giri clarified. "A ghost? A wraith? What?"

"Something like that," the old mage shrugged. "This place, these caves, they have seen many years, and many things call them home, safe from the purifying effects of the sun."

"It was hungry," Dello rasped. "It was looking at me."

"Me, too," Iyai whispered.

"It was looking at all of us," Master Himes corrected. "You two are just the ones sensitive enough to know it."

"And look back," Dello added with a shiver. "I can't describe what I saw, because I can't remember, but it was horrible, like a nightmare you can't remember, and you just wake up terrified."

Master Himes pulled her apprentice up into her arms, and he sat there, shaking much like Iyai. Vor found herself shivering, too. The intense cold was fading, and she could move again, but she felt weak. If whatever it was had been hungry, had it fed on them? Had it eaten their energy, or something else? Vor was afraid to ask. No one seemed seriously hurt, just shaken, some more than others. Giri gave her hand a squeeze, and she squeezed back.

"I think we're done sleeping," Lanisala commented softly.

They shuffled into line again and kept going, but Vor didn't feel rested, and doubted anyone else did, either. Their path was more of the same: lots of rocks, a little water, no light. The next break came when they reached a place where the path turned almost straight down, through a contorted crack-like hole full of sharply angled rocks and twisting gaps. A little stream of water ran down it, but not so much it could drown someone, just enough to be really annoying. Everyone stopped and stared, but there was no other path. The way forward was down through the crack.

Iyai shivered and reached out to cling to Vor's arm, hiding her head against her shoulder.

"You can do it," Vor said.

"No, I can't," Iyai whispered.

"I'll go first," Ramikar said, deep voice calm and soothing. "If it's too tight I'll reshape the rocks a bit."

"The invaders made it through; we can, too," Master Himes declared. "Save your strength, Ramikar."

He nodded, and began the descent without any further delay. Vor watched from above as he wedged his long body through the gap, reaching for foot holds, turning his shoulders or hips to fit through and ducking his head around spurs of rock. Iyai clung more tightly to her arm.

"If the invaders and Ramikar can all make it through, so can you," Vor repeated, "just like Master Himes says. Besides, you're much smaller than them, so it should be easier for you. Gather your courage now. You're a wizard."

Dello volunteered to go next, and began the descent as soon as Ramikar's head was out of view.

"I wonder how far this goes," Giri muttered. "I mean, how long is this vertical section?"

"So how long will we be in there," Vor nodded, "feeling trapped?"

Lanisala went next, carefully managing her hurt leg. Somewhere down the crack, Vor heard a loud scrape, smack, and muffled curse. Vor thought it must be Ramikar, but no message of disaster was relayed up.

"Frimillin, do you think you can fit?" Master Himes asked in an undertone.

"I'll be fine," the hefty wizard smiled and patted his waistline. "I've lost some girth since we've been down here on short rations."

Vor thought Frimillin was more muscle than fat, but didn't dispute him. She hoped his joke would calm Iyai. Gamely, he began squeezing himself into the jagged hole that served as the start of the descent. There was really very little space between him and the rocks. Master Himes looked between the remaining mages.

"I'll go," Craduticus said. "Giri, would you help me manage Breeka?"

"I will," he nodded.

Giri was a good choice for it, since he was slim and short, but also had a stronger physique because he was male, so could probably exert the strength to move Breeka in the pack through awkward angles if needed. Giri actually ended up going down first, with Craduticus following.

"Alright ladies," Master Himes said.

Iyai still clung to Vor's arm. She was shaking her head.

"You have to do this," Master Himes affirmed. "You will get through to the other side."

"And then I'll have to come back this way," Iyai whimpered.

"Well, yes. Maybe. There is still the chance of another exit or alternate path. We don't know."

"I don't want to go down there." Iyai hid her face against Vor's shoulder again.

"Stay calm. Go one step at a time, and you'll get through it," Master Himes soothed. "Come now. You follow Craduticus. If an old, weak man can do it, surely you can. You're smaller and stronger and more flexible."

"Iyai, you have to do it, we all do," Vor encouraged. "Let go of me and go get it done."

But Iyai just shook her head, her whole body shaking, and clung even tighter. Vor and Master Himes exchanged a look. Master Himes could try to pull her off, but she couldn't shove the girl into the crack and force her to climb down. Vor knew what could be done instead, what might be the only solution. Frimillin had calmed Pirossa when she was hysterical with a light touch of mind magic, but Master Himes did not like that kind of magic. Vor had never applied such a technique. Their eyes met while Iyai trembled.

"I'm afraid if I try it, I'll mess it up," Vor breathed.

Master Himes grimaced with obvious distaste.

"You know how?" Vor continued softly. "We can't just go and leave her behind."

The older woman turned, ran her hands into her hair, and after a moment heaved a heavy sigh. After another few moments, she turned back, face set in a disgusted scowl.

"You're right. It's the best solution. Don't tell Frimillin," she gritted out.

"I won't," Vor promised.

Master Himes approached. Iyai was still trembling, but the master wizard set a hand lightly on her head, and in an instant, the trembling stopped.

"You can do this, Wizard Iyai," Master Himes said softly. "Go get it done, like Vor said."

Iyai's arms slowly relaxed, and she lifted her head. "Alright," she whispered.

She let go of Vor and went to the gap in the floor where the twisting tunnel began. Vor could see her take a calming breath, and then she looked over her shoulder.

"You did something to me," she accused lightly.

Master Himes looked at her feet. "I did."

"Thank you. I can do this now. I didn't like being afraid."

Iyai crouched and put her first foot into the hole, and began her descent.

"Can't hide it from someone as sensitive as she is, especially when I'm not that good at it," Master Himes muttered to Vor once Iyai's blonde hair had vanished into the tunnel. "It'll wear off quickly. You're next, but you don't need a nudge."

"No, I don't," Vor agreed, and walked herself to the crack that looked impossibly tight.

"Vor," Master Himes said abruptly, and Vor paused to look back. "In case there's not another chance," she was frowning.

"Yes?" Vor asked, suddenly worried the master wizard knew she'd overheard her talking with Dello about rather personal details.

"You have two marks of five. Would you like your third?"

Vor straightened from where she'd been crouching by the hole. "Are you sure?"

"I doubted you, and questioned you," Master Himes admitted, "but through this all, you have shown integrity and courage and skill. The techniques you use are uncommon, but you use them well, for the right purposes. I can wholeheartedly confirm you as a wizard, if you would accept that from me. I've been wanting to offer, ever since the bone pit, but there hasn't been a good opportunity."

Vor needed only a moment to consider. "Yes, Master Himes. I would accept a mark from you."

"Then." She beckoned, and Vor stepped close.

Quickly, because the others were already drawing ahead, Vor tugged her shirt and jacket aside to expose her left shoulder, and Master Himes pressed her thumb there, placing one of the two bottom petals of the flower-shaped scar. Vor bore the pain—not so significant compared to other pains she'd known—and in the space of a couple breaths, it was done.

"Thank you," Vor said.

"You'll make an excellent wizard. Colby is lucky to have you, and Giri, too. Now down the hole. I'll follow you."

Vor nodded and began. The rocks were rough, and the water was going to soak her clothes again, though the coolness might feel good on her burning new scar. She increased the magic light from her clothes now that the light from others wasn't there to help her. Vor got into the hole feet first, feeling for footholds with her toes. She eased down and scraped her back, but she bit back a curse. She figured she'd be well bruised and scraped by the time she made it to the bottom. Water dribbled into her face. Her view of Master Himes was cut off as she worked her way deeper, and then it was just her and the rocks.

Each movement had to be calculated. She had to have space to bend her arms and legs. If the walls of the tunnel blocked her elbows or knees she had to find another way to move them. In places the way turned or angled, so that she wiggled along on her side, and then sometimes had to roll herself so she could bend at her hips in the most useful direction. The sharp edges of rocks bit into her over and over as parts of her body not intended to be weight bearing took the load. She couldn't see Iyai ahead of her or Master Himes behind her, but she could hear their movements and occasional muttering over the gurgle and patter of the water.

The whole time, fear fluttered just beyond her consciousness: fear of getting stuck, trapped. The recent warm glow of Master Himes's approval helped to combat it a little—and Vor wondered if that was another reason she'd awarded her the mark when she did—but still the fear threatened to engulf her. She couldn't let it in. If she did, she knew she'd cry and scream and panic, and struggle to go up or down and not really get anywhere, until she was exhausted and hurt.

She had to focus on one movement at a time and nothing else, and keep the steady faith that she would get through to the other side. At one point, her foot seemed to get stuck at an angle she couldn't pull it out of, and the fear began to crowd her, but she forced herself to breathe, backtracked, and pulled herself back up. She had to take a moment and then try a different way of making the step down.

The worst moment came through a section where the rock pinned her belly and back as she was working herself horizontally through the crack. She slid down too much and the pressure of the rock prevented her from taking a breath. Only by pushing at terribly awkward angles with her arms and legs was she able to push herself up into the wider part of the crack and breathe again. She made it through that spot and kept going. It felt like the gap-crawl would never end.

Then the space opened up under her feet and she found herself searching for a place to put her foot next. It wasn't a big room, just a widening of the tunnel, enough that she had to strategize, and eventually lower herself with just her arms until the next jut of rock could take her foot. If she fell, she could land badly and injure herself. The stream of water was also causing her problem. In some parts, it ran along a path that avoided her, but in enough places it was falling on her to have made her clothing soaked, as she'd expected, and the cold was making her shiver. Even the new scar on her shoulder had stopped burning.

And then after what seemed an eternity, perhaps a full hour, she heard quiet talking below her.

"Vor, you're almost out," she heard Giri say. "There's a bit of a drop. Go slow."

She kept moving, and when she reached her foot back a moment later, felt only air. Then a hand touched her ankle.

"I'm here," Giri said. "Lower yourself. I'll grab your hips."

She did as directed, and felt his supporting hands take her weight. One at a time she let go her hands and settled into his arms. Her feet found the floor. He was smiling at her. His cheek was smeared with dirt.

"Well done," he praised.

"Thank you, and you as well," she told him.

Then his smile turned startled. "Did Master Himes—?"

"Yes," Vor confirmed, "my third."

He smiled again. "Well done."

"Alright, my turn," Dello said, ready to move into where they were standing.

Vor and Giri stepped away.

"Unfortunately, not everyone came down so perfectly," Giri said.

Frimillin looked scratched up. His arms and face had raw scrapes, and his robes were torn and dirty. Iyai and Lanisala seemed fine, but Ramikar had a clotted cut above one eye, and was leaning against the wall, keeping his weight off his left foot.

"Twisted my ankle when I dropped," he explained. "There was no one to catch me."

"I'm afraid I dislocated a few fingers," Craduticus mentioned, rubbing his hand. "Got them stuck. I popped the joints back in. We'll all have to manage."

The group was in a larger tunnel this time, and it was suspiciously round, like a tube, though with a level floor. It ran off to both the left and the right, oddly straight after all the rough twists and turns of the natural caves they'd been working their way through. The floor was damp but the water was running away into little troughs on each side of the tunnel. They were obviously put there intentionally for just that purpose.

"What is this?" Vor whispered. "It looks sculpted."

"We're not sure," Ramikar answered, "but I agree. Something or someone made these tunnels."

"These?" Vor confirmed.

He nodded. "It branches just a little ways that way."

Vor looked, and she, too, could see the darker shapes of two tunnel mouths.

"I'm right below you, Master," Dello was saying now. "Just lower yourself and I'll help you down."

Vor glanced over to see Dello accomplish the maneuver Giri had just done with her, but with his master. Master Himes gave his shoulders a quick pat, and stepped away, shaking her wet robes down to her wrists.

"Everyone alright?"

They reported on injuries again, but there was really nothing to be done about them. None were so terrible as to prevent them from going on. Even Ramikar said he could manage on his injured ankle.

"So, left and right," Master Himes said softly. "Any footprints?"

"We can't find any," Frimillin answered. "The floor is too clean and wet."

A breath of air suddenly swirled through the tunnel, enough to make any hair that wasn't wet sway and chill any exposed skin. It startled Vor, but there was no feeling of aggression with it: just air.

"It keeps doing that," Frimillin shrugged.

"Curious," Master Himes commented. "We'll split up: half to the left and half to the right." She looked around the group. "Ramikar, are you sure you can walk?"

"I'll be fine," he repeated.

"Good enough, then. Traskitandi, Holstor, Hearthsraven with me; the rest of you'll be the second group. Go that way. Wait, one more thing."

She looked down at the floor, searched for a moment, and collected several small rocks, or large pebbles. Master Himes took them in her fist and concentrated for a few moments. Then she opened her hand, palm flat.

"Took me all night to do that to our rings, using a circle," Giri muttered. "Now she's done it to four times as many items in as many seconds on the fly."

Vor managed a smile.

"Everyone take a pebble," Master Himes instructed. "Holstor, stop whining. If you find the invaders, heat up the pebble. Two pulses for 'come quick' and three for 'save yourselves.' The others will do their best to follow the source back to you. Don't engage them unless you have to. Wait for the others to reach you."

Eight hands reached in, each taking a pebble, and Master Himes kept the last one for herself. They all tucked the pebbles into an inner pocket, so they'd feel the heat better.

"I think," Master Himes said softly, "we're nearing the bottom. I can sense strong power from somewhere. Is anyone else feeling it?"

"Yes, Master," Dello murmured, "but I wasn't sure if I might be hopefully imagining it."

"You're not."

"I feel something," Iyai whispered. Her face was still oddly calm since the mind magic Master Himes had worked on her. Vor just hoped she wouldn't be ignorant of real danger if—when—it came.

"The earth magics are burdened here," Ramikar said. "I think you're right. It's probably the key to the city, but it's definitely something."

Master Himes looked sharply at the oldest member of the party. "Master Craduticus?"

He was holding Breeka in his arms again. The bat-cat seemed to be unconscious, and its breath was raspy and slow.

"Yes," he concurred. "This feels like the end."

Vor darted a glance at him, not liking his wording.

"If you find the key without the invaders, guard it and call everyone else," Master Himes instructed. "Understand?"

"What if they're about to pull the key out?" Iyai asked.

Master Himes's face went hard. "Do what you must. Let's get moving."

On impulse, Vor stepped over to Craduticus and took his wrist. "Master Craduticus," she said, and then didn't know what to say next.

He smiled at her, making his eyes nearly vanish into wrinkles, and patted her hand without dropping Breeka. "Not to worry," he told her. "You'll be fine."

"What about you?"

"Yes," he said. "Everything will be right. I feel a great sense of power and peace down here."

Another breath of air moved through the tunnel, and it somehow prompted Craduticus to nod knowingly.

"That's right," he sighed. "You'll be fine, Vor Hearthsraven. I know you will be. Let me go now."

"Would you like me to carry Breeka?" she offered.

He shook his head and looked away, into the darkness. "No, no. Breeka and I need to be together."

"You're talking like you're going to die," she growled bluntly.

"Everyone does, Vor," he replied, still staring into the dark.

He started to walk off, and Vor reluctantly let go of his wrist.

"Come on," Giri whispered. "They're getting ahead of us."

Vor turned and followed him down the tunnel, to where Dello and Master Himes were reaching the fork. The other group of five wizards and one bat-cat moved into the darkness in the opposite direction.

Chapter 13
The Circle

Master Himes was staring at the two ways of the crossing tunnel as Vor and Giri came up to her.

"We'll split," she said. "Traskitandi with me. Holstor and Hearthsraven, that way."

"Is that a good idea, Master?" Dello asked. "We're a lot stronger together."

"We're only locating the invaders, like I said before. Don't go trying to fight them. Call back everyone else and we'll face them together."

Vor was already thinking that if the tunnels turned out to be labyrinthine, as Ramikar had suggested, locating other members of the party could be challenging.

"And if the tunnels branch again," Vor said, "do we split again and go alone?"

"We must search until we find them," Master Himes insisted, "diligently. Make your best call."

Giri nodded, and Vor didn't see the point in arguing, but she knew she didn't want to be alone in this place. They were so far below the ground, and had come through so many obstacles that she already felt like she'd never get out. If she were lost down here by herself, she might truly panic. Giri bumped fists with Dello, and took her hand as they began walking the path Master Himes had indicated.

"Alone at last," he joked.

Vor tried to smile, but in the dark she doubted he could see it. The tunnel was nearly black, the only light coming from the residual glow of their clothes. It was just enough to allow their dark adapted eyes to see the way, faintly. Vor hoped the invaders would be using much stronger lights and they would see them before they stumbled upon them.

The tunnel was also nearly silent. There was a faint trickle from the water making its way down the walls and through the carved channels at either side of the path. Vor and Giri both tried to keep their footsteps as silent as possible, and their breathing as well. So when Vor heard what sounded like a scrape against rock it came as a surprise and made her startle. Giri also twitched, and they paused. She felt a pulse through her ring.

"Me, too," he'd sent.

Vor looked back, looked ahead, and could see nothing moving. It was just a plain black tunnel, but something had to have made that noise. They waited for several breaths, Vor watching their backtrail and Giri looking ahead, but the sound did not repeat and nothing moved.

Vor sent the pulse signal she'd used at the bottom of the bone bit for "wait." Giri seemed to understand and stood quietly. With as little volume as possible, she breathed the words to a cantrip, and summoned a darkling sprite. Her reserves of energy were getting low, but she thought it was a wise investment of power. She gave the sprite its duty, to first go back and search behind for anything living or magical.

Beside her, Giri nodded and sent "yes," through their rings.

Giri began walking again and Vor went with him, feeling only slightly better now that she'd dispatched a magical scout. The dark and silent tunnels were just too deep and alien for her to feel relaxed. Then another breath of air went through the tunnel, like had happened a few times before, and Vor nearly jumped as it hit her and washed around her, but it was harmless, she told herself.

Vor found herself wondering what that was. Air didn't move by itself. In general, temperature or pressure could make it move, or an animate object could—so one of those had to be present—unless it was being done magically. It was a big breeze, too, and it wasn't constant. For a while she racked her brain, trying to figure out what could cause bursts of intermittent wind, but she could think of no inanimate source.

Her darkling servant returned, reported a negative for magic or living creatures behind them, and she sent it on ahead with the same instructions. The tunnel turned in a wide curve, so gradual it was hardly noticeable. There were no cross tunnels, at least not yet, which was a relief. Then she noticed an anomaly ahead and pulled Giri to a stop. She reached out to point, and he nodded. There was an object in the distance, on the floor against one wall of the tunnel, but the darkling had not alerted on it, so it was probably benign.

It was paler than the rock and irregularly shaped, spread across a bit of floor, and not very bulky.

They kept walking and it came slowly into focus until Vor knew what it was. They came up on it and paused to look. It was human remains: bones and fragments of cloth. There wasn't a hint of flesh; down here it was so wet, everything that could decompose must have done so long ago. Even the bones looked stained, though still pale enough to show up in the near darkness.

Another sound of scraping, like a boot sole against the floor, made Vor and Giri twitch and look back. A muffled sound followed, almost like a voice, but rough. Vor strained her eyes against the darkness, but could see nothing but blackness. A chill went over her, like she'd just stepped out of her warm cottage into the night, like when the hungry presence in the cavern above had so recently fed on her—maybe.

She squeezed Giri's hand and sent "winter," not having a pulse pattern for "cold."

He didn't reply but began backing away from the remains, and she went with him. The cold gradually faded but both of them cast more than one look back at that sad pile of bones. The tunnel continued to curve and they followed it. It remained featureless. Vor's darkling came zooming back to her, this time reporting humans ahead. Vor instructed it to lead them and they followed it, a tiny blob of utter blackness against the slightly lighter darkness thanks to their glowing clothing.

A cross tunnel came into view. Their curving tunnel appeared to continue on, while another tunnel led off to the left at a near perpendicular angle. Vor and Giri hugged the inner curve of the wall, approaching the junction cautiously—and then Giri released his held breath.

"It's Dello and Master Himes," he murmured.

They walked with a little more confidence then, and soon Vor could see the lighter shapes in the dark that were the two other mages. She saw them lift their hands in greeting and she mirrored them. Shortly they were meeting in front of the left bound tunnel.

"Nothing," Master Himes reported in a soft breath.

"Human remains," Giri replied, "old."

"Did you hear anything?" Dello asked then.

"We did," Giri answered, "and it got really cold, and there was another breeze."

"We heard things, too," Dello replied.

"It's just the darkness getting to us," Master Himes countered. "We're short on food and sleep, and this place inspires fear. So it seems we walked a circle, each pair of us doing one side."

"So it seems," Vor agreed.

"Why would there be a circular tunnel?"

"Does any of this make sense, Master?" Dello murmured.

She put a hand on the damp, mineral-encrusted wall. "And did you notice, it's a perfect circle? Do you have any idea how difficult it would be to tunnel through solid rock and make a perfect circle?"

"I'm sure it could be done with enough measuring and math," Giri said, "but I see your point. Why do it at all?"

"Perhaps there is something in the middle of it," Vor suggested. "Could it be the base of a pillar of some kind?"

"It's a thought," Master Himes acknowledged.

"But it's not why we're here," Dello nudged.

"Right. Let's keep going."

Vor kept sending her darkling forward and back to check for magic and life. It kept returning negatives. After a few minutes walking together in the left bound tunnel, it forked again.

"Alright," Master Himes said, "just like before."

The pairs parted, with Vor and Giri going left again. It didn't take long for Vor to notice certain similarities.

"This tunnel is a circle, too," she whispered.

"Why do it once, much less twice?" Giri breathed back.

Vor had no answer for him, but at least there were no human remains in their half of the circle this time. They were just finishing their arc when Vor felt the contact stone in her pocket heat up. Dello and Master Himes came into view ahead, also reaching for their pockets.

"It's not us," Dello whispered as they approached. "They aren't sended pulses, either, only the steady call."

"We go back to where we came down, and then the other direction?" Giri supposed.

"Since we don't know where this is going," Master Himes pointed ahead with her chin, at another completely dark tunnel leading away from their current circle at a near perpendicular angle, "yes, let's go back and follow the way they went, but no need to split up going around these circles this time."

Vor sent her darkling ahead of them as they turned and followed Master Himes and Dello the way they'd come. They moved at a trot now, trying to keep their footsteps silent. Since the floor was pretty bare, it wasn't that hard to do, but still the slight sounds they made seemed to echo and bounce back at them from the walls, multiplying. Another breath of wind rushed over them as they ran, but Vor was getting so used to it, she barely paid it any mind.

Then they ran into a patch of cold air in the connecting tunnel between the two circle tunnels they'd explored. Dello stumbled and swatted at the back of his neck with a muffled exclamation.

"Traskitandi?" Master Himes hissed, stopping as her apprentice staggered into a wall.

"Dello?" Giri asked. "What is it?"

Vor stopped, too, concerned as Dello uttered a low moan, grabbing at the back of his neck with both hands. The cold intensified. Giri and Master Himes both went to Dello, but the tall, skinny mage was buckling over now, coughing. Vor's senses shrilled with alarm as she sensed something moving nearby—something she couldn't see. Her darkling dashed behind her, and she detected sharp, spiky fear from it. Her own adrenaline kicked up and she turned her back to her companions, facing out, and started gathering power.

A frigid blast of air hit her as her gaze raked the darkness, sensing something, but unable to get more than a hint. It was like looking into a pool and knowing there was something just below the surface of the water, the faintest shadow. She was afraid to extend her magical senses to touch it, and backed up another step. Then the oddest sensation began to creep over her skin, like something rough rasping over her. She coughed and her breath came ragged. She heard the scrape of boot soles on the floor, and a hoarse voice she couldn't understand.

The cold made her shiver, but her heart pounded. Something growled in her left ear and she jerked away. Behind her she could hear Dello gasping after his breath. Nerves jangling, Vor released her gathered energy, lighting up the tunnel in a flash, like Craduticus had done in the cavern above. It blinded her, but against the searing light she saw a dark shape like a tattered blanket full of holes and trailing threads and shreds closing in around the group.

Master Himes cursed, but Vor couldn't tell if it was because of the sudden light or if she saw what Vor saw. The light faded and Vor felt more than heard a low rumbling roar mixed with the creaking of old hinges. Whatever she faced, she'd angered it, but it hadn't gone away.

She gathered power again, into her right palm, and infused it with light. She lifted her hand, opened her fingers, and with a hiss of fury released not a flash, but a slender beam of cutting brightness. She had to squint, but against the light she saw her foe, closer now and starting to boil with blackness.

Dello let out a tortured cry.

"Release him," she commanded.

It moved in and she felt it seize her ankles. Ice gripped her feet and began crawling up her legs, and she almost fell. Vor slashed with her beam of brightness, severing shreds of the nebulous enemy. It recoiled, but she could see the cut pieces reattaching. The light wasn't working.

"Vor," Giri called, voice sounding choked. "It's not high magic."

"What does that mean?" she growled back.

"Light won't work."

"I figured that out."

She shut off the light, saving her energy. There was nothing else for it. Vor extended her senses to touch the freezing fragments of whatever-it-was. It was like touching nothing, touching emptiness, not even air, but something that sucked in all else. Pouring power into it only made it stronger. She gritted her teeth and tried to pull back her touch, but it clung to her like sticky strands. No kind of flashy magic was going to do anything but feed it.

"Dark," she breathed.

Vor closed her eyes—not that she could see much, but it was the principle of the thing—and reached down deep into her soul. In the deepest reaches dwelt the powers she didn't often draw on. There was despair. There was death, just waiting for its turn. There was the end of her time. There was rot and waste and the disgust that went with it. She pulled it all up, and darkness that could not be seen crackled between her fingers.

That which was not, which was absent, which was over or not yet begun, was what she sought, and what she opened in the space before her, keeping it from touching her companions. Invisible, silent, and yet still there—the way she could walk into an empty room with her eyes shut and just feel how large it loomed—the dark power sighed into the tunnel, opened, and ate that which had been trying to eat her.

The pervasive shreds of foe were sucked in, and it went with a scream that Vor could only feel along her skin like a thousand claws. When it had gone there remained only the dark energy she had called into being. It floated, not quite in the world, but close, obedient for the moment, but still hungry.

Vor's hand shook a little as she spread her fingers in its direction. She queued more power, and this time released it in a gentle glow. The walls became visible, and the darkness waiting just on the other side of the fabric of her world dissipated without a whimper, taking with it the dark wraith she'd had it swallow, to wherever darkness went when light came to displace it.

Behind her, she heard Master Himes curse again, but softly.

Vor lowered her hand and shuddered. Her stomach cramped with hunger and she wrapped her arms around her middle, afraid she might try to vomit.

Giri came up beside her and embraced her, helping to hold her up. She shivered convulsively.

"Wizard Hearthsraven," Master Himes breathed, "well done."

"Thank you, Vor," Dello panted. "That got it. I'm alright now."

"I've never seen the darkness used like that," Master Himes murmured.

"We all carry it around," Vor grunted through chattering teeth. "No one exists who doesn't have that dark energy in them, right along with the light. I put it to work. If I'm going to carry it, it might as well earn its keep now and again."

"And it might have been the only weapon that would work against whatever that thing was," Giri added.

"It's just another tool," Vor said, trying to get her shivering under control. "It's only evil if you use it for evil, just like any other flavor of magic."

"We need to keep moving," Giri urged. "The contact stones are still calling us."

Master Himes trotted off again, with Dello following her. With a gesture, Vor sent her darkling, which had hidden behind her through the whole fight, to check the tunnel ahead.

"Can you run?" Giri asked Vor.

"Yes," she nodded, and made good on it by pacing him.

The movement helped to warm her, to dispel the sense of sucking nothingness she'd felt. They started on the next circle, and Vor noticed—despite the weariness of her body—that the air felt lighter, the tunnels emptier. That feeling of being watched or followed was gone. She didn't suppose she'd ever know what that adversary of tattered shadows actually had been, if it was the same thing that had attacked them when they were sleeping, or if it was what Breeka had referred to as the thing that followed them, or if it was what members of the party had glimpsed down dark hallways ever since they'd entered the tunnels below the city, but it was gone now.

They slowed down when they reached the crack in the ceiling that they'd descended through. As they paused, her darkling zipped back to her and reported no humans ahead of them.

"They're still some ways away," she translated for the others.

"But this is where we left them. Let's keep going, a bit slower," Master Himes said.

They walked on, and shortly saw the tunnel branch, in a very familiar way.

"More circles," Dello breathed. "Why? Why make all these circles one after the other? This clearly isn't a place people lived. There's no need for these tunnels to be here at all."

"The key is hidden down here, though, somewhere, right?" Giri added. "We can all feel it, a strong magical signature in this area somewhere."

"Let's just find the others. Split up again, two to the left, two to the right," Master Himes said.

Vor obeyed, with Giri at her side.

"It is a question," Vor muttered, "but this isn't the only illogical thing we've seen. Remember that area of intersecting halls, all at right angles, after the bone pile and before the swim?"

"I was wondering if that might be symbolic," Giri replied softly. "Perhaps they held some kind of ritual."

"For what?" Vor asked.

"The stairs that go nowhere, that we had to swim through, I was thinking maybe the people who lived here believed their dead journeyed down into the earth after they died."

"After you die?" Vor echoed. "But when you die, you just die. You don't go anywhere, you're just done."

"That's what we know now," he nodded, "or think we know, but I've read that older cultures made up stories for a sort of life after death."

"Like the celestial dragon?"

"Like that."

Another breath of wind passed through the tunnel and Vor found herself shivering. The darkness did not relent, and again she had a feeling like winter had suddenly fallen, though she couldn't see her breath steaming, but then, it was so dark, she might not have been able to even if it was. She might have feared it was another dark wraith, but now that she'd touched one so closely, she could tell the difference. This was something else, but not necessarily without its own kind of danger.

Then came another sound of scraping against rock, softer than before, but prolonged, then it stopped, and then resumed, becoming irregular. Vor and Giri both stopped walking to listen, hands clasped tightly.

"What is that?" Giri hissed.

"Like someone staggering, struggling to walk, dragging their feet," Vor breathed back in a barely audible babble.

"Yes," Giri agreed, "but how?"

Without consulting about it, they moved so their backs were against the nearest wall. Vor's gaze swept back and forth over the darkness. Was there a darker shape in that darkness, moving at the very limit of her vision? She shut her eyes for a moment.

"My darkling said there was nothing nearby," she whispered. "It's our minds inventing things."

"Then why are both our minds inventing the same thing?" Giri asked back.

The sound hadn't stopped, except for pausing every third step—if it was footsteps—or so.

"Is it coming closer?" Giri breathed.

"I can't tell," Vor replied.

"Is it another one of those things?"

"I don't think so."

She opened her eyes to the blackness again. She could see the opposite wall, the ceiling, the floor, and Giri beside her, because of the remaining glow from their clothes. Something moved to the right, the direction they'd come from, but she couldn't resolve it. It was like a smudge—maybe just a floater: the occasional odd shape she'd see cross her vision that she knew was just some kind of harmless artifact in her eye.

Then something flicked her face, like she'd been splattered with drops of water, and she jerked away, her adrenaline spiking. Beside her, Giri jerked, too. Then she felt a hand grab her upper arm, but it wasn't Giri, and the fingers were hot.

"Come on," Giri gasped.

Vor had the fear that she wouldn't be able to run because someone had grabbed her, but Giri crossed in front of her, pulling on her hand, and she turned and followed. The ghostly grip did not hold her back, and she went with him. After a few hurried steps, just short of a run, the feeling faded, but she couldn't quite speak.

"Are you alright?" Giri asked, still hurrying them along.

The sounds of scraping footsteps had stopped but before Vor could gather herself to answer, a pale huddled shape came into view, and Vor recognized her darkling hovering over it curiously.

"That's Iyai," Giri said.

The darkling sped over to Vor, magically conveying its message that it had found someone.

"A lot of good you are," she muttered, but she sent it off again to check their backtrail.

"Iyai," Giri called softly as they approached.

The young mage was sitting against the wall, knees pulled up, head ducked down, and arms crossed over her head. She was rocking a little side to side.

Vor and Giri knelt beside her.

"Iyai? It's us," Vor tried. "Where's Ramikar? Are you alright?"

Giri stood up. "I'll go get Master Himes and Dello."

Vor's hand darted out, almost without conscious intent, and grabbed his wrist. She wanted to tell him not to go, that no one should wander alone—that he mustn't leave her. Vor set her other hand lightly on Iyai's shoulder, and sensed the despair that had paralyzed her. Whatever had happened to the young mage, it could probably happen to any of them.

"Please," Vor breathed, "be careful."

He nodded. "I can sense Dello close. They must be at the intersection just out of view. I'll be right back with them. You have the ring. We can keep in contact."

"Alright," Vor agreed reluctantly.

She watched him turn and walk into the blackness, and then she stroked Iyai's hunched back, and tried to send soothing energy into her aura. It seemed like every heartbeat was a whole minute of waiting. Iyai kept rocking, shivering, and Vor began to wonder what she would do if Giri never came back and Iyai never responded. Try to escape, leaving everyone else to their fates here down below, and hope the invaders didn't pull out the key and crush everything? Or go on alone, leave Iyai rocking in the dark, and try to stop the invaders herself? What if she walked into whatever took her companions? What if the invaders had already been stopped by whatever was down here in the dark? Or had the invaders somehow done this to Iyai? Or had another dark wraith hurt her?

Vor could still feel the steady thumping of Giri's heart through the ring. It was elevated slightly, but not as it would be were he running or fighting for his life. Then three shapes emerged, approaching from the dark, and they matched the relative heights of Giri, Dello, and Master Himes. In another moment, they were close enough for positive identification, and Vor stood. Giri grabbed her in a quick hug, as if he'd been as scared as she by their brief separation.

"Wizard Iyai," Master Himes commanded. "Report on what happened to you."

Iyai shivered harder, but didn't reply. Master Himes crouched and grabbed her shoulders, forcing her to sit up and lift her head. Iyai gave a whimper but didn't resist. Her eyes and mouth looked like dark holes in her pale face, and she didn't seem to be focusing on anything.

"Iyai," Master Himes said, more gently. "Where is Ramikar? Did he leave you here alone?"

Vor saw the girl's throat work, like she was trying to swallow. Softly, Master Himes cursed.

"Something's happened to her," the master wizard muttered. "Her mind is all muddled. Me putting that calming on her before the climb down surely didn't help."

"You did what to her?" Giri asked.

"She worked a little mind magic," Dello whispered, "very gentle."

"I saw it," Vor confirmed. "Iyai was too scared to climb down without it. It was gentle, like Dello says." She eyed the tall mage. "I'm guessing you were able to just sense it on her?"

"It was nearly worn off by the time she got to the bottom of the crack," Dello said. "I can't sense any of it now, but yes, she's been so upset by something that her mind is adrift. She's trying to get a grip on herself, but she just can't. She needs to be somewhere she feels safe."

"Right, and we have so many of those kinds of places handy right now," Master Himes grumbled.

Vor bit back a sigh. "This is going to be the best we can do."

She got down on the damp floor beside Iyai, and pulled her into her arms.

"Oh," Dello uttered.

"She trusts me more than the rest of you," Vor explained, "so I'm the best choice for this, though admittedly not optimal, but we don't have any of her real friends handy. Someone dry her robes. I know it's energetically expensive, but she's not going to be functional otherwise. Some of this shivering is from the cold."

Master Himes reached down and touched Iyai's shoulder. A few moments later Vor felt her robes warm and start to steam. Iyai's shivering lessened. In another minute, Iyai was starting to grab onto Vor's still damp robes, and Vor guided her arms around her. Iyai held on, and started crying. Giri made a sound of sympathy, but Master Himes patted his arm.

"Tears are good," the master mage explained. "It means she's starting to process her emotions, moving from shock to resolution."

Iyai sobbed against Vor's neck for several minutes before beginning to gather herself.

"Vor, thank you," she sobbed.

"Of course," Vor replied. "Take your time."

There might not actually have been much time to spare, but trying to rush Iyai wouldn't help. Shortly, though, the young mage was taking deep breaths to calm herself, and then drew away from Vor, who let her go.

"I'm sorry," she whispered to the group at large.

"It's alright," Master Himes said. "But now can you tell us what brought you to that state? And where's Ramikar?"

Iyai nodded, stood up, and wiped the tears from her face with her sleeves.

"Master Ramikar and I were exploring, like we were supposed to. The others split off to take the other path," Iyai began.

"We haven't seen any sign of them," Dello contributed, only to get shushed by his master.

"I heard noises, like footsteps, but didn't see anyone," Iyai went on. "Ramikar was concentrating, walking with one hand out, touching the wall, and then he suddenly stopped, just here." A sob escaped her. "He said, 'it's not a key, this is the key.' And then he told me he had to check something, and to stay right here. He looked excited, like the most wonderful thing had happened. I didn't know what he was talking about, but then he turned to face the wall, put both hands on it, and walked into it."

"When you say 'walked into it,' you don't mean this." Dello took three steps and bumped face first into the wall, bouncing off it a little.

Iyai shook her head, making her messy hair twitch. "It was like the wall absorbed him, like if you stick your fingers into bread dough. The wall was like bread dough, and once he went in, it went back to normal."

Master Himes put a hand on the solid wall of rock and cursed fluently. "What was he thinking?" she hissed, and then called Ramikar a number of rude names, calling mainly into question his intelligence and judgement.

"And you stayed here to wait for him to come back?" Vor asked Iyai.

"I did," the young woman answered, and her voice wavered. "At first, I thought I should veil myself, but that takes so much energy, and I don't have much left. So I sat, but I heard things, and saw things, and something touched me, but I couldn't see what it was. It was just like shapes of smoke. And then something started talking to me, but I couldn't understand the words. I wanted to run away, but I didn't know where anyone else was, and then suddenly Vor was hugging me."

Master Himes was still staring at the wall, but now she took a break to ask, "You didn't activate the stone, did you?"

"No, I didn't," Iyai replied. "I forgot about it. I was too scared."

"Then the others, Craduticus, Lanisala, and Frimillin are the ones who did."

"We need to find them," Giri said.

"What about Ramikar?" Dello asked.

Master Himes shook her head. "None of us have the power over earth magic like he does; we can't follow him. I can't believe he'd do such a thing.

I'm tempted to think something drove him mad or confused him—maybe whatever was after Iyai. He'll have to get out of this by himself."

"Should I stay here?" Iyai asked. "He told me to wait."

"You're coming with us," Master Himes declared. "Otherwise, whatever happened to you while you were waiting the first time will just happen again. I'm sorry about Ramikar, but we can't help him. Let's go help those we can."

The group of five now headed for the next intersection.

"What did he mean, 'it's not a key, this is the key'?" Dello asked quietly as they walked. "It's bugging me. It doesn't make sense."

"I don't know," Iyai replied.

"I think something must have affected his mind," Master Himes said promptly. "That's why it doesn't make sense, and why he'd seal himself into solid stone. How did he expect to breathe in there?"

"You think he's dead, don't you?" Iyai whispered.

"He's a resourceful wizard, but I think something tricked him into doing something very stupid. Alright, intersection: Traskitandi and me to the left; you three to the right. Go carefully."

Master Himes walked off at once. Dello gave one helpless glance over his shoulder at the other three before following her.

"Dello has a point," Giri muttered. "I think Ramikar realized something. Just because he doesn't talk much doesn't mean he's not brilliant. I wish he'd told you a little more before he disappeared on us, Iyai."

Vor was thinking on that very question, and had been entertaining an idea ever since the pattern of tunnels became obvious. They started walking, and she took the chance to drill Giri for more information as the one most likely to have it.

"Did anyone ever record what the key looked like?" she asked. "The key that the ancient wizards set down here to keep the city from falling—is there a drawing somewhere?"

"Not that I've seen," Giri answered. "I never made a study of this event, but it was mentioned in my classes. No instructor ever produced a drawing, and you'd think they would if they could."

"But it's definitely true that they had to bring something down here from above to make the link, because there is so much rock between here and there that an ordinary spell would never hold."

"Right," he agreed.

"So we, everyone, have assumed that the key was a magical construction, made of metal or carved of stone or something like that, that was then planted down here somewhere, shoved into the bedrock like a key into a lock, and that anyone of some small magical talent—provided they could get to it—could just grab it and pull it out again, and the city would fall apart when the rock it stands on breaks into pieces."

Giri shrugged, "That's more or less the gist of it."

"That seems like a very easy spell for keeping however many tons of rock standing for millenia."

"Yes," Giri agreed slowly, "but we always assumed the old wizards spent ages crafting the perfect key before coming down here, and knew things we don't."

Vor raised her eyebrows. "Why? Has knowledge been lost since then? Have libraries burned or been destroyed?"

"Not that I know of," Giri admitted.

Vor glanced at him in the darkness. "Weldom has stood for thousands of years as a major power. Don't you think it's more natural for a society that is a good husband of information to accumulate it, not lose it?"

"Yes," Giri agreed again, though even more slowly, "but I have never seen, and as far as I know no one has, a book that exactly details how this key was made or placed, so something must have been lost."

"Or the wizards who did it never wanted anyone to know, so no one could undo it," Vor countered.

"You think they withheld information?"

"Maybe even gave out a little false information," Vor nodded, "and never wrote down exactly what they did to save the city."

"So the key?"

"There never was a key," she guessed. "If you were going to pull off magic like this, how would you do it?"

"Me?"

She smiled, though doubted he could see much of it. "Sure. You're a very smart wizard."

"But I have far less experience and knowledge than someone like, say, my—our—master."

"All the same," Vor persisted. "I want to hear if you'd do it the same way I'm thinking I'd do it."

Giri walked for a while in silence. Vor had an idea, she just wasn't exactly sure how it could be done practically.

"You want to hold the city together," Giri began.

"More importantly, the rock the city sits on," Vor prodded.

"Yes, because the city could change. Buildings are created, modified, maybe even torn down."

"The general theory Craduticus spoke about, like tying the city together, that makes sense, but using the rock it sits on."

"I agree," Giri said, "but if there's no special artifact so you're not tying it to one central point—"

"And how do you anchor the ties onto the rock of the city itself?" Vor nudged.

They reached the other side of the circle, where Master Himes and Dello joined them. There were still no signs of the invaders or their missing companions. Giri paused and stared at Vor, and she could almost see the thoughts cascading through his mind, as he picked up and discarded ideas. Then she saw his enlightenment bloom.

"What once touched," he began.

"Always touches," she finished.

Master Himes frowned at them. "What are you talking about?"

"They didn't use some kind of magical glue to tie the city together, centered on a magic artifact," he mused.

"They used the rock itself. That's what I think," Vor said, and nudged a little more. "And when you are linking objects to objects what do you use for an anchor?"

"These circles are a magic circle," Giri concluded, voice turning excited. "They are a huge magic circle. That's why everywhere we go down here, we feel like we're near the key. This is the key, just like Ramikar said."

"And inside each circle, somehow, is a bit of rock from above," Vor guessed. "They carried down a sample from above, from several different parts of the city, and bound them together down here, in this permanent circle."

Now Vor saw the enlightenment blooming for Master Himes and Dello, too.

"As long as those bits stay bound here in the circle," Master Himes realized, "so does the city. It cannot fall while the circle endures and continues to be powered."

"That's a very powerful spell," Dello breathed, clearly impressed.

"The earth itself is powering it, I think," Vor said. "It's just a guess."

"That's a stretch," Master Himes countered. "No, there has to be something else. Where does the wizard stand in grand conjurations? The items of interest are around the edge of the circle. If the spell is not being cast on something that is in the center of the circle—"

"Then the wizard stands in the center," Dello completed.

Master Himes began pacing around the intersection. "The key is the circle, and I agree that using an associative magic with samples of rock from the corners of the city makes sense, but there still must be a center."

"No wizard from that time could still be alive," Dello muttered. "That's preposterous."

"Even if there is something in the center, how do we get to it? There are no tunnels to the center, at least not that we've seen yet," Master Himes fumed. "They came down as far as that crack led them and decided they were deep enough. They carved these tunnels with pure power. Somehow they put a chip of rock from the surface into the center of each circle."

"An earth elemental could have done it for them," Vor suggested.

"Likely," Master Himes agreed.

"Then they activated the key, the circle," Giri frowned, "and it's still working. We can all feel it."

"You activate it from the center," Master Himes growled again.

"What if they spaced themselves out, and stood around the edges?" Vor asked.

"No," Master Himes refuted. "They'd interfere with the connection between the pieces of stone. They had to be in the center."

"Did they walk through the walls," Iyai whispered, "like Ramikar did?"

Master Himes halted her pacing, knuckles pressed to her teeth. Two facts clicked into place in Vor's mind.

"Iyai," she said, "you said something spoke to you while you were huddled there waiting for Ramikar to come back?"

"Yes," the young mage confirmed.

"But you couldn't understand what it said."

"I couldn't."

"Ramikar is a scholar of ancient languages," Vor stated. "He read the writing left behind by these people. Could he have understood whatever it was—"

"No one speaks the old languages anymore, though," Master Himes dismissed. "The languages are dead and the phonics forgotten."

Vor grimaced. "Somehow he knew how to pass through the wall."

For a moment no one spoke. Then Master Himes heaved a sigh.

"Let's go look at the walls."

The group spread out, each finding a different bit of wall to touch, while still within sight of each other.

"This is pointless," Dello grumbled. "Earth is my weakest element."

"Focus, Traskitandi."

Vor put a hand on the wall, and walked along it, mimicking what Iyai said Ramikar had done. The walls had endured water dripping down them for longer than Vor cared to think on. The water had both eroded the rock and left deposits of minerals, so the texture had long been altered—and yet, she felt something. It was so dark, closing her eyes was mostly a symbolic gesture, but she did it anyway, and reached out with her magical senses. As she walked along, it was like inked letters appearing on parchment, one at a time, as if dropped there by an invisible author.

"Of course," Vor exclaimed, making everyone flinch at her volume. "Of course," she repeated, more softly. "When you make a circle, you write runes around it. They carved them into the walls. The water has worn and obscured them, but that doesn't matter. The runes carried the magic, and the magic is still in the walls. The earth remembers."

"What do they say?" Dello asked.

"We'd have to walk a ways to read enough to understand, like Ramikar did."

Giri snapped his fingers. "Crossing circles ordinarily breaks them. My master was just teaching me this a month ago. You can build a door into your circle, if you know you'll need to get in or out. It does create a weakness in the circle, but you can also put a lock on it that requires a particular bit of spellwork, or potion, or anything really. Then you can pass through. Ramikar found the key to the door."

"Then let's go back where—" Iyai blurted.

"The door isn't in a particular location," Master Himes overrode her. "It can be used anywhere along the circle if you know how to open the lock. Though I suppose you could link it to just one bit of the circle." She scrunched up her face. "I can't think of a reason why you'd need to, though. Sounds like extra work to me."

"So the invaders found the way in. I'll bet Craduticus found the way in," Vor rattled off.

"And now Ramikar's found the way in," Dello piled on.

"And we're late to the party," Master Himes seethed.

She spun about swiftly enough to make her damp robes swirl out. A hand on the wall, she began walking. The others paced her, their own hands on the wall, too. Vor concentrated on the runes, on the feeling of the runes, as they dropped one at a time to the receptive surface of her mind. For some, she could guess what they were, and visualize them. Others tasted familiar, but not exactly like runes she knew. Others completely baffled her. She wished for a way to write them down, for there were quite a lot of them and she struggled to hold them all in her head.

"I don't know all these," Giri muttered, and got shushed by Master Himes.

They walked another minute or two, until finally their brave leader stopped with a grumbly sigh.

"These are almost all earth runes," she said, "and I know most of them."

"Not all?" Dello breathed.

"Enough," she growled at her apprentice. "I can get us in."

"Into the center of the circle," Giri said carefully. "What will we find in there?"

"Whatever is holding this circle together will be in there, plus some invaders and our companions, I hope. Not to mention, power. As you know, circles contain power; they are active magic at work. I urge you all: don't touch anything." She glared around at the group. "Or you might mess something up."

"Like the capital city of our country," Dello muttered.

Master Himes's glare shifted for a moment into an amused smile.

"Oh, well, if that's all," Giri shrugged, and Vor found a weary chuckle.

Then her smile melted off, as she heard scuffles of movement in the dark. Giri lifted his head.

"You all heard that?" he whispered.

"What is down here?" Master Himes growled through gritted teeth.

The temperature dropped.

"Another one of those things?" Dello asked, a quaver in his voice.

"It feels different," Vor said. "It grabbed me, back before we found Iyai, and it was hot, not cold."

"I need you all to grab onto me and hold tightly," Master Himes instructed. "Hurry up. You should probably also take a deep breath, and possibly close your eyes."

The four of them crowded close to her back, all trying to get an arm around the master wizard's waist. They packed in snug, with Vor between Giri and Iyai, doing her best to also hold Iyai close against Master Himes's right side. Vor heard more shuffling footsteps, getting closer.

"As soon as I tell you we're through, be ready to fight," Master Himes continued. "We might be walking into a battle." Then she cleared her throat. "And if anyone has extra energy to spare, this isn't going to be easy, and I could use it."

Vor didn't really, but she donated some anyway, feeling light headed for a moment afterwards. Everyone else donated, too. A shadow moved in the darkness, and she silently urged Master Himes to hurry up and get them through—not that whatever was on the other side would be any less dangerous. She felt Master Himes take a deep breath, and the magic began to move.

The rocky wall changed its nature. Master Himes put her hands on it, and Vor watched her push them into it: just like bread dough, as Iyai had said. As Master Himes stepped into it, Vor felt Iyai flinch. She closed her eyes, Giri holding tightly to her, and shuffled forward, just as something hot as a branding iron touched her back, and she struggled not to scream.

The soft rock encased them all briefly. When it sealed over Vor's face she was the most afraid. The hot touch on her back vanished. It was a strange sensation, stepping through rock. It was cold, cooling the new burn on her back, but not as cold as water, and the pressure of it made Vor have to fight to move. Under her arm, she felt Master Himes take a breath, hopefully because the master wizard had emerged from the other side. After several seconds the rock rolled off Vor, leaving no residue, and she was able to take a breath, too. The rock released her body, leaving her right foot at the last, and Vor opened her eyes to take in the situation before moving.

"We're through," Master Himes whispered.

The first thing she saw was light: vibrant purple light. It couldn't have been as bright as daylight, but after the near blackness of the tunnels, lit only by the faint glow of their clothing, it was almost painful. The room before them was huge and open. It was perhaps three hundred feet across to the other side. They stood on a ledge several feet wide that rimmed the outer bulge of the sphere-shaped wall behind them.

"The outside of one of the circles," Giri whispered as he looked behind at the wall they'd just passed through. "Each circle with the sample rock in it is actually a sphere, and they ring the anchoring master circle—"

"Hush," Master Himes hissed.

In here, each of the spheres touched, like seven balls pushed into a circle. The walls of the spheres, like the one they'd just passed through, must have been so thick that the connecting tunnels they'd walked between each circle tunnel had no visible evidence here. The ledge they stood on continued around in the inside of the space, at the equator of each sphere, forming repeating curves that arched towards the center of the room. At the innermost point of each of those arches, the ledge widened and a ramp of rock led down towards the center of the floor in an elegant arc as if the room had been rotated, dragging the ramps into trailing curves.

"Seven spheres," Dello muttered, "seven ramps down."

"I said hush," Master Himes repeated.

No one had attacked them at least and, seeing as how there was no need to fight and the ledge seemed perfectly sound, they spread out a little, releasing their tight grips on Master Himes. From where they stood, they couldn't see what was down at the bottom where the ramps must lead without going to the edge and peering over, which no one had been brave enough to do yet. The purple light was also coming from below, but the walls were reflecting it, making it ambient enough to see by. The walls were still wet, and glistened in the light.

Vor was listening hard, but she didn't hear the sounds of battle, not even mage battle, which didn't usually include the clashing of metal weapons and so was often quieter. There was however, a sort of roaring, like a waterfall in the distance. She reached out with her magical senses, and jerked them back with a whimper she bit down on. Beside her, the others winced in turn.

"There is a power source here, incredibly strong," Master Himes breathed, nearly silent. "I am all but magically blinded."

The others murmured their agreement.

"We go down?" Iyai asked. "Ramikar must have gone down."

"They all went down," Master Himes agreed grimly. "Do we want to share their fate?"

"The stone is still calling," Dello mentioned, pulling his out of his pocket.

"With this much power flying around, everything magical would be activated. It's probably not a conscious call. They could all be dead."

Vor took a moment to regard the ring she wore, and indeed, it was now just emitting a constant magical tone, lit up with power that wasn't coming from her. Still, it was power, and that meant—

"Do we dare gather this energy?" Vor wondered. "We could recharge, but I can hardly bear to sense it, much less touch it."

"It will burn you out," Master Himes growled. "Don't you dare."

Iyai moaned a little and put her hands on her head. "It hurts," she whispered.

"You're staying up here," Master Himes ordered. "Ramikar was right to leave you outside, you're so sensitive. This is like swimming in acid for me; it must be far worse for you. Traskitandi, are you alright?"

Vor looked over at Dello. The tall, skinny mage had a look of calm concentration on his face.

"I can handle it," he said softly.

"Can you handle it when we get down there? Closer to it?" Master Himes asked.

"I'll handle it," he repeated.

"And you two?"

Vor exchanged a look with Giri. "I'm fine as long as I don't touch it, I think," she said.

"I'm afraid the longer we stay here, the more it's going to hurt," Giri said. "We need to do what we must and get out. You think anyone is alive down there?" he asked of their leader, almost demanding. "You think anyone could possibly stop this? Whatever the ancient wizards did here, I'm not surprised it killed some of them."

"I'm going down," Master Himes said. "I have to see if I can bring anyone back up. And what if this isn't what the ancient wizards did? What if this is happening because the invaders are undoing what they did?"

Dello stepped up beside his master and touched her arm. "I'm going with you."

Giri looked at Vor and she saw his determination written plainly on his face.

"We're going, too," she said.

Chapter 14
The Key

Iyai stayed behind, huddled in a ball tucked into a corner where two spheres met and trying to hold up shields to resist the pressure of magic in the air. Holding Giri's hand, Vor walked behind Dello and Master Himes to the nearest ramp. As they approached the edge, they could see more of the purple light streaming up from below. She could see it had a center, an intense source at the bottom of the room. The floor seemed only a few stories down, but too far to jump safely, so they took the ramp. As they descended, Vor could begin to make out a column of nearly white light coming up from that bright center. It was nearly constant, not flickering, and yet the roar in her ears began to intensify, as if it were a bonfire, but without the radiant heat. As they got closer to the floor, however, she saw that there were lower level spills of light around the central column that did wave and pulse, and which were much more purple.

Around the purple and white bonfire was a dark ring, as if the light did not reach out to the sides, only up. Vor knew it had to be a magical source of light. No natural fire would behave like that, even if a natural fire could burn purple. In that dark ring of space, Vor saw shapes, bodies: there were people there, and scattered fragments of debris as well. Beyond the dark ring were the walls and the bottoms of the curving ramps. The walls bulged inward and up, outward and down—the lower hemisphere of the spheres—and up them crawled heatless flames of black-violet. Vor wondered if it could be just a trick of the light playing on the wet stone, but it really did look like flames licking along the walls.

"Wait," Master Himes ordered before they stepped down off the bottom of the ramp. There was one step, half a foot above the floor. Even from so close, the floor looked black: the dark ring where no light entered.

The darkness crawled over the shapes of people. There were at least a dozen bodies within view. More could be hidden on the other side of the central magical bonfire.

"That's Lanisala," Dello blurted, darting out a hand to point.

Vor looked, and indeed she could see the woman between their ramp and the end of the next. Lanisala was standing, facing the bonfire, leaning towards it, hands slightly raised and lips parted, as if about to say something. She stood so still, but Vor thought she was still breathing.

The bonfire flared, and a breath of air washed the room, throwing back unbound hair and making robes sway. Vor realized that somehow it was the same as the breaths of air they'd felt in the tunnels above; it passed through the walls. The roaring of the bonfire was more audible here, closer to it, and the wind had a sound to it, too—much like an exhalation, like an actual breath of a living creature, or a hundred creatures breathing all together.

Beyond Lanisala was a cluster of three people—surely invaders since Vor didn't recognize them—clinging to each other, also standing, but with far less aplomb than Lanisala. They looked terrified, but they did not move. In front of them, nearer to the bonfire, was a body on the ground, flat on its front, with no obvious injury. That one did not look to be visibly breathing, and since Vor didn't recognize it either, it had to also be an invader.

There were more shapes beyond them, but they were harder to see, some on the ground, some standing or sitting. Looking in the opposite direction, away from them and Lanisala, Vor could see Ramikar. He was in the midst of one of his long strides, head up, confident, heading around the bonfire, away from Lanisala. He had an arm out, as if to cast magic or hail someone. Beyond him, Vor thought she saw Frimillin, on his knees, hands over his face, also facing the bonfire.

"You get a little time," Master Himes muttered, "before it catches you."

"What?" Dello asked.

"Whatever this is, here." She flung a gesture at the purple bonfire.

"How do we get them out?" Giri asked.

"Your guess is as good as mine, Holstor," Master Himes snapped. "You think I've seen this before? You think I know what this is?"

"The spell holding the city," Vor said carefully, "it's intact, isn't it?"

"For now, yes, I think so," Master Himes answered, still vigorously.

"All the invaders we can see look trapped, too. I don't think they—"

"They could have done something first," Master Himes spat. "This could be the result of what they did and it trapped them after they did it. Maybe this is burning through the power source that keeps the city together, and when all the power is gone, it falls apart."

"We can't reach anyone who is trapped from here, so we can't ask them," Giri said. "What if one of us steps onto the floor, and stays right by the ramp, within arms reach, until they get trapped, and then the rest of us pull that person back onto the ramp, and ask what happened."

"You're assuming that person could come back," Master Himes pointed out. "Once trapped, their mind might stay, even if we could pull their body back."

Another breath of air washed over them. The violet-black wall flames flickered. The central bonfire flared and warped like phantom fire, with the tall central column of light still unmoving.

"Someone goes down to find out," Vor said, "or we abandon them all here. What if we joined hands, and one person stayed on the ramp. The others venture out, as fast as we can, until we can grab someone who is trapped, and then we pull them back."

"Like I said," Master Himes repeated, "we don't know if we can bring them back."

Vor turned on her. "Well, we'll never know until we try."

She stepped off the edge of the ramp.

Giri grabbed her shoulders, trying to pull her back.

"Let go of me," she ordered.

Nothing happened immediately, except Giri urging her to get back on the ramp, and she resisted both his words and tugs on her shoulders. The floor was warm under her feet. The warmth traveled up her legs. The sensation of Giri's hands faded. The bright bonfire of purple and white began to shrink, and the wild undulations of light calmed. The walls weren't on fire any longer, and as she looked around, she could see the other people on the dark ring much more easily, but still they did not move.

The bonfire continued contracting, the purple bled away, leaving only a shimmer of white, a pyramidal column about twice as tall as Vor was. Even the white faded, until it was a colorless cone of energy continually rippling across its surface. Vor breathed easy; she did not feel afraid. But when she looked around at the other people again, she was surprised to see that while she'd been watching the bonfire, everyone else had vanished. She stood alone on the dark ring, though it wasn't dark anymore. It was just an ordinary stone floor: mostly smooth, maybe a little gritty, and a nice even gray.

Vor looked back to the bonfire that now appeared almost like a small mountain of water. Its shape was changing. Pointy parts and rounded parts stuck out and then receded, as if it was adjusting its shape. Then it seemed to make up its mind. The rippled surface contracted, as if sucked down into its hard shape, and Vor saw a broad, deep chest sporting four forelegs, two on each side, one behind the other. A long sloping back led down to long skinny hips, again with two legs on each side. Three impossibly long tapered tails ran from those hips and spread out across the floor, looping around the room. Four wings opened and stretched, lined with long, flexible scales.

But only one thick neck arched up, with one large head atop it.

Vor knew what she faced, from Giri's description, but it was still colorless and slightly blurry, as if it hadn't finished judging her yet. Fear crowded in on her. What if it turned black? She'd done terrible things. She'd murdered her master. The death dragon in its coat of black would execute her in a wash of fire.

But, no—she'd thought about things, too. She'd been aware. She hadn't been completely thoughtless. Maybe moments had been, maybe she hadn't chosen the best path every time, but she hadn't willfully wanted to hurt any-one—only him. That was why, conscious or not, she hadn't fought her hardest to keep Jessika from escaping. She hadn't told her master about Karolan. She'd done what she could to protect innocents.

She'd been limited. She'd been scared. She'd done what she could. She'd tried to make the best decisions—

Vor realized suddenly that she was speaking aloud. "I did what I could."

Surely that would at least grant her the death dragon in its pink form. Surely it would just put her to sleep, and give her the chance to relive her mistakes, to figure out if she deserved the black or the silver. A little moan slipped from her. She wanted the silver. She wanted to be told she'd done her best—that she had not done things wrong, things unforgivable.

"So," a voice rumbled from nowhere. "Death dragon? That's what you think I am?"

"Celestial dragon," she whispered, hardly a sound at all, for her mouth was completely dry.

The entity turned silver, and Vor felt a shudder of relief go through her. Her hands were clasped to her belly, and it was a struggle not to fall to her knees.

"You and most of the others here," it said. It glanced around, apparently towards the other people Vor couldn't see anymore. "A few had different ideas."

Its voice was sexless, and it didn't move its lips when it spoke. Vor thought she probably wasn't hearing with her ears. Somehow it was speaking directly into her mind. Her relief built, and she tried to take steadying breaths. The dragon was silver. So killing her own master had not been—

Its scales rippled. As though ink had been dripped onto it, the dragon began to turn black. It looked at its own arm curiously.

"Oh?" it observed.

"No," Vor moaned.

It looked back at her, the blackness spreading. "Guilty conscience?" it asked, almost sounding amused.

"No," she begged again. "I, I didn't—"

"You didn't mean it?" the dragon completed for her.

Vor's heart twisted. "I meant it," she forced out. "I'm damned."

The dragon shrugged shoulders and wings. "If you say so."

She shook her head desperately. "I don't want to be."

"Then don't be."

"It's my choice?" she asked, utterly confused.

"Who else's?"

She stared at it, still mostly black, but now a few pink patches were appearing. "Yours," she uttered.

"Mine," it laughed and examined a hand on which two talons were black and three pink. "You think I care? You think I'm capable of caring about what you've done? Things are, and I am. You're the one that cares."

Vor took a moment, trying to unravel what it was saying. "So I shouldn't care?"

It eyed her sharply. "Shouldn't you?"

She stood, unable to figure out how to reply, until the multi-limbed patchwork dragon set down its hand and gave the impression of taking a deep breath.

"What matters," it said slowly, "is that you care."

It stared at her, and she stared back, at its luminous eyes. She tried to assemble its meaning. She still had no idea what it really was, but she could sense its enormous power. It had energy that strained the life around it, just by being in its presence. It acted like it was wise, like it knew the secrets of existence. It had told her that what mattered was that she cared.

She'd done some horrible things, including taking another person's life, premeditated and violent. She was tormented over the act, even now, even though the one she'd killed had killed, tortured, and maimed many others without caring that he—

Vor stopped, and found herself drawing an easier breath.

"Ah," the dragon said softly.

She looked up at the creature, still feeling troubled, still a little confused, but—

"You found the difference," it said.

Vor wetted her lips. "I am not my master."

The dragon nodded.

She said, a bit stronger. "I am not Altare."

From nose to tail, the silver spread, a darker pewter along the spine and in the wings, brightening to palest platinum on the belly. The dragon looked itself over, lifting its legs, opening its wings, as if admiring its new coloration.

"Well done," it murmured.

Vor tried to gather herself. This hadn't been what she'd come here for. A different urgency gripped her.

"Please," she rasped, "will you tell me, is the spell breaking?"

"Spell?" it echoed, sounding relatively unconcerned, and now examining its shining tails.

"The spell that holds the city of Anchoria together," she clarified.

It eyed her with some confusion, and then appeared to put some pieces together and straightened up. "Is that what they pinned a bit of me here to power?"

"You," Vor stuttered, fear turning to confusion of her own, "don't know about the spell?"

"I have no interest in spells. Something caught a bit of me, tucked me down here, or up here." It lifted a clawed hand and turned its palm up. "I might have known about it, but I have forgotten. Not that it matters."

Vor was thinking furiously, trying to figure out what was going on, and with the application of logic, her fear faded further. "You're not the celestial dragon?"

"Well," it said with a shrug that moved all four wings, "I am, and I am not. You decided I am."

"It's just, one of the ancient wizards wrote that the death dragon was down here."

"You apparently believed him."

"I don't know," Vor affirmed.

The silvery dragon gestured at itself with one clawed hand, and tilted its head in a way that could only indicate amusement. "It would seem you do."

Vor followed the line of thought. "You're suggesting you will shift your appearance based on what I think you should be and look like."

"Not think," it replied, "expect and hope. So far it's been working, wouldn't you say?"

She had to be sure. "But you're not actually the celestial dragon then."

"Oh I am, for you make me so."

A trickle of fear returned, although she still wasn't certain exactly what was going on. "You're going to kill me, then."

"Really?" Its look of amusement vanished, and it lowered its head to look much more intently at her. It asked carefully, "Is that what you expect and hope?"

Its scales were beautiful, shining silver, perfectly fitted to its nose and cheek, and around its brilliant silver eye, like overlapping polished coins. Vor could see her reflection in that eye. It looked completely real, completely solid. She thought, if she reached out and touched it, it would feel real. So would its claws and teeth, if that was the way it would kill her. She expected though, that a being like this could flatten her with the slightest puff of its power.

"No," she managed to answer it. "I want to live. I hope you will let me live."

The amusement came back, perhaps at her wording of "hope", not "think". It straightened back up to regard her evenly. "That isn't in the story, though, is it? The silver aspect of the death dragon talks to you, and then takes you away under its wing, and into what comes after."

Vor nodded. "That's what Giri said."

"And you believe him."

"Well," she revised, "he did say it's just a myth, but no one really knows what happens after death. I mean, we know it's over. Life is over. You end."

"But no one wants it to be the end," the silver dragon said, sounding weary.

"What are you?" Vor asked. "You're not the celestial dragon, but you are. You changed colors as I felt different things, but you haven't burned me, or put me to sleep, or—"

"I won't kill you," the being said. "Where in the myth that Giri told you did it say anything about the dragon killing those who come before it?"

"It didn't," Vor answered. "He said you come before the dragon after death."

"And are you dead?"

"I don't think so." She put a hand to her own chest, over her heart, but she couldn't feel any thumping. She was suddenly terrified.

"You won't feel anything," the dragon assured her. "We are speaking not with bodies."

Relieved, she relaxed again. "But I'm breathing."

"Your mind thinks it needs that, to talk."

She wasn't in her body, yet she was still herself, able to talk to this magical whatever-it-was. So her real body must be standing there by the ramp, waiting for her return.

"You're talking to everyone," she accused, "everyone standing in the dark ring, at the same time."

"They came to me," it shrugged. "They can walk away at any time. Some will be able to. Others will never want to stop talking, but eventually they will. Others already believed I killed them."

Vor stared at the floor, away from the most gloriously beautiful being she'd ever seen, trying to think.

"I want to leave here with my friends," she said.

It shrugged again. "Then do so."

"Some of them are talking to you. How do I get them to stop?"

"Ah. You can't. You have no power over others, not here, no more than I do."

"You can't bring me to where you are talking to them, so all of us can talk, so I can talk to them, too, and try to convince them to walk away?"

The celestial dragon stared at her curiously for a few moments, twitching its wings. "Well, there is no reason I couldn't do that. Your friends won't be able to see me, however, and you won't be able to see what they see, or hear."

"Even though they are also talking to you?"

"Well," it winced. "It's a little difficult to explain: concurrent versions of a perceived expression of that which is infinite, but which suffer contradictory collapse when—"

"That's fine," Vor agreed.

The dragon nodded, humanlike, and seemed to concentrate. A milky mist spread behind it, obscuring its hindquarters, and the other people who had stood frozen in the dark ring began to appear, but they were moving now. Vor walked towards where Lanisala had been, and found a dim shape standing there, appearing to speak and gesture, but she was blurry, and her words mushy, so that Vor couldn't understand her.

"Lanisala," she called.

The shade of Lanisala paused, as if startled, and then resumed whatever conversation she'd been having. Vor reached out to grab her arm and got a shock when she touched it. A vibrant string of images flashed through Vor's mind, no image lasting more than a second, but they were nothing she'd seen before. She saw a tall bearded man in fine clothes, and a kind, weary woman in servant's clothing, an immaculate home, the Citadel, an older woman in mage robes—and scenes, interactions, bits of conversations. The kind servant woman was braiding her hair. The tall bearded man was scolding her. The older lady mage was teaching her, showing her magic.

Giri, bare and beautiful, long dark hair scattered across a pillow, was arching below her.

Vor ripped herself away, panting though she knew she didn't need to breathe in whatever space she was in. Memories: when she'd touched Lanisala she'd seen the woman's memories. She couldn't get that final image of Giri out of her head and she rubbed at her forehead.

"Vor?"

She whipped back around. Lanisala's image had firmed up, looking almost natural. Her eyes were wide and her rich skin a little pasty. Vor realized that as she had seen Lanisala's memories when they touched, Lanisala must have also seen hers. Vor wondered what she'd seen, but there was no time for it now.

"Lanisala," she said. "Do you understand what has happened to you? I saw your body, frozen, standing before the lit center of the room. This is happening only in your mind. You must return to your body and walk away, back to the ramp."

Lanisala's gaze went towards the light, where Vor's celestial dragon was still partly visible.

"I still have questions," she murmured.

"That's too bad," Vor growled. "We all do. No matter how much we learn, we always will. Get back in your body."

Her gaze went back to Vor. "What about you?"

"I'm going to try waking everybody up. We've found the key, here, that holds the city together. I don't think the invaders have the power to undo whatever the ancient wizards did, but I'll try to wake them up, too."

Lanisala looked again at the central brightness. After several moments, she returned to Vor. Now her face was creased with concern.

"I see," she murmured.

"We can share what we've learned with each other when we awake," Vor suggested as a compromise for leaving so many mysteries unanswered.

Lanisala stared at her, much of her usual arrogance gone from her face. Vor wondered if she, too, looked different. Her sense of Lanisala had changed in that one touch, in the sudden download of flashing memories. She couldn't remember them all, but it was like there was a new flavor when she looked at Lanisala. She didn't despise the woman quite so much anymore.

"I'll help you," Lanisala said. "It will go faster with two of us. I don't think we should be away from our bodies too long."

"Alright," Vor agreed. "I'm afraid, to get someone's attention, you might have to touch them, and that thing might happen, that happened with us."

Lanisala nodded. "Yes," she said softly, "but it can't be helped."

She turned to walk to the next nearest person, and Vor turned around to go back the way she came, towards where Ramikar had been. She found him sitting cross legged on the floor, smiling, she thought, though his face was a little blurry. She waved her hand in front of his eyes and called his name. He seemed to notice something, and investigate, looking around. With repetition, Vor noticed his outline become firmer, and she was relieved when he focused on her without her having to touch him.

"Vor?" he asked. "That is you?"

"It is I," she answered.

His expression shifted from happy to concerned. "Are you alright? Where's Iyai?"

"Iyai is safe," she told him. "We found her. She's not trapped down here. You know what's going on?"

"I am speaking with an entity of energy," he replied. "It has attained consciousness and can interact with my energy. It's absolutely fascinating."

"Yes, it is," Vor agreed. To one side, her partial celestial dragon seemed to grin. "But we have to get out. Being down here too long will kill our physical bodies."

Ramikar sighed. "I know."

"You're not planning to stay?" Vor gaped.

He took a moment to answer, running a hand through his hair. "I know," he said again, although Vor didn't think he was talking to her. Then he quirked a smile her way. "Yes, I know. I will be back, one day, and then many questions will be answered, and many more created. It won't be that long, only a handful of decades. That's nothing, really."

Vor eyed him. "So, you'll go back to your body?"

He shrugged. "I suppose I must. Who will be Iyai's master, if I don't?"

"Thank you," Vor told him.

"I'll go get Frimillin, first. He wasn't very far from me."

"Again, thank you," Vor repeated.

He walked away, and Vor could see Frimillin, on his knees, hands over his face, just like he'd been in the physical world. Then beyond him, Vor saw

Craduticus. As Ramikar went to Frimillin, blurry again since he was no longer focusing on Vor, she walked past, heading for Craduticus. The old wizard was standing tall, head tipped up, and he was perfectly in view. When Vor drew up to a few feet away, he glanced at her.

"Hello, Vor," he said kindly.

"Master Craduticus," she said.

Beside his feet, she saw Breeka. The bat-cat was curled up, its outline barely holding together. Craduticus followed her gaze.

"Don't worry," he said gently. "Breeka will go with me, so we won't be alone."

"Go?" Vor whispered, suddenly struck with distress. "Master Craduticus, you don't have to go. Come back, please. We need you."

"No, you don't," he smiled.

"Yes, we do."

His tone did not turn sharp, but it was still final. "Don't argue with me, Wizard Hearthsraven." Then he lowered his head at her, to give her a firm glare, like he might give to a disobedient student. "You, however, need to get back to Giri. He is trying to wake you, and can't."

A prickle of fear went through her, but overriding that, she stared at him, not knowing what to say. She found it impossible to imagine a world where he wasn't there to turn to for advice, for wisdom, for help.

"This is the way of it," he said kindly. "We pass, which does not just mean we die. We pass along the world, and what we've learned. We pass it on to those who follow, like a gift. I've written down everything I know. It's in a box in my room. Your touch will open it. Take it. Read it. Decide what you should teach to your apprentices."

Now his expression turned hard. "That is not a decision to be taken lightly, and I don't mean only what it is in my book. There is much more to teach than just facts, just knowledge. There are things that are much harder and much more important, and there is only so much time, but it must be passed on."

"Yes, Master," she said. Her gaze once more turned to Breeka. "I could carry Breeka out, if you are willing to go alone."

Now his composure cracked. "Dear Vor, Breeka's body has already gone cold."

Vor's throat choked, her chest ached. She felt the heat of burgeoning tears. "No," she whispered.

"Breeka will go with me," he said, and summoned up a smile. "It will all be alright."

"What," Vor fumbled, "what was Breeka?"

"It is a sad story," Craduticus said. "Are you sure you want to know?"

Vor nodded.

"Your late and unlamented master Altare, my former apprentice, was try-ing to make a demon, a tame demon, of course, that would obey with no other payment than room and board, a demon of this world, not one summoned from another plane. He thought he could breed an army of them, if he worked out the right recipe, the right spells. He wouldn't listen when I told him that was folly. As he tired of each of his flower girls, he'd breed on her, trying to get a demon child."

"Breeka?" Vor gaped.

Craduticus nodded. "Breeka was one of the few that lived more than a few days, and the only one with any awareness, but it wasn't what Altare want-ed. He began experimenting on Breeka, trying to see what had gone wrong." The mage rubbed at his brow. "To me, it looked like cutting up a baby. Breeka's cries I could not stand. When Breeka reached for me, for help, I could not tol-erate it any longer. It was the final act that broke through to me, and I couldn't not care any longer."

Vor took that in. Beside her, the silvery dragon nodded solemnly.

"I remember when you fought him, when you left the castle," Vor said.

Pain streaked his face. "I should have taken you. I took Breeka, but I should have taken you, too. I should have killed him that night. Instead, I saved myself, and left him for you. Vor, can you ever forgive me?"

She centered herself, and considered her feelings, and how she and Craduticus carried much the same fears, much the same pain. "You cannot save everyone," she said. "You tried. You do what you can, what you must. You have protected Jessika, and Breeka, and you helped me when I fought Altare. I could not have defeated him without your help. I survived, and I forgive you."

"Thank you," he declared solemnly.

Vor put her hand to her shoulder. "I will carry your mark that says you believe in me. I thank you for all you've done. I wish I could have known you better."

"You have read my journals in my cottage. Read the book I have left for you in my room here. Whenever you miss me, read my words, and there I am. Now, you should get along."

Vor nodded, but still had to force herself to say the words. "Goodbye, Master Craduticus."

"Goodbye, Vor Hearthsraven."

"Bad girl," came a sudden exclamation from Breeka. The bat-cat, now far less blurry, peered around Craduticus's legs, and Vor broke into a smile. "Bad girl not bad," it said. "Good girl, go back to dumb boy. Help dumb boy be smart. Breeka goes with master."

"Thank you, Breeka," Vor said. "I will miss you, and remember you fondly."

The permanent stubborn expression on the bat-cat's face softened. "Breeka, too."

Craduticus was still smiling. Vor managed a smile in return, bowed, and turned to go.

"Now," she heard from behind her as she walked back towards her body, "where were we?"

She knew where she'd come from, where she'd stood as she first looked upon the celestial dragon, and returned to put her feet on the spot. The big silver dragon sat before her again, having watched in silence. She could no longer see other dim shapes of the people trapped in the dark ring. It was just her and the dragon.

"Going now, are we?" the being asked.

"Yes, but I'm not sure how," Vor confessed. "Craduticus said Giri is trying to wake me up, but I can't feel his hands on my shoulders."

"That is because he has pulled your body out of the dark ring, as you put it," the dragon replied. "You aren't standing where your body is anymore."

Vor turned to look behind her, but couldn't see the ramp, only blackness.

"There is nothing there," the dragon said. "The influence of, shall we say, my presence only extends as far as what you call the dark ring."

Anxiety began to prick at her. "Then how do I get back to my body?"

"They need to put it back into the ring."

"But I can't tell them that."

"No, you cannot. You have forgotten the plan you made with them."

"One of us goes into the ring, and then the others pull them back out," she said, a chill of dread settling over her. "It didn't work, just like Master Himes thought. I'm trapped here for real now."

But then she felt warm tingling on her feet.

"Ah," the celestial dragon purred. "There you go."

She looked back over her shoulder at it.

"Follow that feeling," it told her. "Just close your eyes, and let yourself follow."

Vor ran her eyes over the creature, trying to memorize its beauty and grandeur. "Thank you," she told it.

"Thank you," it replied, "for a lovely conversation. In gratitude, allow me to show you something."

"And what's that?"

"When you came into this room, you reached out to touch my energies and were burned by them."

"Yes," she agreed, thinking back to standing on the ledge assessing the situation and all the power filling the room.

"You were burned because you reached out with the wrong part of you."

"Alright," Vor said, trying to follow.

"Reach out now. Don't be afraid."

Vor sought her personal mage power—and found it missing.

"Don't panic," the being said. "Your mage energies are in your body, which you're not in right now. Reach out with what you are now."

Vor frowned, and not knowing what else to do, put out her hand.

"There you go," the dragon purred.

The dragon leaned its head and neck towards her, and touched its nose to her fingertips. There was no shock, no warmth, no sensation she could blame her five senses on, and yet there was something within her, something that was her. Vor looked at herself, supposedly standing there in stained and torn clothes, and sensed purple light shimmering on her every surface inside and out. She reminded herself that she wasn't seeing anything with her actual eyes—that she only thought she was because it was what she expected and hoped.

With that thought, the look of her skin and clothes vanished, and she was shimmering light, just like the celestial dragon. Then for a half a second she felt something more than herself; she felt everything, a part of everything, while she herself became nothing, and yet everything. A word she'd rarely had cause to use, and didn't even fully understand, came to mind: universe.

Just before the feeling could overwhelm her sanity, the energy that had appeared to her in the shape of a multi-limbed silver dragon drew its nose away, and she returned to being just a person, standing there in stained and torn clothes, horribly exhausted, so hungry she felt sick, and yet hopeful. Vor stared at the creature before her. It gave her a slow little nod, and she was smiling without knowing why.

Then it said its farewell. "One day, many years from now, in a place far distant from here, we shall meet again. I will look forward to it."

"As will I," Vor said, feeling awkward and unsteady, "but not so much that I can't wait a lifetime."

The dragon shape evaporated back into the bonfire of light. Vor closed her eyes and concentrated on the warmth on her feet. She had no feeling of dissolving or flowing down through her feet and into her body, but suddenly she was in it again, feeling the hard rock ramp against her back and Giri's hands on her face.

"Kiss her," Lanisala's voice ordered. "That works in nursery tales."

And she felt Giri's desperate mouth on hers, flavored with the salt of his tears. Vor smiled against his lips and wrapped her arms around his neck.

"See?" Lanisala declared triumphantly. "It works."

Then Giri was pulling back, babbling over her, touching her all over to be sure she was whole, and she was trying to convince him she was fine. When he finally let her sit up, her feet were still in the dark ring, and she saw all the others except Craduticus, Breeka, and Iyai gathered around at the end of the ramp. Just beyond them a few feet up the ramp, were a half a dozen of the invaders, looking scared and sheepish. Vor got to her feet, standing in the dark ring, and everyone gasped and called her back.

"It's alright," she told them, chuckling inwardly. "I can walk on it now. I have an agreement with the purple bonfire."

She felt the energy, but she knew what part of her to touch it with, and what part to keep her distance with, and so it did not pull her from her body again.

"I'm going to go up to Iyai," Ramikar announced, and without another word pushed past the invaders and headed up the ramp.

"I'll go, too," Lanisala said, and followed him. "Iyai must be frightened."

"They were saying," Dello spoke up, jerking a thumb over his shoulder at the invaders, "that it was like this when they got down here. They didn't do anything to it. They were just trying to figure out how to turn it off, when it caught them. I guess some of them, somehow died from it."

Vor nodded and walked out into the ring. She circled the magical bonfire, finding the bodies of several invaders. She checked for a pulse on each one, and felt nothing. What she did not find was the body of Craduticus or Breeka. She could only guess that Craduticus had walked into the bonfire with Breeka in his arms. Perhaps their bodies lay in the center, but she wasn't about to go look, or perhaps even their tired, exhausted flesh and bone had melted into pure energy, and there would never be remains to find.

Vor returned to the others. "Do you want to bring their bodies back?" she asked the invaders.

Vor recognized a few of them. One near the front of the group she thought had been called Tallie, when Vor and the other mages had been their prisoners. Most of the others were hunched over or turned away, hiding their faces.

"How would we carry them out, even if we wanted to bring them out?" the woman called Tallie asked sadly.

"How are we getting out, for that matter," Master Himes grumbled, and then to Vor, "And what happened when you were trapped?"

"One thing at a time" Giri encouraged. "Vor and all the others who were trapped will have to give a full accounting, once we're back at the Citadel, so that will come out in time."

"You think, oh, just snap our fingers and we can go back to the Citadel?" Master Himes rounded on him now. "Coming down was hard enough. Now we have to do everything we just did, in reverse, against the pull of gravity, when we're hurt and tired and hungry."

"I can move the bodies together, so they lie in company," Vor said to Tallie. "Perhaps under the curve of one of the spheres?"

"Can we put them in the fire?" Tallie asked, pointing at the bonfire.

Vor looked and winced. She had some immunity now to the pull of the power, but she didn't think it would extend to approaching that close to the center.

"Under a sphere is fine," Tallie revised.

"I'm sorry they have to rest down here, so far from their homes," Vor offered.

Tallie lifted her chin with a hint of defiance. "Most of them didn't have homes. In most cases our families either reject us or are scared for us and of us. Lying together will be enough."

So Vor went out onto the dark ring again, and one at a time dragged the bodies to the sphere nearest the ramp everyone still crouched on. She noted that the invader called Vittara, who had seemed to be one of the leaders and had cut off Master Himes's wizard marks, was not among the bodies. Nor did she see the woman among the survivors. The two men called Kardy and Granken were among the dead. She didn't know any of the others' names.

"Is there anything they have on them that you want to bring back?" Vor asked when she was done.

Tallie shook her head, but two of the other survivors exchanged a look and stood up. "We'll go get our packs," one of the men said, and the two got up and began ascending the ramp.

Finally, Vor stepped off the dark ring, back onto the ramp, with a sigh of relief.

"Can I ask," she said to Tallie.

"Where's Vittara?" the woman guessed. "She walked into the fire, first thing. She didn't even say anything. I don't know if she thought she was going to break the spell, or if she was compelled by something, or what. She never came back out."

"How did the others die?" Giri asked.

Tallie shrugged helplessly. "We all walked into the circle almost at the same time, to try to start examining the spell and taking it apart, and then things started happening to us, I guess, different things. Some of us died. I don't know why."

"I want to know what happened when you were all out there trapped," Master Himes demanded, standing up in order to loom better. "What did you see?"

"I'll tell you all about it later," Vor promised.

That didn't seem good enough, and the master mage whirled to face the bonfire.

"No, Master," Dello said calmly, but firmly, stepping between her and the dark ring. "You're not going out there."

Master Himes's face clouded with a building reprimand.

Vor sighed with as much grumpy drama as she could put into it. "I would have to go and fetch you, and I already did that with Lanisala and Ramikar, and I'm tired. Be a good master wizard, and stay here. There's nothing out there you need that you won't learn in time."

Master Himes's face when she turned to Vor was approaching outrage.

"How dare you tell me what to do, both of you," she hissed. "This is an opportunity unlike any other. You took advantage of it and now you want to stop me from getting to know what you know?"

"And now you know how the magic-gifted commoners feel," Vor said.

Master Himes's outrage faded somewhat, but her mouth firmed up with stubbornness. Vor gave in.

"I don't have the energy to argue with you," she sighed. "Alright. Master Himes, Dello, Giri, do you want to see?" she asked. "I can guide you."

"Yes," Master Himes answered immediately.

Dello and Giri were more cautious, eying each other and the mysterious bonfire-like energy swirl.

"It doesn't hurt, and it's not dangerous unless you make it so," Vor assured them, "but I'd like to ask that when you get trapped, do not move from where you started. If you walk away from your body, it's harder to get back and I might have to come out there with you."

Dello blinked at her. "If I walk away from my body?" he echoed.

"Just step out here," Vor directed, "and once you're on the ring, just stay here, exactly here. Don't move your feet anywhere. I'll give you a little while, but then I'll wake you up, so keep the conversation moving."

Understanding now what happened, and having touched the power that flowed through the bonfire-like eruption of energy, Vor thought she would be able to wake the sleepers up without having to get trapped herself. After a moment, Dello moved forward beside Master Himes, ready to step down onto the ring. Giri gazed at Vor for a few moments.

"There's something different about you now," he murmured. "I trust you can get me out."

"I will get you out," Vor promised, "all three of you, even if I do have to get down there with you."

"What is it?" Dello asked nervously. "What are we going to see?"

"What you expect and hope to see," she told him. "When you're ready, step down."

Master Himes went first and crossed her arms over her chest. Vor sensed when the power took her and watched the stillness come over her. Dello and Giri stepped down together, and after a few breaths, they went still as well. Vor stood behind them, on the edge of the ramp. After a few breaths it seemed they weren't about to drop dead, or whatever had happened to the deceased invaders, and she relaxed a little. She wondered if the being, or entity, whatever it was, had been protecting itself, or if it had judged the invaders and executed them as evil, maybe when they started trying to break the spell—but then, it had spoken to Vor like only her expectations were realized when she stepped into the dark ring. Had they expected that approaching the key would kill them, so it had?

"Thank you all for getting us out," Tallie said from behind her.

Tallie and two invaders were still sitting there. Vor saw the two others returning burdened with a half a dozen packs. Frimillin was also still sitting on the ramp, his face in his hands, utterly silent.

"We would have died out there," Tallie went on, "and you wizards could have left us there, just got your own companions and got out, without any danger to yourselves. Those other two came and woke a couple of us, so we could get our companions, too. They said it was only because you woke them. Then you even fetched our dead for us."

"It's not right to let someone die, when you can save them, especially with minimal risk to yourself," Vor replied. "That's as bad as murdering someone."

"We hurt you, though," Tallie went on, "back up in the caves. We were going to leave you to die. It would only be fair if you did that to us, too."

"Yeah, well, life isn't fair," Vor declared wryly. "Get used to it."

She turned back to watch over Master Himes, Dello, and Giri. She'd give them another few minutes. She'd had quite a while with her celestial dragon, after all. That sort of fairness she'd support. They were perfectly still except for breathing, just as seemed to be ideal.

Then Frimillin cried out, followed immediately by Tallie and other voices, and Vor spun about to see one of the invaders who had fetched the packs trying to drive a knife into Frimillin. The wizard was still seated, the invader standing over him. They were struggling for control of the blade. Meanwhile, the other pack-carrying invader ran for Giri's undefended, unaware back, another knife in his hands.

As the man leapt, Vor set her feet and launched a step-through thrust kick directly into the center of his body, putting her whole weight into it. Her adversary was airborne, with nothing to control his path but his own velocity, gravity, and Vor's redirecting kick. He missed his target, tumbling past Giri's right shoulder, and rolled into the dark ring. The man cursed as he hit, lost the knife, and started to get to his hands and knees.

Then he went still as the bonfire reclaimed him.

Vor turned back to where Frimillin was now wrestling with the man who had tried to stab him. Tallie was shouting and trying to grab the knife-wielder's wrist, while the other two invaders who'd been sitting with Tallie had shrunk back, as if afraid to get involved. The knife-wielding invader was on top of the struggling trio. Vor braced her feet, wrapped her arm around his neck from behind and grabbed her other forearm as she put her other hand against the back of his head. Then she tightened. He struggled, but Tallie had his knife hand now and was hanging on like a stubborn dog in a tug-of-war. In a few more seconds, he stopped fighting, and Vor pulled him off of Frimillin.

"What should I do with him, Tallie?" Vor asked, panting. "He's your friend."

Tallie had wrestled the knife away, and stood now halfway between fury and tears.

"You all saved us," she half shouted, half sobbed, "and they tried to kill you. I don't know why—why he'd do this."

Frimillin was sprawled on the ramp, groaning. He had a hand clasped to his right trapezius muscle and blood was leaking between his fingers.

"He got the first stab in before I realized what was happening," the husky wizard gritted out.

"You commoner mages killed dozens of us," Vor assured Tallie. "When you put up the shield over the Citadel, and released the golems and blade-tails, you killed many wizards. Wasn't that your objective?"

"Yes, I mean, no, I mean, I didn't know," Tallie pleaded. "Vitta said," she whispered at last and trailed off, head drooping in shame.

"You didn't know that some of us are just as human as you, that we'd save you if we could? Some of your friends still don't know that," Vor said roughly, trying to manage the unconscious knife-man's weight. "No matter what group of people you have, or how you try to label them, there is going to be a mix of people in there. They won't all be the same. But there's a lot of that attitude going around, not just with you and your friends. I'd like to declare a truce, at least until we can get out of here."

"I will declare a truce with you," Tallie nodded.

While she'd been talking, Vor's grip had shifted, and the recovering invader she held threw an elbow back into her gut as he regained consciousness. Vor grunted at the sharp strike.

"Wizard bitch," he snarled. "No truce. Never!"

Vor immediately tried to tighten the choke hold, but he'd tucked his chin so she couldn't get her arm against his throat. She already had him on his knees, being on one knee herself, but she knew he wouldn't stay there long. His hands went straight for her arms, and she knew she couldn't let him get a grip on her; he was much stronger and would win that struggle. She whipped her arms back out of his reach, and drove a swift fist into his kidney with as much strength as she could find.

Teeth gritted, letting the anger that he'd stabbed Frimillin fuel her, she repeated the strike, into his kidney again and again as if she were practicing on a hanging bag, making him snarl. She only got a few strikes in before he started to turn, and she saw his hand reaching back for her head, probably to grab her hair. Vor stood up, much easier for her than for him, because she had one knee up already.

She set her right foot back, and delivered another kick, this one to the back of his head, snapping it forward, and he fell forward to catch himself on his hands. Vor reset and kicked out one of his supporting arms, so he half fell to the ground, spitting garbled curses at her. Still, she wasn't sure what to do with him. He still had some fight in him, and in a prolonged struggle, his size and strength would probably see him the victor. He was stunned right now; she might be able to drag him into the dark ring, but—

"Here," Frimillin growled, and his free hand landed on the man's head.

In a blink, the invader stilled, not dead, but perhaps deeply asleep.

"He'll wake up in a few hours," Frimillin said, still panting with pain. "Hopefully, we'll all be gone by then. He'll have his own chance to escape, but from what I sensed, his skills might not be enough to get him through the wall." The wizard shrugged his uninjured shoulder. "But then again, desperation can bring out heretofore unknown abilities."

Vor was panting now, and bent over to brace her hands on her knees. The lack of food, all the power she'd thrown around recently, dragging the heavy bodies by herself, and then a couple tussles had worn her out.

"Wake those three up," Frimillin ordered. "I'll watch the scum."

Vor nodded. She went to Giri first. Laying her hands on his shoulders, she reached out with the same part of her that had reached out to the celestial dragon, and touched that same part in Giri. She couldn't speak to him in thoughts, but still the message passed.

"Come back," she murmured. "Come out, come up, come back to me, to here."

She sensed his return, that the body below her hands was no longer empty, and then he was stepping back up onto the ramp, and taking her for a hard hug.

"Thank you," he whispered.

"You're welcome," Vor replied. "Now will you help watch the mages?"

"What happened to you?" Giri exclaimed upon seeing Frimillin.

Vor went next to Dello while Frimillin filled in Giri on what had happened. It took a little longer to bring Dello up, just because Vor wasn't attuned to him the way she was to Giri, but then he, too, was joining them on the ramp again, shaking his head in wonderment. Master Himes took the longest to rouse, and as the minutes passed, Vor began to fear that she wouldn't be able to do it. Dello came and joined her, though she wasn't sure he was reaching out in the same way she was.

Then at last, Master Himes took a deep breath and lifted a hand to pat Vor's where it rested on her shoulder.

"Don't worry," she said, "I'm back. And that's my hurt shoulder."

As Master Himes stepped back up onto the ramp, Vor slumped down to the floor, pulling up her knees and resting her head on them. She was very nearly out of energy now. She felt so drained, even the walk back up the ramp sounded like a trial. And after that, once someone helped her pass through the rock wall, she was going to have to climb back up that natural crack in the rock? And after that, crawl through the long cave tunnel, and the swim again? Then find a way to get herself up out of the bone room pit? What if the drakes were back?

She needed food and sleep. If she could get alone with Giri for a few minutes, they could possibly generate some energy together amorously—if they weren't too flat out exhausted—but that seemed unlikely in their current environs—

Suddenly the bonfire flared, bathing the group in a torrent of light and making everyone flinch.

"What in the world?" Dello exclaimed.

Everyone was looking at it when the next flare happened, so they were all blinded by the flash.

Then the room shook for a moment.

"Impossible," Master Himes breathed.

Ramikar came half running, half sliding down the ramp.

"You feel it?" he demanded.

Another flare shocked their vision again, and Vor felt the power of the spell falter. The room shook again, more violently.

"What's happening?" one of the invaders quavered out.

"Exactly what you wanted," Master Himes snarled.

"The spell's coming apart," Ramikar said. "What did you do?"

"We didn't do anything," Tallie pleaded.

Another shake came with another, more extended torrent of light, and the rasp of pure magical energy from the bonfire felt like a cheese grater against Vor's senses. Giri's hand landed on her back, and she felt him merge his energy with hers. She sensed him begin building a protective shield, but she didn't think that would work. Sure enough, the next flare of power—with another tremble of the stone below them—burned the shield away.

A triumphant and totally insane cackle of laughter came from the direction of the bonfire.

"I've got it!" the voice, shrill and female, trumpeted. "I've got it!"

A spear of white-hot mage-fire flashed over Vor and into the blinding glare of the bonfire, but it seemed to get lost in the light, and Vor couldn't tell if it hit anything. The subtle roar of the bonfire began to increase.

"She's spreading open the conduit," Ramikar shouted. "It will overload the spell and break it."

"Vittara!" Tallie screamed. "Stop it!"

A lash of power circled out from the bonfire, like a long whip, striking around the room. It missed everyone who was crouched down or lower on the ramp, or who dodged it, but it hit Tallie in the face and knocked her flat.

"We have to close it back up," Master Himes declared.

Another lash circled the room, this one lower, and everyone ducked.

"Traskitandi," Master Himes ordered, "block those attacks."

"Here," Ramikar called, kneeling down beside Master Himes and taking her hand.

Frimillin scooted over to them, too, and the trio of master wizards literally put their heads together. Dello landed on his knees beside Vor and Giri.

"Shields won't work," Vor cautioned.

"Yeah, I already tried," Giri confirmed.

"We'll have to redirect it, deflect it," Vor suggested.

Giri gathered Dello's energy into their meld just as another vibrant lash began circling the room. Giri took the lead, building up an angled barrier of power, so when the lash came around, it ran up off the barrier, flashing upwards to hit the ceiling, but it burned the barrier down to motes of energy.

"We can't do that too many times," Giri gasped after his breath.

"Master, hurry up," Dello urged.

It was a sign of her deep involvement in the work, that she didn't even tell him to shut up. Another tremblor shook the room, this one longer. Vor, Giri, and Dello began gathering energy again. One of the commoner mages who hadn't been hit with the lash attacks crawled over to the trio. He was young and skinny and clearly scared.

"Can I help?" he rasped out.

"You can donate," Dello snapped, grabbing his wrist.

Another lash of power whipped out from the swelling bonfire, and again Giri built an angled shield. Vor helped him hold it, bolstering it from below, and felt when the lash hit it, but this time the lash was sticky, and it ripped at the shield, tearing at the energies supporting it, and Vor cried out as it yanked at what was left of her personal energy. It tore at her like it was tearing off a limb, and only when Giri threw his power against it, cutting at it like a knife, did the lash slap away into a wall.

"This isn't working," Dello grunted. "That really hurt."

Spears of hardened power came flying from the bonfire, driving out like rays of light, directly into the gathering of mages on the end of the ramp. There were no shields in place, the recent lash having just ripped all shreds of the last one away. Vor felt one skim past her ear, making it burn and tingle. The commoner mage by Dello grunted and fell back. Giri choked down a cry, grabbing at his thigh. Behind them, Master Himes gasped, and Dello immediately turned to check on her.

Vor looked to Giri. There was no blood. The magical spear had been pure power and had attacked him on a magical level, searing his energy and turning it to pain signals. Merged as their energies were, she could feel the echo of the injury in her own leg. He had both hands clasped around his thigh, as though trying to stop bleeding that wasn't there. He shook, swallowing his cries. The pressure of his hands could override pain signals, which was what he was probably trying for. The pain would be breaking his concentration, keeping him from working any magic to try to fix it.

"Hurts," he gritted out.

Beside him, the commoner mage who had been struck was writhing, moaning, hands pressed to his chest, but if Vor was going to help someone, there was no question who. She detached her energy completely from Giri's and the phantom pain vanished. She clapped her hands over his, on his thigh.

"Stop trying to fix anything and let me do it," she commanded.

Giri shuddered, taking gasping breaths, and Vor sent her attention to the energy patterns in his leg. It was chemical energy, lighting up all his nerves, so she would have to convert it to something less harmful. She couldn't make it heat instead—that would only burn him. His muscles were already locked up, so kinetic energy was out. She couldn't convert it back into his personal energy; he would have had to do that himself. What she could do was steal the energy from him, and convert it into her own energy. Then she could give it back.

She only hoped another attack didn't come while she was doing it.

The room shook again, a prolonged vibration. Vor tried to ignore it. Taking Giri's energy and making it hers wasn't difficult, and it only took a few breaths of time. She saw him begin to relax as soon as she started. It would leave his thigh numb for a little while, but at least he'd be able to focus again. She drew on the energy, swirling it into her own like mixing liquids in a potion. She changed its nature, converting it from chemical energy to basic life energy.

Giri slumped, trembling, but breathing easy now.

"Thank you," he stuttered.

"Take it back," Vor encouraged.

"No," he argued. "Vor, we can't stop these attacks. The next one will finish us."

They both looked over where Dello was cradling his master, one hand behind her back and the other over her sternum. Her face was twisted with agony. Ramikar and Frimillin still had their heads together. She could see sweat coating their faces in a fine sheen.

Giri grabbed her hand. "You can walk into the dark ring. Go take her out."

Vor snapped her gaze over to the bonfire. It was twisting, fluttering, flaring, as if unstable. At its base, just in front of it, she thought she saw a slightly darker figure standing.

"I can't face this power alone. It's too great," Vor objected.

"Just how you took down Altare," Giri suggested.

She considered quickly. Mages were experts at slinging power about in various forms, but mostly they were not skilled in physical fighting. That vulnerability had allowed Vor to defeat Altare in a way he was not prepared to defend against: with an actual spear.

"If I can get through the magic," Vor muttered.

It seemed like the best chance. If nothing else, she could maybe distract Vittara long enough for the master wizards to stop her from whatever she was doing to break the spell holding the city together. If Vittara succeeded, they'd all die.

A deep rumble went through the rock around them. With a shocking pop, a crack zigzagged its way up the side of one rounded wall. Vor got to her feet. Another lash of power came slashing through the air, but she ducked it and stepped out into the dark ring. The effects of the flashing bonfire were worse on the ring. Spurts of wild power buffeted her as she struggled to keep her feet. Just a couple yards away the invader who had attacked Giri with a knife still posed on all fours, but his face was grimacing in fear. Whatever he was seeing, Vor didn't want to know.

She snatched up the knife he'd dropped when she'd sent him tumbling, and wove her way towards the center of the bonfire and the figure standing before it. More spears of energy went flying past, luckily missing Vor, as she'd had hardly any warning. The roar of the bonfire was so pervasive now, she couldn't have heard if the spears hit anyone behind her. Step by step, she came closer to the blinding white center. Tears streamed from her eyes and she squinted them almost completely shut, trying to look only at the slightly darker figure that was her target.

It was like walking through a wind storm: blinded, deafened, and barely able to stay on her feet. Vor didn't bother trying to put up any shields, knowing that the wild flares of power would only rasp them away. She just tried to hold onto her personal power—that which gave her body life—even as the magical winds ripped at it.

As she got near the center, she began having to lean in, against the terrible pressure erupting out. The human figure she'd seen loomed before her, the power of the bonfire wrapping around it as if consuming it. Whatever was happening, Vor didn't think this person would survive it. She could only assume it was Vittara—the only missing invader—but she couldn't make out any facial features. After a moment, Vor realized the person was turned away from her, facing into the magical fire.

There was another person there, on Vittara's other side, facing her from deeper in the bonfire. Vor felt a faint contact, not against her mage energies, but against that which she'd touched the celestial dragon with: her deeper self. She recognized it.

Craduticus was standing there, in some form, stopping Vittara from doing whatever she was trying to do.

Vor gripped the knife handle, reminding herself that she didn't have to strike to kill. She just had to break Vittara's concentration. Magic required focus. Vor, however, could barely keep her feet, and found she couldn't manage another step closer, but she also couldn't reach Vittara yet.

A blast of magic wind and flame hit her and she slid backwards, falling to her hands and knees. Vor gritted her teeth. So she'd crawl. On her hands and knees she crept closer, trying to hold the last of her energies in. She came within reach of Vittara's ankles and raised up the knife against the gale of power.

Then the pressure lessened. Vor looked up. Behind Craduticus spread wide bat-like wings, blocking the torrent. With a spread as wide as a good-sized griffin, the wings deflected the horrible wind, but Vor sensed they wouldn't hold for long. She drew back the knife, and drove it down into one of Bellara's feet.

The blade went all the way through, so the tip hit the rock she stood on. Vittara buckled, and Vor stabbed her other foot for good measure. Bellara dropped to her knees, catching herself on her hands, any cry she made lost in the roar of the bonfire.

"Get out, Vor," she heard in her head.

Vor looked up again. The wings were folding back in, the membranes between the bones thinning and starting to rip. The white fire took the image of Craduticus, of Breeka's somehow massive sheltering wings. Vor left the knife and started to scramble blindly backwards.

Vittara's kick hit her in the jaw, dazing her. She felt someone grab her tunic. Sharp pain bit into her shoulder, and Vor thrashed her body, trying to wrench away. Vittara's weight shoved her back and Vor saw that there was a knife now in her upper arm, hence the pain. She caught a glimpse of Vittara's face, snarling, all sense gone from her eyes.

"I'll have it," she yowled. "Give it to me!"

Vittara yanked the knife out and went for a second strike, but Vor twisted away and the blade hit nothing but stone. Vor tucked up her legs and kicked out, catching Vittara in the face, breaking her nose, sending out a spray of blood.

Freed, Vor scrambled back again. The bonfire roared. Two long, clawed limbs emerged from the fire, grabbing Vittara's ankles, and pulled. Vittara screamed and scrabbled at the floor with her hands.

Vor rolled back to her belly and crawled away as fast as she could, until she could gain her feet, and stagger the rest of the way back to the ramp. She could hardly see, her eyes were so light-dazzled. She tripped over the step up and half fell on Giri. The bonfire roared, nearly a shriek, and Vor felt Giri lay his body over hers.

She heard Frimillin shout something and Master Himes answer, and then gradually, silence fell.

Except it wasn't exactly silence. The roar of the bonfire went on, but it was subtle again. The rasp of power over her energies faded back to what it had been when they'd entered the room: annoying, but tolerable. Giri got off her.

"You're bleeding," he said.

"Vittara got a hit in," Vor mumbled back. "Bad?"

He poked at her shoulder. "I can wrap it. It's not squirting or anything."

She heard ripping cloth.

"Your energies are really low. Rest and let me handle it," Giri said.

"Traskitandi, are you alright?" Master Himes asked somewhere above her head.

"I'm alright, Master," Dello answered, sounding wearier than she'd ever heard him.

Vor let herself lie still while Giri wrapped some cloth around her upper arm and shoulder. The other members of the group checked in with each other, and Vor was able to hear that everyone was alive.

"Vittara?" Master Himes asked eventually.

"It sucked her in," Vor reported. "Pretty sure she's dead."

"And everything seems normal again." The master wizard heaved a deep sigh, coughing on the exhale. "Alright, let's start thinking how we can get out of here."

Vor let them start to discuss it. Her energies were perilously low now, and she was hurt. Like Frimillin, she'd need her arms and shoulders to be working in order to climb back up that crack they'd descended through. She closed her eyes and wondered how she'd do it. She also desperately needed energy, and there was no source of it—

Then an idea occurred to her. If she knew how to touch the energy of the magic bonfire, if she could move into it without being hypnotized by it, perhaps there was a way now that she could make use of it. It was obviously powering the spell that held the city together, so it was a type of energy that could be used for magic. How, she wasn't sure, but the ancient mages must have figured it out. Vittara had figured it out. Perhaps there was a way to take it in and convert it. It had burned her before, but she knew more about it now. She'd nearly been inside it, and it hadn't fried her to a crisp—just toasted her a bit.

Vor sat up at the end of the ramp, though it was hard, like a griffin was sitting on her chest. Behind her the others were talking about how they were going to make the exit. Vor turned her head to look at the bonfire. She let her eyes unfocus so it was just a white and purple blur. She put a hand down on the edge of the ramp, so her fingers dangled above the outermost rim of the dark ring. With the slightest effort, she brushed at the energies there.

One thing she knew, she needn't worry about depriving the spell of energy if she took some. All that central column of white light, the black phantom flames dancing over the spheres, even the effect of the dark ring itself, was all magical overflow. The ancient wizards had needed a steady stream of power to turn the metaphorical water wheel of their spell, and by accident or design got a roaring cataract instead. Vittara had been trying to enlarge the flow to overload the spell, but it was back to normal now. There was still extra energy spilling out. There was no reason she couldn't take some.

Carefully, she opened a pin prick in her aura, and reached out to siphon away some energy with that which was essentially Vor—that which she had touched the silver dragon with. She siphoned it through, let it take on her own personal vibration, and when it reached her drained power well, it tingled, but it didn't burn. Excitement made her tremble. She was taking it in like a slow drip into a huge barrel, but she was indeed taking it in.

With forced caution, she opened herself to it a little wider—two pin pricks, then three. The energy dribbled in and she nearly moaned with relief; it was working. She shut her eyes and let it continue. It would take a while at this rate, but if they left her alone for—

Giri touched her uninjured shoulder. "What are you doing?"

He was whispering, so he'd lowered his face close to hers.

"Refueling," she whispered back, and felt him brush her replenishing energy with his.

"What is that?" he murmured in awe.

"I'm taking it from the bonfire, from that thing, whatever it is," she replied quietly.

"How are you doing that?"

"That part of me that spoke with it has to handle it first," she tried to explain, "and transform it to a type of energy my mage powers can use. I'm guessing Vittara did the same thing, but maybe she went too fast, and it burned her out."

Giri didn't reply right away but she felt him examining her and what she was doing, as though lightly touching a craftsman's hands as he worked to understand his process.

"I don't think I can do that," he said after a minute.

"I touched it before, or it touched me," Vor murmured. "For a moment, I fused with it. That's why I can walk on the dark ring. It did something to me. It's like I know the vibration now and can work with it. That's why I could wake you up earlier, and walk almost to the center, to fight Vittara."

"Remarkable."

"Take some."

"What?"

"You can't touch the source, but once it's in me it's mage energy like any other and you can take it, and use it to replenish yourself." That wasn't completely true; the energy still felt different, sort of effervescent, but she knew she could use it like any other.

He put a light hand on her back. "Are you sure?"

"Just let me sit here and keep drawing," she nodded against her knees.

Vor hadn't filled herself up by any means, but Giri took about half of what she'd gained, and she knew that would help him a lot. When a person was starving, they might need a feast to recover fully, but even a single apple was a huge help while they waited for the feast to cook. Once she was full, she'd give him some more. Hoping she could handle it, she opened herself a bit more to it. It made her whole body tingle, but it still didn't burn.

Perhaps Giri gave some explanation to the others, for nobody disturbed her. She only hoped they wouldn't all ask for energy donations. To refill everyone she'd be sitting there for an hour. Still, maybe that was what she had to do for them all to be able to start the climb back to the surface. How far—how horribly far away it seemed. Then again, perhaps they only had to reach the drake cave; there was an opening to the outside there. If they could only get a message out, the griffins could come and fetch them.

And there would be daylight and greenery: life. Vor longed for that cave, visualized it, smelled it, wishing she were there already—

And suddenly her marked shoulder began to heat and ache: not burning like fire, but like—

"Scrying," Giri exclaimed. "I'm being scryed."

Vor lifted her head. "Me, too, I think. Is that what this is? My shoulder?"

"Your mark?" Giri asked, looking befuddled. "No, I feel it all over. Anyone else?"

The others indicated negatives. The last time someone had scryed on her, it had been Altare, trying to find her so he could come kill her, and she'd felt it all over, like Giri was saying, not just in one spot: her partially completed wizard's mark in this case. In fact, it was only one of the three thumbprints— the one Giri had given her—where she felt it. Vor was baffled, but when she looked at Giri, he did not seem dismayed. In fact, he was smiling.

"It's Colby," he said to the group at large. "I can feel it. He's scrying me, but it's picking up the mark I gave Vor, too, because that's a little bit me. He can probably see me, and maybe a bit of Vor. I need a mirror or a bowl and some water, and I'll try to scry him back. Then we can, well, not talk, but figure something out."

The others shook their heads and opened their hands to indicate their lack of handy mirrors and bowls, but Ramikar knelt down.

"Alright," he said. "It's a good thing there's water everywhere here. I'll make you a bowl."

The earth mage set his hands on the stone of the ramp and began to push. Vor meanwhile kept drawing in bonfire energy, but watched as Ramikar used earth magic to put an indentation in the rock the width of his two palms. He sat back, panting, and the indentation slowly began to fill with the water running down the ramp.

Vor put her free hand out and touched Ramikar's arm. She gifted him some energy, and the lean, tired man turned a gaze of profound gratitude onto her. Meanwhile, Giri was kneeling by the little pool of water.

"I need something of his to scry back with, and I don't have anything," he was fretting. "I don't even know how he's reaching us this far down, or how I'm supposed to have the energy to reach back to him."

"You've never scryed using your bond?" Frimillin spoke up.

"My what?" Giri asked.

"Your master-apprentice bond," the husky wizard clarified. "That's what he's doing, sort of, scrying the one he's marked. You have something of him, right in your mark. Do the reverse of what he's doing. Use his mark to look for him."

Giri hissed through his teeth. "I can almost understand that."

"And then add your thoughts and feelings," Frimillin went on. "Use your loyalty, respect, and admiration. The mind is a powerful tool in wizardry, and not just for memorizing spells. It has assets you can leverage. Leverage them. Those bonds of yours are with him. Send them seeking."

"I know what to do now," Giri replied this time, but he looked like he was concentrating. Vor moved her hand from Ramikar to Giri, and gave him some more energy. From her angle, she couldn't see the surface of the pool much at all, and wished she could, but she knew she had to keep collecting power, especially if Giri was trying to punch that scrying spell all the way up through the stone and into the Citadel, so leaving the edge of the dark ring to go see was out of the question.

It took several minutes, and then Giri let out an explosive breath, but not in defeat: in victory. Vor felt when the spell found its target and locked in.

"Master," he whispered. "I don't think I can reach his mind. I've just never been very skilled at that. I can't convey words."

"You're a broadsword with all the power needed to swing it as easily as a broomstick," Dello commented, "but you can't do surgery with a broadsword, my friend. You need a scalpel for that."

"Like you," Giri acknowledged.

Dello shrugged. "But I don't have the connection to Master Srawn, so I can't help."

"He's looking through a mirror I think," Giri reported. "He's moving it around to show me." His voice turned excited. "He's in the drake cave. Thornwing is with him."

"I was thinking of the drake cave when the scrying hit us," Vor mumbleld curiously. Perhaps her attention there had actually helped the spell find her and Giri.

"Alright, now he's writing something on a bit of slate. How many? He's asking how many. People? Yes, there he clarified."

Giri looked around.

"Eleven?" Dello provided. "Iyai, and Lanisala are up there. I hope they're alright."

"I'll go see," Ramikar said, and began a fatigued walk up the ramp.

"And this guy?" Master Himes prodded the sleeping invader who had stabbed Frimillin.

"That one's still alive, too," Dello added, pointing at the invader on his hands and knees in the dark ring, the one that had tried to stab Giri.

"I don't think I'm interested in fetching him," Vor muttered.

"I'm not sure why he wants to know, but I'll tell him thirteen." Giri held up his hands in front of the puddle and indicated on his fingers.

A few moments passed.

"Where are you?" Giri reported. "He wants to know where we are. How am I supposed to tell him that? I can't lift the pool of water to show him the room."

Perhaps Colby had observed the frustration on Giri's face, for he apparently wrote something else.

"Did we stop the rogue mages? Yes, I'd say that's a yes." Giri nodded. "Did we find the key? Yes, another yes. Is there still danger? No, that's a no. Can we easily get back?"

He looked around at the others for input.

"No," Frimillin stated. "I barely made it down that crack with two good arms. Now I'm supposed to climb back up it with one? Hearthsraven is hurt, too, and Ramikar's ankle also, and Lanisala's leg. We're all pretty banged up, really."

"We are all worn, but we'll have to do it," Master Himes said, "but easily? No."

Giri shook his head at the puddle on the ramp. Another moment passed while he waited for whatever the next message was.

"What?" he gasped. "No. Impossible."

"What's he saying?" Master Himes demanded, and moved around to stand behind Giri so she could see into the puddle, too. "Teleport," she said incredulously. "He wants us to teleport out of here?"

"Through all this rock?" Frimillin gaped.

"That's what we were going to do," Tallie whispered, "but our expert is dead."

"He's showing me a departure circle, inked on paper," Giri went on grimly. "He must want me to chalk it out."

"Where?" Master Himes gestured around at the oddly shaped room. "And we can't step back down on the floor, well, except for Vor. Colby," she shouted at the puddle, "it's insane. We can't move thirteen people through all this rock. Do you have any idea how far down we are?"

"I don't think he can hear you, Master," Dello murmured, but Master Himes speared him with a glare and he jerked a thumb over his shoulder. "I'm going to get Ramikar and Lanisala," Dello said, and began hurrying up the ramp as quickly as his weary body could go.

"I'll have to memorize the circle," Giri was saying. "I've nothing to write it down on, but it's similar to others I've chalked."

"I'll help you," Frimillin grunted, getting up to nudge in beside Master Himes. "I've chalked some circles in my time."

"You're not seriously thinking of trying it?" Master Himes declared.

"Tessa, I can't climb out of here," Frimillin told her. "I'll try it. With Master Colby on one end of the warp, it might just work. You know, he's a brute when it comes to teleporting. It'd be better if you helped, though."

Dello came back with Ramikar and Lanisala behind him. He was filling them in as they approached, and they all crowded in behind Giri, almost toppling off the ramp. Master Himes stepped back, clearly caught in distressing indecision.

"Help me memorize this," Giri told the others.

"How are we going to chalk it?" Lanisala lamented. "We haven't got any chalk, or even any rocks big enough to scrape with."

"I can carve it into the floor," Ramikar said, "but it will take a lot of energy."

"I'm gathering," Vor spoke up. "I'll give you more."

She'd increased her draw again, to the point that she was nearly vibrating. Her own energy stores were almost full now. At this rate, she really could fully charge everyone else within the hour. The group stared at her briefly, incredulously.

"I'd expect nothing less from the brilliant Hearthsraven," Ramikar said simply, and turned his attention back to the puddle.

"We'll help, too," Tallie offered tentatively, as if she wasn't sure they were invited, even though the number Giri had reported had included them.

"The more the better," Frimillin said. "Everyone who's going has to pull their weight on this. It will be a warp like I've never done before, nor ever heard of."

Dello tapped Ramikar. "I'll help you start the circle, if you want. I have the basic structure."

"I'll work on the runes," Lanisala said, still concentrating on the puddle. "My runes are pretty good."

"Take some power before you go," Vor said, holding out a hand.

Ramikar approached and touched her fingers. Vor let the energy flow, giving him most of what she'd stored up—but she had to give it away, so she could keep drawing more, even though it left her feeling weak again.

"Thank you," Ramikar said. "That's lovely."

The two men went up the ramp to find the widest spot on the ledge that encircled the room.

"This is madness," Master Himes said as they all ran—or walked as quickly as their weariness would allow—off. "We'll get stuck halfway and die. I know everyone wants to get out, but this isn't the safest way."

"Master Himes," Vor said softly, "it might be the only way. A lot of us are hurt. You're hurt, too. We've hardly eaten for several days. We're frightened."

"So we're not thinking straight," she argued back.

"But Colby and the other wizards, the ones outside, are. They're healthy. They can help."

"They have no idea how deep down we are," Master Himes shot back.

"Can Colby sense Giri?" she asked gently. "If he's able to scry him, is he also able to sense his location? I'm not really experienced with scrying, but do you know?"

Master Himes stopped her pacing and took a heavy breath. She rubbed her forehead with a hand. "Yes," she admitted finally. "Yes, he probably has at least a vague idea. Still, it's a lot of stone—a lot. I would never try such a thing myself, not even with an inanimate object."

"But Colby is good at it. You're going to have to trust him."

"With my life? With everyone's lives?"

"You've done an excellent job leading us, Master Himes. With Colby's help, I think you can lead us through this, too."

She blew a breath out through her teeth and cursed. "They're going to do it with me or without me. Fine. I'd better help or the whole thing will fail."

"Here, take some energy," Vor invited.

She held out a hand, and Master Himes touched her fingertips, accepting the flow of power Vor offered.

"Thank you," the master wizard said. "That makes me feel a little better, but I just thought of something. I hope we don't blow ourselves up by putting our departure circle within the key circle. That's not exactly standard practice for circle-making."

Still, she walked off with the energy, to begin helping to build the circle for departure. For the next quarter of an hour, Giri held the scrying spell, Ramikar used his earth magic to carve the departure circle on the ledge, and most of the others ran back and forth between the puddle and the ledge, checking runes and structure for Ramikar. Vor donated energy to them whenever she had enough to share, and they shared it among themselves, making sure Ramikar got all he needed.

"There's a problem," Master Himes announced as the circle neared completion. "I mean in addition to trying to teleport a dozen exhausted humans through miles of stone, using a circle placed within another circle. I don't think we all can fit in it at once. The circle is just too small. We'll have to go in two groups."

Ramikar was putting on the final touches, and Lanisala was double checking all the runes, but everyone else except Iyai, who still couldn't bear to be close to the bonfire, gathered back on the ramp.

"Colby will be pulling us through," Master Himes went on. "But what he found us with was his bond to Giri and through Giri to Vor." She looked between the two of them. "He'll use you as anchors to pull on. You'll have to split up, one of you in each group. Vor had better go first. If Giri goes up there first, his connection to the mark he left on Vor might not be strong enough to reach anymore."

Vor stared at Giri, and he stared back. She had expected to be teleported with her arms around him. She'd never teleported herself before, or been teleported by another mage, but knowing she'd be with him had taken away some of the fear. What Master Himes said made sense, though, and she knew she couldn't argue against it.

"The strongest of us will also have to split between the groups," Master Himes went on. "I can teleport humans; I've done it before. Who else?"

Ramikar and Frimillin both lifted a hand.

"Who is more confident?" she asked.

The two men looked at each other and discussed it in low tones Vor couldn't hear. Then Frimillin took a step forward.

"Can you concentrate through your pain?" Master Himes asked him.

"Put us together," Ramikar suggested, "in the second group. Together we're probably your equal at this."

"Traskitandi with me, first group," Master Himes said.

"Iyai will go in the second group," Ramikar said, "with me."

"Master Colby is writing something," Giri interrupted. "Are we done?"

"The circle is made," Ramikar said.

Giri nodded yes. "He says he's going to go up to the third teleportation platform on top of the Citadel. He wants us to arrive there. He says there are already wizards there making the circle. They'll help pull us through."

"So he expected to teleport us out from the beginning," Master Himes muttered wryly. "But that must be twice the distance from here to the drake cave. He just doubled the difficulty."

"But if there are more wizards there, plus an arrival circle, that will lower the difficulty," Ramikar soothed. "It will be alright, Tessa."

Meanwhile Giri held his hands up and repeated the counting gesture he'd done before, to indicate how many, and then he moved his hands apart. Vor could tell he was trying to convey that there would be two groups.

"Here," Lanisala said, and dragged a few others around behind Giri.

She mimed separating the group into two, pushing wizards to the left and right, and then indicated one group and held up a single finger, and then the other group and held up two fingers.

"Colby is confirming," Giri reported, "that we'll teleport in two groups. Thanks, Lanisala. He says for me and Vor to go in separate groups, just like you said, Master Himes. He's going to fly up to the platform now. We should get the first group ready."

"Should we take them?" Lanisala asked, indicating the unconscious invader and the one in the dark ring. "If we leave them, they'll die here."

"We've made them a nice teleportation circle," Dello huffed. "If they want to leave they can, through the circle, or they can walk through the wall and climb out."

"But even if they have the skill and power to get to the top, they won't be able to open the final door," Ramikar pointed out, "the one into the water basement. They'll join that dead ancient wizard in his room."

"Fine," Vor huffed. "I'll fetch the one in the ring. Frimillin, please knock him out as soon as I extract him."

By then, she'd donated enough of the filtered energy that everyone was nearly full. She had a good supply, too, so broke the feed and got up. Frimillin stood ready, and Vor went into the dark ring one last time and sought the invader's self. She winced at having to touch his shoulder, but there was no other way. It took her a couple minutes, and when she finally got him back, she grabbed his hair before he realized what was happening, and dragged him the couple feet over to Frimillin, who promptly knocked him out. Dello helped Ramikar drag the man up to the circle.

"Colby has reached the platform," Giri reported from where he was still in contact at the pool. "It's harder to see him now; the spell is tenuous. It looks like they're preparing. Half of you get in the circle."

Master Himes marched up as Dello came back down. The tall, blonde mage put a hand on Giri's shoulder and gave him a bracing squeeze.

"Traskitandi," Master Himes called. "And this piece of shit mage, and Lanisala, another two commoner mages, fine."

"Vor," Giri said. "You have to go with Dello."

"I wish you could go," she replied quietly. "If both Dello and I go in the same group, and we don't make it through, you'll lose both of us."

His expression was tight as he looked at her. "It's just as likely my group might fail. The wizards will be tired from the first spell when they do my group. I need to hold the connection with Colby. I'll see you arrive safely. Then I'll follow with the second group."

"Traskitandi, Hearthsraven, get your asses up here," Master Himes called.

"See you soon, my brother," Dello said softly, giving Giri another little squeeze. Then he walked up the ramp.

"Go on, Vor," Giri encouraged, trying to smile.

"I've never teleported myself before," Vor whispered.

"Don't try to do anything. Just donate power to Master Himes," he said. "There are enough wizards on this to pull you through. I can see them; there are something like a dozen. Besides, Colby can pull on your mark through me. If anyone will get pulled through, it's you. It's the others who should be worried."

"Hearthsraven," Master Himes called again, with more of a growl.

"Alright," Vor agreed recklessly, her sanity questioning what she was doing.

She bent over to give Giri a kiss. "I love you," she whispered.

"I love you, too," he whispered back. "I'll see you shortly. Now go, before Master Himes bursts a vessel or something."

Vor forced herself to turn away from him and walk up the ramp. She saw the circle for the first time. It was indeed small, though it was in a wide spot on the ledge where two spheres met. The unconscious invader was on the ground in the center, with everyone else standing over him. Dello held out a hand in welcome, his other around his master's waist. Lanisala stood crammed in on her other side discussing something with Master Himes in low voices. The other two invaders, one of them Tallie, were fitting themselves in at the back of the group, looking quite nervous. Vor took Dello's hand, stepped carefully over the carved runes, and got her feet tucked inside the circle.

"Vor," Dello said, voice close beside her ear.

"Yeah?" she mumbled back.

"Colby will be pulling on you," he whispered, "so you're likeliest to make it through."

"I guess so," she replied. "That's what Giri said, too."

"If I don't get pulled all the way through, you'll take care of him?"

She flicked her gaze up to his. "Yes," she promised. Looking into his scared, exhausted green eyes, she couldn't say otherwise. "But I won't let go of you, so you'll get pulled through, too."

"I wanted to help you with your mark," he mumbled.

Vor nodded. "I remember. You will."

The invaders had already cut the shoulder of her clothes to reveal her partial wizard mark. Dello's thumb went to it and found the next empty spot in the mark.

"Now? Are you sure? The energy," she protested. "It can wait."

"But what if it can't? I want you to always remember: you're worthy, Vor," Dello breathed.

"We're ready," Master Himes called down.

Humbled and touched, Vor didn't know what to say, but it turned out she didn't need to say anything. Dello sensed her consent, and her fourth mark blazed with burning pain that helped to calm her jumbled emotions.

"They're ready up at the platform," Giri called from below.

Vor hoped fervently that it wouldn't be the last time she heard his voice. She wrapped her arms around Dello and opened her energy stores to the group. As she felt Master Himes begin to draw on her powers, she hid her face against Dello's shoulder, and shut her eyes.

Chapter 15
The Rescue

The experience of teleporting was something Vor would learn to be comfortable with in the years to come, but this first time was a shock. Master Himes controlled it from the departure circle, like tossing up a rope to someone waiting at a clifftop. Though Vor had successfully teleported inanimate objects, she'd never done animals. She sensed that Master Himes was doing a more advanced form of teleportation, with extra steps and extensive buffering, to keep the people being teleported alive.

On the other end, Colby was preparing to catch, and then all the wizards on the clifftop pulled. Vor felt the tug on her second mark—the one from Giri—grow stronger, like a hook in her shoulder, and she held tightly to Dello, afraid she might somehow leave him behind. Master Himes began drawing hard on her energy and Vor didn't resist.

The spell took effect all at once. All Vor's senses were blinded. She couldn't even feel her arms holding Dello or her clammy, gritty clothes against her skin. Even the fresh pain of her fourth mark and the stab wound in her arm vanished. She couldn't breathe. There was no gravity, no up or down, and afterwards she couldn't recall how long it had taken, an instant or a few seconds or several seconds.

Suddenly the light was blinding. The floor hit the bottom of her feet, though she had no sensation of falling—it was just suddenly there. She fell against Dello and felt him fumbling about—he'd made it up alive. Several people spoke words her ears registered only as raucous nonsense. She felt gapingly empty, with only dregs of power remaining, as though her insides had been scooped out. Now her shoulder and arm hurt again, but that was just one agony among many.

From the corner of her eye she saw a few people catch the two invaders at the back of the group; both were unconscious. Someone was helping Lanisala stagger away. Master Himes was holding up Dello. Vor began sinking to the ground. Her legs were numb, unable to hold her. Her hands lost their grip on Dello.

"Here, here, my apprentice," she heard.

Hands caught her under her arms before she hit the floor. She had a brief glimpse of Colby's face. He was smiling, holding a small, round mirror. It reflected bright light into her face and she flinched.

"Good, good," he said. "Just showing Giri you made it through. Off you go now."

Vor tried to lift her head, tried to say something, an expression of gratitude or a request to see Giri for herself through the mirror, but then she was falling down a dark hole and the empty pit of her stomach suddenly contained ice. She almost moaned: not more darkness, not more underground, not more tunnels and caves. Belatedly, she tried to struggle and reached for the light.

"Easy, Vor," someone said.

She recognized the voice, but couldn't place it.

Then— "Here." That was Master Himes. "I'm sorry I took so much. I wasn't sure if we'd make it through without a heavy punch."

Vor felt a gritty hand on her gritty forehead, and then lovely energy flowed into her, not a lot, but enough that she stopped falling down the dark hole. She managed to get her eyes open. Master Himes was squinting and filthy, but smiling.

"I have to see to my apprentice," she said, and then glanced past Vor's shoulders. "Will you—?"

"We've got her," said that familiar voice again.

"Get off the platform, they're going to pull the next group." Master Himes turned away. "Get up, Traskitandi. This is no place for napping."

Vor made the gargantuan effort to turn her head and focus on the person half behind her. "Andra?" she croaked.

Giri's sister gave her a glowing smile. She was supporting Vor on one side. Somewhere in her muddled head, Vor realized there must be a second person on her other side, but turning her head back to see who it was felt like an effort that might kill her, so she just left it turned to the left.

"Come along with me, sister," Andra coaxed. "Here's someone to help you."

Vor blanked out for a few seconds, and then felt fur under her hands. Then a few someones were lifting her up and laying her down on something rounded, furry, and warm. Stiff feathers brushed her face.

"I am so glad you are safe, Vor," another familiar voice said, and something plucked at her tangled mess of hair.

"Joy," Vor groaned, and tightened her hands on the griffin's fur.

"It is I," the griffin said. "I have got you."

She was on her belly, arms and legs straddling the griffin's back. Hawkjoy started walking.

"Wait," Vor objected urgently—or, as urgently as she could. It was more like a pathetic moan. "Giri."

"I know," Andra said near her head, while Joy kept walking. "We have to get off the platform so the wizards can get back in their circle and bring the next group."

"Giri," she repeated, more weakly, but she was blanking again, and didn't have the strength to stop them from taking her away.

She resurfaced again, a little, when Andra was helping strip off her ruined clothing and get her into a bath, no shower this time; she wouldn't have had the strength to stand up for it. The hot water and soap felt fantastic, and revived her enough that she could wash most of herself, slowly, though Andra took on the effort of combing out and cleaning her hair. Vor was able to recline against the sloping wall of the tub with a neck roll behind her head. It was almost comfortable enough for her to fall asleep, even with Andra tugging on her hair.

While Andra scrubbed, two other women Vor didn't know came in. One carried a tall glass of dark tea and a square of something edible on a plate. Vor's stomach clenched painfully even before she knew what it was. It turned out to be a dense cube of grains, honey, nuts, and dried fruit. The other woman had a medical kit and sat down where she could work on the leaking stab wound in Vor's upper arm.

The food-bearing woman broke off bits of the dense square and fed them to her, and Vor made what seemed a nearly impossible effort to chew and swallow, but her body was demanding the sticky, high-energy substance, and somewhere found the energy for her to do it. In between bits, the woman held a glass up to Vor's mouth, and she took swallows of some kind of strong tea. The bitterness helped balance the extreme sweetness of the food, and Vor guessed the tea was half potion, meant to rejuvenate her.

The healer meanwhile began the task of thoroughly cleaning the wound—which stung—and then stitching it closed—which did a great deal more than just sting, even with a smear of skin-numbing salve. The procedure did, however, keep Vor awake. As soon as the healer finished tying off the bandage, and the tea and food had both made their way into Vor, her energy ebbed again. When trying to dry herself off, she nearly fell. Andra wrapped her in a bathrobe, put her back on Hawkjoy, and Vor faded into full unconsciousness.

❀❀❀

Air: fresh, delicious air, pleasantly cool, and scented with spring brushed softly over Vor's face. What seemed the most luxuriously soft pillow ever made cushioned her head. An equally indulgent mattress supported her body. A billowy down-stuffed comforter over a clean, silky sheet topped her, surrounding her in gentle warmth. A tiny corner of her mind noted that these furnishings were in fact rather common and ordinary, but compared to sand and gravel and rock, the comfort was pure luxury.

Vor floated up towards consciousness and noted the afternoon daylight sneaking into the room. Above her head, the window was open a few inches, letting in the breeze and gently tossing a white curtain. She smelled books, mixing with the spring scent, and Giri. Her hand reached out under the covers, but she was alone in his bed. Her eyes drifted open a little more, and she looked around, taking in the ordinariness, the peace of the room. It nearly made her cry. She was safe.

Vor could see fresh clothing folded over the back of the chair, but that was for the future. More immediately, the little table by the bed, where his mage-stone horse statue sat, held a pitcher of water, a glass of more tea, and a plate with something on it, covered by a tea towel. She decided that sitting up was something that sounded useful, and managed to push herself up with her arms, quivering only a little, and discovering aches in her back and shoulder. The wound was still bandaged, and didn't seem to be leaking blood anymore.

Once she had herself balanced, the plate proved to hold that rarest and most wondrous of things: food. Unlike the block of high-energy stuff she'd been fed after the teleport, this was light food: berries, bread, and some mild cheese. She took her time eating and drinking, and was careful that her shaking muscles didn't topple the glass or pitcher.

There were a great many thoughts, questions, worries, sorrows, and hopes waiting to ambush her, but she kept her focus on the present moment. There was only one thing as urgent as food, and that was the mage-stone ring she wore. It took almost no energy to listen to it, and she felt the steady pulse—Giri's pulse—that meant he was alive. It didn't surprise her. Somehow she thought, if he had died in the second teleport, she would have known. Even unconscious, she would have known.

When she finished the food, she gathered what energy she had and sent a message through the ring, a simple contact call, and felt him respond right away. A few minutes later, he was at the door. His smile greeted her, but as they met she could sense that he was barely more recovered than she. She scooted over for him, and he sat beside her with a weary groan. For some time they just leaned against each other, sharing energy and company.

"Colby wants to see you," Giri murmured eventually. "Should I call him, or not yet?"

"Alright," Vor consented, "but help me dress first."

"I will."

When the master wizard knocked politely at the door frame several minutes later, Vor was fully dressed and sitting up at the head of the bed, atop the covers, so she looked less like an invalid. Giri had taken a seat in his desk chair but Vor had the sense he'd rather be horizontal.

"Come in," he called to his master.

"You two have had quite an adventure," Colby said upon entry. "Saving Anchoria and defeating the commoner mage invaders: most impressive."

"And on our days off, too," Giri quipped.

"Fear not, I shall alot you the time again. After all, I didn't get my vacation either. I had to come back here and break a shield, chase down golems and blade-tails, and then hunt down the Magical Liberation Front—at least, the ones you didn't eliminate or capture."

Colby made a little salute. "I hope you are on the mend, Vor Hearthsraven."

"I am, sir," she answered. "Giri said you wanted to see me."

Colby clasped his hand loosely before him. "I have heard the tale of your adventure and you seem to have acquitted yourself well," he replied. "I assure you, this is not what wizards do all the time, or rather, it is, but on a less literal scale. There is a rumor that you intend to stay in Weldom, in Anchoria, in the Citadel even, as a wizard yourself. Is that your plan?"

Vor hardly had to search her feelings to know that she was now certain. Weldom wasn't perfect, and nor were all the wizards that served it, but by being among them she had a chance to improve both. Besides that, fighting beside Giri was a thrill like no other, and she felt optimistic about their growing partnership after a week with him.

"Yes," she answered. "I have to stay."

Colby's lips curved in a half-smile. "To stay, you will need the recognition of five fellow wizards. I sense that you only have four."

"Would—" she began.

"You'll also need to apprentice," Colby went on. "For though you are brave and talented, you have yet much to learn."

"I know," she got in.

"Have you given thought to your options?"

Colby had already called her "my apprentice" up on the landing platform, when he'd pulled her through the teleportation, but she knew it had to be made official.

"What is the procedure for picking a master?" Vor asked.

"Normally masters are selected in the final year of group classes after a great many tests, but as what you have just endured was a far greater test than any of those, just ask," Colby said softly.

Slowly, because she was still weak, Vor swung her legs off the bed and pushed up to her feet. She walked to face Colby. It didn't take a lot of courage, because she knew what his answer would be.

"Master Colby Srawn, would you accept me as your apprentice?" she asked.

Now he smiled fully and bowed his head. "I would be glad to, but you'll need your fifth mark."

Vor tugged at her shirt, exposing her shoulder and the four marks she had already.

"Follow what I do," Colby instructed. "After this, you will have the right to award such marks to others and you'll need to know how."

"Yes, Master," she breathed.

She felt something heavy fall into place within, and almost shivered. Giri had once spoken to her about bonds of duty. Her former master, Altare, had made her his apprentice. Though he had given her empty words suggesting it was her choice, it really hadn't been. This time she was choosing it herself, and unlike Altare, she knew that Colby would never try to manipulate or abuse her. She wouldn't stand for it if he tried, either, master or not. It was a mutual pledge, and though it felt heavy, she did not feel that it encumbered her.

Her master gave her another nod. "Brace yourself now."

Vor was able to observe magically how Colby left not only a shiny scar but also a hint of identity in that scar tissue. Any other mage would be able to touch the scars and sense who had given them.

Now, if Vor committed any crime and was caught, those marks would be read. Giri, Master Himes, Dello, and Colby—not Craduticus, for he had passed—would all be told of it and asked why they had approved a criminal to be a wizard. Responsibility, accountability: such things had never laid so heavily on Vor before, but then she had never felt camaraderie or loyalty to her former master, only fear and disgust.

Finished, Colby drew away, and Vor looked down at the completed flower petal pattern of scars. There was no going back now.

"You'll tell me, will you," she said, "what constitutes a crime, so I know how not to get you in trouble?"

Colby chuckled. "First lesson when we get back from our well-earned vacations. Welcome," he went on, "Wizard Vor Hearthsraven, my apprentice."

✿✿✿

A couple weeks passed before Vor and Giri were able to get permission to finally take the trip to see both their families. The Citadel was in a state of distress. The death toll due to the golems and blade-tails had been considerable. Nearly half the wizards and apprentices who had been at the Citadel during the attack were dead. Naturally, many others had been away on assignments, or in the city but not in the Citadel, and luckily, the youngest apprentices had sealed the doors and windows to their dormitories, keeping the blade-tails out, and—not being very powerful yet—the golems had not sought them.

Still, dozens had died, including Pirossa's master. Lanisala's had escaped only by lucky chance. She'd been in the greenhouse, where the abundant life energy had disguised her mage power, so the golems hadn't sought her, and the greenhouse doors and windows could be tightly sealed, so no blade-tails had gotten inside. She'd made use of the time she spent trapped, gathering a bushel of herbs she knew repelled blade-tails, rubbing some on herself for protection, and then venturing out to find other wizards before they were overcome by the swarm.

Pirossa was well on her way to healing, and wouldn't lose her arm, though it was unlikely to recover completely. The wound to Master Himes's shoulder, where her original wizard mark had been cut away, took a long time in healing, and left an ugly scar, but she lost no use of her arm. Frimillin's shoulder stab, the cut to Dello's arm, Lanisala's leg wound, and Ramikar's twisted ankle and head wound had all been tended promptly, and would leave no lasting damage.

Vor's stab wound to her upper arm had missed any major vessels or nerves, so it would heal fully except for a scar. The griffins, too, had suffered no permanent damage, except for the large, circular scar left by the parasitic cave scorpion on Hawkwind's arm, where fur would never grow again. Other scrapes, bruises, and strained muscles among the group would also heal in time. Psychological trauma from the experience was a harder wound to forecast, however, for all of them.

Vor had been asked to write a report of the whole journey, including what had happened with the magical bonfire-being at the end, just like everyone else. Senior wizards had formed a committee, the Key Committee as it was being called, led by Master Himes, and would be analyzing the various reports. Mages from the Magical Liberation Front that had cast the shield and summoned the golems and blade-tails had been caught. In the fight that followed, many had been killed, including a few more wizards, but some were in cus-

319

tody, along with Tallie and the four other invaders who had been teleported back from the key chamber. Their reports were taken, too.

The fate of the invader mages was scheduled to be decided, but not until after all the investigation and analysis of the events was complete. Vor and Giri had both filed reports that reflected their perspectives, and would be called on as witnesses in the court proceedings that would follow, but that wasn't scheduled for another month. There was nothing more they could do for or against the MLF until then.

Master Himes had already questioned them both for hours in front of the Key Committee until she'd finally told them they were free to go. Now, they stood back on the largest platform above the Citadel, with Thornwing and Hawkjoy, their bags packed and on the floor beside them.

"Well," Thornwing said with a jaunty tilt to his head, "shall we try this again?"

He extended his wings and gave a few practice flaps, sending wind gusting across the platform. Since the griffins and wizards had all had time to rest, heal, and feed, none of them were any worse for wear, though both Giri and Vor sometimes woke from dreams of being in the caves again, and Vor had occasional nightmares about drowning or being tapped under the pile of bones, with no Breeka to dig her out.

She'd also done as Craduticus had requested, and gone to his rooms and found the book he'd told her about. It had opened at her touch, just as he had said it would. It was now on a shelf in her room—one of her few books so far. She hadn't started reading it just yet; the loss of Craduticus was still too raw, and she wanted that to heal first so she could read his words without pain.

Jessika, too, had taken Craduticus's loss hard. Last week, two diplomats had arrived from Northborn—one who had been a part of the Weldom invasion, and one who had been an advisor to the king before the invasion and had been among the mine slaves until Vor and her allies freed him last year. With their arrival, Jessika had given up her efforts to take back the country and be recognized as the next ruler. With Rikah, Hawkwind, and Snowdark, she had returned to Northborn. Eagelgrace and the two griffins who had brought the diplomats had stayed on at Weldom.

Vor picked up her pack and went to Hawkjoy to strap it on. She really didn't care much what became of Northborn now, as long as it was logically and compassionately managed. Her life was now in Weldom, and after this journey to meet Giri's family and rediscover her own, she would return to the Citadel as Colby's apprentice and Giri's partner, and then she would see what came next.

"Yes," Giri replied to Thornwing, carrying his own pack over. "Let's go face the danger, excitement, and surprises of visiting family."

"Can't be worse than spelunking for a week to find an ancient magical key, now, can it?" Vor grinned at him.

He grinned back. "Yes, I think that magical bonfire was considerably scarier than your grandmother."

"How about yours?" she teased as she got herself onto Hawkjoy's back and began strapping herself on.

"Just wait and see," he said. "Ready, Thornwing?"

"Ready," the griffin nodded, prancing a little in place and fanning his tail. "No magic shields this time."

"I sure hope not," Giri muttered.

Thornwing launched, flapping to catch the wind, and Hawkjoy followed as soon as Vor patted her on the shoulder to indicate her readiness. Vor clung gamely, and the griffins caught the thermals over the city, kettling up so they could coast to the next one. The morning sun at their tails, they wheeled about, and flew on into the west.

❀❀❀

Epilogue 1
Trivale

They started the policy of landing away from people after their first landing sent villagers screaming and brought a few confused bowmen running out, trying to decide if they should shoot. Now Vor and Giri would walk beside their griffin friends as they approached any other humans, trying to share jokes or funny comments, or anything to help them smile and look friendly. The griffins had trouble looking friendly, because raptorial faces just tended to look fierce by default, but they did their best to seem playful and harmless.

But they'd drawn the line at collars and leashes.

And so they walked into the town of Trivale, drawing stares and trying to avoid spooking the livestock. The griffins had already hunted, so weren't hungry, but the livestock didn't know that. They found their way to the town hall, which was a public building with one wall that could slide back in warm weather, and a large hearth on the opposite wall for cold weather. There were several older residents sitting in the sun spinning or carding wool, or carving bits of wood, or doing any other number of small tasks. A dozen small children, too little to be of much help at chores, played with toys either in the hall or in the yard before it.

Everyone stopped, looked up, and stared when the griffins approached. Vor and Giri had taken pains to try not to appear as wizards or nobility, but their clothing—even their simplest items—were finely crafted. However, with the griffins drawing everyone's attention, Vor figured they could have come naked, or in their most elaborate mage robes, and not be noticed. Giri put an arm around Thornwing's neck and ruffled his feather-fur playfully, and Hawkjoy rubbed her cheek against Vor's shoulder like a cat.

A tall, broad shouldered man with a little grey in his hair stepped out of the hall. He looked confident, and didn't need to visibly gather himself before he walked up to the strange quartet in his town center. Vor found herself admiring his control.

"Good morning," he greeted. "Pardon my bluntness, but might I ask what business travellers as distinctive as you have in Trivale?"

Vor bowed her head. "I'm looking for my family, the Hearthsravens. Are they still here?"

She had everyone's attention now, except for most of the children. One older boy was edging closer to the griffins with unconcealed curiosity, and the others were still staring, mouths open, though a few had gone to hide behind one or another of the old folks. Hawkjoy lowered herself to the ground and lounged like a dog, putting her head at about the level of Vor's belly.

"Hearthsraven," the town's man echoed. "You're a Hearthsraven then, yourself?"

"Vorella," she nodded.

A few people gasped, but others gave no reaction. One old lady leaned towards her neighbor and asked, "what did she say?"

"Is that so," the man said. "And your companions here?"

She put a hand on Hawkjoy's head. "This is Hawkjoy. That's Thornwing. And the human is Giri."

"They're well trained, I take it?"

"I do everything she says," Giri winked.

"I've always disappointed my matriarchs," Thornwing drawled. "They say I'm reckless. I call it adventurous."

Several people, including the head man, jumped at hearing not only speech, but sarcasm from what they had assumed was a trained beast of burden. Vor scratched behind Hawkjoy's crest, and the griffin purred.

"You may do that forever," she instructed hopefully.

Then Vor's gaze was attracted by an old man emerging from inside the town hall. He walked with a cane, but was only a little bent in his upper back, as though he had spent a lifetime hunched over a workbench. He stepped down onto the porch in front of the open wall, and into a patch of morning light. He looked at Vor over Hawkjoy's head, and she looked back. His hand holding the cane trembled, and he came closer, stepping down onto the dirt.

He hardly glanced at Hawkjoy, and didn't seem to fear her, coming much closer than the head man had dared to come. His eyes were wide and incredulous, his brow deeply lined. His white hair was receding a little, but was still thick. His hands looked knotted with arthritis and heavily scarred with a lifetime of nicks and cuts. Vor stared at him—and then realized that his eyes were the same color as hers, only a little paler. He stopped right in front of her. Hunched as he was, he was still taller, but not by much.

Vor searched his face. His wide eyes crinkled now. When he lifted his free hand and touched her cheek, she didn't pull away.

"You look so much like your mother," he said, voice hitching. "And you have my boy, Stratus's, eyes."

Vor discovered her throat had choked up, burning, and she couldn't swallow.

"You're Vor," her grandfather said, looking caught between joy and tears. "You're Vor, and you've come back to us."

She nodded. "I'm Vor."

He seemed about to burst into tears, and then mastered himself.

"You'll bring all your friends over for lunch," he said.

Vor's grandfather turned to lead them through the village, but Hawkjoy stepped up beside him.

"Would you like a ride, sir?" she asked cheerfully, doing her best impression of a cute kitten—a kitten weighing a couple hundred pounds who could eviscerate a deer with one claw swipe.

He came to a halt and gave her an appraising look. Vor held her tongue, finding herself suddenly relying on an instinct that said to let her grandfather handle the question on his own. His face bloomed into a smile.

"Imagine the look on Helena's face when I come home riding a griffin," he stated.

Hawkjoy lay all the way down, and Vor and Giri helped him get on. Vor carried his cane, and Hawkjoy stood up, carefully keeping perfect balance.

"You rode here on griffins?" he said to Vor incredulously, and then revised: "Of course our Vor rode here on griffins."

"We flew, sir," Hawkjoy contributed. "We carried them through the air."

"In our claws," Thornwing added brightly.

"You did not," Vor scolded, finding herself caught with laughter.

They walked through the town, collecting quite a number of children and other young people who abandoned their tasks to get a look at the strangers. Even more people leaned out of windows, or looked up from their gardens. Vor, her grandfather, and Hawkjoy led the parade, while Giri dropped back with Thornwing. Vor could hear Thornwing showing off and telling lies, and Giri trying to set things straight. Pretty soon the word spread that Vorella Hearthsraven had returned to Trivale with two griffins and a handsome young man, and Vor heard it being whispered all around.

"I didn't know everyone knew who I was," she confided to her grandfather.

"Your mother was famous," he replied, "and your father a bit, too. Naturally folks would be following your future, especially when you showed signs you might have magic." He looked down at her and lowered his voice. "You did turn into a mage, didn't you?"

"I did," she confirmed. "It's a long story, but I'm a wizard now."

"Keep that quiet if you will. Your gentleman friend is one, too, isn't he?"

"Yes."

"And nobility, too, by the looks of him. Can't hide that under plain clothes."

"He is," Vor admitted.

"Which house?"

"Holstor."

Her grandfather sniffed. "Not a bad one, as houses go. You're going to wed him?"

She shrugged. "We've no plans for that, but he's my partner."

"He's a good gent, then?"

Vor glanced back at Giri. He was helping a brave little girl balance on Thornwing's back.

"He's no more flawed than I am," she said.

Her grandfather patted her shoulder. "As we all are. Good enough, then. Ah, and here we are."

The Hearthsraven home was no noble estate, but it was far finer than many of the other houses they had passed.

"Right," Vor said slowly as the house cued her memory. "You're all wood workers."

"That we are," her grandfather preened. "Not even my youngest son stealing a daughter of the nobility and getting the Mrandises all enraged could ruin our business. In fact, it might have helped. We're the best around, and a good thing, too, with how many grandchildren I ended up having."

The house was two stories with what looked like a generous attic. A long workshop was attached to one side, with the walls drawn open like the town hall had been, to let in the morning air. Three men of varying ages were at work, and two boys just old enough to be cautious around all the sharp objects were assisting by sweeping up sawdust and wood shavings, holding boards in place, or fetching tools. On the other side of the house was an extensive garden. Three women and an older girl were weeding and planting. On the front porch in an exquisite carved rocking chair sat an old woman darning socks.

They all couldn't have helped but notice the parade approaching their house. Work stopped as they stared and some walked out to the waist-high fence. The woman on the porch stood up in confusion, and then threw down her mending into her basket. She marched with youthful energy down the path to the main gate.

"Husband mine," she started in, "what sort of ridiculous nonsense have you gone and—"

Then she trailed off; her eyes had found Vor. She stood completely still, staring, mouth still open. Then she made a little, abrupt sound, and her fingers flew to unlatch the gate. She swept out it, and Vor didn't resist as her grandmother clasped her tightly to her chest.

"Thank all that is green and good," she babbled. "Vor, our Vor, whatever has brought you back to us: you're alive. Oh, our little girl, you, you."

There was more, a string of endearments and praises, and Vor didn't struggle against it. Old, buried sensations and memories were stirring, both anxious and tender, under the scars put there by the war, by Altare, by her recent journey through the bowels of Anchoria.

"Let the girl breathe, Helena," her grandfather fussed.

Helena drew back, holding Vor's shoulders at arm length. "Oh, look at you. You're too thin, but strong enough. Oh, my dear, you're like your mother, look at you, like our Juleena. Oh, but there's my lost little boy in you, too." Tears slid down her face. "I never thought I'd see you alive. Oh, look at me, falling apart."

"It's alright," Vor assured her. She was having to blink back tears of her own. "I'm sorry it took me so long to get back."

"Oh, nonsense, you're here now. And look who you've brought. Griffins, then, aren't you? Oh, and a young man, as well? Good job then, Vor."

Giri was helping Vor's grandfather down from Hawkjoy, who had laid down again to make it easier. The rest of the family was gathering at the fence now, and had overheard some of what was said.

"Vor?" The youngest of the women said in wonderment. "Really?"

"Oh my goodness," the oldest of the three garden-working women gasped. "Vor?"

"Yes," Vor confirmed, feeling awkward. "I've come back to Weldom finally. I wanted to come see everyone."

The garden-working girl tugged on the sleeve of the oldest garden-working woman to ask who Vor was. Vor heard a reply of "she's your cousin, lost in war."

"Do you remember me?" the young woman went on, now sounding urgent.

Vor stared at her, struggling to remember. Her face did look familiar. She looked like she was probably about Vor's age, but her hair and skin were both much lighter. All the rest of the Hearthsravens were watching eagerly for Vor's reply.

"We used to pretend we were unicorns," the woman went on softly. "It was our favorite game. You were a black one and I was a white one, but we were twin sisters, and we'd fight off the harpies that came to steal food from the garden." She shrugged, smiling. "Well, the crows and ravens anyway."

Vor reeled as a fragment of memory hit her. It was blurry. She looked over towards the garden, at the neat rows and mounds and the worn path around it. She closed her eyes as the memory grew stronger and took a shaky breath. She recalled the smell of earth and plants and water, and running about with a carved wooden horn on a strap of leather tied to her forehead, and jumping up and shouting like she imagined unicorns would shout. Was that here? This place? This was a whole piece of her life that she'd locked away and forgotten about, refusing to look at for fear it would cause pain and weakness.

"You've moved the compost pile," she murmured, "and the fence. You replaced it. I got a big splinter in my arm off the old one."

Dreamily, Vor touched the spot. There was a little scar there, inside her right elbow. She'd forgotten what it was from.

"Yes," the young woman across the fence from her confirmed, hands clasped under her chin, while others whispered in agreement. "Oh, Vor, I thought you were gone forever."

Her name came to her. "Evalyn," she said.

"You remember me." She broke into tears and held out her arms, and Vor hugged her across the fence. "We're cousins, but we grew up like sisters. I'm only older by a few months."

"I only remember a little," Vor confessed, feeling like her mind was being stirred up, and a multitude of old memories that had settled to the bottom were now floating up into view.

"That's alright. That's alright," Evalyn assured her. "We can make new memories."

"I'll start some tea," the woman who had told the girl that Vor was her cousin announced, voice sounding choked, and scampered back to the house. Vor wondered if she was using that excuse so she wouldn't cry in front of everyone, and then tried to remember her name.

"Come in, come in, all of you," Helena insisted, "oh, but I don't think your griffin friends will fit through the door."

"Not to worry," Thornwing piped up. "We can have a nice lie down out here in the yard and keep the harpies off the garden. It'll be a nice change of pace. Do you know these two expected us to fly all day every day to get them here?"

"We did not," Giri objected. "You two set the pace and took plenty of rests, if I remember right."

"Your memory is going," Thornwing said with finality.

Some of the Hearthsravens laughed nervously, and one of the two boys turned to a man who was probably his father to ask, "can I pet them?"

The man grinned hesitantly. "I think you'll have to ask them."

"Well come in, then," Helena ordered again, halfway up the path to the house.

Vor's grandfather led the way through the gate, and the griffins half spread their wings to hop over the fence—a simple act that nevertheless brought gasps of awe. The people who had followed the newcomers to the Hearthsraven house began to disperse. The remaining Hearthsraven woman who wasn't Evalyn and hadn't gone to fetch the tea went back to the garden to tidy up anything urgent, and one of the men put a few things in order in the workshop, and then all thirteen humans gathered in the main room of the house.

There were two tables, a long rectangular one, and a smaller circular one. The two boys and one girl went straight to the circular table and sat on the three stools waiting there for them. Meanwhile, two additional chairs were fetched for the rectangular table, and all the others there were scooted closed together. Vor felt Giri touch her arm.

"Are you alright?" he whispered.

"I'm not sure," she confessed. "I'm having so many memories."

"Come have a seat," one of the women invited them both: the woman who had seemed to recognize Vor at the fence, and had told the girl she was Vor's cousin. She had a sweet face, ruddy brown hair only showing a few strands of grey, and dark umber eyes that glinted with good nature.

"I'm sure you're going to hear this over and over," the woman said ruefully. "Do you remember me? I'm Ona, your aunt."

"You're Ona," Vor nodded with relief. "I remembered your name, and you look familiar." She frowned for just a moment, and the information came to her. "You're married to Uncle Tam."

One of the men from the workshop came over and clapped Ona on the shoulder. He was taller than Vor, with a dark blonde beard cut short and his hair in a long braid.

"So you remember me, do you?" he grinned.

Vor found herself grinning back. "We used to have races. I'd ride my dad, and Juri rode you, and," the fragments were coming quicker, "Evalyn rode Uncle Mag."

The room had gone quiet listening. The youngest of the adult males, one who looked not much older than Vor, who stood with a woman of equivalent age who Vor definitely didn't recognize—the one who had gone back to tidy up the garden before coming in—raised his hand and pointed at himself.

"Juri," he identified with a grin remarkably like his father's, "only my wife calls me that these days."

"And I'm his sister," a voice called from the circular table. The girl, who looked to be about ten years old, had her hand up. "Mama said you're my cousin," she stated.

"Tam and I had trouble having another child after Juris," Ona explained, "and thought we never would. Then little Alaurie showed up and surprised us."

"Alaurie," Vor echoed. "No, Alaurie is my other aunt."

She saw Evalyn's smile fade. The young woman was standing by the oldest man in the house except for Vor's grandfather. His blonde beard was going grey, and likewise his short cut hair.

"We had a sickness about a decade ago," Vor's grandmother explained. "It hit Trivale hard, and Lenali, too."

"It also reached Croun," Giri mentioned.

"It took about one in five here in Trivale," Vor's grandmother went on. "We lost Magnus's wife Alaurie; Dansen, their only son; Dansen's wife, Tania, and their newborn baby girl."

"Most of us got sick with it," Uncle Tam added, "but we recovered, even Pa, and we thought he was a goner for sure."

"Somehow, I pulled through," Vor's grandfather sighed. "I would rather have died and Alaurie or Dansen or Tania or the baby lived. I'd trade myself for any of them, if I could." He raised a defiant finger and glared, "and it was heartbreak that killed Dansen, not the red fever."

No one disputed this, and Vor got the impression that it was one of her grandfather's convictions that he'd tell everyone, whether it was true or not.

"My sister, Glory," Evalyn spoke up. "Do you remember her, Vor? She was a bit older. She got married and moved to be with her husband's family, but we got word that her and her husband and children all survived. It was his parents who died. It was a hard time for everyone."

"We haven't seen the red fever for years now, though," Vor's grandmother spoke up, trying for a cheerful tone, "and Vor has come back to us now, so let's celebrate what we do have: our lives and our health."

"I'm sure the tea is ready," Ona said, and worked her way through the crowd towards the stove.

"We have some mumfruit tarts left over," Juris's wife, the woman Vor didn't recognize, said. "I'll just warm them." She pulled up a trap door in the far corner of the room and went down the ladder within.

"Hey, so are we your cousins, too?" one of the boys from the circular table called out.

"No," little Alaurie refuted immediately. "She's my cousin, and your dad's cousin. I'm your aunt; you can't be her cousin, too."

The fact of a girl only a handful of years older than them being their aunt was apparently a sore spot and they retorted with what were probably standard objections. Juris's wife emerged from the trapdoor and scolded them into silence.

"I've heard enough of that," she said firmly, "and in front of guests, too. Settle down, the both of you."

She set a tray of tarts on the stove where the tea kettle had shortly been. She gave her husband Juris a look that apparently conveyed a message, and he cleared his throat as he took a seat at the table.

"I didn't introduce my wife," Juris said, glancing at Vor. "This is Millie, proper name Millinda. She joined the family six years ago. As for our obedient little boys over there, they joined the family about five years ago." He cleared his throat again. "We of course didn't know Millie was carrying twins, until the midwife suspected it, and we had of course heard that Stratus and Juleena had died a couple years before that. And, I hope you don't mind Vor; we named our two boys after them, though they have a long way to go to live up to the names."

A pleased smile grew on Vor's lips. She eyed the two boys. "Really? I hope they didn't really name one of you Juleena."

"I'm Julean!" one of the boys corrected vigorously.

Several people, including Vor, chuckled, but she apologized. "Pardon me, Julean. May I say I'm glad my cousin, your father, in his great wisdom, did not name you Juleena."

"See?" Julean growled, and shoved his brother.

"So you're Stratus then?" Vor spoke over the hubbub. The shoved boy scowled at his brother and nodded. "Then I suggest you live up to the name. My father was kind and fair to everyone. I hope you are, too."

"I am," he said sulkily.

Giri spoke up then. "I'll bet it took Stratus some time to grow into the man he became. I'm sure young Stratus, here, will get there, too."

Little Stratus nodded in agreement. "That's right. I'm working on it."

Everyone agreed by word, nod, or smile. Ona began handing out tea cups, and shortly Millie was taking the tarts off the stove and plating them.

"I think that recounts everyone who Vor would have known when she lived here as a little girl," Vor's grandmother summed up. "Mag and Tam are both running the carpentry business now, and Juris is apprenticing to them. Young Stratus and Julean will be walking in their footsteps, it looks like. Ona, Millie, and Evalyn are doing wonderfully running the garden and house. Evalyn seems to have picked up Juleena's skill at embroidery and has been selling pieces to supplement the carpentry income."

"I hope you don't mind, Vor," Evalyn put in quickly. "Your mom left behind so much floss and unfinished pieces. My first pieces weren't very good, but now they're alright. I remember your mom tried to teach both of us, and I liked it. I just thought, it all shouldn't go to waste."

"That's great," Vor assured her. "I'm glad you're carrying on what my mother taught you."

"Evalyn says her pieces are alright, but judging by the prices she gets for them, I'd say they're quite good." Helena spread her hands and grinned. "With everyone helping out so much, there's hardly anything for me to do these days, which is just the way I like it."

A few people chuckled. Evalyn had gotten the seat next to Vor. Now she leaned over and nudged her, wearing a big grin.

"Vor, you have to introduce him." She nodded her chin towards Giri, who was seated on Vor's other side.

When she glanced at him, he raised an amused eyebrow and took a sip of tea. The room had gone expectantly quiet, and everyone seemed entertained except Vor.

"I hate our culture," she muttered under her breath. "This is Giri," she said shortly. "He's with me."

"Does he come with a last name?" Millie teased.

"Holstor," Giri spoke up, with an awkward smile. "Yes, that Holstor, but it's really not a big deal, and I like how you've been treating me, so please, if you could all just keep ignoring my surname," he really did look uncomfortable, "I'd prefer it, if you don't mind."

Eyebrows went up all around the table, from those who knew of the nearby noble houses. Evalyn stuck her hand across in front of Vor.

"Nice to meet you, Giri," she said.

He shook her hand. "Nice to meet you, too, Evalyn."

"Too bad for me Vor saw you first," she smirked.

Across the table, Millie snorted.

"What?" Evalyn retorted.

"Now you're going to start paying attention to men?" Millie drawled.

"Evalyn is still single," Vor's grandmother said archly, "if young Giri has any unattached brothers at home."

"I'm afraid not," Giri replied with a smile. "I only have a sister, and she's taken."

"Just as well," Evalyn said firmly. "I'm staying right here."

"You'll be going to visit your mother's family as well?" Millie asked, turning her attention off needling Evalyn and onto Vor. "Speaking of noble houses."

Vor got the sense that, while she was a lovely lady in general, Millie liked poking and tugging on topics that maybe she should have left alone. Vor recalled how her grandfather had said not to mention her magery, and decided it was good advice to follow, with Millie around and the current public dislike of wizards coming from some quarters.

"You're half a Mrandis after all," Millie went on, pausing for a sip of tea and a nibble of tart.

"My maternal grandmother actually came to see me, a few weeks ago, in the capital," Vor said lightly. "I'm afraid we didn't get on."

"Vor," Helena said, more seriously, "you should visit the branch house. Your great uncle Damarin is still around. Do you remember him at all? He only met you a few times, but he helped your mother escape from Mrandis House, and he stood as witness when your parents married. I'm sure he would like to see you."

"There have been rumors," Magnus contributed, "that Mrandis House is falling on hard times, maybe even failing. Of course they're not acting like it, but some of us in Trivale are concerned."

"Mirassi said something to that effect," Vor shared. "They haven't been able to produce any children recently."

"Serves them right," Helena opined. "If they had let your mother marry Stratus and bring him into the family, like she asked, they'd have you, and maybe Juleena and Stratus could have given you brothers and sisters, too. He certainly wouldn't have been sent off to that senseless war."

"I'm not planning on rejoining House Mrandis," Vor revealed. "They didn't want me. They can do without me."

"So," Tamarus said hesitantly, "you'll be marrying into House Holstor?"

Vor flicked a look at Giri.

"We're," Giri began, and then paused at the look of caution on Vor's face. "We're figuring it out as we go along."

She was afraid he'd been about to blurt that they were wizards and would be living at the Citadel and going on magical assignments all over the country—not a typical married couple. Vor hid her relief by taking a bite of mumfruit tart, and found it pleasantly crisp and sweet, even though it had apparently been made previously and sat chilled in the cellar.

"I hadn't heard," Millie put in, "that the noble houses were flexible like that."

"They aren't, usually," Giri confirmed. "I'm even the oldest child, but my little sister married well and already has two children, twin girls, in fact, and very healthy. I refused all the women my parents tried to get me interested in, so now that there is someone I'm interested in—"

"They'll go along with whatever you want," Vor's grandfather—and his name finally came to her: Ruslin—chuckled.

"That's what I'm hoping anyway," Giri nodded. "We came to visit you first. Vor hasn't met my parents, but she did meet my sister and her husband, and they're going to the house ahead of us."

"So they can prepare the soil," Ona grinned.

"But don't noble houses usually require a spouse price, or something?" Millie frowned.

"There's no wedding planned," Vor insisted, but she didn't miss the look that came over her grandmother's face then, like she'd just recalled something long forgotten and perfectly helpful.

"It's quite clear that the situation for Vor and Giri isn't the ordinary kind," Helena said firmly. "And if Holstor House is prepared to be reasonable, then I'm sure all will be well. Now, isn't it about time to prepare lunch?"

"Yes," Ona confirmed. "We were just gathering what we needed. Millie, will you come help me finish up?"

Millie went along as Ona led her out, and Vor thought that Helena and Ona had quite a good partnership when it came to blunting Millie's nosy personality.

"Alaurie, why don't you go help?" Helena instructed, and the girl got up and followed her mother.

"I'll help, too," Evalyn started to say, but Helena overrode her.

"No, Evalyn, I'll need you and Mag and Tam. We're going up to the attic."

"Oh," Evalyn said, sounding a little surprised. She turned to Vor. "That's where my room is."

"Come along, Vor, and you, too, Giri," Helena said, already heading up the stairs and wincing like her knees pained her.

The six of them wound their way up to the second floor and down the narrow hall, which had three doors on each side. Just past the last set of doors was a steep stair going up to a tiny landing below the house's peak. They stepped off to one side into what appeared to be a storage area. The rest of the attic was partitioned with a wall going part of the length of the peak, which met up perpendicularly with a wall going crosswise that hid the far end of the attic.

"Because of the slanting roof," Evalyn explained, "not so many people can sleep up here, and we use some of it for storage besides. This is my room." Evalyn indicated the partition directly across from the storage area, with the wall that ran just under the peak. "It used to be your room, if you remember, Vor."

Helena was directing Magnus and Tamarus to shift boxes and bags and trunks, and Vor stuck her head into the little attic room. Evalyn had a narrow bed tucked against the wall, and a little desk by a window at the end. Shelves and storage were built into the slanting roof side of the room—as could be expected from a family of carpenters—and there was even a bar from which a few sets of clothing hung. It looked cozy, but Vor didn't find herself remembering it.

"You only spent a couple years in this room before you left," Evalyn said. "Before that you were down in the nursery with me."

"We converted the attic for your parents," Tamarus told Vor. "It used to just be Stratus's room, with lots of storage stuff all over the place, since he sometimes slept in the guard barracks anyway. After they got married and came to live here, we put a bigger bed up here, but you slept in the nursery, like Evalyn says. Only when you got old enough for a room of your own, there weren't many options, so we put the walls in up here."

"My dad sleeps up here, now, too," Evalyn said quietly.

Vor realized that must be because his wife had died. He hadn't remarried, so maybe it made more sense to yield a bigger, better room on the first or second floor to a married couple, and maybe he hadn't wanted to continue living in the room he'd lived in with his late wife.

"There we go," Helena said with satisfaction.

She'd unlocked a trunk that Magnus and Tamarus had apparently unearthed from behind several other stored items.

"This got buried up here," she said, "after so many years. Kept it locked to keep you kids out of it. What little girl, or boy for that matter, can resist a game of dress-up?"

Magnus helped Helena lift the lid, releasing the scent of old herbs used to keep out insects—though the trunk looked very sound, and Vor wondered if insects could have gotten in if they'd tried.

"There's something else to show you, too, but it's downstairs. For now, these," Helena explained, "belonged to your mother."

She lifted out a folded gown in emerald and forest green and handed it to Tamarus.

"Don't unfold them just now," she instructed. "It took a lot of effort to get them folded just right in the first place. These should be yours, Vor. You're a bit leaner than your mother, but that's better than being plumper, as it's much easier to take in clothing than make it bigger."

Vor knelt down beside the trunk. It was not a small trunk. She checked her fingers to be sure they were clean, and then reached in to lightly touch the wealth of fabric inside.

"How did you get all these?" she asked. "My mother took them with her when she left Mrandis House?"

"No, your grandmother was going to burn them, but the head of the Mrandis servants smuggled them out instead, and sent them to us."

Giri looked over Vor's shoulder. "I'm amazed she was going to burn them. Dresses like these aren't cheap, and with the loss of Juleena's spouse-price, selling them could have helped compensate."

"You should sell them," Vor suggested to her grandmother. "Why did you keep them?"

Helena smiled, and reached in to take a few more out, handing them to her sons and Evalyn. "That's just what Juleena said. She told us to sell them, and we did sell a few, when we had bad years, but we couldn't do it in Trivale. We had to sell them to traveling merchants, who would take them to distant towns, so that Mistress Mrandis would never see someone else wearing them. Merchants like that have to be able to mark up the price to make a profit when they sell, so we never got what they were actually worth. I made sure to keep what I thought were the prettiest ones, especially the ones that Juleena had embroidered."

"But why?" Vor repeated gently.

Helena was digging deeper in the trunk now. "Sentimentality, I suppose. I think I also felt special, having them. We're not a noble house; we're not rich. We've never gone hungry, but that's largely because we have such a big garden. There isn't always a call for carpentry, you know, and we have expenses. I think it made me feel special to know that we do own something of such value, hidden away. I sometimes regret that I sold any of them."

"But no one can wear them," Vor said.

"Now you can." And Helena lifted out a heavy gown of red and black, with yellow and light blue poking out under it, all of it densely embroidered.

"That's a noble's wedding gown," Giri identified immediately.

"It was your mother's," Helena said. "She was making it for her wedding to House Salasis, if memory serves."

"Light blue and yellow are their colors," Giri confirmed.

"Then her secret love with my son resulted in you," Helena told Vor. "She finished it, all the embroidery is hers, but she never wore it."

Vor glanced at Giri. "You said blue and yellow are Salasis's colors?"

"That's right," he nodded. "See, there's an outer gown of red and black,

Mrandis's colors, and the inner gown is yellow and blue. During the ceremony, the spouse that is leaving their house and going to their spouse's house sheds the outer layer. For men they wear a double layered long coat, though the design isn't much different from the double layered gown, really."

Vor stared at it, and shook her head a little. "Even if I were going to join Holstor House, you know, officially, I'm not a part of the Mrandis House, and yellow and blue are Salasis colors."

Giri had stepped up to where Helena was holding the wedding gown, still folded. He was looking at the fabric of the inner gown where a bit of it was exposed.

"I'm not an expert on fabric," he said, "but it looks like the embroidery thread is a different textile from the fabric of the dress, so a clever dyer could pick a dye that would affect the one and not the other." He eyed Vor. "Do you know what my house's colors are?"

She eyed him back, observing the little smile that was starting to curve his mouth. "I didn't know your silly little houses had colors," she prodded, "but I'm sure you'll tell me."

His smile bloomed. "Blue and gold, a darker blue than this. I'm sure my sister would love the challenge of finding a dyer to make the adjustment."

Vor felt her cheeks blush. "She can do as she likes," Vor said archly. "Maybe one of her daughters can make use of it."

Tamarus guffawed and slapped Giri on the back, making him stagger. Beside her, Evalyn bounced and stifled a squeal.

"That's settled then," Helena sighed, grinning. "Shall we have the trunk carted to House Holstor? I am guessing it's too heavy for your griffin friends to carry."

"I'll handle it," Giri said confidently.

"Do I get a say in this?" Vor grumped.

Everyone ignored her, except Giri, who winked.

"Then shall we take it downstairs?" Tamarus asked Giri.

"No, you can leave it here." He looked around the space, assessing, and Vor realized what he was thinking.

"Giri," she said low, a warning.

He met her gaze, and she realized he was thinking they should tell them. "Your grandfather already knows," he said softly.

"Millie is the one that gossips," Helena offered, also quietly, and then took a steadying breath. "Vor, your uncle Damarin told us that you showed early signs of mage talent: sitting and staring at fire or water, as though you were about to make it do something, as though you could feel something in it." She looked between Vor and Giri. "You're both mages, aren't you?"

Giri reached for the collar of his shirt and tugged it over, revealing the five scars on his shoulder in the flower petal pattern, so Vor braced herself and did the same.

"We're wizards," Giri whispered, "still apprentices, but I can teleport the trunk to my room at House Holstor, if I have enough floor space to chalk a departure circle. I'm good with teleporting inanimate objects. The trunk should arrive there fine. It's how I usually send anything big that needs to go home."

Vor's throat was tight. Evalyn was staring at her wizard marks, fascinated, and she self-consciously covered them back up. Magnus spoke into the silence.

"We've heard of the tensions between the wizards and the common-born mages," he said in his rough voice. "We've had no reason to take sides."

Vor met and held his gaze. "We wouldn't bring trouble onto you, Uncle Mag," she promised.

"We'll keep it quiet," Helena smiled, and then sighed. She stood up, joints popping a little, and went to take Vor in a big hug. "Wizard or not," she whispered, "you're our Vor, and we love you, and you are always, always welcome here."

Evalyn patted her shoulder, nodding, and Tamarus was smiling at her, too. Magnus still had a neutral expression, but Vor didn't get the sense that he was displeased, just cautious. The overall welcome was more than Vor had ever thought she'd have anywhere, and had to fight down another surge of tears. Giri was grinning.

At last, Helena let her go and started repacking the trunk.

Vor watched her, wondering if she ever did want to wear any of those dresses. Maybe someone else in House Holstor would fit them? A few of them had colors she didn't mind, but she was a mage, not an ordinary lady of a noble house. She caught herself smiling a little at a thought. "I suppose I shouldn't go walking up to House Mrandis wearing one of my mother's dresses. Mirassi already hates me enough."

Evalyn snorted with mirth.

"They need tailoring anyway," Helena said from behind a smile.

"So then, do you want to send it now?" Vor asked Giri.

"Can I watch?" Evalyn begged.

"Ah," Giri looked between Vor and Evalyn, suddenly seeming shy. "Sure, let's do it now," he said. "I have some chalk in my pack, and, um, alright, I guess it's fine if you watch. You won't see much."

Evalyn bounced and stifled another squeal. Giri trotted back down to fetch his chalk, and Helena went down, too, saying something about supervising lunch. Magnus followed without a backwards glance, but Tamarus stayed and helped Vor and Evalyn put away all the other stored items that had been moved around to get to the trunk.

"Don't mind Magnus," Tamarus said. "He's been like that since he lost so much of his family."

"That's one reason I stay," Evalyn said, now somber. "I'm sort of all he has left. Grandmum says I should get married and have some babies to make him happy, but Glory has babies, and Pa doesn't seem to care much, even though she brings them to visit all the time. I really think he misses Ma. He loved her so much."

"Some wounds can't be healed," Vor said in agreement.

Evalyn's hand was suddenly on Vor's arm, and Vor paused to regard her.

"Oh, Vor," Evalyn whispered, "you have wounds like that? Of course you do, but I didn't even think of it. I'm so sorry. Your parents died, of course that was horrible. What happened, all these years you've been away? Was it very bad?"

Vor put her hand on Evalyn's. "I'm alright," she assured her. "I'll tell you about it sometime."

Vor and Tamarus moved the trunk into the center of the room. Giri returned with the chalk, and Tamarus asked if he could watch, too. Giri, perhaps feeling he had to agree since he'd already said Evalyn could stay, said it was alright.

"Back up into the doorways, if you would," he said.

He'd also brought a slim, handbound book, which he opened to a page showing a magic circle and laid atop the trunk.

"You can help, if you want," he told Vor. "This is the circle I use for departures."

She took a piece of chalk, and referenced the book to begin drawing the simpler aspects of the circle. Giri apparently had it memorized and went straight for the complex runes around the outside. Tamarus and Evalyn watched silently. It took them several minutes to finish, and then Giri stood for another couple, looking over the circle to check for any mistakes.

"It's good," he said at last.

"You can do this without an arrival circle?" Vor asked.

He smiled. "There is an arrival circle. I chalk it on my bedroom floor whenever I'm home, and the servants have orders not to disturb it, but to check it every day in case I've sent something, and take it out of the circle." He took her hand. "You want to help?"

"Of course I'm helping," she muttered back.

Teleporting anything took a lot of energy, so sharing the cost would mean Giri wouldn't be so exhausted afterwards. Plus, it was a chance for Vor to observe the process. She'd teleported small objects short distances in the past, but teleporting was difficult, and involved making the world think that the areas inside the departure and arrival circles were the same place, and then allowing them to separate again, having moved the object from the departure circle into the arrival circle.

Vor contributed energy and followed along with what Giri was doing magically, and then between one blink and the next, the trunk was just gone. A faint breeze moved around the room, and Giri and Vor both let go a breath.

"That's it?" Evalyn asked.

"That's it," Giri nodded, and leaned back against the wall. "I told you, you wouldn't see anything."

"But the trunk is in your bedroom now?" Evalyn confirmed, "in Holstor House?"

"Yes," he answered. "Everything felt right, so it should be there, and not, you know, on fire or anything."

Evalyn's eyebrows made a run for her hairline.

Giri shrugged. "It happened once, when I was first learning. I still don't know what I did wrong. I've had trouble with accidentally setting things on fire," he muttered, rubbing at his head, and then perked up to reassure them. "Not recently. I mean, when I was a lot younger."

"Don't worry," Vor said, also feeling the magical drain and leaning back against the wall. "After this Giri doesn't have any energy left to set anything on fire, accidentally or on purpose."

"Oh," Evalyn said, nodding and trying for a smile. "Good."

"Shall we clean this up then?" Tamarus asked.

"Might as well," Vor said. "It's of no more use."

"I'll do it," Evalyn volunteered. "You two look tired."

"Teleportation is expensive, energetically," Vor told her.

"Lunch then," Tamarus said.

They followed him downstairs where the women were busy with preparations, while Evalyn quietly fetched a bucket of water and some rags. Tamarus directed Vor and Giri to a couch against one wall and began setting the table.

"The children are out playing with the griffins," Ona called over to them. "I take it, that's alright?"

Ona had the composure not to look like she was afraid the griffins would devour the children.

"Thornwing's likely to hamstring himself showing off," Giri said. "Perhaps we should go check on him."

Vor followed him out the main door, through the mud room, and onto the porch. Her grandfather was sitting there now, in the rocking chair Helena had earlier occupied, watching the antics of the three children and two griffins. Giri took a seat on the railing and Vor leaned against one of the supports for the roof. The two boys, Stratus and Julean, were romping around with Thornfire, trying to catch him. Alaurie had gotten up on Hawkjoy's back and was taking an easy trot around the yard, with the boys and Thornwing dodging around them.

"I still sometimes wish I'd died in the red fever," Ruslin said, just loud enough to be heard over the laughter, "but now I'm so grateful for this day, to know you're alive and see you again, Vorella. Your mother and father were so very dear to me, and their loss might never heal, but I see both of them in you."

She went and knelt by the rocking chair, and put a hand atop his on the arm of it.

"You'll go visit your mother's family after lunch?" he asked.

"I suppose so," she agreed.

"But you'll not ask to be taken back in?"

"No," she confirmed, and kept her voice low. "Giri and I are both wizards, and that makes us not quite like ordinary nobility. Our real home is the Citadel."

Over on the railing, still watching the griffins and kids, Giri nodded.

"You think you'll have a family of your own?" Ruslin asked gently.

Giri shrugged. "It's not really necessary, and could be inconvenient, but who's to say, really?"

"We'll have apprentices," Vor said, "someday. For now, we are apprentices. To wizards, the apprentice-master bond is stronger than parent and child. There's work to do, and I wouldn't have a child just to dump it in Holstor House, ignored, so I can attend to my work."

"In noble houses, most children are raised by the servants, as Vor says," Giri contributed, "so parents and children sometimes barely know each other. Holstor House isn't so much like that, we're smaller, but it still happens to some degree. I question sometimes whether the system of noble houses is the best for the country and the people in them, but I can do that, because I have seen inside them and outside them."

"It certainly caused problems for Juleena," Ruslin muttered.

"She must have had great happiness here," Vor offered, "with you."

"For a short while," he agreed. "How I wish Stratus hadn't been called to the war. How I wish she hadn't insisted on going with him, and taking you."

Now her grandfather turned to look at Vor, his expression both serious and sad.

"Can you tell me how they died?" he asked.

Vor hesitated. She'd expected the question would come up. It wasn't something she'd told anyone, not even Giri, but if anyone deserved to know, it was Stratus's father.

"We marched all the way to the capital," she began. "Other towns and cities fell more easily, but the fighting at the capital was horrible."

"You saw a lot of it?"

"I was with my mother and the other camp followers, and she tried to shield me from it," Vor said. "But when the casualties came in, she helped tend them, and she couldn't watch me at the same time. There were some other children with the camp, too, and we got sent to fetch and carry and clean. I wasn't very big or strong; I couldn't do much. Of course, there were guards at the edges of the camp, so I couldn't get out, but I still saw, as we marched, and I saw the injured and the dead brought back. I heard the screams and saw the fire."

These memories, too, were ones Vor had tried to forget, but talking of them brought back the sights and sounds, even the smells: smoke, blood, the stink of the latrine ditches, horses, leather, the polish the soldiers used, and many others.

"My mother did her best to protect me. It was like the men fighting weren't human anymore. When they fought, they were just animals, when they were hurt, they were hurt animals. Not all of them," she revised. "My dad was good at fighting, he hardly got hurt. We had a tent when we camped, and he'd come back and clean up and be with us. I remember what scared me the most was when he'd cry. My mother never cried. She'd just hold him. Me, too, sometimes."

Ruslin and Giri were both silent, neither looking at her, but she felt waves of sensation through her ring, coming from Giri. She also sensed without turning around, that Helena stood in the doorway behind her, listening silently.

"At the capital," Vor went on, "the drakes fought the griffins. The wizards brought in storms. My mother and I huddled in the tent, waiting for the rain and the fighting to stop. Everyone was confident we'd win, since we had won so far, though lots of people had died. They still called it winning."

Vor paused to breathe. She'd reached the hard part.

"Then the call came for help with the casualties. They had brought back the first group of dead and injured, so my mom went out to help. After she went, I snuck out, too. I wanted to see the griffins. It was too dark and rainy, though, and it didn't look like there were any griffins in the air. At least, I couldn't see any. The storm was getting worse and some of the tents were starting to come loose. Someone saw me and made me start helping to tie them back down, but there were a lot falling over and we couldn't fix them all. The ground was wet, so the stakes weren't holding. I remember being really cold, so I ran off to go back to our tent, but it had collapsed, too, so I went to find my mom."

Vor took another breath, and reminded herself that it had all happened long ago, and could not be changed now, and was over. Feeling pain over it wouldn't change anything, and wouldn't benefit her. That helped a little, just a little.

"The tent for the injured was still standing. It was a big tent, and well secured. There were a lot of injuries this time. The tent was full. There were men outside it, in the rain, dying. I didn't see my mom outside, so I went in, and it was crowded with everyone who could help. I had to push my way through. There were men on cots and men on the ground. I couldn't think of anything but finding my mom.

"I finally did, and she was trying to help a man on the ground, and when I got to her, I saw it was my dad." She had to stop. The vision of it was before her eyes. She'd seen a lot of injuries, being with the army. When she'd seen her father, she'd known he wouldn't survive, yet her mother had been frantically bandaging, trying to slow the bleeding, as if bandages could put back together a body so cut to pieces.

"I held his hand," she managed, not mentioning that he'd only had one hand left to hold. That was a pain her grandparents didn't need to know. "He died. They dragged him outside so another man could be brought inside, one who was still alive, who still had a chance. They lined him up with the other dead, in the rain. My mom and I stayed with him, but they tried to make her go back inside to help others. She wouldn't go."

Vor also kept to herself the sounds of her mother's weeping and screaming. It was a sound she'd never forget. For herself, all she'd been able to do was sit there, mute, holding her father's hand, in shock. She'd seen many men die, but she couldn't believe it would ever happen to her father. She took a breath and kept going,

"Someone grabbed her and tried to drag her back, but she fought them. They hit her, but she still fought, until finally one of the officers ordered them to stop. The day got darker, and I was so cold, but I didn't want to leave my dad. The fighting stopped, but the casualties kept coming. They kept adding more dead men to the line, making rows. There were other women and children sitting with their dead men. Eventually, I needed to get warm so badly that I had to get up, get out of the rain, but I started to think my mom would never get up. I tried to get her to go back to the tent, but she wouldn't.

"Finally, I saw a soldier who had been my dad's friend, and I went and begged him for help. He went with me and put our tent back up, and I went inside and lit the brazier and changed my clothes. A little while later, he brought my mom inside. I tried to get her to change into dry clothes, but she just lay on the bed. She wouldn't respond. I went out and got food, but she wouldn't eat."

Vor left out another section of the story: the days her mother lay, unresponsive, while the army finished its conquest, as the tents began to thin around them. All she would say was "I'm sorry" over and over.

"She got sick," Vor had to say. "Sickness went through what was left of the camp. Some of the soldiers said it was punishment for going to war on a country that had never done us harm. There was unrest. Some of the Northnest people were still fighting back, in little pockets, not soldiers, just regular people. They buried my dad with the other soldiers who had died, and started another grave for everyone dying of the sickness. I got it, too, a little, but I recovered. My mom died of it. They buried her."

Vor felt her grandmother's hands on her shoulders and she took a deep breath.

"And you?" Helena asked, voice rough.

Vor had been alone, so alone. She hadn't been able to find anyone she knew. The soldier who had been her father's friend was nowhere to be found—dead or alive, she didn't know, but not there. The pain and fear had been so great, after a spate of hysterical screaming, she'd gone numb. The army had packed up the empty tent. She'd no more known how to get back to Trivale by herself than she'd known how to fly.

"I realize now, I should have found an officer, that maybe they would have found a way to ship me back to Weldom, but I was afraid of everyone I didn't know. I went into the city, and joined the other orphans," Vor said. "I begged for food, or stole it. My mage powers were starting to emerge and I learned to make heat, to keep myself warm."

She abridged the story again, leaving out how some soldiers had assaulted her as she ran through the city one night after curfew, desperate to get to a healer because she'd started bleeding—her first cycle—and hadn't known what it was, and had thought she might be dying. The orphans did die from time to time, from disease, from hunger or cold, and Vor had thought it was some kind of sickness.

She kept her voice soft. "One of the mages living in the Northnest palace sensed my powers, and came and fetched me. He made me his apprentice, but he wasn't a good man. He did a lot of cruel things, and I did some cruel things, too, when I had to. It's a long story, but it ends when I fought him and killed him. Giri and his master and some other wizards had come to see what kind of nonsense he was getting up to, and that's when they found me. That was just around a year ago, or a little less."

Vor looked up, realizing now that she'd been staring at the plank floor of the porch, unseeing, during her recitation. She was holding her grandfather's gnarled, scarred hand. Giri had adjusted his seat and was looking at her.

"I met Giri," she said, feeling the pain of all her history lessening with that joy.

He smiled a little, but his eyes were slightly swollen, as though he'd been crying. Vor realized then that her internal emotions—that she'd been trying so hard not to express—must have reached him in some form through the rings. She should have taken the ring off before talking about this, so he wouldn't sense her old pain. Of course, he could have taken his ring off, if he'd wanted to, but it gleamed on his finger; he'd left it on.

"Around a month ago I came back to Weldom, and became a wizard, and went with some other wizards down under the capital to stop a group of common-born mages from pulling out the magic key that keeps the capital from falling."

"And now we're here," Giri said softly.

"Now we're here," Vor echoed.

Helena gave Vor's shoulders a little squeeze.

"And now lunch is ready," she said. "Thank you for telling us, Vor. As awful as it is, I am glad to know how their story ended. It is better to know than to keep making up possibilities, one more horrible than the last. Now we can come to terms with it. After lunch, there's something else you should have. The army did send a package back to us, though it took a few years to reach us, of belongings that Stratus left behind."

"That's right," Ruslin mumbled. "It's been in our closet for a long time."

He wiped his face with his free hand, and Helena bent over him to kiss his forehead. They all got up, Helena called in the children, and they sat down to have lunch.

Lunch was a spring vegetable soup and rounds of bread Ona had baked, with butter that must have been bought since the Hearthsravens didn't have any livestock. It was all hot and wholesome and Vor enjoyed it.

"Do your griffin friends need anything?" Ona asked nervously.

"They can fly off whenever they want and find something in the forest," Vor assured her. "They'll go well beyond the nearby area."

"Oh, good," Ona said, obviously relieved.

After lunch, Ruslin called Vor and Giri into one of the rooms behind the kitchen, which turned out to be the master bedroom that he and Helena shared.

"As I mentioned, a parcel did arrive a couple years after the war," he said. "It was only then we knew for certain that Stratus had fallen in battle, and that you three would not return."

He went to a shelf high in a closet and brought down a thick sack. From it he pulled a paperboard package that had clearly been opened before and rewrapped.

"Unfortunately, his sword, which belonged to my brother before him, was not recovered. I am supposing he lost it in battle, and his body was carried back, but no one picked up the sword. It can't be helped. I hope another is caring for it and using it for honorable purposes."

Ruslin began to open the package, and Vor began to feel a magical vibration from the vicinity of it that made her own personal energies resonate in sympathy.

"You feel that?" Giri muttered softly, and she nodded.

"There was a note," Ruslin went on, apparently not having heard Giri. "It told us Stratus had perished in battle, but made no mention of Juleena or you. His armor was only issued to him; he didn't own it, so it was reclaimed. He was buried in his uniform, the note said. His tent and most of the contents were also army issue, so they of course were reclaimed. There were two items, however, that they made the effort of sending back to us."

Ruslin handed the first to Vor. It was a thin, narrow package about as long as her forearm. She began to unwrap it.

"This was your mother's," Ruslin said. "Stratus gave it to her. Before they were married there was some kind of festival among the nobility that Juleena went to, and Stratus was assigned as a guard for the Mrandis party. One of the days, a trio of harpies attacked the festival. Stratus and the other guards fought them off, and Juleena also had just been out hunting with the other noble ladies and shot one of the harpies off Stratus with a brilliant eye shot from her bow."

The paper wrapping fell away and Vor saw that she held a long, slender dagger in a sheath.

"Stratus was rewarded for his valor with a harpy feather."

"I've heard this story," Giri contributed suddenly. "My parents told me about it. They were there. I was still in the nursery, and setting it on fire regularly, so there was no way I'd get to attend a summer gathering, but I remember hearing about the harpies."

Vor eyed him. "You set your nursery on fire? You were serious about that, accidentally setting things on fire a lot?"

He shrugged. "I had night terrors, and couldn't control my powers. They came on me early."

Ruslin chuckled. "At least Vor didn't do that." He pointed. "Your parents never let you handle that blade. Harpy feathers are extremely sharp, and never need honing. It'll never rust, either. Be careful with it."

Vor pulled the blade from its sheath. It did indeed look like a feather. It even had a rachis running down the middle, and was curved just slightly, but though it was shiny and sharp like a forged metal blade, it was a little too flexible to have been metal.

"I wonder why they sent it back," Vor mused. "Who wouldn't want a blade so fine? Someone could have claimed spoils of war and kept it."

"I think they sent it back because of the other item," Ruslin said. He lifted a vaguely circular package out of the box. "You may remember this; you used to play with it."

Vor sheathed the dagger and set it on the bed. This second item she thought must be the one giving off the magical vibration, for the harpy feather had produced next to nothing, hardly any more than an ordinary metal blade would. She took the package and immediately felt its song in her fingertips and rapidly moving up her hands. Her grandfather, meanwhile, rubbed his hands together and shook them, as though shaking off an unpleasant sensation.

"I don't know if you recall," he said, folding up the empty paper package, "but only you and your father could ever touch that without discomfort. I am guessing they sent it back along with the harpy dagger because of superstition. No one could touch the one, and they were together, so they were afraid of a curse or some such if they kept either one."

Vor unwrapped the item, sensing a memory poised to pounce on her, and revealed a milky white disk, slightly oblong, but close to circular, about the size of a dinner plate, but thinner. One edge, about a quarter of its circumference, was slightly squared off and rough, while the rest was smooth.

It continued to emit its subtle magical hum, but it wasn't unpleasant at all. In fact, it felt good, and made her want to keep holding it. As she stared at it, the memory came swirling onto her, of sitting and running her hands over the slick surface, and staring at it, holding it up to the sky or a lamp or a fire to see the light shine through it, and thinking she could see things in it.

"Yes," she said. "I played with this as a child."

She showed it to Giri, but he took a cautious step back. "I can tell I mustn't touch it," he said. "It wouldn't like me."

"Stratus told the story many times," Ruslin said. "You remember what it is?"

Despite Giri's aversion to it, to Vor the disk seemed to be begging to be touched. She stroked it. It felt almost alive in her hands.

"Yes," she said slowly, as more memories connected to the disk began to surface. "The mist dragon gave it to him. It's a scale from the mist dragon's belly. My father spoke with the dragon and negotiated peace between us and the Wild Ones. The mist dragon gave him a scale in thanks. It was before I was born, but he told me about it."

"That's right," her grandfather nodded.

"Your father spoke to a dragon?" Giri echoed. "He negotiated with it?"

Vor nodded as more of the story came back to her. "It landed in the Mrandis courtyard, after the army had killed a bunch of Wild Ones. It was angry, but my father gave it back the golden krine horns and agreed to get the army to stop killing Wild Ones that weren't violent, and it agreed to try to keep the Wild Ones away from where humans were. Then it gave him a scale from its belly and flew away. This is the scale."

"You have a dragon scale," Giri marvelled, eyes wide. "I've read about them. I've even seen one. There's one in the Citadel vaults. I got to see it on a tour when I was still an unbonded apprentice, but it was dark and rough and pointed: nothing like this. They said no one could use it."

"Use it?" Vor asked. "Use it for what?"

"Dragon scales are better than mage-stone for storing power," he said. "You can also use them as scrying mirrors, and they have a huge range, much farther than water pools or glass mirrors, or even polished metal mirrors. I also read, though I didn't fully understand it, that they have an amplifying effect on magic that is worked through them. The problem is that they are keyed to one person and their descendants. That's why no one could use the dragon scale in the vaults anymore. The last wizard to own it left no living mage-gifted children, at least that anyone knew about."

Vor frowned. "I guess that means I have to have a mage-gifted kid before I die."

"Well," Giri said, voice cautious now, "maybe. Dragon scales are powerful and lend that power to the wizard that can hold it. Not all wizards use their powers for beneficial goals. Imagine if Vittara had reached the key with a dragon scale in hand. She might have succeeded in destroying it. I have no doubt you will only use the scale for good works, and a child we raise, we might be able to depend upon to be as good—if it is even a mage—but what about generations from now, long after we're gone?"

Giri shook his head doubtfully. "We can't know what the dragon was thinking when it gave this scale to Stratus. It must have had a good reason, and it must have known what it was doing, but— Oh, I should mention, scales have to be willingly given for the powers to come through. Hunting down and skinning a dragon won't get scales that have any power in them, and finding scales a dragon has shed won't give you anything special either, though the scales are so tough and light they make excellent armor.

"For the keyed magical connection to happen, the scales have to be willingly given directly from one dragon to one person. There's something special about that connection. Anyway, as I was going to say, I don't know if the mist dragon could foresee the destiny of its scale, if it knew it would only come to those who would use it wisely. It could be better to let the power die with you, Vor."

She turned the scale over in her hands, still captivated by it. "Well, it's something to think on."

"Take it, Vor," her grandfather urged her. "The harpy blade, too."

Vor shook her head. "You should keep the harpy blade, as something to remember my parents by. You're giving me all my mother's clothes and these? What will you have?"

"No," Ruslin said simply, picking up the harpy blade and offering it to her. "We have our memories. These have sat in my closet ever since we received them and wept over them. Stratus and Juleena would want their daughter to have them, to use them. You will use them, won't you? You are a wizard. The capital is going to send you all over on assignments. It could be dangerous. These could help keep you safe."

"He has a point, Vor," Giri said softly.

She did want them, especially the dragon scale, but knowing the history of the harpy blade, that it was a gift between her parents, made it precious as well. Still, she felt overburdened with gifts this day, and overwhelmed with emotions and memories. It didn't feel fair for her to be so greedy.

"Alright," she surrendered, "if you're sure."

"I'm completely sure," Ruslin smiled. "Vor, the best thing we have to remember Stratus and Juleena by, is you. Your return is worth far more than your mother's dresses and dagger, and your father's dragon scale combined. So you keep them, alright?"

Vor felt her throat choke, but she nodded. "Alright."

Ruslin made a sound like his throat was clogged, too. "Now, perhaps you should make your journey to Lenali. It is not a long walk, and an even shorter flight, I'm sure. However," he held up a finger, "you should not wear that blade openly on a trip to Mrandis House. Your grandmother will remember it."

"Ah," Vor nodded, setting it back down on the bed. "You can hold onto it for me?"

"Of course. Pick it up before you leave Trivale."

Vor tucked the dragon scale inside her tunic and hoped it wouldn't be too obvious.

"Will you be back for dinner?" Ruslin asked as he set the blade back up on the shelf, out of reach of any children that might come into the room. "We can also arrange sleeping space for you."

Vor hesitated. She could see that the house was full. Sleeping there would surely inconvenience her family, even though they would be welcomed, but they would need to sleep somewhere. Surely Lenali would have an inn, even if Trivale was too small for one, and they did have coin.

"If we're visiting the Mrandis branch family," Giri spoke up, "and they are likely to be friendly to Vor, as you've indicated, they should have guest rooms available, and they will likely offer. I wouldn't depend on the main house, though I could probably lean on them enough to make them feel obligated, but I'd rather not trade on the Holstor name if I don't have to, and even if they complied in deed, it might not be in spirit, and that could make for an awkward night. The branch house is our best bet."

"That sounds ideal," Ruslin smiled, "putting you close enough to visit the main house, without you having to stay there."

"Yes," Giri nodded, apparently still thinking. "I expect the branch house will make the offer without us even having to mention it."

"You will come back and spend a day with us before you leave the area," Ruslin encouraged.

"Definitely," Vor agreed, and winked at Giri. "After a visit with my mother's side of my family, I am expecting to need some sanity before I fly off and meet Giri's crazy family."

"I didn't mean," Vor assured Giri as they took their packs off the griffins, "that I think your family will be crazy."

"Oh, I know," he smiled. "You were just trying to reassure your grandfather, but you are right, my family is a little crazy. I think all noble houses are. Too much inbreeding."

"What does that say about you?" Vor muttered at him.

"Apparently you like my crazy."

She had to smile. "Apparently I do. Now we get to go see the kind of crazy I would have been if my mother had married Salasis after all."

She was tucking her dragon scale into the outside of a pack, trying to keep it away from Hawkjoy's skin, in case the vibration irritated the griffin, when she felt Giri's hand on her shoulder, and she paused to look at him.

"You wouldn't be here," he said, almost sadly, moving his hand to her cheek.

Vor was touched by his sudden tenderness, and stood still, letting him look at her and gently stroke her face.

Giri shook his head a little. "No, my precious, unique Vor, no amount of inbreeding among inbred noble houses could produce the special kind of crazy that is you."

He couldn't keep a straight face and broke into a wide grin. Vor growled, but she was grinning, too.

"I'll kick your ass," she mock-threatened.

"You'll have to catch me first."

He took off running around the yard, leaving her standing there.

"You're serious?" she called. "You want me to chase you?"

"Usually, the matriarch has the male chase her," Hawkjoy remarked.

"I could drop him for you," Thornwing offered, "maybe while flying over a lake? I'm sure you wouldn't want him permanently damaged. Who else could you find that would treasure your special kind of crazy?"

Vor growled at the griffin, but it was only half-hearted. Giri disappeared around the back of the house, and Vor felt him send a series of little teasing pulses through her ring.

"I can't believe I'm doing this," she muttered, and she took off after him.

Giri was waiting for her around the corner of the house, but she sensed him before he leapt out at her, and she dodged, passing him. There was the bathing room tacked onto the back of the house, and she had to swing wide to run around it.

"Now who's chasing who?" Giri called, pelting after her.

"Hawkjoy told me," she panted back, "the male is supposed to chase the matriarch."

They rounded the end of the workshop where the menfolk were crafting again, and Giri called out to little Stratus and Julean, "get her!"

The boys needed no second invitation, dropping whatever they were doing to race off, and they were surprisingly fast. While Giri was perhaps not putting on his fastest turn of speed, those two boys sprinted with all they had.

"Alaurie, Evalyn, help me!" Vor summoned as she passed the garden.

Evalyn jumped out, laughing, and snatched up one of the twins—Vor couldn't tell them apart—swinging him about, and Alaurie ran out, chasing the other one, who took evasive action and went over to run behind Thornwing. That left Giri chasing Vor without interference, and she got to decide if she wanted him to catch her.

Of course she wanted him to catch her, and if they didn't quit running about, they'd be mused and sweaty and that was no way to greet members of a noble house, even a branch house. She only had a couple seconds' lead. Behind the bathing room, she spun about, lifted her hands, and sent a stiff wind—not enough to lean against, but plenty to slow Giri down. He ran right into it, staggered a little, and Vor released it just in time to let him land in her arms. He seemed completely happy to be there, and got his arms around her, too.

"You are crazy, you know," he said, breathing a little heavy. "You stepped right off into that circle of doom around the key, just to see what would happen. I thought I'd never get you back. You really scared me."

"I'm sorry," she apologized, holding him a bit tighter. "I have no excuse. It just needed to be done. No one else was going to do it. They were all just talking while Iyai was up there dying, and who knew what was happening to the others in the circle."

"I know," he assured her. "Could you just, tell me, next time, when you're going to do something like that, so we can do it together? Or at least so I have some warning?"

She nodded against his neck. "I'll try, if you promise not to stop me."

"I'll try," he echoed.

Then came little running footsteps and something collided with Vor's legs. Little arms wrapped her and clung to her knees.

"Gotcha!" the twin who had just ran up and grabbed her declared, apparently having evaded little Alaurie in the end.

"You win," she groaned.

"I win, I win!" the boy announced, letting go just as fast, and running back the way he came.

They stood there for another minute or two, but there was a noble house to visit, and putting it off wouldn't make it any easier.

Epilogue 2
Lenali

Vor and Giri had decided that bringing the griffins into the small city of Lenali was probably not the best idea. They did, however, give the griffins magic stones that would heat up if Vor or Giri encountered some kind of trouble and needed rescue. There was always the concern though, that humans had bows. Projectile weapons were not the best friend of flying creatures. Hopefully, aerial rescue would not be needed.

So Thornwing and Hawkjoy gave them a quick lift from the Hearthsraven home to just beyond bow range, outside the Lenali city walls. There, Vor and Giri took their overnight bags, and the griffins said they'd go back and sleep in front of the Hearthsraven house. Both were comfortable sleeping outside, the night was not likely to get too cold for them, and they could curl up together to share warmth.

"Plus," Thornwing said, "if we but shiver in view of any of your family, Vor, I think they will come fling blankets on us."

"At the expense of their own beds," Vor pointed out, "so please only shiver if you must."

Thornwing nodded. "Noted. I don't think it'll be too cold, though. When you grow up atop a mountain, the weather down here is perfectly balmy."

Hawkjoy preened a bit of Vor's hair—though it was in braids so it was a bit awkward—in farewell, and the two griffins flew back towards Trivale. Vor and Giri finished the walk up to the gates of Lenali.

"I've never visited the Mrandis House," Giri said. "I don't think they've ever hosted a gathering in my lifetime."

"If they really are as poor as my grandmother said," Vor offered, "it would make sense that they can't afford it."

The guards at the gate stopped them.

"Were those griffins friends of yours?" one of the men asked.

"That's right," Vor told him.

"They're not violent?"

"Not unless you're a plump buck deer," Giri winked. "We've suggested they don't come into the city, so no one gets scared."

The guard nodded. "I'll spread the word not to shoot them then. We've had a healthy respect for the Wild Ones, these past two decades. I wouldn't want there to be a misunderstanding."

"Nor would we," Vor agreed.

"You're strangers here?" the guard asked next, sounding professional but also friendly. "Might I ask your business?"

They'd changed into a nicer set of clothing, not their mage robes, and nothing so fancy as the gowns Vor had inherited, but it marked them as middle or even lower-upper class.

"I'm visiting family," Vor told him truthfully.

"Can you direct us to the Mrandis Branch House?" Giri asked.

The man's eyebrows rose a little, but he didn't seem too alarmed. They figured asking for the main Mrandis House directly might attract too much attention, and they wanted to visit the branch house first anyway. The guard instructed them to head down the main street behind him and turn left at the end. The street climbed up the side of the small mountain that Lenali was built on, though not unbearably steep. There was another wall around the Mrandis House itself, at the center of the city, and around that, the guard said, were the houses where the branch family and many of the servants lived.

Vor and Giri thanked the man, and headed up the road. The city of Lenali was not overly large, but the simple fact that it had roads paved in stone, a sturdy outer wall, and a noble house in it gave it the distinction of a city. All the buildings they saw were well made as well, and got finer as they went further into the city, passing dense houses where lived the farmers and unskilled workers, then the homes of craftspeople and merchants, markets, and then dealers and makers of more luxurious goods and providers of services, before the homes of the middle class and rich began.

The end of the main street was obvious, terminating where it ran into a circular road that looped the walls of the Mrandis estate. Within that road was a ring of parkland with a well-used walking and riding path, directly outside the walls. Whatever was inside the walls, Vor couldn't see more than a glimpse through the main gates.

"These will be the branch houses, then," Giri said, nodding towards the nearer buildings on their side of the looping road. "The finest one will be for the closest relatives to those currently leading the main house, but they will all connect a bit. At least, that's how they are for my house."

He turned left and began walking towards a grand set of stone stairs not far from the road they'd followed up to the loop road. Vor went with him, and they mounted the stairs up to the double doors. There was a door knocker there, and Vor gave it three firm raps. She only got a few breaths to enjoy her anxiety before the door opened, revealing a stately man who had the look of a manservant.

"Good afternoon," he said politely. "May I help you?"

"Good afternoon," Vor replied. "I'm looking for Damarin Mrandis."

The man almost spoke, hesitated, and then looked her up and down. His eyes went next to Giri. Vor could tell he wasn't dismissing them, but assessing.

"Your name, Miss?" he asked with a little bow.

Her heart gave a few particularly strong beats. "Vorella Hearthsraven," she told him.

"You are expected," he said without a twitch. "Won't you and your companion come into the parlor?"

"Gladly," she said, hugely relieved, but also a little puzzled. How could word of them have gotten to Lenali so quickly? And why?

She and Giri followed the manservant into the hall, and to the first door on the left. The room behind it held a few options in seating and had a view of the road they'd just come from through large, clear windows veiled only by a sheer drape.

"Please take your ease," the manservant said. "I'm afraid Master Damarin is not at home at the moment, but the lady of the house will attend you shortly. I shall send in a maid with some tea in just a moment."

"Thank you," they told him, and he bowed himself out.

"My grandparents didn't mention Damarin's wife," Vor whispered as she took a seat on a couch behind a low table. "I don't even know her name."

Giri joined her. "Then I suppose we will learn it shortly."

The tea came surprisingly fast, brought by a woman who must have been a little younger than Ona. She came to a sharp halt in the doorway and stared at Vor. Her skin was pale, but well-freckled, and she had red hair that was bundled up in braids under a white cap. She also wore an apron, but her dress was no servant's well-worn smock. It was a fine dress like any well off woman might wear, not fancy, but of quality material and tailored to fit. Vor had the impression that this woman might help out in a servant's capacity, but that she was much like a member of the family.

Her hands trembled and the cups and saucers on the tray rattled. Her face pinched, and Vor jumped up to go take the tray from her as Giri leaned forward with murmurs of concern.

"Are you alright?" she asked.

The woman put her hands to her mouth when Vor took the tray. When Vor turned back to her after setting the tray down, she saw the woman was weeping, shoulders and chest jerking with sobs that she was struggling to keep silent.

"What is it?" Vor asked, concerned.

Giri got up, too. "Should I fetch help?"

The woman took a shaking breath and wiped her face with her apron. "No," she hiccupped. "I'm so sorry. Please forgive me. I didn't think I'd fall apart like this. So silly."

"It's alright," Vor assured her.

She continued dabbing at her eyes. "It's just, you look like your mother." She sobbed again, and struggled to get herself under control.

"Oh," Vor said, as gently as she could. "Please, come sit down. You knew her well?"

"I grew up with her," she said, allowing Vor to lead her over to the couch.

Giri moved to a chair, and the red-headed woman sat down near Vor.

"We were in the nursery together. We grew up together. All my life I was her playmate and then her ladies maid, but it was never like master and servant, you know? I mean, it was, but Julee wasn't like that. We were like sisters, the very best of friends."

Finally, she managed a smile and looked over at Vor.

"I was her confidant. I helped arrange her meetings with Stratus, your father. When she got pregnant with you, I helped her keep it a secret as long as possible. That's why I'm in the branch house now—oh, not that it's your fault, nor Julee's. Of course I would have helped her no matter the consequence, and I'm so much happier here anyway."

Vor didn't know what to say. The woman dabbed at her eyes some more.

"I'm sorry for crying," she apologized again.

"You don't need to apologize," Vor managed to say. "It must have been very difficult for you to lose her."

"Not nearly so difficult as for you, I've no doubt." She took a few steadying breaths, and smiled again. "I'm Samira."

Vor offered her hand to shake, and gave her best smile. "I'm Vor."

Samira shook her hand. "It's not true. You don't look exactly like Juleena, but there's a strong resemblance. I was just shocked. I never thought I'd get to meet you. I didn't think what you must look like. I wasn't ready."

"Samira?" asked another voice, and Vor looked up to see another woman, this one probably a few years younger than Samira, standing in the doorway. "Is everything alright?"

"Oh, yes, I'm sorry," she said. "I'm really being a silly goose."

"Everything's fine," Vor agreed, and she stood up to greet the newcomer. Giri did, too. Vor assumed this must be the lady of the branch house. Her dress was a bit finer than Samira's and she held herself with the poise of the nobility. "I heard I was expected. I came to see my great uncle Damarin. I'm Vorella Hearthsraven. My mother was—"

"Juleena," the newcomer smiled. "She was my cousin. Damarin is my father." She stuck out her hand. "I'm Yusani Mrandis."

Vor shook. Yusani was a little bit taller than Vor, with skin almost the same color, and hair a very dark brown. Her eyes were dark hazel and looked cheerful.

"I'm sorry my father's not here right now," Yusani went on. "He's over at the main house, in discussion again. He should be back soon, since he's been there since this morning."

Vor gestured back towards Giri. "This is Giri Holstor."

"A pleasure to meet you," he said, giving a little bow over Yusani's hand.

"Ah, of the main Holstor House, aren't you?" She dimpled. "Well, what a surprise to have you in our parlor. Vor has done well, then."

Before Vor could decide whether to protest or agree, Samira gave a gasp, causing everyone to look at her. The woman had her hands pressed to her face again, eyes wide and almost rolling.

"Samira?" Yusani asked, going so far as to put a supportive hand on her shoulder.

"Giri Holstor," Samira repeated.

"Yes?" Giri said, curiously.

"I met you," the maid went on, almost breathless. "Juleena met you. You were little, maybe four or five at the most. You'd just set your nursery on fire."

Giri seemed to be trying to regroup. "I did do that a few times," he admitted, "when I was small. I don't really remember it."

"Oh my goodness," Samira exclaimed, suddenly shoving to her feet. Yusani stepped back so Samira could pace unimpeded. "Oh my goodness," she said again, and then stopped, turning to look between Vor and Giri. "Are you," she hesitated, "are you two, um?"

"Samira," Yusani scolded softly.

"Yes," Giri answered simply.

A laugh bubbled out of the freckled maid. She even arched back a little, raising fisted hands, as if in victory, still chortling.

"Samira," Yusani said again, a bit sharper, but with an air of confusion that suggested to Vor that the maid normally had impeccable manners and was acting quite out of the ordinary.

"I'm sorry, I'm sorry," Samira said after a few moments. She wiped another tear, but this one from laughter. "So," she gathered herself, looking again between Vor and Giri, "do you know?"

"Know what?" Vor replied suspiciously.

"You don't remember?" she asked Giri directly.

"How nice to have someone else getting asked that," Vor put in dryly.

"I don't remember meeting you or Juleena," he said, "though now I wish I did. I would like to recall a meeting with Vor's mother."

"So you don't remember what you said to her? The agreement you made with her?" Samira pressed, still grinning.

"An agreement with Juleena?" Giri repeated back, incredulous. "No, I don't remember anything like that."

Samira clapped her hands, bouncing a little. "Oh, should I tell you? I wonder if your parents remember. I suppose they threw it out when Juleena married Stratus, and doubly when she died, if they even heard of that." She shook her head. "I am just amazed."

"I am completely confused," Vor commented.

"And I as well, cousin," Yusani muttered. "Samira, I think we should show a little more courtesy to our guests, especially to Lord Holstor."

"Of course," Samira agreed, and made a curtsy, though she was still grinning.

"I don't mind," Giri said, looking amused, "and please call me Giri."

Samira knelt by the low table, tucking her apron under her knees, and began pouring the tea. "Perhaps Lord Holstor might consider asking his esteemed Master and Mistress Holstor what the agreement was that he made with Lady Mrandis, which they witnessed and was witnessed by Mistress Mrandis as well."

"I shall," Giri said, accepting the tea she handed to him, "unless you'd like to tell me now and get the suspense over with."

"Oh, it's not my place, Lord Holstor," Samira simpered theatrically.

"Samira," Yusani sighed, but Vor could see by the twitch of her lips that she was amused.

Samira glanced at Vor and winked.

"I think my mother was very lucky to have a friend like you, Samira," Vor said, accepting her own cup of tea now.

"It was mutual," Samira assured her. "There was no lady kinder, gentler, and braver than my Juleena. I miss her desperately."

"I hope you might tell me more about her," Vor asked tentatively.

"I would love to," Samira smiled. "And you must tell me all about you, and how you met Lord Holstor."

Vor found herself smiling back. "And I want to hear about how my parents met."

"It's so romantic," Samira gushed, now handing a cup to Yusani. ""I will tell you all the naughty secrets about when they had their first kiss, and other things," she raised her eyebrows, "until you are blushing scarlet. Oh, and Lord Holstor must be a wizard, mustn't he," Samira realized. "And you, Vor, Lord Damarin said you showed signs of mage talent."

"We're both wizards," Giri confirmed.

And just then a handsome, dark-skinned man with black hair turning to salt-and-pepper came into the doorway behind Yusani.

"Having a party in the parlor?" he grinned.

Vor stood up. Giri copied her.

"Father," Yusani said, confirming Vor's guess.

The man's quick eyes swept the room and landed on Vor.

"And there she is," he said with evident satisfaction. "You took longer to get here than I had expected, but it is no matter. You are here at last, and with Lord Holstor in tow, just as Mirassi reported."

"We had to stop some people from destroying Anchoria first," Giri explained wryly. "We do apologize for the delay."

"There's always something," Samira giggled.

"So my grandmother told you about me," Vor concluded.

"Vociferously," Damarin nodded, still grinning. "She said you're just like your mother, and it went downhill from there."

"She said as much to me," Vor admitted.

"I expect, despite your presence in my parlor, your decision not to rejoin House Mrandis still stands."

Vor nodded. "It does. I didn't come here to ask to rejoin. I came to meet my family. I confess that I don't remember you, any of you, but my grandparents on my father's side have told me you helped my mother, and took an interest in me."

Damarin leaned back against the door frame and folded his arms. "How your mother was treated by House Mrandis was wrong, in my opinion. It is an unfortunate consequence that often children of the main houses cannot marry where they wish, and get forced into marriages they not only aren't suited for, but vehemently do not want. It was the case with your mother, and she had a strong enough personality that she stood up to it."

He gave a little shrug. "I hoped, when I found out, that I could convince my sister to allow Juleena to marry Stratus and bring him into the branch family, but she wouldn't have it. She insisted on sending Juleena to Salasis and getting the spouse price. She over spent on Ledren and Myra's spouses." He spread his hands. "And look what has come of it. She had to sell both Myra's sons to have enough to buy a spouse for Ledren's daughter, and there has been no issue from that pair."

Yusani sat down on the edge of the couch, her hands clasped nervously in her lap. "Has there been any progress in your discussions?"

Damarin gave a wry half-smile. "Someone put the idea in Mirassi's head that she should look to the branch family and invite them back to the main house. She shouted all about how preposterous that was, but my nephew Ledren—your uncle, Vor—thought it had potential." He chuckled, shaking his head. "There have been very few times that Ledren has applied pressure to my sister. He's arguing to bring Yusani back into the main house."

Yusani explained for Vor and Giri. "I have two daughters and a son. They're too young to marry just yet, but they're all healthy. They could be the future of Mrandis House." She straightened her back. "But I won't have Mirassi dictating their futures, and neither will Nirai, my husband."

"Mirassi is fighting it," Damarin said. "For a little old woman she has an amazing amount of energy."

"I'm fine staying in the branch house," Yusani said. "I've never felt ashamed of it or wished I were in the main house. The main house comes with a lot of extra restrictions and I've never cared much for power, which is the only benefit I see."

"Plus, this would disgrace Ledren and his daughter and her husband, to be removed from the line of descent," Damarin sighed, and then chuckled. "I always hated the main house. They're such a lot of pompous fools. I was relieved when Mirassi pressured me to leave, and I'm not going back to be the master of it. That's another discussion: who will be master and mistress. I don't blame you at all, Vor, for not wanting to get involved."

"Will you marry into Holstor?" Yusani asked Vor then, clearly wanting a change of subject.

Vor and Giri exchanged another weary smile.

"I won't marry into Holstor," Vor said. "If I'll marry Giri is another question, however. We're both wizards and we have things to do. We're not going to live at Holstor House and make a bunch of babies, even though Giri is firstborn."

"That's right," Damarin said, giving his thigh a slap. "You showed signs. Oh, this is perfect. I didn't even think of it. Can either of you look for the latent talent?"

"I can," Giri said promptly.

"I've never tried," Vor admitted.

"Do you need someone looked at?" Giri asked. "I'd be happy to do so, and I can show Vor how at the same time."

"Daddy," Yusani objected. "Hyldi is just a little unique. She can't possibly have mage powers."

"You should meet the whole family," Damarin smiled. "You'll stay the night?"

It turned out that Nirai, Yusani's husband, had taken all three children out to play in the parkland ring around the Mrandis estate, with the help of a couple other members of the household. Samira settled Vor and Giri in adjoining bedrooms in the meantime.

"We have to put you in separate rooms for appearances," she said conspiratorially, "but no one will stop you from sneaking into each other's after dark."

Samira showed them around the house and then sat with Vor and demanded to know her whole story over tea and cookies. Yusani joined them and a few other household members came in, too. Giri vanished somewhere with Damarin, and Vor wondered if he was getting himself involved in Mrandis politics when he shouldn't, but she also saw no reason to stop him; he could make his own decisions. Besides, he certainly knew far better than she did how to navigate noble house politics, and she could trust his judgement.

After her story was told—edited to avoid some of the most violent or intimate bits—the listeners were left wide-eyed and mostly stunned to silence. Luckily it had been easier recounting her parents' deaths this time, but Samira had still wept. Yusani managed to gather herself first.

"It sounds like your grandmother isn't happy with you, but do you want to go see your uncles and aunt and all? Your grandfather, Rodreric, died from the red fever. It was very sad. I lost my mother, too. But there are still others, much nicer than Mirassi. Maybe you want to meet them?" Yusani asked Vor.

"I'm willing," Vor said, "but I'm not expecting much, and if they lay into me trying to make me stay or want to drive me off by calling me names, I'll just leave. I don't want anything from them other than a pleasant chat. If they can't give me that, I want nothing to do with them."

"I don't blame you," Samira contributed.

Then Nirai arrived with three somewhat dirty children, varying in age from a teenage girl, to a boy perhaps ten years old, and another girl, who might have been about five, and hid behind her father's legs. Nirai turned out to be a lean, tall man with lightly tanned skin and reddish-brown hair. His eyes were blue. He had a wide mouth and large hands and looked sort of like he'd never grown out of his gawky teenage years. He smiled generously and frequently, reflecting what seemed to be a mellow temperament.

Damarin and Giri came in, too, making the parlor remarkably crowded, and the other less related people left, leaving just Vor and Giri, Damarin,

Samira, and Yusani and Nirai with their brood. Yusani began making introductions.

"This is Bethriana, our oldest," she said. "And Shorin, our middle child, and over there is Hyldi."

All three children had been blessed with skin a tone close to warm olive. Bethriana had her mother's dark brown hair and hazel eyes, though they were a bit lighter. Shorin clearly had a lot of his father in him, and was almost as tall as his older sister. His hair was dark but with reddish highlights. His eyes were also hazel. Hyldi was still trying to hide behind her father, and had somehow ended up with strawberry blonde hair and her father's blue eyes.

Yusani went on to explain who Vor and Giri were, and Shorin had no hesitation in sticking his hand out to shake. Bethriana was also bold enough to say hello and shake, but Hyldi held back.

"So how does this testing work?" Yusani asked frankly.

Giri leaned forward a little. "I think Bethriana would have shown obvious signs by now if she was born with mage ability."

"Like what?" the girl asked.

"Like setting things on fire when you're scared or angry, with just your inner powers, no fire-striker involved," he told her. "That's usually the most obvious sign and can happen to children as small as four or five. That's what happened to me. I burned out my nursery a few times until my grandfather came down to help me learn not to."

"There are subtler signs," Damarin prompted.

"There are," Giri confirmed, "but a lot of them can be caused by things other than mage powers. Being fascinated by water or fire and staring at it for long periods is a common one. The ability to somewhat control animals is another, but less common. Sometimes children learn how to heat up objects, or even make them emit light. Vor taught herself how to do that. It's also possible, if a child is on the path to developing a high sensitivity to energy and auras, it can make the child cautious and shy, because he or she is sensing a lot of things they don't understand and can't stop."

Damarin glanced down at Hyldi, who had her face hidden in her father's trouser leg.

"Bethriana, it's unlikely you have any mage powers," Giri said simply, "if you haven't shown signs by now, but I can still take a look if you want."

"How do you look?" she asked warily.

"I hold your hand and look for any personal mage power you're carrying, using my own mage senses," Giri said. "You won't feel anything if you don't have any. If you do have some, you'll feel me touch them, but it won't hurt."

"Where?" she asked, still wary.

"It's hard to describe," Vor answered. "Not on your physical body, like on your skin, but within. As some might say poetically, in your heart, or in your spirit."

Bethriana seemed to take a few moments to think that over. "That's alright then," she said at last.

"You don't have to do it," Giri told her firmly. "It's up to you."

"No, I'll do it," she replied, lifting her chin. "It'll help Hyldi feel comfortable, won't it?"

Giri nodded and held out his hand, palm up. Bethriana put hers on his, palm to palm.

"Ready?" Giri murmured, but to Vor.

"Ready," she said.

She figured this first bit would be just like touching anyone's aura, like she'd done many times before, and indeed that was basically what Giri did. Vor hadn't sensed any hint of mage energies from Bethriana, and didn't expect she'd touch any. When she touched another mage's aura, there was resistance, and often a reaction. When she saw Giri's energy touch Bethriana's though, there was no resistance. She had energy—the energy of life, in every cell—but she had no ability to hold and store it. It was like a membrane was missing, and instead her energies were a cloud bounded only by her skin. A mage's energies sometimes also extended beyond their physical body. That was often necessary to perform magic; the energy had to be leveraged and connected with outer forces and objects.

Giri drew back.

"I didn't feel anything," Bethriana reported.

"You have vibrant energy," Giri told her, "but no potential to use it to do magic. Your talents lie elsewhere."

Bethriana did look a slight bit disappointed, but she nodded with good nature. "That's right. I'm a baker. I can bake all kinds of things. You don't need magic for that."

"And I can't bake anything," Vor told her. "You have your own type of magic, and you should be proud of it."

"My turn," Shorin insisted.

Bethriana stepped back and Shorin took her place.

"I think I have magic," he declared. "I've seen signs of it."

"Really?" Giri asked, without a hint of patronization. "And what signs have you seen?"

"I can predict the future," he whispered, eyes going large with drama.

Giri smiled at him. "Perhaps you can, but that's not a skill that comes with magic."

His face fell with confusion. "It's not?"

"No. Mages, wizards, cannot predict the future. Maybe you have that skill, but it's more like fortune telling. Let's test you anyway. You're younger. It's possible you still have potential that hasn't revealed itself. When a child's body matures towards adulthood, his energy changes, and he—or she—will be more able to start using his magic to actually make things happen consciously. Before then, it usually only happens unconsciously, if at all, or with great practice, because the energy isn't mature and isn't very available."

Giri glanced at Vor. "This is difficult to describe," he said "It's more something you can feel, or not. The best I could say, is that it's like a seed or a cocoon deep within a child's core of personal energy. It's alive, but dormant, and it feels different than ordinary life energy. It's made of energy, but it's like, hmm, Colby told me once it's like if life energy is a cloud of wool, there's a dense woven ball of it at the center, for a child-mage. As the child matures, it expands and becomes like a very fine web, moving outwards in all directions and encompassing the life energy cloud, holding it, storing it, and making it tangible to the adult mage. When that web has finished expanding, we say a mage's power has settled. That usually happens around twenty years of age. With Bethriana we would be able to feel that expanding web, were it there, and she'd feel if we poked it."

"But it's not there," the young lady said.

"It's not," Giri said. "Now, with Shorin, if he has mage potential, we won't feel the web yet. We have to look for the core, the potential, and he won't be able to feel anything, probably, whether it's there or not."

"I'm ready," Vor said. "Show me."

Giri held out his hand and Shorin eagerly put his in it. Vor followed Giri, sort of like looking over his shoulder as he worked. Shorin's life energy was a cloud much like Bethriana's had been—much like all non-mage humans. Giri didn't stop at the surface, but sent his careful energy touch deeper, and made a filter-like pass through Shorin's aura, the way he might drag his fingers through water.

"What do you think, Vor?" Giri murmured.

She shook her head. "No anomalies."

"What does that mean?" Shorin asked, almost sounding demanding.

"You have a standard set of energies," Giri pronounced. "Very healthy, but no hidden mage potential."

"Aww," Shorin groaned.

"That doesn't mean you don't have other talents," Giri repeated, "and maybe you can see the future, but I can't tell if that's true, not with my abilities. Even magic has its limits."

"Fine," Shorin heaved a dramatic sigh. "Hyldi's turn then."

The little girl had emerged slightly—she was no longer completely hidden behind her father's legs—but didn't look eager to come over to the strangers.

"Hyldi is sensitive to the emotions of others," Giri surmised, glancing at the adults for confirmation.

He got it, from nods and murmured affirmatives.

"It's possible she's just very observant," he went on. "If something badly scared her at some point in the past, she might just be cautious and in time she'll get braver. My friend Dello, though, is highly sensitive, and a mage. Those who are highly sensitive don't tend to have a lot of power as far as throwing fireballs and so on, but that doesn't mean their skills aren't useful. They can become skilled healers. They tend to be good at communication and reading other people, as long as they learn to control their abilities, which makes them excellent diplomats, negotiators, and spies."

"Is that what Dello does in Lackland," Vor asked him in an undertone. "He spies on them?"

"I didn't say that," Giri said carefully, but Vor could tell from the taste of his energies, that was exactly what he'd meant, regardless of what he'd said.

Yusani tried to coax Hyldi to come out, but the little girl wasn't having it. She held tighter to her father's trouser legs the more her mother begged.

"Here," Giri said, getting up off the couch. "If she really is highly sensitive to energies, she won't be able to resist this."

He got down on his knees a couple feet in front of Hyldi. Giri held his hands in front of him, together, cupped, like he was holding a ball from below. Even from a distance, Vor could see him pour nearly colorless energy into his cupped hands. Non-mages wouldn't be able to see it or tell that he was doing anything, but Vor saw him charging it with non-differentiated energy. It was just his own life energy, different from heat or electricity or anything that might hurt someone, but concentrated in one spot.

For a minute, he just sat there, and Hyldi stared at him, at his hands. As he made the energy denser and denser, she started to seem agitated. Hyldi nibbled her lower lip and began to inch out, only to recall that she was hiding and inch back again. To Vor, it seemed obvious that Hyldi could sense something. If she couldn't have, she would have just hid deeper from the strange man doing some strange thing and not moving, for no reason. Giri seemed to reach the same conclusion.

"It won't hurt you, Hyldi," he said softly. "I'm calm. It's calm energy. You can come look at it, or even touch it, if you want."

To the apparent surprise of most everyone in the room—though they stayed pretty still so as not to startle the girl—Hyldi stepped out from behind her father's legs and walked up to where Giri was kneeling. She looked intently at his hands.

"What is it?" she whispered.

"It's my life energy," Giri told her. "It's just like yours. I just moved a bunch of it into one place."

Slowly, she lifted her hands and hooked her fingers over the edges of Giri's cupped hands. She bent and peered closer.

"How do you do that?" she breathed.

Now that Hyldi was touching him, Vor sensed Giri do what he'd just done with Shorin: extend a filter-like brush of searching energy through her aura. It was more difficult for Vor to follow, since she wasn't touching Giri now, but she could sense well enough when he brushed something different: a dense center to her energy.

Hyldi twitched. "What was that?" She put a hand to her chest.

"Are you alright?" Giri checked.

"I felt something," she said, half uneasy, half accusative.

"Miss Hyldi," Giri said, slowly and gently. "I just tested you, like I did your brother and sister. I hope it didn't hurt."

She shook her head. "It just felt funny."

"You can see this energy in my hands, can't you?"

"Sort of," she mumbled. "I don't really see it, but I know it's there."

"That's right," he nodded. "Does everyone around you seem really loud?"

"Yes," she whispered, looking timid again, but she was still drawn to the energy Giri held, and she didn't back away. "But Daddy's the quietest."

"You're doing magic," he told her with a little smile. "You aren't just hearing them with your ears, or seeing them with your eyes. You're touching their energy with yours, but you don't know you're doing it."

Now she looked up at him with big eyes. "I don't like it. How do I stop it?"

Giri reabsorbed the energy and put his hands down on his thighs, but he didn't get up. "You probably can't, and if you try, you might hurt yourself. But," he held up a finger, "there is a really easy solution my friend Dello told me about. He did the same thing as you when he was a kid, and his aunt saw what was happening and gave him a fix for it."

"What is it?" Hyldi asked, almost begging.

Giri smiled and looked up at Yusani and Nirai. "Hyldi needs some jewelry, some mage-stone jewelry. She needs a couple bracelets and a necklace with nice big beads. Mage-stone absorbs energy, and Hyldi has got so much that she's been reaching out with hers and touching everyone else's without knowing it. The mage-stone will suck up any overflow, so she shouldn't feel so raw and tender anymore."

He looked back at Hyldi before him. "The mage-stone will fill up though, so whenever you start to feel overwhelmed again, you have to take the jewelry off and run it through the fire. The fire will set free all the stored energy, and you can put the jewelry back on and it will start filling up again. Just be careful you don't burn yourself, and the beads will need to be connected with wire, not string."

"And I won't feel everything anymore," she whispered, "in my head?"

"That's right, but this treats the symptom just for a while," Giri explained. "Things will change when you get to be eleven or twelve." He looked up to Yusani and Nirai again. "She should go to the Citadel for training," he told them, "if she wants to, and if you can afford it. It's not too expensive, but there is a fee for room and board until the students become apprentices and start working."

Giri sighed and visibly gathered himself. "Or, if that isn't possible, just let her keep wearing the mage-stone. Without training, her powers will fade by around age twenty. Then she can take it off and she'll be ordinary, like anyone who never had mage potential."

"Well," Yusani said softly, "I can tell what you think is the best course."

Giri shook his head. "Having this power, this ability to feel and sense so much, and the strength to make changes, to help people, to protect people— to have it gone, to have it fade feels like a tragedy worse than having an arm cut off. It's a part of me. It's a part of her. She was born with it. She should have it forever, and she should get the training she needs to master it. Even if she doesn't work as a wizard, even if she comes back here and marries and raises a family, and develops other skills," he shook his head again, "this shouldn't be taken away from her."

Hyldi had put her hands on her head, and now she whimpered.

"I'm sorry," Giri realized, and took a calming breath. "I was emoting too much. You're feeling it, aren't you?"

She nodded, hands still on her head.

"Here," Giri whispered, and he put a hand lightly on her crown.

Vor sensed the magic moving, but it was too subtle for her to follow from a distance. She could see the result though. Hyldi lifted her head, took away her hands, and gazed at Giri like he'd given her food when she was starving.

"You fixed me," she whimpered.

"Just temporarily, and you're not broken," he said. "I borrowed some of your extra energy and wove it into a shield around you. It'll wear off in a day or so, but that should be long enough for your parents to take you shopping."

Hyldi flung herself at Giri, and he caught her. Her short little girl arms couldn't go all the way around him, but she hugged with all her strength.

"There, there," he said, patting her back. "You'll squeeze me in two."

She let go and turned about to look up at her parents. "Mommy, Daddy, I want the necklace and the bracelets, and I want to go to the training."

Both Yusani and Nirai looked a little surprised at her sudden demand, as though she had never demanded anything before.

"The training can't be for six or seven years," Giri said.

"Then I want the training in six or seven years," Hyldi revised.

"We'll get you some mage-stone," Yusani promised, petting Hyldi's hair, "and we'll talk about the training."

"Yay!" Hyldi celebrated, jumping up and down with childish enthusiasm. She pivoted and flung herself at Giri again. "I love you," she declared.

He patted her back again, and just as quickly she released him and ran off. Vor heard her running down the hall, yelling, "Becka, Becka, the fire stopped!"

"That was what she called it," Nirai explained. "She said it was like fire in her head."

"This is remarkable," Yusani whispered, looking like she was about to cry. "I haven't seen her so happy in ages. The closest she's ever gotten was playing by herself, away from other people, but she likes other people."

"She just couldn't be around them," Nirai added. "It's been hard to watch."

Giri got up and went back to the couch. "There's another option, if you can't send her to the Citadel. You have a wizard come here regularly to train her. She probably wouldn't attain the skill to become a wizard herself, but it would be enough for her to keep her abilities and keep them from driving her mad, and enough for her to make some use of them. She could be a great healer, because she'd be able to touch someone and know exactly what's wrong."

"You've given us a lot to think about," Nirai said. He glanced at his wife. "We should get everyone washed up and take a trip to the market before it gets too late. If Hyldi is going to be wearing it all the time, she should probably get to pick her jewelry."

Vor and Giri decided to delay their trip to the Mrandis Main House until the next day. That afternoon they went with Yusani's family to the market and watched Hyldi pick out two bracelets and a necklace. Mage stone had become scarce as the mines were exhausted, and prices were up, but Vor slipped the shopkeeper a portion of her first wizard's stipend when no one was looking, and the woman did her the favor of acting like she was so charmed by Hyldi that she gave her a special, lower, price. Nirai glanced at Vor like he knew what she'd done, but made no comment.

The branch houses were not poor, and were provided funds by the main houses, who were in turn provided funds by the central Weldom government based on the size and population of the areas they oversaw. Some houses also had income from other sources. Most owned land and buildings in their home city and residents paid rent. But that didn't mean the Mrandis Branch House had a lot of spare cash to spend on frivolous purchases like jewelry. Plus, this was an unexpected expense, and Vor didn't want negative feelings associated with Hyldi's magery, that might make the family more inclined to let her magic fade instead of training it.

They wandered the market for a while longer, but didn't really have any other shopping to do, though Bethriana fawned over fabrics and sent pleading looks at her mother and father. Yusani and Nirai seemed immune to this behavior, but did purchase some new spices for her to try in her baking. Shorin rambled along, lost in thought and apparently bored by the market. Hyldi either ran around, looking at everything, or walked beside Giri, holding his hand.

"I think you have some competition," Samira teased Vor.

But Vor didn't mind the little girl's fascination with Giri. "She has good taste," she said.

"He is a charming young man," Samira agreed.

"I wonder sometimes," Vor confessed, "what he sees in me."

"Says the woman who just gave half her pay to make sure a little girl could stop being unknowingly traumatized by everyone around her," Samira replied promptly, and then gasped. "Ooh, come look at these. A little village up the mountain makes these."

And so Samira tugged Vor all over the market, showing her all the wealth and wonders of Lenali and the surrounding region. As dinnertime approached, the market closed down and the group headed home. The cook, who turned out to be the person named Becka that Hyldi had run off to earlier, had the evening meal all but ready, leaving them just enough time to wash up.

The Mrandis branch house had its own garden, just like the Hearthsravens, and indeed just like every family that had some spare land and the hands to tend it. Becka had made a salad with their vegetables, and had an egg, potato, and cheese pie to go with it. After dinner entertainment was games and music in the parlor and library. Bethriana disappeared for a couple hours and then brought out some cookies still warm from the oven, to great praise from her family and guests alike.

Samira showed Vor the bathing room for the ladies before bed, while the manservant they'd met earlier—whose name was Baylen—took Giri away to the one for men. The bathing room was good size, with four big tubs screened by curtains, and was shared by Damarin's family and the servants that lived in the house beside them.

"Most of the people who act as servants," Samira explained as they soaked in hot tubs of water, "are actually Mrandises, but generations back, and of course with spouses that came from elsewhere. I'm not. My family was hired at the main house, and my father and brother still work there."

"Mirassi sent you here because you were so close to Juleena," Vor recalled.

"At first she just demoted me to the kitchen, but then it turned out that any sight of me reminded her of your mother, and she suspected me of plotting with Julee, so she sent me out. It worked out alright. With Yusani getting married and there likely to be babies, Damarin needed the extra help."

"It doesn't seem you had any children of your own," Vor said cautiously.

"No, not me," Samira confirmed. "I like taking care of babies, but it wasn't something I ever wanted for myself. I like taking care of people in general." She grinned. "I guess that's lucky for me since I'm a maidservant, and that's my job."

"Are there other things you want to do with your life?" Vor asked, thinking that just being a servant could get tediously boring.

"I'm starting to help Bethriana sell her baking," Samira offered. "It's actually quite fun, helping her adjust her recipes and seeing how each item sells. There's a baker just down the main road that has agreed to take on some of her sweets. They mostly sell savory breads, so it's not really competing with them, and they get a cut of the profit, of course. It gives Bethriana pocket money, and she gives some to me, too, for helping her: not that I have much I want to buy. I'm quite content, really. My youth with Juleena was enough excitement to last a lifetime."

Samira sighed contentedly. "I feel like a part of the family, and I have a lover, too, Baylen, you met him, the man who answered the door for you. I'm lucky. The red fever that came through a few years back got me very sick. Maresta, Damarin's wife, your great aunt, and two other servants died from it. We thought we might lose Shorin to it, as well, but he's a strong boy, and he fought hard. We're really lucky here."

Then she frowned a little. "I actually hope Yusani doesn't go to the main house. I don't want to go back there."

"Surely you could stay here if you wanted to," Vor suggested.

"Yes, but who will take care of Hyldi?"

Vor gave a little shrug. "Maybe Hyldi should continue growing up in the branch house, where she's comfortable, even if Yusani and Nirai are brought into the main house," Vor said. "It's not like people can't come and go between here and the main house. It's a two minute walk away."

"That's true," Samira agreed, and sat up to wash out the conditioning solution she'd had soaking in her hair.

"Besides, if Hyldi becomes a wizard, she won't be living in Lenali much, and as third born, maybe she's not as important as Bethriana and Shorin?" Vor wondered.

"Oh, no," Samira corrected. "If she's a wizard her value goes up. We'll try to shield her, but for sure Mirassi will try to use her to make a good match, either selling her off or getting a really good spouse from a powerful house, and keeping her in the family, probably with the hopes of more wizardly babies."

Vor frowned. "My uncle is Ledren, right? My mother's brother? Why isn't he master of Mrandis? Why is Mirassi still running things?"

"He doesn't have a wife," Samira explained between dumping cups of water over her head. "She died before you were born, and he never remarried, and I think Mirassi has trained him to be a good boy."

"Hmm," Vor pondered.

She hadn't intended to get involved in any Mrandis House politics, but now that she had concern for Hyldi, she suddenly found herself feeling like she needed to go make her voice heard. Samira finished rinsing her hair and got out to start drying off. Vor figured she'd better do the same. As she bundled herself up in a robe a few minutes later, Samira eyed her.

"You're thinking hard," the maid commented.

"I'm thinking," Vor sighed, "I might speak up about the future of House Mrandis after all."

Samira smiled. "I knew it."

Vor and Giri wore a more formal set of clothing for going to the Mrandist estate the next morning with Damarin. Actually, Giri had brought formal clothing, but Vor hadn't owned any of her own to bring—other than the set of mage robes she'd worn for Colby's wedding. Yusani and Samira had helped Vor sort through everything in the branch house's storage and every closet to find a suit that both fit her and managed not to be too masculine, while avoiding anything so feminine it made her gag. She hadn't wanted a dress, even though they had some very pretty ones, because they made her feel more decorative than effective. She hadn't worn her one set of mage robes—and Giri wasn't wearing his—because she didn't want to set herself apart as something other than what everyone else was.

Her grandmother knew she was a mage already anyway, so she had to figure the whole house knew, but she didn't want to flaunt it. Giri had agreed. Neither of them had any authority to order Mrandis House about—which showing up as wizards in all their glory might bolster. Instead, they were going to have to be persuasive and logical, appealing to both sense and empathy. Looking like a foreign sort of person wouldn't help them there.

It turned out that Yusani and Nirai had decided to accompany Damarin this day. Samira was going to attempt to keep the children contained at home, with the help of the other servants. Hyldi's new exuberance since the taming of her overactive unconscious sensitivity was going to present a novel challenge in that respect. The gathering of five spent a moment appreciating the morning air on the steps of the branch house, a satisfying breakfast behind them; Bethriana had made some scrumptious scones.

"Shall we then?" Damarin said after everyone had gotten several breaths of the bracing new day.

He moved slowly down the steps, and Yusani and Nirai fell in behind him. Vor and Giri went after them. Giri didn't ask if she was ready for this, but she could practically taste him wondering about it.

"I'm ready for this," she muttered, in the hopes of easing his pinched expression.

"I know you are," he said simply.

"Then what are you so worried about?"

"I'm not worried about you. I've seen you face enough challenges to know you'll rise to this one."

"Then what?" she persisted, keeping her voice down, though if Yusani and Nirai overheard, she wouldn't really mind.

"I've only met your grandmother once, just like you, and she was a bit infuriating even in that brief meeting."

"She was," Vor agreed.

Giri lightly took her hand. "To get results here, fury will not serve. I've seen your fury, and it is as bold as a griffin and fierce as a unicorn, and nearly as powerful as both, but you must use something else here."

Vor let a breath out between her teeth. "I know it, just as you say. It makes me angry that she will be free to demean and refute, but I, no, I must try to be reasonable, to convince and cajole, and if I free my griffin or my unicorn, as you put it, it will only drive her to greater heights of malice. The worst of it is, this is a game she has been playing her whole life, so I sense."

Giri nodded, and they reached the gates. "She might be a lovely person, but for her game: the way she keeps and holds power over others."

"And now I must play it, or forfeit."

There was a guard at the gate. Vor and Giri joined the other three to be introduced. This guard was fairly old, probably in his fifties, but looked remarkably fit.

"The spearhead on his coat means he's a captain," Giri whispered for Vor's benefit. "Probably the captain of the house guard."

The captain apparently knew Damarin, Yusani, and Nirai well, and greeted them with smiles and handshakes.

"And here we have a surprise," Damarin said with a grin. He held a hand out to Vor and Giri. "Juleena's daughter has returned to Lenali."

"For a visit," Vor corrected quickly.

"Of course," Damarin revised without rancor, "for a visit. Captain Petersil, may I present Vorella Hearthsraven."

The captain removed his helmet, which was only a leather cap with lining, revealing his bald head. His eyes went round and he bowed.

"Your father, Stratus, served in my command when he was stationed at the house," he said. "He was the bravest, wisest man I ever had the honor of leading. He faced the mist dragon with me, and though it felled me with strength, he subdued it with words. That he was taken for that war was a great injustice. That he was lost in it is greater still. I wish I could have been there to protect him and your mother, and you."

He tucked his helmet under his left arm and gripped his left wrist with his right hand. Vor noticed his left arm seemed stiff and less muscular than his right.

"I lost some use of my arm when the mist dragon kicked me," the captain went on. "It broke my collarbone, and never did heal right. They wouldn't take me for the army."

Vor wasn't sure what to say. Perhaps Petersil realized this, for he smiled and chuckled.

"And now, here I am, an old man guarding a house I could never protect, were the mist dragon to show up again." He gave Vor another little bow. "But I remember your mother and your father. House Mrandis did wrong by them, and lost its heart when they left. Perhaps your coming is a sign of better days ahead, and I can only be humbly grateful that I have lived so long I might see them."

"I hope there are," Vor said, "better days ahead."

"Go on in with you then," he gestured, "to face a different sort of dragon in the shape of your grandmother."

"I've faced a dragon recently," she told him.

He nodded somberly. "I hope it has prepared you. One other thing I should convey: you are not the only guests today."

Damarin's focus sharpened. "Other nobility," he said with understanding.

The guard nodded. "Two curricles: each carried a young man and his father."

"Unmarried young men," Damarin clarified.

He shrugged. "I would assume so, sir."

Vor suddenly found everyone looking at her. "It can have nothing to do with me," she protested.

"If someone told her," Giri said, "yesterday morning when we arrived, she could have sent fast messengers to the nearest houses. Are there houses within a day's ride? Holstor is too far, I know that."

"She could have used her birds," Yusani contributed.

Giri looked perplexed, so whatever Yusani meant, it wasn't something well known. "What does that mean?" Vor asked.

"It's a fad," Damarin sighed. "Some of the older ladies of noble houses have started keeping doves. When they meet, they exchange a few. If they release someone else's dove, it will fly back to where it hatched."

"All they need to do is tie a message to it," Yusani said tightly.

"Mirassi brought back several doves from her trip to the capital last month. Well, this will complicate things, but perhaps we can find a way to turn it to our advantage." Damarin said.

He eyed Vor again and she fought not to bristle. "Why are you all looking at me?"

"You should have married your Holstor boy before you came here," Damarin said bluntly. "I suspect your grandmother is thinking of trying to bargain with you."

"I will make it clear that is pointless," Vor replied, just as blunt. "I already told her I would not rejoin the family."

"Yes, but now you're here," Giri said. "You came back. Word may have even reached her about your role in saving Anchoria. If you're young, pretty, healthy, a wizard, and a hero, you're extremely valuable to her if she can entrap you into rejoining Mrandis and bringing in a quality spouse—or selling you in marriage to a rich house that will pay handsomely for you."

Vor's jaw was aching from where she was clenching it. "But I won't do that. How could she think she can just make a decision like that for me and expect me to submit to it?"

"Welcome to dealing with Mirassi," Damarin said dryly. "I have never been able to convince her that she actually doesn't know what's best for every person around her. What I have learned is this: she knows what she thinks is best for her, and then somehow in her logic she thinks if it's best for her, it must be best for everyone else, too. She tries to make it so, and then can't understand why all the people she's manipulating aren't grateful."

Damarin turned back to the guard captain and gave him a nod. "Thank you for the information. We shall go forewarned."

"Luck to you, Lord Damarin," the captain bowed.

The group turned, and headed up the sloping path to the Mrandis House.

They were met by a pair of house servants, a man and a woman, who both looked like they wanted to greet Damarin with enthusiasm, but were keeping themselves to restrained politeness. They were shown to a parlor and swiftly supplied with tea, juice, cookies, and other light snacks. Damarin, Yusani, and Nirai sat, but Vor felt too anxious to sit, and it seemed that Giri felt the same. He stood at the window, looking out at the Mrandis gardens.

"I should have worn my mage robes," Vor heard Giri mutter to himself.

"Now you think we should have?" Vor said.

"Not we, me," Giri corrected.

She arched an eyebrow, but he was turned away and couldn't see it. "Just you? Why?"

He glanced back over his shoulder, perhaps taking in her raised brow. "To look more important. You need to look less good, and I need to look more good now."

"Giri," Vor said carefully. "Are you actually thinking that these other two men who have been brought here, whoever they are, are your competition?"

He tugged nervously on his tunic and faced her. "Well," he prevaricated.

"You really think I would change my mind because my grandmother asks it of me?"

His cheeks colored a little and his gaze dropped to the floor.

"I am not Vorella Mrandis," Vor said softly. "I will tell my grandmother that as many times as necessary, and no two random boys, no matter how noble, are going to make me question my choice of companion."

"Well said," Damarin commented, and took a sip of tea, looking supremely unconcerned.

"If I looked more impressive," Giri began, "I would count for more, and so would my words, when we go in there."

"She knows you're a wizard," Vor said. "She knows who you are. Soon everyone else will, too."

"Appearances are very important when it comes to the politics between noble houses," Yusani offered in tacit support of Giri.

Vor shrugged one shoulder. "Throw a fireball then." She felt a smile tug at her mouth. "We could summon some elementals to accompany us, or maybe make a windstorm to disarrange everybody's hair."

"They will have done their hair very carefully," Damarin confirmed. "That would be quite a blow." He chuckled. "Ah, pardon the pun."

Vor didn't walk over to Giri, but she sent several firm pulses through her ring to him. "I'm a Hearthsraven, and a wizard, Colby's apprentice, friend of griffins, a little darker than some wizards like, and the killer of my own master—in self-defense, mostly. I also spoke with the death dragon and lived to tell of it. On the other hand, my mother was once a Mrandis until she was disowned. That's nothing to do with me. Mirassi will get nothing from me, and those young men have come all this way for an equal amount of nothing."

"We shall see," Damarin said then, standing up.

He nodded towards the doorway, and Vor turned to see a servant standing there, no doubt having come to summon them.

"Let's go then," Vor said.

Damarin followed the servant out, with Yusani and Nirai behind him. Giri came up to Vor and took her hand, looking a little abashed.

"You're right," he whispered as they walked. "It's just instinct, having seen how the houses bargain with their children. I'm sorry I got worked up."

"No one's going to take me away from you," Vor promised. "I cannot be commanded or bargained with. Mirassi couldn't do it to my mother, and she's not going to do it to me."

Giri gave her hand a little squeeze.

"I defied Altare," Vor concluded, and grinned. "Mirassi can't get up early enough in the morning to come close to him."

Together, they stepped into the Mrandis House's main audience hall.

The room could have been used for banquets or ceremonies or dancing, but on this day it was mostly empty, but for a rectangular table, and a dozen or so chairs. The table had the look of one that was regularly used for business, not something special that had been dug out of storage and recently polished. One wall had multiple windows, and all the window coverings were drawn back to let in the light. A couple of the windows were swung slightly open, letting in the morning air. The room was also dramatically blue. The curtains were blue, the wallpaper was blue, the chair cushions were blue, the table runner was blue, even the ceiling tiles were blue.

Mirassi sat at the head of the table. To her right was a tall man who looked to be in his fifth decade. He was standing as if too nervous to sit. Though Mirassi barely glanced at Damarin and his guests, this other man sought among them with his eyes, and arrived at Vor. His brow was creased, his expression troubled. It looked like a common expression for him, and was leavened with weariness.

There were four other men in the room, all seated, and came in pairs of a young one and an older one. Both pairs had the familial resemblance of father and son. Vor guessed these were the men who had arrived last night from other noble houses. They gave Damarin's party a thorough looking-over.

"Uncle Damarin," the tall, standing man said, and came around Mirassi's chair to greet him. "I hope you are well this morning."

Damarin shook his hand with a smile. "I am, thank you, Ledren," he said.

"Miss Yusani, Mister Nirai," the tall man, Ledren apparently, which meant he was the brother of Vor's mother, and thereby Vor's uncle, went on. "How nice to see you."

Nirai shook hands and Yusani curtsied.

"And allow me to introduce you to your niece," Damarin said, clear and loud enough for the whole room to hear. "Vorella Hearthsraven and her betrothed, Giri Holstor."

Ledren's skin was a rich, warm bronze, but seemed to pale as Yusani and Nirai parted, so that he was face to face with his sister's child. Vor winced inwardly at Damarin's choice of words, but knew it was a strategic move to try to head off her grandmother's matchmaking. There hadn't been an official betrothal, and quite honestly she was getting tired of all the madness about marriage. She hadn't even met Giri's parents or made any public declaration— but it didn't matter anyway. She could do whatever she wanted with herself.

"Vorella," Ledren croaked, and then cleared his throat.

"I go by Vor," she said, trying for level politeness, "or you can call me Wizard Heathsraven."

Ledren's throat worked, but no sound came out. "I'm sorry," he managed finally, "for what happened to your mother."

Vor narrowed her eyes. "Which thing? You throwing her out of House Mrandis, or her dying from plague in Northnest? The latter wasn't your fault, and the former I'm actually grateful for."

"Do sit down, Ledren," Mirassi ordered, an exasperated huff in her voice.

He obeyed, and Giri spared a glance for Vor. "It's knives out already, is it?" he muttered from the corner of his mouth.

She snorted with amusement.

"Won't you all sit down?" Ledren invited.

Damarin immediately went to take the seat to Mirassi's left. Yusani sat beside him, and then Nirai. Vor followed and sat beside Nirai, with Giri on her other side. Across the table sat the four other nobility: the father and son pairs. Vor noted that they wore jackets trimmed in two colors each. Two wore purple and white, but the other two wore yellow and light blue—sending an alert straight to the front of Vor's brain. Hadn't Giri said—

"Won't you introduce your other guests, Sister?" Damarin was saying to Mirassi.

"Of course," she said coolly. "Master Felixi and his son Lord Goranis have come from House Pramindin."

The two men with white and purple trimmed jackets gave short seated bows. "We're honored that House Mrandis was able to accomodate us on such short notice. We'd miscalculated on our way north to hunt but luckily found a slight detour here to be our salvation," the older man, Felixi presumably, lied smoothly.

Both men had lightly tanned skin and dark blonde hair brained back in the common traditional style of western Weldom, though the son was slightly darker than his father in both skin and hair. The father had a subtly sly expression in his sharp brown eyes, and his rather large hooked nose did little to improve Vor's impression of a bird of prey watching carefully for scurrying mice. The son looked a bit more lost and confused, but also had his father's nose.

As for the other two, Vor hadn't taken her attention off them, and she could feel Giri's warning tension beside her.

"We're honored as well to receive a visit from Master Terkari and his son Embris," Mirassi continued, "of House Salasis."

Vor found herself skating right over the son and fixing her gaze on the father. He looked vaguely familiar, like she'd seen him somewhere before. He was tall, even sitting down, with broad shoulders, a neat black beard and mustache, and hair to match, though he kept it cut short instead of long. He smiled at her, his teeth white against the dark tone of his skin, and Vor got a creeping, rolling sensation in her belly.

"So you are sweet little Juleena's daughter," the Master of Salasis said. "I knew your mother, briefly."

Not even Mirassi had a reply to that.

"Had she been more pliable, I'd have been your father," he went on, and picked up a cup to sip its contents. He twitched his head slightly at the boy beside him. "As you can see, I did not lack for suitors willing to comfort me when your mother broke our engagement, and I still got a beautifully crafted case full of harpy feathers for my trouble."

He set his cup down and began toying with a jelly tart.

"It has left bad blood between Salasis and Mrandis for all this time, though," he frowned. "You could mend that, however, if you would consent—and keep your promise as your mother did not—to marry into Salasis."

Still the room was silent.

"Embris is an obedient boy, perhaps a little young for you, but that hardly matters. I need strong leadership for my house, which I doubt I shall get from my firstborn. You, Miss Vor," he purred, "look like you could provide strong leadership."

"You'll call me Wizard Hearthsraven," Vor said softly.

Terkari's slight smile widened. "Strong leadership," he repeated.

"Young Mister Embris is not your firstborn," Giri spoke up clearly.

Master Salasis's gaze shifted to Giri without any drop in pleasure.

"You are forgetting Lanisala," Giri said.

That was where Vor had seen Terkari Salasis before: in Lanisala's memories, for the brief moment that she had touched her inside the dark circle.

"She is forgettable," he replied with a little flick of his fingers. "An accident that has done me the favor of turning out to be a mage, which is always a benefit to the house: nothing more."

"If you want strong leadership," Giri specified, "you should look to her."

"Lanisala does as she is told," Terkari countered, a hint of iron in his voice now. "As she was told when she confessed an interest in a certain firstborn boy of Holstor House, and I made clear to her what her options were."

Vor felt a surge of anger from Giri. He seemed locked now in a staring contest with the head of Salasis.

"However," Terkari said, tone light again, "I might give her new options, if she still had such interest, if it would get that Holstor boy to stand up and leave the Mrandis estate now."

"No," Giri said softly. "It wouldn't."

The Master of Salasis gave a little sigh and broke the stare, rolling his eyes. He lifted the tart and took a bite.

"As I expressed to Vorella in Anchoria," Mirassi spoke into the pause, "Mrandis has come to challenging times. She has deigned to join us here that we might discuss a plan to restore it to its former glory."

Vor kept her expression even, but felt her jaw tighten. "I will not rejoin Mrandis House," she said evenly, "as I told you, Grandmother, in Anchoria."

"That was not what we were given to believe," the Master of House Pramindin muttered in a displeased tone.

"Vorella need not join House Mrandis," Mirassi said. "It is my wish that she join Pramindin or Salasis."

All four pairs of eyes of the visiting men turned speculatively onto Vor. Terkari licked a morsel of red jelly from his upper lip. Vor was recovering from the shock, trying to put some appropriate words together, when Damarin spoke.

"Mirassi," he said, "she is not yours to give."

"She is Mrandis blood," she shot back. "There is no greater claim."

"But you disowned Juleena. You struck her name from the books as though she were dead. The same applies to her unborn child of the time."

"Juleena can be reclaimed," Mirassi argued. "It was a hasty mistake. Vorella can be put back into the bloodline. Then she will be available as a spouse for a noble marriage."

Damarin lifted an open hand toward Vor and Giri. "Vor has made her selection of life companion already."

"Preposterous," Mirassi sneered.

"And what is wrong with House Holstor?" Damarin pressed. "If you are determined to arrange a noble marriage for her, it is as good a house as Salasis or Pramindin."

"Mrandis owes Salasis," Terkari rumbled.

Vor pushed to her feet. "But I don't. If anything, you owe me."

Terkari's face registered slight surprise. "Why do you say that?"

"I saved your daughter's life," Vor told him. "Dear little Lanisala has been returned to you, so you could pump her for information about Giri and me, because I pulled her out of a trance spell. Not to mention that Giri and I both, with help," she added fairly, "fought off a tentacular sand monster that would have eaten her."

"Lanisala does not count," Terkari said firmly.

"She should," Vor refuted. "She's brave and strong and passionate. If you start showing her some respect, there's a chance she might find some loyalty for you." Vor shrugged. "But I rather hope you don't. In my opinion she'll make a much better master wizard than she will a mistress of Salasis. I would hate to see her talents wasted."

"Vorella," Mirassi scolded. "Sit down."

Vor stayed standing, and turned her head to look down the table at her grandmother. "You don't get to tell me what to do. I know it would be polite to sit, but I don't feel like it. I'm also not going to marry Embris or Goranis."

"But Vorella—"

"No, Grandmother. I already told you I wouldn't."

"Mrandis House needs—"

"What Mrandis House needs, I can't give."

Mirassi got to her feet, too. She pointed a sharp finger in Vor's direction. "You have an obligation—"

"No, I don't," Vor denied. "I told you, I am not a part of House Mrandis."

"But you can—"

"No. I won't."

"But—"

"No, I won't."

Mirassi's dark skin was getting darker with anger. Her eyes flashed. "You will—"

"No," Vor repeated firmly, "I won't."

Mirassi's restraint broke. "Vorella," she screeched. "You'll marry and be house mistress. You'll be in power, in control, with a family, safe, secure, with every luxury. You'll be happy the rest of your life. Don't you want that?"

Vor took a breath. "I will work towards my happiness on my own. Perhaps I will make wrong choices, but they'll be mine. I'll have no one to blame but myself if I go wrong, and if I succeed, it shall be by my own doing. You have no power over me, and I have no power to save Mrandis House. The people who have that, are sitting right here."

Vor unfurled an arm, gesturing to Damarin, Yusani, and Nirai.

"But," Mirassi stuttered, her fury draining away.

"You don't get to have me," Vor told her. She looked at the men from Pramindin and Salasis. "And neither do you, and honestly, you wouldn't like it if you did have me. I'd cause you nothing but trouble."

"Just like your mother," Terkari muttered.

"So, is that understood now?"

Mirassi glared, her thin chest heaving as though she was panting.

"Sister," Damarin said gently. "You have worked long and hard to serve Mrandis House. Since Rodreric died, you have been struggling alone. It is time to turn the leadership over to Ledren."

Mirassi's mouth fell open like a fish gasping for air. "To Ledren?" From her face, Mirassi looked as though her brother had suggested she turn the leadership over to a mutt from the kennels, or the butter dish.

"He is your son, and he has had many years of experience assisting you,"

Damarin said. "I'm certain he can lead well, with you and me both here to help him should he need it."

Vor saw her great uncle give Ledren a wink, with the eye on the side away from Mirassi, so she wouldn't see it. Vor interpreted his words to mean that Damarin would keep Mirassi out of Ledren's way, and support his decisions. Ledren, for his part, did not look so confident.

"I have no grandchildren," he said.

"But you have always been kind to Yusani," Damarin countered. "She carries the Mrandis bloodline as much as your daughter does, and so do her children. Bethriana will be old enough to wed soon."

"This is your plan," Mirassi accused. "I knew it. You intend to supplant the true line of House Mrandis."

"Sister, what you call the true line has been cut."

"It is alive in Vorella," she insisted.

"We've been through this," Vor declared. "Besides, I don't know that I will choose to have children. I can stop it from happening, you know. I'm a wizard."

Vor took a casual, leisurely sip of tea. Mirassi looked positively incensed. Damarin, meanwhile, was looking beseechingly at Ledren. He needed to step up now. Here, in front of two other houses—three counting Holstor— Mrandis House was looking weaker and weaker, and its mistress was coming apart at the seams.

"This is what the branch houses are for," Giri contributed calmly. "Holstor House has done it before, and so have many others. Probably all of them have at one time or another, if you look back far enough. When there is trouble with the main line, the branch house is there to give support."

"That is true," Master Pramindin concurred. "Pramindin has done it, several generations back. It is no shame. It may be we shall do it again soon. Without it, it is clear that this would be the end of Mrandis House."

House Salasis did not contribute an opinion. Terkari lifted another tart and bit it sharply, his gaze unfocused on the middle distance. Embris looked warily towards the head of the table and gave a tiny, hesitant nod, before looking back down at the tablecloth.

"Yusani," Ledren's voice cracked on her name, as though he were a boy and not a man grown into maturity, "would you and Nirai join us here in the main house? Would you bring your children, when they are ready, and if they so choose, to carry Mrandis forward?"

Yusani and Nirai shared a glance, but it was clear they'd already discussed it.

"We would be honored," Yusani said with perfect grace.

Mirassi was still puffing, and Vor began to worry she might work herself into a true fit, or have a heart attack. "Of course they'll come," she spat suddenly. "All three of them. Bethriana is lovely. She'll need to be tutored. Shorin we'll have more time with. Hyldi of course will be a beauty—"

"No," Vor declared, and all eyes turned to her. "Uncle Ledren," she said, more quietly. "Hyldi will be a mage. She has the talent for it. I'd like you to sponsor her at the Citadel, when the time comes. I'll watch over her there."

"We can't afford that," Mirassi spat, predictably.

"I'm sure my stipend could cover the cost," Vor bowed her head, "if that is what's needed."

"Please, Wizard Hearthsraven," Ledren said, voice only a little shaky, "I will ask your advice for when Hyldi should go, and we will discuss what is needed for her care. If she has the talent, we cannot let it go to waste."

A tight ball Vor had been carrying, unknowing, in her chest loosened. "Thank you, Uncle," she said, and finally relaxed into her seat.

That was what she'd needed. Under the table, Giri nudged her knee with his, encouragingly, and she gave him a little smile. Damarin, Ledren, and Mirassi continued their discussion at the head of the table, with Yusani and Nirai both chiming in from time to time. Vor listened, but felt no need to interject again. The men of Pramindin and Salasis seemed to lose interest, too, now that it seemed that neither of them would be marrying their son off that day.

"I like my sister," Embris blurted suddenly, at Vor.

Vor looked at him in surprise, and Terkari made a little growl.

"She's not your sister," the Master of Salasis rumbled.

"Lanisala, I mean," Embris bumbled on. "She was always nice to me, even though I was a whiny little brat when I was young."

Since Vor had estimated that Embris was perhaps fifteen years old, she thought it was a little too soon for him to be talking of when he was young, as though he weren't still young, but figured there was no benefit to pointing that out, other than to embarrass him.

"I think you're right, that she would make a good Mistress of Salasis," Embris continued, "but maybe a better wizard. She's very good at the wizardry."

"Yes, she is," Giri agreed softly. "Very powerful."

"She shows me tricks when she visits," he said. "You're both wizards, too?"

"We are," Vor confirmed.

"What can you do?"

He was as eager as a child asking for a sweet. Terkari rolled his eyes again.

Vor looked down the table towards the head. "I don't think we're needed here any longer," she said, and Nirai glanced back at her with a smile and a nod. "Let's go get a tour of the grounds, and maybe we can show you a little."

Vor and Giri stood up, barely beating Embris.

"We'll just get some air," Giri announced.

"No need for us to sit here and be privy to Mrandis politics," the Master of Pramindin grunted, "if there's to be no betrothing." He stood, too, and prodded his son.

Terkari huffed, but followed Embris from the room. A servant appeared to lead the group out to the gardens. She was a mature woman, tall and slender, and seemed surprised at the relatively civil discussion happening among Mirassi, Ledren, Damarin, Yusani, and Nirai. Vor didn't miss how Ledren caught her eye and gave her a smile. She smiled back—much more warmly than a servant would ever smile at her master unless—

"Ah, that's how it is," Vor murmured under her breath.

The woman heard her, her pale cheeks flushing red. Vor gave her a nod and a little smile of her own, subtle assurance that her secret was safe with her. Probably every servant knew that this woman was warming Ledren's bed with more than just a warming pan, but Mirassi probably didn't. Vor wasn't about to do anything to put her in Mirassi's line of fire. Her blushes fading, the woman led the six of them through the house to a side door, and out onto the grounds.

It was turning into another beautiful day.

"We've had good weather on this trip," Giri observed as the group spread out.

The father and son of Pramindin didn't seem inclined to conversation and walked off by themselves. Terkari and Embris, however, didn't wander far.

"Pramindin is having trouble of their own," Terkari volunteered abruptly. "That boy is the only heir, so I hear."

"It doesn't make much sense," Giri commented, "wedding a solitary heir to a solitary heir. That's putting the final eggs of both houses in one basket."

"Pramindin has fallen on hard times, just like Mrandis. They're struggling to find a spouse and can't pay much." The Master of Salasis shrugged. "I'm guessing the deal would be to breed Wizard Hearthsraven like a prize mare and Mirassi gets the firstborn."

Vor's lips curled in disgust. "That's never happening."

"As we learned," Terkari chuckled.

"What was the deal with Salasis, exactly?" Giri asked.

"Mrandis owes me," he said, all signs of mirth evaporating. "They promised me Juleena and then broke the promise."

Giri frowned. "So you wanted Vor to marry Embris, and then, what, also surrender the firstborn back to Mrandis? That's not something ordinarily done."

"I would have provided a large spouse-price," Terkari clarified.

"But that still wouldn't have gotten an heir for Mrandis."

The Master of Salasis took his time before replying, and Vor began to wonder if he would at all. However, she sensed someone come up behind them and turned to see the tall lady servant—her uncle's apparent beloved— had lingered outside and apparently overheard.

"Ledren's daughter has not kindled, though she has been married for seven years now," she said simply. "This could be her own fault, or could be the fault of her husband. It is not because of dislike in the pairing; they get on well enough."

"The tradition of fostering has fallen out of practice in the last several generations," Terkari said, "but my brother has a spare son. He might as well be put to some use, so I thought. A year here might improve the young woman's fertility."

Vor found herself mildly surprised, and Giri made a sound of distaste.

"My brother also has a daughter," Terkari shrugged, "also an extra. He really has bred far more than he should have for a second son."

"Mistress Mirassi thought to pressure Ledren into remarrying," the woman servant concluded.

"But Lord Ledren is in his forties," Giri pointed out, "and Master Terkari, your younger brother's daughter surely can't be more than—"

"Fifteen," he provided promptly, and without a flinch. "I shall see her married off somewhere else, it seems. We've made a journey for nothing, and at short warning, too." He arched his back a little and took a deep breath. "Still, it is nice to get out from time to time, except that my wife will probably have redecorated our bedchamber yet again by the time I get home."

He chuckled, but Vor still found herself staring at him with a lingering sensation of shock and revulsion. Giri and the servant woman seemed much the same. Embris only looked cowed and cautious.

"Perhaps I'll see then if this Bethriana would make a suitable spouse for Embris," the Master of Salasis went on. "Mrandis does still owe Salasis for the broken vow after all. They must repay it somehow."

"Lanisala's life is not enough payment for you?" Vor spoke up.

Terkari raised an eyebrow at her. "You just repeatedly emphasized how you are not a part of Mrandis House, Wizard Hearthsraven. If such is true, your actions are completely irrelevant to the Mrandis debt, even if Lanisala were not."

He grinned at her twitch of frustration.

"Unless you'd like to renegotiate marrying my son?"

"No," Vor said.

"As I thought. I think I'll have a stroll. It is such a nice day."

Terkari Salasis walked off, his long legs carrying him swiftly into the gardens.

"That's not going to cause problems in the future," Vor said dryly, "no, not at all."

"There's only so much he can do, Wizard Hearthsraven," the servant woman spoke up again. "He makes big of the debt and the broken vow, but he really was injured very little. He found another suitable spouse at the next summer gathering, and she's provided him with three children already. They also seem, from what I have heard, to be a much better match than Juleena would have been for him, so I don't see that he has much to complain of. Besides, once Ledren gets his feet under him, he won't let that smart-mouthed braggart get away with anything."

Giri slid a glance at Embris, who was still in hearing range, having not followed his father. The boy looked a little embarrassed, but not surprised.

"The boy should hear what people think of his father," the servant woman went on, "so that he might have inspiration to do better when he is Master of Salasis."

"You sound like you might make a good Mistress of Mrandis," Vor prodded experimentally.

The woman's cheeks colored again, and she neatly clasped her hands before her. "Forgive me. I have spoken too freely."

"You're not offending me," Vor assured her. She stuck out her hand. "Please, call me Vor."

The woman bowed her head. "I'm not sure that's—"

"You're going to marry my uncle, so you'll be my aunt," Vor retorted with a smile. "You should call me Vor."

She shook her head, but did reach out to shake. "I'm Vanissa. Lord Ledren and I are," she hesitated, "friends, but it's impossible that I should ever marry him."

"But he's a widower," Giri pointed out, "and he's old. Old enough, anyway. Older nobility can often get away with things the younger ones can't, especially when they are the master of their house." He turned to Embris. "Now, come young Embris, I promised you magic tricks."

Giri led Embris away, leaving Vor with Vanissa.

"I liked your mother," the servant woman said, "but I didn't know her well, not like Samira. I was just a kitchen wench until after Juleena left. Then I was promoted to help in the nursery, when Lady Myra had her children. Viola, your cousin, Ledren's daughter, was there, too, of course. After Lady Cindra died, Ledren came often to the nursery, to see Viola, so I saw him often, too.

"He was very sad," Vanissa said softly. "The only time he ever smiled was at Viola. When she moved out of the nursery, I was assigned to her. Ledren says I was like a mother to her, and I suppose in some ways I was, but perhaps it wasn't fair to Viola. I was showering all my attention and affection on her, because of course I could not show any sign of my infatuation with her father."

"You were redirecting it," Vor said.

"Yes, to Viola," the servant nodded. "After Viola married, several years ago now, it was the end of a time for both Ledren and me. I didn't think he knew," she blushed again, "how I felt about him, but he knew. Perhaps because I was so dedicated to turning my focus away from him, I hadn't realized that he felt the same way. I hadn't paid attention. I had thought it impossible that he could have any—"

Vanissa seemed to catch herself. She laughed dismissively and took a few steps away. "Pardon me, please, Miss Vor. I don't know why I'm telling you this." She took a steadying breath. "What I wanted to tell you was that I liked your mother, Juleena. She was a fine lady, spirited, smiling, and full of energy. I wish I could have known her better, and I'm so sorry that you lost both her and your father in war. Please, don't take anything Mirassi says to heart. You must live your life how you see fit."

"Thank you," Vor said, trying to sound both polite and friendly. "So should you. You should marry Ledren if you both want to. I don't think Mirassi can do anything to you now, either. It seems that her time is over."

They returned to the branch house for the afternoon. The household was all a bustle with preparations to move some of the members of the house into the main house, and Vor and Giri did their best to stay out of the way, or help in any way they could. Later, Vor got the chance to talk some more with her Uncle Ledren about Hyldi's future, and met her other aunt, Myra, as well as Camin, Myra's husband and thereby Vor's uncle. Both her male cousins, Myra's two sons, had been given in marriage to other houses, so they weren't around to meet, but Viola, Ledren's daughter and so Vor's cousin, and her husband also introduced themselves.

Several other servants of the main house had come to Vor to tell her they remembered Juleena fondly, but the woman who had raised her in place of her real mother had been called Mum Hyldi, and had died several years ago. Little Hyldi, Yusani's daughter, had been named in her honor. That evening Vor and Giri joined in for a fairly formal dinner with the main house—including now most of Damarin's family—and again were accommodated in the branch house, but on the morning of their fourth day in Lenali she and Giri found themselves alone in the branch house dining room.

"I'm glad we came here," Vor told Giri.

It was a resumption of a discussion they'd had the previous evening in the darkness of Giri's guest bedroom. The days had been tumultuous for Vor, especially meeting her Mrandis relatives who she hadn't remembered at all, or in several cases had never met before. Mostly, it had exhausted her, and Giri had been good enough to sit patiently, letting her mumble out all her weary frustrations.

"You feel like some things have been resolved?" he coaxed.

"I do feel better that Mrandis House is going to be more stable." She shrugged one shoulder. "Even if I'm not a part of it, I still feel connected, I suppose. I'll be glad to leave, though."

Giri nodded and took another sip of tea. "You want to leave today? I'm fine with that."

"I'd like to go see my other grandparents again before we go, but yes, soon. If not today, then tomorrow."

So they left word with Samira, and walked back to Trivale. It was another lovely day, with just enough clouds to keep the sun from burning too brightly. Vor found herself breathing more easily, like a weight of stone had come off her chest.

"Does it feel stressful to you to be home?" she asked Giri. "Do you feel like you can't breathe when you're there?"

"Home, you mean at Holstor House?" Giri confirmed. "It can, sometimes."

"Your parents and grandparents expect a lot from you?"

Giri gave an uneasy grin. "My parents aren't too bad, especially now that Andra's had some babies. My grandparents aren't around much—really I only have one. My father's mother has already passed away, and my father's father isn't at the house very often. I almost never see my mother's parents." He took a breath. "You've felt stressed here, but it's all over now. My stress will start when we leave here for Croun."

"I don't want you to be stressed," Vor said. "I wish you didn't have to be, but after seeing some into House politics, I can relate a little."

"Holstor is nothing like Mrandis, I must say. We don't have a Mirassi try-ing to bully everyone around."

"That's good at least."

"I still don't really know what they'll say about you, though. We'll just have to see. We can always leave, if we have to."

She reached out and briefly held his hand. "I don't want to cause prob-lems between you and your family."

Giri gave her a sunny smile that almost concealed his anxiety. "You won't."

They reached the Hearthsraven home to find Thornwing lounging indo-lently in the front yard, while Hawkjoy flew loops and tricks above the house to the accompaniment of squealing children. It looked like most of the town's youngsters had shown up to look at the griffins. The Hearthsraven children came running to the gate though, when Vor and Giri approached.

They spent the day there, helping out in the garden and a little bit in the woodshop—but neither Giri nor Vor had any experience with wood craft-ing and mostly just watched. Tamarus was carving little wooden griffins with wheels instead of feet and a string to tow them with.

"A shame I can't make them fly," he smiled.

Giri insisted on buying two of them, though Tamarus tried very hard to give them away, for his nieces. That evening most of the adults sat around the table after dinner and painted the wooden griffins in an attempt to look like Thornwing or Hawkjoy. Evalyn even tried inventing new color patterns based on other birds and house cats she'd seen.

"You'll be leaving tomorrow then, I expect," Ruslin said.

It was late, and Vor and Giri had to walk back to Lenali for the night.

"That's the plan," Vor confirmed.

"You'll be back to visit," Helena said as a matter of course.

"Definitely," Vor nodded. "And we'll be back in the morning for our horses."

She winked in the direction of the griffins, who were curled up together by the porch in a fluffy ball of fur and feathers for the night.

"Did you hear that?" Thornwing muttered to Hawkjoy. "It is as I thought. We are nothing but flying horses to them."

"Talking flying horses," Hawkjoy corrected.

Then she and Giri endured a number of hugs, which she expected she'd endure again the next morning, and they retraced their steps back to the Mrandis Branch House. They passed a pleasant night, and the next morning Samira must have snitched on them, because Damarin, Yusani, Nirai, and all their children were there to see them off.

"You didn't think you'd leave without a goodbye?" Yusani grinned.

The family pressed food on them and many thanks and even a few tears. A promise was extracted from Vor that she would come visit regularly—which she only gave because she figured she'd need a place to sleep when she came to visit her Hearthsraven family. Just as reluctant was little Hyldi, who fastened herself to Giri and didn't want to let go.

But at last their bags were packed and they shouldered them for the walk back down to Trivale. With much waving and farewelling, Vor and Giri left Lenali. The griffins were stretching their wing muscles when they arrived, and Vor and Giri passed over much of the food they'd been given to the Hearthsravens, because it was too bulky and heavy to be flying with. Besides, they would be in Croun before dark and the Holstor House was sure to feed them well.

As expected, Vor endured more hugs and tears and gave her promise again to come back and visit. They strapped down their packs to Thornwing and Hawkjoy, mounted up, and with a great sense of relief, Vor held tight as Hawkjoy powered her way into the morning air.

Now all that remained was to meet the family of the man she intended to run around slinging magic with for the rest of her life—or marry or whatever. After Mirassi and reuniting with the family she'd spent the first several years of her life with, that just didn't seem that scary.

Epilogue 3
Croun

Unlike the Mrandis House, the Holstor House was not located in the center of a city. It wasn't even in the center of a town, or a village. The tower-like building perched atop a high, windy moor, with a tall wall making a wide circle around it and embracing gardens and some bushy fruit trees. Two massive oaks flanked the main gate, but they were the only large trees in sight. Heather and other shrubs formed clumps around scattered, smaller, twisted trees, but most of the land was covered with grasses and other low growing plants, all currently sporting flowers in a riot of colors. The moor undulated, rising and falling in steep inclines: not quite a mountain, but still elevated over a pair of intersecting valleys, where trees grew more thickly.

From Hawkjoy's back, Vor was able to see it all with a quite close to literal bird's eye view. Down in the valleys she could pick out clusters of buildings and some agriculture fields. There was no central city, but clearly the area was well occupied by loosely linked farms. From the valleys, two roads led up to the Holstor gates, but Vor's party of course had no need for roads. Giri pointed and the griffins began fighting the wind to get down to the ground.

Vor kept watch for any signs of archers—though what arrow could make a straight flight through this wind, she had no idea. Giri had felt confident they wouldn't be fired upon, and the griffins had such good vision they'd probably see danger long before Vor did, but still, if anyone did attack them, all the griffins could do was try to evade. Vor, however, could try to defend. The air was pleasantly occupied by various air elementals, and if the wind didn't turn an arrow by itself, an air elemental certainly could.

Some people did come running out of the house and outbuildings, pointing and shielding their eyes to look up at the bright sky, but no one appeared armed. Hawkjoy held back and let Thornwing get down first. The smaller male griffin had a little more trouble with the wind, and did indeed slew about trying to make a controlled landing. He nearly fouled a wing on an apple tree, but at last got all four feet on the ground and his wings and tail safely folded. Giri slung himself down from Thornwing's back after undoing some buckles, and Hawkjoy began her final descent.

Vor clung tightly, noting that Thornwing was scampering out of the way. They'd been aiming for the main courtyard in front of the house, where carriages and the like would ordinarily arrive, but a number of fruit trees ringed it—probably an attempt at a windbreak. That only added difficulty for airborne arrivals. Hawkjoy was still a young female, compared to Thornwing, who was a mature male, but she was around a quarter larger than he was, and her wide wingspan made for more chances to hit something. Vor thought they should have planned to land on the wide open moor instead, and just walk the rest of the distance, but it was too late now.

Giri was hugging his family while at the same time urging them to step back. Hawkjoy dropped below the height of the encircling wall, and then into the ring of trees, and Vor felt the wind drop, and drop some more, while Hawkjoy flexed and flapped and adjusted her wings and tail until she landed with only a bit of a bump. Vor immediately set to unbuckling herself. The torrential wind was only a temperamental breeze down at ground level, and she felt immediately warmer, but her frozen fingers were stiff.

Giri came trotting over to help with Thornwing beside him.

"Good landing," Thornwing praised.

"Did you hurt your wing?" Hawkjoy asked back in a tone that sounded almost smug.

Thornwing flicked his crest. "I merely did that to demonstrate where the strongest slip current was coming from, so you'd be ready for it, little Hawk. My wing is fine, and apparently my demonstration helped you land safely."

"Make sure you stretch it," Hawkjoy murmured.

"I assure you," Thornwing purred smoothly, "I'm perfectly fine."

Vor levered herself off Hawkjoy's back and slid down to find her feet. Beside her, Giri unbuckled the packs Hawkjoy carried, and Vor saw that he'd already grabbed the ones off Thornwing. She also saw at least a half dozen people waiting near the front doors of the house.

"Come along," Giri said softly to the griffins.

The breeze tugged at his words, but their hearing was so good they at once stopped flicking their crests at each other and fell in behind him and Vor. The two people in the center of the group had to be Giri's parents. They looked about the right age and were dressed in the finest clothes. Not that they wore anything particularly spectacular, but there was still a difference between them and the others, though Andra and her husband were well dressed, too, and grinning from beside the Master and Mistress of Holstor.

"We welcome Giri's friends and companions," the Master of Holstor said. "Andra brought word of you from the capital, and we're honored to be able to meet you all in person."

"Won't you all come in out of the wind," the Mistress of Hostolr added. "You picked a particularly blustery day to fly in."

A pair of servants opened both of the main doors to the house, and Vor estimated that yes, the griffins could fit through. The greeting party turned to go inside. Giri gave Vor an encouraging, though nervous, smile and took her hand. She lifted an eyebrow at him.

"No point in pretending," he whispered. "Andra will have spun tales anyway." Giri glanced over his shoulder at the griffins. "Come inside," he invited. "There's a room we all can fit in."

Vor let him lead her into the home he'd grown up in.

They settled in a large room directly to the right after the entry hall. Vor guessed it was like the blue room at Mrandis House: a multipurpose room that could be used for banquets, dancing, or anything else that required a large indoor space. Unlike the Mrandis blue room, it was decorated by at least a dozen large, intricate, multi-colored tapestries. The colors were remarkably rich. The scenes depicted were mostly of nature, animals, and birds, though one had unicorns, and one was of an outdoor banquet.

There was a collection of small tables and comfortable chairs. Mistress Holstor whispered something to a servant, and a few moments later a quartet of men came in, each pair carrying a mattress. A few women followed with sturdy blankets and cushions. In only a couple minutes, two large, comfy-looking lounges were prepared, and the tables and chairs were adjusted to make them a part of the circle. The servants adjusting the furniture withdrew except for one elderly woman who took a seat behind and to one side of Mistress Holstor.

"Please," Mistress Holstor gestured. "Won't everyone take their ease?"

Andra must have done her job well. The Holstor House members were acting like the griffins were any other guests, and showing little if any fear around them. Vor let Giri lead the way, and took a seat in a chair beside him. The griffins hesitated, but then each went to a lounge and cautiously sat. Vor saw Hawkjoy's neck ruff lift, and then the grey female lay down on her front, head still up but paws tucked under like a house cat and wings neatly folded. Her muscles relaxed with obvious relief. After a moment, Thornwing took a similar posture.

"Very nice, thank you," Thornwing said with a little bow of his head.

A few servants came in with tea and biscuits. As the cups were poured and handed around, and the plates set out on each table with a few different varieties of biscuit, Vor took the chance to get a look at Giri's parents. Neither were very tall, not much taller than he was, though his mother was a little taller than his father. They had pleasant faces that seemed a little weathered from the wind and sun. Giri's father had the rich dark skin common to western Weldom, but his mother was somewhat paler, suggesting she might have come from a more central area, though it wasn't impossible she could be from the west, too. He had hair that was completely black, and wore a tidy mustache. Her hair was more like dark amber, just a little lighter than Giri's. Giri's skin tone was at a midpoint between his parents, and Vor could see hints of his facial features in both of them.

"I'm not sure how we might serve you tea," Mistress Holstor confessed with an awkward smile that reminded Vor strongly of Giri, as she looked across at the griffins.

"Not to worry," Thornwing said easily. "I'm afraid we wouldn't do your tea justice, as we can't appreciate all the subtle flavors you humans can. To be quite honest, we'll get a drink from an outdoor fountain or pool later."

"And probably bathe in it," Giri contributed. "It's quite amusing to watch, and totally ruins this sleek, powerful look he's got going on right now."

"He punctures my vanity," Thornwing quipped cheerfully.

"Which will heal all but immediately." Giri cleared his throat. "Introductions. My mother Sarilla, and my father Davin. I think everyone here knows my sister Andra and her husband Terias." He pivoted a little towards the griffins. "This amusing fellow is Thornwing. In his great generosity he agreed to carry me on this journey. And this magnificent lady is Hawkjoy, who agreed to carry this other magnificent lady," he took Vor's hand again, "Vor Hearthsraven."

Vor bit the inside of her cheeks, suddenly fighting a blush and the urge to run off somewhere far away, possibly while screaming.

"I'm sure Andra has told you every detail she can remember and made some more up besides," Giri continued while Andra stuck her tongue out at him, "but I can tell you I met Vor in Northborn, as you already know, and she has come to Weldom now to live. She's been confirmed as a wizard and since Milsa is a master wizard now, Master Srawn has agreed to take her on as a second apprentice, with me."

Vor braced herself, trying to keep her outward posture and expression unchanged. Now would be the moment for Giri's parents to express disapproval of their son's choice in life-mate, if they were going to do it. Indeed, their faces grew slightly closed—just slightly.

"Andra did bring tidings, as you say," Giri's father Davin said.

"Giri has many allies and friends at the Citadel," his mother Sarilla said with a smile, "and we are always pleased to meet them."

"I believe Andra and Terias left the capital just after a series of remarkable events both Vor and I were a part of," Giri spoke up. "I'm sure they brought news, but might have missed hearing some of the details. Vor and I, along with my friend Dello, his master, and some others, were in the Citadel when it was attacked by a well-organized group of mage-talented commoners. These mages were trying to break the spell that holds the city together, that prevents the rock it stands on from crumbling. We pursued them down into the caves below the city, and stopped them."

Davin frowned. "Your duties have always been dangerous, my son. We know it, and we are grateful you have been able to return to us unharmed."

"Then thank Vor. She saved my life down there, and I hers."

Vor didn't dispute it. Though there had been many more factors involved than straightforward heroic gestures, she could agree that they had both survived it because of each other, and their other allies.

"Of course," Sarilla said at once, with no hint of reticence. "Miss Hearthsraven, we thank you for our son's life."

"I wouldn't have survived without him, either," Vor was quick to say.

"You wizards do well looking after each other," Davin nodded.

"And Vor and I will continue to do so," Giri declared. "Not just because we are wizards. Mother, Father, we are a pair. Vor and I intend to continue protecting each other. I ask that you cease trying to pair me up with anyone else."

Vor sat quietly, again considering the option of running away screaming, or perhaps going to hide behind Hawkjoy. She also got a few moments to question her own sanity. She did love Giri, and trusted him and valued him as her closest ally. She knew that if she faced a foe, he would stand up right beside her, hand her weapons, give her energy, or step forward and smite the foe himself if that was the best tactic. And when the battle was over, he would give her care and healing and accept the same from her in turn. Despite her younger age and smaller experience—in some things—he didn't patronize her, but instead respected her journey and didn't hesitate to trust her when she was confident in her position.

Now he would give up the future he'd been meant for: making a noble marriage and providing children to his house. She knew he'd been on the path of giving that up anyway, but now he was telling his parents there was no hope—because of her: Vor Hearthsraven, half-dark former apprentice mage and murderer of the late villain Altare. Perhaps she was overreaching herself. Perhaps she didn't deserve him. Perhaps she would harm Giri's future, or contaminate him.

Perhaps this was not the right path for her.

Giri seemed to sense her doubt, and his hand tightened on hers. Through their rings he sent pulses, clearly saying "I love you."

"Hearthsraven," Davin said slowly, words tinged with regret, "is not a noble house."

"Not in Weldom," Sarilla added hopefully. "Perhaps it is in Northborn?"

"No," Vor said. "Hearthsraven was my father's name. He was a soldier and came with the Northborn invasion, from Weldom."

"But Vor's mother was nobility," Giri contributed, voice showing hints of heat, "not that it matters."

"She was disowned," Vor disclosed.

Both of Giri's parents wore slight frowns now. They exchanged glances with each other, and Davin leaned forward, resting his elbows on his knees.

Vor exchanged a similar glance with Giri and kept her voice low. "Samira said something about you having an agreement with my mother. Should we mention that?"

Before Giri could reply, Davin spoke. "Son, we have long hoped you would marry, though we always knew that sometimes wizards don't." He made a weak gesture at Vor. "But—"

"We're not intending to marry yet. We might someday, but we might not," Giri said, tone sharp. "It doesn't really matter to us, and it wouldn't be a noble marriage even if we did. Also, don't expect children. We might not have any."

Eyebrows rose all around in surprise.

"I know Vor can't provide a spouse price or some useful alliance," Giri went on, voice rising, "but nor does she cost you anything. This isn't about House Holstor. This is about me, and if you want what will make me happy. Vor and I will be Colby's apprentices, together, for another couple decades, and I love her, and won't consider anyone else."

He paused, took a deep breath, and shut his eyes for a moment, as if trying to calm himself. His next words were gentler.

"So, I just hope you'll be happy for us," he said, "because I'm not going to be Holstor's prize boy any longer." He nodded at Andra and Terias. "You have healthy grandchildren. I expect you'll even get more."

Andra beamed. Terias looked fairly unruffled. The griffins, too, were calm, almost dozing. Into the silence, the old lady servant seated behind Sarilla leaned forward and whispered something into her mistress's ear. Sarilla's frown turned thoughtful, and then her eyes snapped back onto Vor with a new, assessing sort of gaze.

"Wizard Hearthsraven," Sarilla said softly. "Might I inquire as to your mother's name? She was nobility?"

Vor nodded. "Juleena Mrandis," she said. "The house isn't far. We just came from there." She glanced at Giri again, thinking of the puzzle Samira had hinted at.

Davin nodded. "Yes, we know of Mrandis House. We've been allies with them in the past—" but he stopped talking as his wife went pale. "Sari?"

The servant woman behind her was also wearing a stunned expression, and put a supporting hand on Sarilla's shoulder. Sarilla reached up and covered it with her own hand.

"I met Juleena," she said, and glanced at her husband. "We both did. You remember the scandal that year? She was promised to Salasis."

Recall flared in Davin's face and he nodded. "Then Mrandis broke the engagement and disowned her. The rumor was she'd run off with a soldier."

"That's correct. That was my father," Vor confirmed. "You remember her? I heard from her maidservant that you met."

"She stayed here with us during the summer festival hosted by House Tuma," Sarilla explained. Her eyes flicked to Giri. "She met you, too, Giri. You were little, four or five. I suppose you don't remember."

"I don't remember," he declared at once, "but Juleena's maidservant did say I had. Was there something more? Some kind of agreement I made with Juleena?”

Some color began returning to Sarilla's face, and she put her hands back in her lap. All her attitude of shock, the frowns, the raised eyebrows melted away, and she smiled at Vor. Vor stared back, perplexed by her sudden reversal of expression. She was even more perplexed a moment later when Sarilla chuckled and shook her head.

“It seems,” she mused, “we will be keeping the promise I made with Juleena.” When she looked at her son, her eyes crinkled and her smiling lips parted to show her strong, white teeth. “We shall honor the agreement Giri made with her.”

Giri blinked. “What agreement?”

Sarilla turned to her husband. “You remember that while we were hosting the Mrandises, Giri had an episode?”

“An episode?” Vor asked.

“One of those times I burned out my nursery,” Giri explained softly.

“He was so upset he wouldn't be soothed,” Sarilla went on, “despite how much Betta tried.” She patted the hand of the servant behind her. “We all returned from the summer gathering and Giri ran off in a fury and hid behind Juleena. She calmed him when he was refusing to be calmed, and I expressed how much I wished we had a boy of the right age to marry her.”

She turned her delighted attention onto her son. “And then Giri said she should have a daughter, and that he'd marry her, and Juleena agreed, though at the time it might have been mostly in a spirit of fun. Even after she was promised to Salasis, I assured her that if she should have a daughter, we'd hold to the agreement as long as the two children liked each other.”

Now Davin was smiling, too. “Apparently, they do,” he said smugly.

Vor's mouth had dropped open a little, and she turned to stare at Giri just as he turned to stare at her. His skin had gone waxy and his eyes very round.

“I swear,” he said, “I didn't do this on purpose. I liked you before I knew you were a Mrandis, and I don't remember at all that I—”

Vor leaned over and quickly kissed his mouth, just to shut him up. “I know,” she said.

He didn't say anymore, but still looked a little stunned. Vor faced his parents again.

“So, does that mean this is alright then?” she asked.

Davin smiled and sighed. “It wouldn't make any difference if we resisted, except to alienate our son from us.”

“And seeing as how we like him very much,” Sarilla purred, “we shall approve his choice of partner."

"And take me off the market," Giri added, almost a growl.

Davin nodded sincerely. "And we'll make it known that the prize boy of Holstor has been won, and no further suits are welcome."

Vor felt the tension melt from Giri's hand, and he leaned over a little to rest his forehead on her shoulder. She leaned her head against his, unable to fight down a small smile.

"Thank you," Giri murmured.

From the directions of the griffins came a rustling sound as Thornwing roused his feathers and gave a little shake.

"Fascinating," he said.

"It is," Hawkjoy agreed softly.

"Humans have such complex mating rituals. I didn't know they had to get their parents involved, too," Thornwing marvelled.

A few people laughed.

"When I was in heat and wanted a male, I just bit his neck and he complied or flew away," Hawkjoy mused. Her cheek feathers flared. "Usually he complied."

"That works with humans, too," Vor assured her, and had the pleasure of sensing Giri blush. "But it's different for formalizing exclusive, permanent mating pairs."

"And it's not done yet," Davin told the griffins. "Once we can get them convinced to actually marry, there has to be a special ceremony, where everyone will wear fancy clothes. There will be an audience, music, special foods, and some member of Miss Hearthsraven's family will need to come stand as next-of-kin, or maybe Master Colby could do it."

"There will be many plans to be made," Sarilla joined in with a sigh of pleasure.

"I'd rather not have anything at all," Vor said.

Andra giggled. "I'm afraid it's too late for that, Vor."

She caught Terias's eye, and for a moment he shared an expression of longstanding futility with her.

"Oh dear," she muttered. "What have I gotten myself into?"

"Just bear with Andra for a short while," Giri murmured, head still on her shoulder. "There will be no wedding on this trip. Then we'll be back to taking lessons from Colby and getting sent on dull or dangerous assignments. Then I can guarantee you there will be no frills, no dancing, no carefully styled hair or gourmet foods; just a lot of him saying 'that was pathetic, do it again.'"

Andra bounced a little and scooted forward on her seat. "So what's in that chest you magicked into your room, big brother? We didn't open it in case it might explode."

Giri lifted his head and smiled at Vor, with a hint of wickedness. "Oh, that? It's full of gowns that belonged to Vor's mother. There's so many, I don't know how we'll ever sort through them all, or which ones might fit Vor the best."

Vor had time to whisper, "you are a cruel, cruel man," before Andra bounded across the room and seized her arm.

Vor didn't fight as Andra dragged her from the room, but before she was out of earshot, she got to hear Thornwing's next comment.

"You know she will take vengeance," the male griffin said.

"Of course," Giri replied. "I expect she will bite my neck particularly hard."

Then Vor gave herself up to being Andra's dress-up-doll for the next couple hours. Considering how remarkably light her spirit felt—having left her past in Northborn and become a wizard and Colby's apprentice, saved Anchoria from crumbling, come to some peace over her killing of Altare, re-united with her father's family, helped to ensure the future of Mrandis House, placed herself to safeguard a new magical talent in the person of Hyldi, and soothed the Holstor family so they wouldn't make a fuss over her being with Giri—it hardly felt like an imposition at all.

To be continued.

Thank you for reading!

Did you enjoy the journey?

Please leave a rating or review on Goodreads, Amazon, or wherever you talk about books. Reviews help books get to readers who might enjoy them.

You can find more information about me and my books, and updates on future books, at my website or on my Facebook or Goodreads page.

www.elucidationimages.com
Kasmith Art & Books